# SEA OF SOULS

## A DAWN OF FIRE NOVEL

*More Warhammer 40,000 from Black Library*

# SEA OF SOULS
## A DAWN OF FIRE NOVEL

# CHRIS WRAIGHT

BLACK LIBRARY

## A BLACK LIBRARY PUBLICATION

First published in 2023.
This edition published in Great Britain in 2023 by
Black Library, Games Workshop Ltd., Willow Road,
Nottingham, NG7 2WS, UK.

Represented by: Games Workshop Limited – Irish branch,
Unit 3, Lower Liffey Street, Dublin 1,
D01 K199, Ireland.

10 9 8 7 6 5 4 3 2 1

Produced by Games Workshop in Nottingham.
Cover illustration by Johan Grenier.

See Black Library on the internet at

## blacklibrary.com

Find out more about Games Workshop
and the worlds of Warhammer at

## games-workshop.com

Printed and bound in the UK.

---

*To Hannah, with love.*

For more than a hundred centuries the Emperor
has sat immobile on the Golden Throne of Earth.
He is the Master of Mankind. By the might of His
inexhaustible armies a million worlds stand
against the dark.

Yet, He is a rotting carcass, the Carrion Lord of the
Imperium held in life by marvels from the Dark
Age of Technology and the thousand souls sacrificed
each day so that His may continue to burn.

To be a man in such times is to be one amongst
untold billions. It is to live in the cruellest and
most bloody regime imaginable. It is to suffer an
eternity of carnage and slaughter. It is to have cries
of anguish and sorrow drowned by the thirsting
laughter of dark gods.

This is a dark and terrible era where you will find
little comfort or hope. Forget the power of technology
and science. Forget the promise of progress and
advancement. Forget any notion of common
humanity or compassion.

There is no peace amongst the stars, for in the grim
darkness of the far future, there is only war.

# DRAMATIS PERSONAE

CREW AND PASSENGERS OF HIS BATTLE CRUISER
*JUDGEMENT OF THE VOID*

| | |
|---|---|
| Iannis Kiastros | Captain |
| Leroa Avati | First lieutenant, Master of Astrogation |
| Nevus Boroja | Second lieutenant, Master of Signals |
| Heriof Spleed | Second lieutenant, Master of Gunnery |
| Magda Kuhl | Third lieutenant, Master of Engines |
| Mergaux Santalina | Navigator |
| Garg Vandia Ortuyo | Astropath Senioris |
| Slavo Jep | Medicae |
| Aris Garrock | Captain of Armsmen |
| Refad | First lieutenant, Armsmen |
| Hobes | Communications officer, Armsmen |
| Herj | Lieutenant, Armsmen |
| Arfo-5 | Enginarium tech-priest |
| Krujax | Enginarium furnace master |
| Tuo Maizad | Sergeant, Akaida Squad, Iron Shades Chapter, Adeptus Astartes |
| Miriam Isobel | Sister Hospitaller |
| Hastin il-Moro | Interrogator, retinue of Inquisitor Gertruda |
| Xinarola | Navigator's menial |
| Chatak | Captain's adjutant |

OTHERS OF FLEET SECUNDUS

| | |
|---|---|
| Rasmatin Olythaddeus Samil | High Admiral |
| Heila Jovanjiar | Groupmaster, Battle Group Dominus |
| Juleis Hekaon | Commodore, Squadron Acertus |

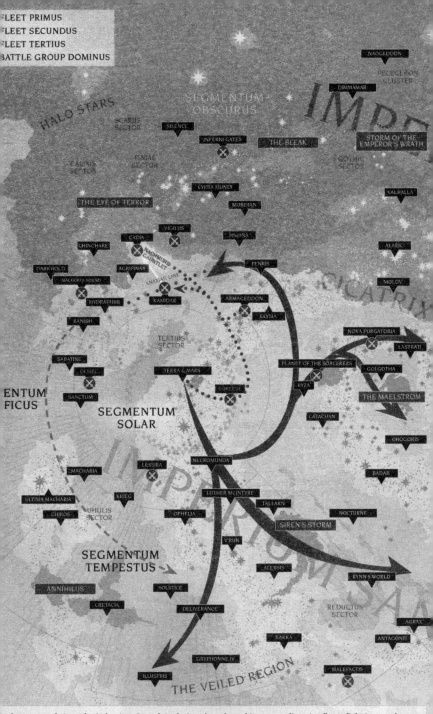

FLEET PRIMUS
FLEET SECUNDUS
FLEET TERTIUS
BATTLE GROUP DOMINUS

NAOGEDDON
PELEGERON CLUSTER
DIMMAMAR
STORM OF THE EMPEROR'S WRATH

HALO STARS
SEGMENTUM OBSCURUS
IMPE

SCARUS SECTOR
SILENCE
THE BLEAK
VALHALLA

INFERNI GATES
FINIAL SECTOR
GOTHIC SECTOR

CALIXIS SECTOR
CYPRA MUNDII
MORDIAN
ALARIC

THE EYE OF TERROR
VIGILUS
VISCANA
MOLOV

CADIA
CHINCHARE
NACHMUND GAUNTLET
FENRIS
SICATRIX

DARKHOLD
AGRIPINAA
ANAMAN LINE
ARMAGEDDON

MACHORTA SOUND
HYDRAPHUR
KAMIDAR
ELYSIA

BANISH
NOVA PURGATORIA
LASTRATI

TERTIUS SECTOR
PLANET OF THE SORCERERS
GOLGOTHA

SABATINE
TERRA & MARS
RYZA
THE MAELSTROM

ENTUM FICUS
OLMEC
VORLESE
CATACHAN

SANCTUM
SEGMENTUM SOLAR
CHOGORIS

IMPERIUM

MACHARIA
LESSIRA
NECROMUNDA
BADAB

ULTIMA MACHARIA
KRIEG
LUTHER MCINTYRE

CHIROS
UHULIS SECTOR
OPHELIA
TALLARN
NOCTURNE

SEGMENTUM TEMPESTUS
V'RUN
SIREN'S STORM

ANNIHILUS
ALEUSIS
RYNN'S WORLD

CRETACIA
SOLSTICE
REDUCTUS SECTOR
AGRAX

DELIVERANCE
ANTAGONIS

BAKKA

GRYPHONNE IV
MALEFACTIS

ILLUSTRIS
THE VEILED REGION

rs have passed since the Indomitus Crusade's glorious launch, and its ever-splintering fleets fight in countless
arzones across the galaxy. No cartograph, even this one, should be considered all-encompassing due to the
measurable scale and fluidity of the crusade as it battles to save the Imperium of Man from total annihilation.

*Haul the chain fast, scrags,*
*Haul the chain fast*
*Slip not nor trip*
*And the void take the last*

– Old Navy work-shanty

# Chapter One

**VEILBREAK**

**THE ENEMY**

**NO STONE LEFT UNTURNED**

'I wish to make a change,' said Iannis Kiastros.

The captain of the Imperial battle cruiser *Judgement of the Void* sat calmly in his command throne, one hand lightly on the granite finial of his armrest, the other cradling a half-full goblet of wine. Ahead of him, overlooked by lines of tall columns supporting a dome of transparent armaglass, the bridge thrummed with orderly energy. Menials carried data-slates from station to station, while dozens of bridge staff kitted out in the squadron's dark blue livery worked away in the cogitator pits among the servitors.

Leroa Avati, Kiastros' second-in-command and Master of Astrogation, looked up at him from her position just below and to the right of the throne. This had not been unexpected – she knew her captain well, and most engagements received some kind of modification before the *horizon of determination*, as Kiastros insisted on calling it, was crossed. Avati, also first lieutenant and Tactical Master, adjusted her position slightly to ensure she understood his intentions precisely.

'A change, lord captain?' she asked.

'We shall break the veil four void-units well-ward, blind-position and closed, ready for barrels out on my immediate command.'

Avati nodded, committing the order to memory and mentally comparing it to her existing preparations. The *Judgement of the Void* was currently in the warp, though rapidly winding down towards re-entry into realspace. Within moments, notification was expected from the Navigator, Mamzel Santalina, that the cycle for veilbreak could be begun. Kiastros' order would not be easy to achieve in the time they had available, but it would be possible. He was never entirely unreasonable, was Kiastros. A pain in the arse, of course, and as rigid as a gunner's jerkin, but not unreasonable.

'Aye, lord captain,' she replied, swivelling back on the throne to make the changes.

Four void-units was a significant shift – twenty-five thousand miles away from their current intended trajectory, angled towards the system's gravity well. Such a course would bring the *Judgement of the Void* into realspace at the so-called blind-position relative to their original insertion point – that is, with the system's star directly behind them, taking advantage of any interference delivered by solar radiation to muddy their position for a few precious seconds. Closed was a pre-combat setting – heat-producing systems reduced to minimal running operation, all shutters down, all venting eliminated. Also useful prior to an action, just to maximise the chances of evading a determinate fix from enemy sensors. Barrels-out, pleasingly enough, was the command given to roll out the broadside guns and ready the lances for firing.

So Kiastros clearly expected trouble. Avati wondered why, but said nothing. She shunted a quick warning to the ship's Master of Engines, Magda Kuhl, who was toiling hard in the depths of the enginarium.

'Course correction incoming,' she voxed on a closed link, her fingers working at the control console to send her the data.

Kuhl's hearty laughter crackled back across the link. *'Are we surprised? How much by?'*

'It's a chunk. Get your stoves primed.'

Kuhl would manage it. Her people were good, and they were probably already lining up to coax some extra juice from the plasma lines. Avati cut the link just in time to see Boroja, the Master of Signals sitting just a few yards away in his own station, direct a quizzical look towards Kiastros.

'Lord captain, shall I notify the *Fortitude in Extremis* of the course change?' he asked.

Kiastros shook his head. 'You shall not. They may have secure comms in place or they may not, but we will not take that chance. No announcements or signals prior to veilbreak.'

Boroja looked unhappy about that. Avati couldn't blame him. Comm-silence was rude, even if it proved necessary, and the Imperial Navy, perhaps alone of all the Imperium's military organisations, took courtesy between officers seriously. Kiastros clearly had his reasons, though – she wondered what they were.

'Orders now in effect, lord captain,' she said. 'All preparations for realspace translation completed.'

Kiastros took a sip of his wine, rolled it around his mouth, swallowed. 'Very good,' he said, not being clear whether he was referring to her summary or to the taste. 'Now for Santalina's word.'

Avati switched back to her terminal and reviewed the mission briefing. The star system was Jophra XI: single sun, no inhabited worlds, convenient Mandeville zones for drops out of long-haul warp runs. The *Judgement of the Void* had been tasked by Commodore Hekaon to rendezvous with a small flotilla of five vessels, all of which were light-cruiser class or smaller, for escort back to the gathering muster at Fixed Point U-93. Most of those vessels had recorded idents and designations, including the command ship *Fortitude in Extremis*, but one didn't. That wasn't unusual – it was probably an Astartes or an Inquisition vessel, neither of which would declare their particulars unless necessary. Still, the encounter appeared entirely routine, just part of the long pulling-together of forces that had been going on now for weeks in response to Admiral Jovanjiar's meticulous preparations for the coming offensive, so Kiastros' last-minute caution was intriguing.

'*His Beneficent Gaze, lord captain,*' came Santalina's tremulous voice next, barely audible over the shared bridge comm-link. '*I sense a change in the pipework – something I need to be aware of?*'

'Not really in your province, honoured Navigator,' replied Kiastros good-naturedly. 'Though confirmation of our imminent return to the real would be of great interest to us all.'

'*You may commence your re-entry momentarily, lord captain. The ether is turbulent, and I suspect it does not wish to see us leave.*'

'When is it otherwise, Mergaux?'

'*These days – never. What an age to be alive.*'

'Indeed. Though preferable to the alternative.'

The link closed. Soon afterwards, warning lumens blinked red across the consoles of all the bridge officers. Locks clunked into secondary positions at the base of the warp-shutters, and the deck beneath Avati's boots began the telltale drum of structural adjustment.

'All hands to stations for re-entry,' Kiastros ordered, sitting back in his throne before taking another sip.

The order cascaded down the decks – from lieutenants to division chiefs to deckmasters to ratings, all the way down to the most scabrous and pox-raddled grunts in the shadows of the gun-bilges. Alarms began to sound as the layers of Geller protection were peeled away, and the hundreds of stokers, lubricators and lexmechanics in the enginarium jumped into action.

Just down from Avati's position, a prayer-servitor started up. Its metallic mandibles puffed out some incense, and then the droning began.

*Eternal master of the void and of the spheres, grant now safe passage from the empyrean to the real, for the warding of your servants and the delivery of your justice, that the domain of mankind may be extended and preserved for...*

Avati pushed it away, and it limped over towards the sensorium crews.

'Approaching translation nexus on exact schedule,' she reported, watching the runes cascade across her station's lenses. 'Five minutes to breach.'

'All hands, brace,' said Kiastros, draining the last of his glass and placing it on the table beside him. A tiny clasp clicked closed over it, locking it and the decanter down.

The bridge rocked as if hit by something solid, and the shutters rattled. Then more hits, booming up from below. Officers rode out the turbulence, none of them deigning to reach out to steady themselves – a neophyte error – but swaying with the deck as the battle cruiser was tossed upon the tides.

More alarms went off, each a different timbre, each warning of another phase of the veilbreak. Avati adjusted the requested feed to the plasma drives by a touch, knowing from experience that trim and thrust would need to be delicately handled to avoid a damaged crossing. Confirmation of Kuhl's completed work came with the soft glow of a new rune on her console, which was reassuring.

Then the moment came, which never ceased to make your stomach turn, no matter how many times you did it. The tiny bubble of reality that had cocooned the voidship for the duration of its journey within the other realm blew outward, its meniscus shattered as the structure hurtled back into the embrace of real physics. The howl and skitter of dream-energies were replaced with utter silence from beyond the hull, a brief interlude before the roar of the plasma drives made everything shake again. You felt the change instantly – gravity was the same, the bitter tang of the recycled air was the same, nothing looked different – but you *knew*, you knew that you had moved from somewhere unnatural and hateful and sickening to somewhere merely dangerous and hostile and unhealthy. The void. The dark. The endless black.

'Translation complete,' Avati reported, scanning the hundreds of missive-bursts that crowded her terminal from all quarters of the ship. 'Underway in realspace, running closed to blind-position.'

'Imperial flotilla detected, holding seven v-u bearing three-one-one, all ships expected present,' reported Boroja, his face glowing green from the phosphor of his lens.

'Hold position ahead,' Kiastros ordered. 'Retain shutters, bring to full stop then turn gunward on my mark.'

'Bring to full stop, aye,' Avati replied. She could already sense Boroja's irritation – the flotilla would be hailing by now, having detected the warp breach opening. Had they fixed on to the *Judgement of the Void*'s position? Maybe.

Avati checked the relative positions on her tactical display. The *Judgement of the Void* had come in a long way out of the agreed position, far closer to the system's star than normal and right on the inner edge of the Mandeville zone. Six thousand miles further in and translation would have started to get dangerous. The Imperial flotilla was in a much more conventional location, just on the far side of the ideal Mandeville locus. It was very probable that they couldn't directly ascertain the *Judgement of the Void*'s position yet, and that would be making their commanders nervous.

'Slowing to full stop,' said Avati.

'Mark,' announced Kiastros, reaching for his decanter to refresh his glass. 'Angle for starboard broadside against flotilla position, barrels-out and prime all lances.'

Avati obeyed instantly, sending the commands that would turn the vast ship on its vertical axis and swing the long rows of macrocannons towards the distant flotilla position. Even as she did so, she heard the Master of Gunnery, Heriof Spleed, initiate the gun roll-out. She knew that he'd be just as flummoxed as her, but no one would say a word, not even hesitate – the captain's command was as final as death.

'Fire now, gunnery master,' Kiastros said, shifting position an inch so he could get a good look at his suspended tactical lenses. 'Maximum spread, scatter pattern, all tiers in sequence. Light the void.'

'*Now*, lord captain?' came Spleed's gruff query – a brave request for clarity.

Kiastros seemed to be expecting that. 'Quite so. Just as I specified, if it please you.'

'Firing, aye,' Spleed announced. 'Solution conveyed and locked.'

The orders shot down the comm-tubes, where they were picked up by the deck commanders, who shunted them to the gunnery-team overseers, who roared them out to the hundreds-strong barrel crews. Chains were yanked tight, covers clanged open, cog-wheels cranked into alignment, shells slammed into open breeches, covers bolted closed with spinning iron bolts that sent sparks skipping off the high-polished steel. The *Judgement of the Void*'s miles-long starboard batteries opened up, the muzzles of macrocannons shot out on their rails, hot from their inner furnaces. Ghostly targeting lattices sprung into life inside a thousand guidance chapels, a hundred priests began chants of accuracy.

The guns fired. Silent explosions, running in tight series, hurling shells into the dark – up, out, down, across. They fired again – scatter formation, primed to explode in penetrative clouds the moment something solid was hit – then again, then again.

Avati watched it all go, tracking across her tactical lenses. There was nothing to strike. Just the emptiness.

Until that changed.

A Geller field discharging at close proximity was always an arresting sight – an explosion of light amid the gloom, a starburst of violated physical laws followed by a flurry of startled radiation and the smallest, tiniest, nastiest sense that you'd just got a glimpse of the forbidden amid the whirl and collision of supercharged particles.

'Signals!' Boroja blurted, his long-fingered hands dancing across his terminal. 'Two masses emerging, profiles incoming.' He looked up at the captain. 'Hulls confirmed. Archenemy allegiance, moving now to full instantiation.'

'Tactical, take the foremost,' ordered Kiastros, putting down his glass at last. 'Signals, hail the flotilla, send my compliments and apologies to the commanding officer and request all assistance in containing the hindmost.' He shot a satisfied look Avati's way. 'Just as anticipated, Astrogation. A dull-witted enemy is the very best kind of enemy, is it not?'

'Dull-witted, aye,' Avati replied, shaking her head a little, already activating the tactical station controls and calculating her attack vectors. 'Emperor be praised, may they all be so.'

Just as she spoke, the spread-pattern of shells hit. Not many – perhaps five per cent of the total with the remainder spiralling harmlessly into the void beyond – but it was catastrophic nonetheless. A ship exiting the warp was vulnerable – systems still heating up, void shields not at full power, plasma drives cold and sluggish. Blindly aimed shells hit just as hard as any other kind, and the explosive charges blasted clean through gossamer-weak shield coverage and deep into hull plating.

How had he known? But that could come later. The action had started now, and Avati worked to fulfil her commission. The *Judgement of the Void* was already coming around, burning its manoeuvring thrusters to angle the broadside guns more precisely. Spleed's people would be doing their work too – registering the hits, triangulating them and scrawling calculations for the macrocannons' machine spirits to respond to. Pistons would already be wheezing, platforms already clunking across the rails.

Avati took a moment to register the tonnage and type of the foremost enemy ships. The long-range visual feed showed them to be capable: cruiser-class, with nasty-looking rows of guns and some torpedo tubes visible on the angled prows. The foremost's flanks were a dull dark green, glistening faintly and underlit with an eerie pale glow from its ranks of portholes. It was a crabbed, ridged thing, ugly and patina-coated, and like all ships of the Archenemy it didn't do to look too closely at it even at range – you might glimpse something that would turn your stomach or give you nightmares for a month.

No doubt its captain – or whatever passed for its captain – had expected to come into realspace unannounced, affording the vessel ample time to turn about and level guns at its target before it could be intercepted. Kiastros' manoeuvre had placed the two cruisers between the *Judgement of the Void* and the void-anchored Imperial flotilla, putting the newcomers in a poor position, and both ships had already taken damage from the speculative barrage. They would be struggling to correct that now, working hard to buy some time and run their own sensor sweeps in order to calculate return fire, so it was imperative they didn't get space to move.

'Break them open, Gunnery,' Avati breathed, giving Spleed the go-ahead to let fly.

The second barrage was properly aimed, using the explosions created by the first one to gauge distance and make an educated guess as to where the target would try to run to. The prey was still picking up speed, so they'd aimed just under the cruiser's ridged prow, knowing that Archenemy ships preferred to stay under the battleplane if they could.

Spleed fired, and the *Judgement of the Void*'s vast structure resounded to the upwelling sound of a full broadside. That was a glorious thing to hear and feel, even insulated by so many interposed decks – the plating shivering, the wellheads ringing and the counter-recoil thrusters booming. Every tactical lens picked up the whistling payload as it streaked off into the void, still spread but now clustered more tightly, zeroing remorselessly in on the slowly turning cruiser.

'Bring us around now, Engines,' Avati ordered the enginarium. 'Maintain distance, turn to sustain broadside face.'

The enemy cruiser would want to come in close, due to its shorter-range weaponry. It would also wish to turn prow-facing, to reduce the flanks it exposed to the larger Imperial ship's cannon banks. Both of those objectives had to be denied – the *Judgement of the Void* would pull away, turning all the while, keeping the distance extended and ensuring the largest target for its weaponry. Such a dance could not be extended indefinitely – a cruiser was a nimbler vessel than its larger battle cruiser cousin – but every moment counted when damage had already been dealt.

Just as the core manoeuvring thrusters reached maximum output, sensors indicated the last brace of shells hitting home.

'Damage report, Gunnery,' Kiastros said.

Spleed buried his hirsute face into the maw of a cogitator funnel. 'Strikes across rear-facing hull sections,' came his muffled voice. 'Enginarium plates exposed, shields compromised.' He emerged from the funnel. 'Shall we disable them?'

Kiastros shook his head. 'Negative. I wish to make them run. Angle barrage over their bridge levels – let us smash some windows.'

Spleed got to work, just as Avati got to work, just as Boroja

the ship – that might take hours, and ran the risk of them ship-
ping damage – but force it back into the warp. The enemy had
clearly come for the flotilla, not expecting to be disturbed by a
much larger warship, so they would no doubt be rapidly calculating how long they could live with this level of punishment.
As Avati took in the welter of tactical data coming her way, she
guessed that the conclusion would be *not long*.

'Strike incoming,' Boroja warned, and all of them uncon-
sciously braced for impact. The deck shook again, this time
from the percussive recoils of dozens of enemy shells hitting
the void shields. An alarm sounded from some distance away,
swiftly shut down. 'We are being targeted by both enemy ships.
Second hull is also in range for countermeasures.'

'Negative,' said Kiastros. 'Our esteemed comrades must handle
that one – they will grow bored otherwise. Gunnery, all firepower
on the lead ship. Discharge when ready.'

Avati approved. A less experienced captain might have attempted
to take both cruisers on at once – the *Judgement of the Void* had
sufficient firepower for it – but that was generally a mistake. Take
out the primary target, then worry about what was left. Spleed was
already on to it, running final calculations and overriding a few of
the more wayward solutions shunted up to him from the decks.

'Fire,' he grunted at last, slamming home the authorisation
runes.

The bridge shook again, followed swiftly by a course correction ordered by Avati. This would roll them away, fractionally
narrowing the face presented to the enemy before momentum
brought them back into alignment again. The margins were
small – predictions, anticipations, all governed by the stately
inertia of colossal masses in motion.

The lead cruiser was hit again, its crown raked by explosions.
Something detonated across its ridged spine, a brief flash of red

that flared for a moment before gusting out, and the ranged scanners picked up debris blown clear. That must have hurt it, for the ship appeared to turn out of attack line, slewing wildly ahead of its main thrusters firing again.

'Enemy bridge struck,' reported Spleed, sounding savagely happy about it. 'Gas vents detected – that hull's been cracked.'

'Maintain barrage, remain at mid-range,' Kiastros replied, looking rather smug. 'Any signals from the flotilla?'

'They are closing, lord captain,' Boroja reported. 'Engagement still out of range of their cannons.'

Kiastros tutted. 'A little slow, do you not think? Never mind – keep on course.'

Just as he spoke, another brace of hits came in from both the enemy cruisers. The impacts scattered down the starboard shields, stressed three of the arrays and blew out two power converters on the enginarium level.

'Void array quintus ruptured,' Avati reported calmly, running rapid calculations. 'Angling now to turn away from danger – broadside still available at your discretion.'

'Very good,' said Kiastros. 'Progress, Spleed?'

'Firing now, lord captain.'

More shells streaked off into the void. Kiastros was keeping some of his powder dry – no fighters, no lances, not a thought of igniting the nova cannon. All of those were power-hungry, resource-hungry options, and at a time of war a prudent captain husbanded his stocks. He judged he could finish this prey off with conventional gunnery alone, and what happened next proved him correct.

'Breach-to-warp detected!' Boroja shouted. More alarms went off, and this time they were left to blare. Avati shunted down priority overrides to the thruster crews to keep well away, though in truth the distance was still perfectly sufficient.

Just as abruptly as it had arrived, the damaged Archenemy

cruiser decided to cut its losses, powered up its warp drives, shut down its battered plasma engines and plunged out of existence. The bridge's viewers flared white-gold for an eye-watering moment, the lenses stuttered with static, and then it was over, the volume of space the vessel had occupied now empty save for a smattering of fizzing ions.

'Status of the second ship?' Kiastros demanded, opening lids that had been screwed shut in anticipation of the flash of charged electrons.

'Ah, a moment...' muttered Boroja, struggling to recalibrate his flare-blinded augurs. 'Here it is. Still in realspace, coming up bearing four-five-three, attack speed, forward lances reaching fire positions.'

Kiastros chuckled. 'Attack speed? Very game of them. Turn to engage on my–'

He never completed the command. A second flash of light bloomed across the augur lenses, less dazzling than the warp transition but still enough to scramble the more sensitive instruments. Avati swivelled on her throne, trying to get a lock on what had happened – the second Archenemy ship was still far off, within augur range but only on the very cusp of non-magnified visual sensors. And it was damaged.

'That's a plasma-core breach,' said Boroja, eyebrows raised. 'We didn't do that. Did we?'

'We did not,' said Kiastros. 'Our friends have caught up with it, it seems – let us not permit them to engage without some sociable intervention.'

Avati keyed in the trajectory correction, bringing the vast battle cruiser around in a wide curve. The manoeuvre was not simple – she had to keep the damaged section out of potential fire-lines while maximising the angles for another full broadside. As she did this, she stole a glance at the ranged tactical cartoliths on Boroja's terminals.

The Archenemy ship was listing, drifting down three points away from its initial position and accelerating into a de-powered roll. Beyond it, still at extreme range, all five ships of the Imperial flotilla were closing, streaming at speed with their prow weaponry flickering. For the life of her, Avati couldn't see how they could have done such damage from their current positions. Could the plasma breach have been an accident? Even on ships as badly maintained as a typical Archenemy cruiser, that seemed unlikely.

'Coming into strike range now, lord captain,' she reported, pushing her own plasma thrusters hard to gain the position she wanted. 'Gunnery, you have your target.'

'Target acquired, aye,' responded Spleed, his face now puffy and red. 'Broadside prepared and ready.'

'Then deliver it, if you please,' said Kiastros. 'Right down their noxious throats.'

The *Judgement of the Void*'s cannons fired again at the remaining Archenemy cruiser. This time, the barrage was joined by counterpart volleys from the other Imperial ships. The scopes filled up with the tracks of macrocannon shells streaking out into the void, all zeroing in on the single tumbling hull between them.

The impacts blazed out across the augur lenses – a scatter of silver-white as the warheads detonated against the void shields. Avati nudged the *Judgement of the Void* in closer – the need for precautions had abated now – and ordered another salvo. After that, the spectacle became rather enjoyable, provoking the intense joy she always felt in witnessing an enemy ship being taken apart. She would imagine the hull cracking under the relentless strikes, the systems failing one by one, the whistle of escaping oxygen and the dousing of the internal lumens. She would attempt to picture the faces of those doomed now to die – the hated heretics, the diseased wretches, the faithless dogs, all shrieking to non-existent gods now, all recanting and weeping and tensing up for the scream of atmospheres dissipating into nothing.

'Fire,' she ordered, echoing Spleed's repeated commands. 'Fire. *Fire.*'

It couldn't go on forever. A voidship was designed to take tremendous punishment, but the barrage was now unrelenting. Something on the Archenemy ship suddenly cracked. Something else snapped. Cascades of breaking followed – struts, bulkheads, core structures, fuel lines. Armaglass blew out from reinforced viewports, glittering like gusts of jewel-dust against the void. Radiation emissions spiked, augur readings entered the telltale crescendo of energy discharges, and then the internal explosions began – blooms of angry red, silhouetting the agonised outer plates, glowing up the scale to orange, yellow, white.

'Not too close, Astrogation,' Kiastros murmured, watching the display with the same keen interest as her. 'Though I appreciate it is an arresting spectacle.'

She hadn't brought them too close, not really, so the gentle rebuke stung her a little. Did he have to be so... uptight?

Avati admonished herself. He was the captain, and she had indeed brought them in just on the right side of the safe distance markers.

'My thanks, lord captain,' she replied, adjusting the course instructions. 'All now to full stop.'

Just as the words left her mouth, the Archenemy cruiser lit up in a starburst of energy, a raging sphere of light and fire that tore through the remains of its structure and blew the fragile shell apart. All Imperial ships held position, ranged like hungry predators around the corpse of their victim, guns still trained and battle stations still active. Wise to do so: you never knew what nasty surprises could lurk amid a cloud of rapidly cooling debris, even in a case of such catastrophic destruction.

So it took a while for Kiastros to announce the engagement's close.

'Ship-kill,' he said at last, reaching once more for his wine. 'Instruct the scriveners to prepare all particulars for the log – I shall inspect them within the hour.'

'Ship-kill, aye,' Avati replied, finally relaxing in her seat. It had been an unexpected encounter – at least for her – but the result was satisfactory: one enemy forced back into the warp, one destroyed. The flotilla they had been commanded to intercept was intact, and already the hails were coming in. 'May I offer my congratulations, lord captain?'

Kiastros smiled at her – a brief flicker of amusement across pursed lips. 'You may, lieutenant. Though we still have some mysteries to solve, I think. Such as, what could possibly have breached a plasma core at those ranges. Any ideas?'

'Not yet,' she said truthfully. 'I shall work on it.'

'See that you do,' said Kiastros, getting up, glass still in hand, now waiting for his attendants to scuttle up and escort him to his private chambers. 'No stone left unturned, as I often say. The slightest thing – *the slightest thing* – left undone is all the enemy requires. I shall prepare now to meet the flotilla's commander.'

Avati mentally rolled her eyes. Throne, he could be insufferable, especially when he'd done something clever.

'By your will, lord captain,' she said neutrally, and began her labour.

# Chapter Two

STANDING DOWN

STRAY DREAMS

VELLUM-WORK

Captain of Armsmen Aris Garrock took the order from his armour's internal comm-bead, checked it against the ship's systems for confirmation, then relaxed.

'Action over,' he grunted to his command group, and reached up to unbuckle his helm. 'Short and sweet.'

The high-roofed chamber around him filled up with the sounds of two hundred men and women slamming and clunking the catches on their heavy boarding gear. Cartridges were switched out and stowed, shotguns were locked back into sheaths. Lumens crackled up to full power, exposing the metal grilles and plates of the holding chamber around them. The tension, which ever since realspace entry had been taut, abruptly vanished, and dozens of conversations started up again.

It was usually like this. It would be like this in dozens of other garrisons across the ship. Naval armsmen were only called into service in the event of a hull breach by an enemy. They were rarely deployed in planetary conflicts, due to ancient ordinances that a captain like Kiastros was keen to observe, and so their combat training was restricted to the close-quarters business of corridor-to-corridor fighting. That rarely happened, since the bulk of void combat was conducted at extreme range, so the standard drill was for hours of preparation, hours of waiting in the cramped garrison despatch chambers, then the order to stand down. You got used to it, though the strange mixture of relief and frustration never quite went away.

'Gun-rats getting quicker,' said Refad, Garrock's first lieutenant, fiddling with the buckle under his helm. 'Someone's been busy with the lash.'

Garrock nodded. The broadsides had sounded closer together than in the past. He'd played a small part in that himself – Kiastros had ordered a purge of the upper bilge levels a few cycles back, rooting out the worst of the filth that scratched out a living down there, and that helped efficiency. The more vermin you had on a ship, the more gummed-up everything got, so it paid to apply a lick of flame or two to the worst areas from time to time.

'About time,' he said, reaching up to check the barrel of his lasgun. 'They were slow as hells off Evra IX. Maybe the king's grown a spine about it.'

The king. The captain. A monarch almost as distant and unknowable as the Emperor Himself, albeit one you'd never think of praying to.

Except that Garrock had met Kiastros. Many times. He still didn't think he knew anything about the man.

Refad chuckled. 'Or maybe he'll come down here and knock your teeth out.'

Garrock hefted his weapon. 'Maybe he'll try.'

Hobes grinned. Garrock's comms officer was a slight woman, compact and tough as flaywire. 'You're so full of shit,' she muttered, shaking her head.

'So full of shit, *captain*,' Garrock reminded her, unfastening the breastplate of his boarding armour and taking a deep breath. He wanted a lho-stick. He felt like getting down to the mess hall and grabbing something hot and greasy from the refectory.

Maybe he was getting old. His body ached from the long wait for orders, all the while locked into heavy armour but barely moving. His eyes felt scratchy and dry, his throat sore. Back in the day, he'd have shrugged it off. He'd have been prouder of his physique, a pit-brawler's body that barely felt the injuries. Now his bulk felt a little too much like flab, his heavy-set shoulders a little too much like a burden.

'No briefing, no advance data,' Refad complained, rubbing his neck where the helm's atmosphere seal had left a mark. 'Maybe they didn't expect to run into anything.'

Garrock grunted. The king wasn't a fool – he'd come hard out of the warp, knowing something would be there to shoot at. The fact Kiastros hadn't deigned to share any of that knowledge with his Captain of Armsmen was no surprise – it hardly bothered him any more.

A voidship was a realm. At the top were the lords and the officers, cloistered away in their glittering domes and spires and surrounded by clusters of ephemeral data. In the middle were the populace – the engine crews, the gun-crews, the armsmen and the menials – all held in line with the crushing weight of deference and regulation. Below that were the shadowy worlds of the bilge levels, the caverns where only the wretched dwelt, breeding and dying in the endless dark like sump-rats. Everyone knew their level, everyone knew their place. Save for those right at the very pinnacle, you couldn't even imagine a world outside it – you were locked in, enclosed, condemned to die on the same decks you'd been born on.

So Garrock didn't think much of Kiastros. But then he didn't have to. Hierarchy was just the way it was, and there was no changing it. He'd fight for the man. He'd defend him with his own body, if he had to. But he'd never love him. He'd never love anything about this Imperium. How could you? It stank, all of it, from the bottom all the way to the top.

'So, what next?' asked Hobes, roughing up her short, sweat-damp hair.

'Rendezvous with scheduled flotilla,' said Garrock. 'We'll take on some people, they tell me – I need to be there for security clearance. Then back to U-93.'

'What are we now, then?' asked Vermidha, one of Garrock's own troopers, a lithe figure out of his armour with an uncanny ability to slip into shadows when you weren't paying attention. 'Running escort duty for the commodore?'

'Looks like it,' said Garrock, shaking off the last of his battle plates and heaping them up for the armoury servitors to collect and service. He got up, and felt his old muscles, the ones he'd been so proud of, protest. 'It's what we were born into. The Navy. The most wondrous institution in the whole wide shitting galaxy. So suck it up, stop complaining, and get moving.'

Captain Kiastros walked the short distance from the command bridge to his private chambers. The route took him high into the ship's spine, curving around from where the bridge-dome rose up from the cluster of heavily armoured defence towers and out across a slender ridge of adamantine. High windows gave a commanding view of the entire forward hull structure, and he often paused before the armaglass to take it in. Here you could look along a significant portion of the ship's great length, take in the immensity of its construction, marvel at its symmetry and beauty.

The void swept above and around the upper hull, rendering every angle in the hard light of Jophra XI's sun. Kiastros picked out the little details – the golden aquila set above Santalina's

Navigator demesne, the stone cowled figures ranged above the officers' chapel, the enormous gilded power lines snaking down to the gaping maw of the nova cannon.

The *Judgement of the Void* was a Mars-class battle cruiser. Over three miles in length, two-thirds of a mile abeam at its widest point. The crew numbered in the high tens of thousands – even he did not know the full complement, for no surveys were ever carried out in the depths of his ironclad kingdom. The core warship had twin rows of macrocannons embedded along both flanks – its main armament – plus dorsal lance arrays and its mightiest possession, the nova cannon, slung under the armoured prow. It also possessed four attack wings of Fury interceptors and an extensive standing garrison of armsmen.

He smiled to himself, as he often did. It was a fine ship. A colossus of the void, a monarch of the deep abyss. Greater vessels existed in the Imperial Navy – the true behemoths of battleships and grand cruisers – but not so very many. It was rare for the *Judgement of the Void* to meet something of comparable heft. It was a titan, a great piece of human-made splendour launched into a galaxy of wonders. Perhaps it was only a fractional part of the Emperor's accumulated might – just a mote, just a speck – but from this vantage it felt mighty indeed.

'And of all your works,' Kiastros whispered, the words of the Navy litany coming easily, 'greatest are these vessels, for they carry the blessed into righteous battle.'

To command such a machine was an honour almost beyond expression. Kiastros felt it deeply. He felt it when he awoke, he felt it when he retired to sleep. He felt it when he prayed in his private chapel, and he felt it when he sat down to inscribe the logs and the records for the scriptorium. Some captains, he knew, chafed at the nigh-endless tasks of documentation, disliking the hours spent with an auto-quill amid heaps of parchment. He didn't. He found it restful. Setting out the ledgers of munitions production, crew rotations, watch-keeping and engine maintenance made him conscious of the operations of the realm he presided over. He would likely never visit the lubrication coils lodged under the rear plasma-drive housings, but he knew just how well they operated. He would almost certainly never tour the nutrient vats where the crew's rations were boiled, but he was perfectly acquainted with their efficiency ratios and raw inputs.

The ship was a body, and he was its head. The limbs could operate without supervision at times, though it took an active mind to ensure that every member had what it required.

'My thanks to you,' Kiastros said devoutly, bowing his head. 'Every hour, I thank you. No greater gift exists, no greater service may be rendered.'

Then he was walking again, his tall frame held erect, his gloss-polished boots clicking on the marble. He reached up to press a strand of black hair back into place, to adjust the high collar of his uniform. Then he reached his rooms, and the two guards saluted as he passed through the door.

He unbuttoned the top two buttons of his jacket, placed his empty goblet on a cabinet and moved over to a heavy hojlwood desk set against a circular window with a view of the stars. He sat in his high-backed chair, spine still straight, and reached for a control-wand from the orderly arrangement of objects on the desktop. A soapstone plinth flickered with a ghost of eldritch energies, before a hololith projection spun into life over the plinth. The translucent spectre of a fellow Imperial commander rippled into life.

'Lord captain,' came a crackling voice. 'My greetings to you, and my thanks. Captain Kenete Yila, at your service.'

Kiastros nodded in acknowledgment. 'And mine to you, captain,' he replied. As the commander of an escort-class vessel, Yila did not warrant the prefix 'lord' to her title, and Kiastros was always careful to observe rank. 'I trust that your vessels are intact and secure?'

*'They are. Mostly. We have taken damage to one, and may have to evacuate certain key personnel before transition. Perhaps you will be able to assist us in the transfer.'*

'By all means. I assume, perhaps incorrectly, the damaged vessel is the one whose designation was hidden prior to our arrival?'

*'By order of its commander. The vessel is Adepta Sororitas, of the Orders Hospitaller.'*

'Ah, how interesting. I have not served alongside the honoured Sisters for many years. May I also take it that the – most helpful – destruction of that plasma core was a result of their actions?'

*'It was. Their weaponry, at that range, is superior to anything we possess.'*

Ah, how that must have smarted. 'Splendid. I should be glad to meet them, when time allows – perhaps before the translation to the muster grounds.'

*'I would commend that course.'* She paused. *'Though may I ask, lord captain – your arrival was somewhat... unconventional. Was there some reason you were unable to respond to our hails in a timely fashion?'*

Here it came. The unpleasant but necessary part.

'You are asking the wrong questions, captain,' Kiastros said, quietly but firmly. 'You should be asking how I knew that your position was known to the enemy. You should be asking why I chose to break the veil on the edge of the Mandeville zone in a position for immediate combat, when you had not asked for any such assistance. Had you asked yourself those questions, the answer to the one that you did ask would have been evident.' He placed his hands together on the tabletop. 'Our astropathic choir detected prayer-visions from your location. Not with the content revealed, of course, but enough for a determined listener to divine realspace coordinates. And in these dark times, there are plenty of determined listeners. If we were able to detect it, then I judged the enemy would be even keener to reach you. Had we attempted to make contact with you prior to our arrival, we would have alerted any pursuers to our presence.' He never lost eye contact with the lithocast's flickering face. 'You were in peril from the moment those missives were allowed to leave. Had we not arrived when we did, running silent and ready for action, you would be dead now.'

Yila looked stricken. She knew the score – if what he told her was true, her captaincy would be forfeit. Possibly even her life.

*There must be some mistake,* she said weakly.

'I have the logs prepared,' Kiastros told her. 'They shall be transmitted to you shortly, and will enable you to make all effective enquiries as to where the leaks originated.'

Yila swallowed. *'If this is true...'* she murmured, clearly calculating if it could be, and who might be responsible.

'Then you will apply the appropriate sanctions, I am sure,' said Kiastros.

*'It shall be done.'*

Kiastros nodded. 'Very good. Then we shall speak again in due course.'

He terminated the link. By rights, the breach of security ought to be reported immediately. The Navy's internal military courts should be convened, Yila relieved of command, an enquiry launched. But this was a time of war, and Jovanjiar's preparations were almost complete. Soon all ships in the battle group would be gathered together for the push beyond the Anaxian Line, and the admiral and his commodores would want no distractions. It might be of some benefit to Kiastros to have a junior captain owing him a favour, given the vicissitudes of battle. And, after all, no real harm had come of it, and advantages could be found in every eventuality, Emperor willing.

He sat back in his chair, pushing his linked fingers up under his chin. Should he tell Avati? Santalina, maybe? Perhaps. In time. For now, he had another victory under his belt, a pliant flotilla commander under his wing, and plenty of upcoming action to plan for. A decision could be made in good time.

He was more interested in the news that the Hospitallers were present in the flotilla. Fostering links to the Sororitas, one of the most powerful and effective branches of the sprawling Imperial military machine, could only be beneficial.

He reached up to the comm-bead at his neck and opened a secure channel.

'Astrogation,' he said, linking to Avati's terminal. 'New orders.'

*'Lord captain?'* came the reply.

'Make overtures to the Adepta Sororitas vessel when it comes alongside. Extend my invitation to its commander to dine, or for prayers, whichever is most amenable. Should she wish to join us for the journey to the muster point, convey that she will be most welcome.'

*'By your will.'*

'Look after them. Make every accommodation.'

*'Of course.'*

He closed the link. Just as he did so, a second pair of doors slid open on the chamber's far side. Three archive-servitors limped through bearing taped bundles of parchment and scrivening equipment.

'Excellent,' said Kiastros, reaching across to a candelabra and pulling it closer. 'Leave them here, if you please.'

They soundlessly did as he asked, then shuffled off. He reached for the first leaf – Spleed's account of munitions expended and estimates of replenishment – and began, enthusiastically, to add his notes.

# Chapter Three

**TWO MUTANTS**

**AMBITION**

**AMASEC**

Almost the entirety of a voidship was built under the auspices of the Adeptus Mechanicus. Its enormous skeleton was laid down under the watchful, unblinking gaze of tech-priests and void-magi, its every spar and beam scrutinised against their holy ordinances. Several critical elements were also overseen by high-ranking Navy technicians, and a few specialised areas were given ritual attention by various obscure branches of the Munitorum and Administratum, but it was Mars that made them. Only two discrete sections were finished out of sight of the cowled masters of the Red Planet, for each of those elements contained secrets older than the Imperium itself. One of these was the chamber containing the astropathic choir, whose grand interiors were always completed under conditions of strict secrecy by sages from the Adeptus Astra Telepathica. Psycho-reactive materials were inlaid over the Mechanicus-built substructure, and various wards against the empyrean were painstakingly carved into metal and stone. The structure of the place itself was unlike anything else in the ship – a series of huge concentric chambers designed to harness and funnel the harmonics of the roiling warp placed beneath a tall psi-resonant spire. Once sanctified by its blinded occupants and their morose servants, few of the regular crew went anywhere near the place. It smelled bad, they said. The decks around it were unlucky. You could read strange inscriptions on the walls that would haunt your dreams even if you never deciphered them. All rumours and gossip, no doubt, but it was enough to keep both officers and crew well away unless they could absolutely help it.

The second reserved chamber was the one occupied by the ship's Navigator. Here also the final details of construction were overseen by the equally secretive representatives of the Navis Nobilite, that deeply recondite branch of the Imperial hierarchy whose precise origins had been forgotten, it was whispered, even by themselves. No outsiders ever witnessed what rites were performed in the hollowed-out chambers reserved for the resident Navigator. Perhaps the ceremonies were mundane enough – some sprinkled incense and a few sacred words of benediction. The deck-rats were inclined to believe that human sacrifice must have been part of it, no doubt as gory and prolonged as possible, and they rehearsed elaborate tales of young ratings being taken behind the gilt-faced doors never to be seen again. Whatever the truth, the Navigator's demesne was just as shunned as the star-speakers' halls by the crew, all of whom would far rather take their chances in the violent and filthy under-decks than risk contagion by whatever went on in those uncanny and unnatural places.

Such concerns were not shared, naturally enough, by those who lived and worked in them. The Navigator's attendants did not know every truth about the chambers they inhabited – who, in this Imperium, ever did? – but they knew the air would not poison them and that the floors did not conceal trapdoors over bottomless wells. They remained cloistered away in their self-contained halls, for the most part, fully aware that the non-gifted humans around them reviled them. They prepared their own meals, conducted their own affairs, played their own little games of politics, all locked away in their ship-within-a-ship.

Whenever the Navigators or the astropaths were forced to leave their homes, most likely it was that one of them had chosen to visit the other, for there was a certain kinship in adversity in being one of the Imperium's barely tolerated mutant classes. The distance between the two sets of chambers was significant – almost half a mile, with the astropathic spire being placed by convention a long way from the cluster of command towers around the bridge – but special-purpose corridors trodden by few others could carry residents from one place to the other in conditions of reasonable secrecy.

So it was that the ship's senior astropath, Garg Vandia Ortuyo, had made his way in silence and with minimal escort from his choir-halls to pay his respects to the ship's lone Navigator, Mergaux Santalina of the House Asheler, in her sumptuous reception chambers. Both of them were old, and had spent many decades of service on the *Judgement of the Void*. Both commanded respect within their respective organisations by dint of that longevity, though perhaps a more critical observer might have noted that a battle cruiser was not quite the most prestigious station to conclude a lifetime of service on, not when there were full battleships in need of navigation and star-speaking services. Still, they were serious people, both carrying themselves with an accumulated patina of grandeur. Ortuyo was enormously fat, draped in robes of a deep forest green trimmed with gold, his jowly features overhung by the heavy cowl that hid his milky sightless eyes. Santalina was, by contrast, stick-thin and withered. She wore a heavy damask robe in gold and walked with an ebony cane. The bandana that concealed her seeing eye was lace-trimmed and carried artful embroidered runic devices amid swirls of hard-to-unpick patterning.

Once they were together, their servants left them alone, shutting heavy doors to insulate against all but the faintest echo of the ship's ever-present engine-growl. They both sat, Santalina perched like a bird, Ortuyo collapsing into his armchair and making the upholstery creak. Candles flickered around them, casting a soft light over the assembled finery. In the distance, an ancient chronometer ticked gently.

'He's pleased with himself,' said Ortuyo.

Santalina nodded. 'He's got every right to be.'

'Too clever by half. I could have got them a message – arranged a new rendezvous.'

'It might have been intercepted.'

'He wanted to make a point.'

'And he did that quite well, as far as I can see.'

They were companionable, the two of them, like an old married couple. Ortuyo's voice was low and phlegmy, Santalina's clipped and aristocratic. A menial of Santalina's court glided in bearing tea in porcelain cups, and Ortuyo helped himself to sucrose-balls with a pair of silver tongs.

'He's become too attached to this ship,' he said, picking up the cup and saucer.

'A captain should be attached to his ship.'

'Not if he's as good as you say he is.' Ortuyo sipped, then belched. 'A battleship command, you told me. Clamber up the ladder, leave this hull to his second.'

Santalina's nose wrinkled. 'Avati? No chance. She's got more ambition than sense.'

Ortuyo chuckled, and his chins wobbled. 'You hate her.'

'I don't.'

'You do. You loathe her. Why?'

Santalina thought about that. He was right, of course – she despised the first lieutenant, and dreaded the day she took over from Kiastros. What was it about her? Too young? A reminder of herself, many decades ago? Maybe. Or maybe Avati was just lax, like all the recent crop of officers – rushed out of schola too soon to service the Navy's insatiable need for fresh blood. Kiastros was the real deal – a stickler for detail, a religious man, like they all used to be when she'd first joined.

Things had been better then. Things had slipped badly since. It made her morose to even think about it.

'I think she'll leave,' Santalina said, taking her own cup. 'She's got eyes on a bigger prize. She wasn't born here, she's got nothing to keep her. One big opening, and she'll go for it.'

Ortuyo raised a shaved eyebrow. 'That's hardly protocol, is it? Unless the king gives her his blessing?'

'I don't know. I don't know how they run things.' She shrugged. 'But she's young enough to make it happen. Never forget it – he fights for the ship, she fights for what the ship can do for her.'

Ortuyo laughed again. 'If you say so. I like her fine. Not up to us, though, is it? Things will unfold as they will.'

Astropaths were fatalistic folk. Their entire existence was bound up in riddles and dreams, and so they learned early on to deal with uncertainty. It was different for Navigators. They had to be sure of everything, all the time. Make a wrong guess, misread a gyre in the Seethe, and you could send the entire ship into one of hell's vortices. Santalina valued certainty, solidity, a certain predictability. Kiastros had always given her that, and it counted for a lot. House Asheler was not one of the most highly regarded houses – some vague mutterings of ancient controversy during the Great Heresy – so it paid to keep onside with the better sort of Navy captain.

'He'll be taking us back into the Seethe soon,' she said, setting her cup down with a clink. 'Time is pressing.'

Ortuyo nodded. 'They've already got my people working hard. So many ships, so many missives, all to be coded and secured. I don't think they realise how hard it is.'

Santalina leaned forward, placed her bony elbows on bony knees. 'But we close on the big one now. One more sector, and we'll be out beyond the Anaxian Line. Victory there, and they'll be pushing for more – the final destination.'

'The place we dare not name.'

Santalina snorted. 'I'll name it. The Eye. The Eye of Terror. It's where Fleet Secundus has always been destined to end up. That's what the primarch wanted, and it's only a matter of time before the order comes.'

Ortuyo looked doubtful. 'But could you even guide us there?'

'Easiest thing in the galaxy. The place screams at me in my sleep – I could plot a course without so much as a single meditation.'

'It scares me. I'll be honest.'

'So it should. But that's where we're headed. Clear the Anaxian Line, take the approach lanes, then it'll be in front of us. Within the year, they say. It's bold. I like that. Would never have happened, not before things changed.'

'True enough. Better days, they were.'

'Stagnant days. Days of slow defeat. Better to go out in glory than suffer all that again.'

'Only if it works.'

Santalina raised an eyebrow. 'You doubt the primarch, Garg? Is that what you're saying?'

Ortuyo laughed heartily. 'Don't try to frighten me with that, you old witch. I'm too fat and tired to be scared of the Inquisition, and in any case I don't think they know what to make of him either.' He sighed, and his great chest rose and fell. 'I'm just fed up of it. All the promises. There's no back to break here, no citadel to capture. We grind and we grind, and still it all erodes beneath our feet. I don't believe him. I don't believe this will be any different. It's just a bigger fleet, a bigger war. They'll never end.'

Santalina shook her head. 'Ah, my good friend. You've been too long in your sanctum with your wicked dreams. This is where it all turns. This is where we've always been headed. I wish to see it.' Her natural eyes sparkled. 'The Despoiler laid low. The nightmare ended. That's his vision. That's the promise.'

'You have more faith than me.'

'I have faith enough for both of us.'

'Is that so? Then that comforts me.'

'I should hope it does.' Santalina took another sip of tea. Nasty synthetic stuff, but that couldn't be helped while on campaign. 'A few more victories, and we'll be on our way, out into the black, with our sights on the Eye.'

Ortuyo raised his cup to her as if in wry salute.

'So you say it,' he muttered, and his expression was sour. 'The Eye for us all.'

Avati headed quickly from her quarters down to the hangar intake bays. She buttoned her jacket as she went: full dress uniform, with its tassels and gold-embroidered aquilas and – worst of all – ceremonial sword, which would have been no good at all in a fight and only served to risk tripping her up as she hurried. A squad of six armsmen came with her, all similarly kitted out in parade-chamber finery. They passed through corridors full of activity, for Kiastros had ordered a swift turnaround and soon the warp drives would be powered up again to take them to the muster point. It would have been difficult to meet the deadline at the best of times, but now she had to receive an official guest, and that made the schedule all the more testing.

When she had first arrived on the *Judgement of the Void*, Kiastros' habit of keeping things to himself had been an unwelcome and irritating surprise. Previous captains had been far more open with their officers, even the irascible and drunk ones, whereas her current commander seemed to derive a strange kind of pleasure from closeness. It wasn't a power trip, as far as she could make out, more a personality trait – a kind of pleasure in the reveal, or a test of his own ability to predict and adapt to circumstances. He wouldn't have risked such a thing on a major engagement, but still – it was frustrating. What if there had been more than two enemy ships? What if they'd been bigger and more capable? He couldn't have known for sure what would have uncovered the flotilla's poorly hidden astropathic chatter. Or maybe he had yet more information that she wasn't privy to. Maybe Ortuyo had dredged some intelligence up from somewhere, or maybe Santalina had. Those two were strange, just as secretive, a mini-cabal within a ship already riven with factions and scheming.

Best to let it go. The warp-touched were always liable to conspire with one another, and Kiastros wasn't that bad really. A taste for the theatrical reveal was hardly the worst habit he could have had, and in any case the *Judgement of the Void* would not be her final posting.

She was ready for a captaincy of her own, she knew. Maybe not a battle cruiser, but an escort certainly, a light cruiser very likely. The muster at U-93 was a great opportunity. A thousand eyes would be on them, a hundred scriveners taking down notes on every ship in Hekaon's squadron. When combat came, she would have to make sure the *Judgement of the Void* was seen, that it performed creditably, because there were certain to be casualties elsewhere. Fleet Secundus had taken terrible damage during the months it had been carving a path out from the Terran sectors, and while that was of course regrettable, it opened doors.

She reached the receiving chamber's locked doors and snappily saluted the sergeant on duty.

'All in order, sergeant?' she asked as the doors slid open.

'All in order, lieutenant,' the armsman replied, making the aquila across an armoured chest. 'One guest, as ordered.'

Avati nodded, and passed inside with her escort. A large, utilitarian chamber waited for her. The floor was blank rockcrete, the walls bare plasteel. Sodium lumens cast a stark light over the panels, and the floor vibrated slightly from the machinery lodged underneath. Beyond the far wall was one of the battle cruiser's main shuttle hangars, a cavernous space capable of taking anything from an Arvus lighter up to a void-capable Astra Militarum troop carrier. Out on the apron stood a transport from the Adepta Sororitas already crawling with servitors prepping it for take-off again. Its lone passenger stood before her in the bare reception chamber – a woman clad in pale battle armour, her helm off to reveal a muscled and tanned face.

Avati walked towards her, keeping her head up. The Sororitas were like the Astartes – perhaps not quite as ludicrously big, not quite so aggressively proportioned, but still capable of giving off that aura, the one that informed you very clearly that you were oh-so-very fragile, that this figure here was capable of snapping you in half without so much as a thought, that she was built for nothing else, and even as your blood cooled on the floor she would be moving on to the next target without a pause. Her armour was battle-scarred, pitted with projectile gouges and old stains, but for all that it remained magnificent – a tautly overlapping collection of finely sculpted ceramite encrusted with a panoply of purity seals and stamps.

'Honoured Sister,' Avati said, bowing. 'We are blessed by your presence.'

The Sister had a severe face, short-cropped hair, metallic implants down the left cheek, a trefoil tattoo on the other. Her nose looked to have been broken and reset. The impression was brutal, but also impressive. Such warriors were some of

His finest fighters, tempered physically, mentally and spiritually to go up against the very worst enemies imaginable. The holiest. The most pure.

'Glad to be here. Fine ship. Could do with a drink, though – rough passage over.'

Avati blinked. 'I can request anything that you require.'

'Amasec, then. If it's good. If not, wine'll be fine. Your captain invited me for dinner with him. I'll take him up on that. You coming? That'd be fine too. Miriam Isobel, Hospitaller, Order of the Jewelled Sceptre. Your name?'

The torrent of words was hard to keep up with. Isobel's accent was thick, too – a throaty, abrasive burr that made catching the words tricky.

'Leroa Avati. Master of Astrogation. I shall inform the captain of your–'

Isobel started to march ahead, arms swinging. 'So where'll you berth me? Nothing fancy. I can sleep on a rock. Have done too. But you have an apothecarion – a good one? I'll want to look at it.'

Avati scrambled to keep up. 'Master Jep is our medicae. I can make an introduction at your convenience.'

The two of them passed back through the doorway, out into the corridor, and Isobel went like she already knew the way.

'Is there anything else you would–'

'Just a drink, when you can. My equipment is already being transferred to my chambers.'

'Very well. I shall–'

'Smells clean.' Isobel gave Avati a wide grin. 'Smells clean! A battleship ought to be clean. You'd be surprised how many aren't. That's half the war over – more troops die of infection than bullets. I like this ship.'

'That's... good.'

'How long have you served here, Leroa Avati?'

'Seven years, Sister.'

'You've seen plenty of action.'

'By His grace, yes.'

'And now we come to the main event, eh? The main event. If your captain is amenable, I plan to spend it with you.' She halted, drew closer to Avati, gave her a sly look. 'You can grow tired of an Order warship. My Sisters can be... very serious. It's good to have a change of scene when the mood takes you – you agree?'

Avati didn't know. Moods weren't something that ever affected what she did. There were orders, and exigencies of combat, and chances for advancement, that was all. 'He will be honoured,' she said, hoping that was true.

'Your captain,' said Isobel. 'I spoke to him – just a few words. Religious man, I think.'

'We are all devout.'

Isobel snorted. 'There's devout, and there's devout. I think he's the real thing. I think his soul is secure. I wonder if yours is?' She laughed again. 'Don't worry. I'm here to stitch up bodies, not examine souls. But I'm glad you have a commander who knows the litanies. That's a kind of weapon. A kind of shield. More powerful than cannons. We'll see. We'll talk.'

Avati couldn't help but glance at the warrior as they walked. Isobel was tall, broad, her physique boosted by the heavy plate armour. A faint aroma of machine unguents and human sweat came from her, not an unclean smell, but a fighter's smell, the combination of bodily and mechanical power. The woman was almost absurdly vigorous, striding out with a swagger Avati had only really observed in Space Marines. Those were far heavier, though – like miniature tanks, really – so Isobel was intriguing, a marginally lighter version of the same basic template.

They took an elevator shaft up a few levels, then a mag-train down the mainline conduit to the accommodation decks. Isobel talked the whole time, observing liberally, generally enthusiastic about what she saw. Crew members passed them, bowing reverently or making the aquila. They were used to all kinds of specialised warriors on board, including the Astartes, and so were respectful without being overawed.

Eventually they reached the Sister's allocated chambers – three rooms, well appointed, close to the officers' decks and secured with two armsmen at the door. Avati smiled at her, hoping she'd be able to get away quickly now – so much still remained to be done.

'Well then, I...' she started hopefully.

Isobel smiled, and thumped the door release. 'You'll show me around the place, Astrogation,' she said. 'And when we're done with that, you'll share a glass with me while I ask you some more questions. Throne of Light, I have a thirst on me. What do you say?'

Wearily, Avati nodded, and prepared to followed her inside. This would cost her – tasks would not be accomplished, and soon enough Kiastros would want to know why.

Still, what could she do? She'd been given clear instructions.

A menial scurried up then, right on time, bearing a bottle of amasec and two glasses from the ship's stores. Avati took them from him, drew in a deep breath, and followed Isobel inside.

# Chapter Four

UNDERWORLD

THE GREATEST TRIAL

OBJECTIVE PRIME

An engine. *The* engines. People with no knowledge of a void-ship tended to make simplistic assumptions. They pictured a few fuel tanks leading to a drive chamber or two. They pictured some pipework spreading out to thruster housings. They assumed such things would be big. Very big, even.

They had no idea. Not even the bridge crew really understood the guts of a big warship – they spent their time dozens of levels up, glued to the tactical displays and read-outs, knowing what the engines could *do*, but not what they *were*. How could they? It was a different world below the command decks, where the lumens flickered weakly and oil residues pooled in the corners.

The engine *was* the ship. Almost all of it was, one way or another. The systems snaked and curled up through every conduit and shaft, vast and boiling, spreading like a contagion. You could never escape it, not really – even the most heavily protected chambers suffered from the distant thrum that couldn't be eradicated, the faint vibration that never went away.

On something like a Mars-class battle cruiser, the main enginarium halls were vast. Absolutely vast. A menial could get
lost in their pits and towers and never come out again. Arcs
of energy snapped between conductor vanes, each one the
length of a hab-block, briefly illuminating subterranean cities
built of valves and tubing, injection-spikes and coolant lines,
intake grilles and heat exchangers. The air was always hot down
there, punishingly hot, tanged with stinks of grease and metal.
You might drop a turbo-wrench and hear it clang and spin for
ages, gradually tumbling into chasms you knew nothing of
and never wanted to go to. The furnaces never went out. The
forge-hammers never stopped ringing. The promethium pipe-
lines gurgled ravenously forever, the plasma halls roared and
flared, the reinforced warp-chambers throbbed. It was everywhere, the engine. It was never-ending, rebuilt and patched
and refined, always failing, ever-renewing, *alive*.

At least, that was how Magda Kuhl thought about it. The
Master of the Enginarium knew as much about the *Judgement
of the Void*'s great propulsion chambers as any living soul. To be
sure, the tech-priests of the Machine Cult understood more of
the specifics than she did – the chemical reactions, the operation of the intricate control devices, the precise mix of vapours
and liquids in the thousands of tanks and cylinders – but no
one had walked more miles in the dark places than her, no one
had spent more time analysing the clunk and grind of pistons
in their corroded sleeves, and no one else could gauge the
health of a component just by resting a palm on the casing,
inclining a head, listening. It would have been more usual for
a full Priest of Mars to occupy her position, and all knew it,
but appointments were in the captain's gift and Kuhl had more
than earned her position. She lived and breathed the enginarium. She slept within it, she woke within it. Some distant parts
were dangerous, crewed by semi-feral gangs who only barely

obeyed commands from the remote bridge, but even they knew her, and bowed their heads when she came among them, and listened to what she told them. She was the Lady of the Great Machine, the one truly essential component.

And now she was very busy. Order bundles had plummeted down the tubes from on high, demanding the kindling of the mighty plasma drives to bring the ship back towards the core of the Mandeville zone. The coordinates were not her concern, but the delivery of requisite power was. The lower relays had taken some damage during Kiastros' brief little fight, and several hundred menials were now crawling all over them trying to staunch the bleeding. She had to re-route power from a dozen humming generatoria and watch the temperature of the overloaded plasma chambers. Worst of all, Kiastros had ordered a rapid warp transition, fearing that more enemy ships might show up. That meant even more power, even more complication, even more likelihood of something going wrong.

She turned aside from the bank of valve indicators and brass-cased chronometers to see Krujax lumbering towards her. The furnace master was wearing his full environment suit, a bulky swaddle of faded orange heat-resistant fabric. His exposed face was glossy with sweat, splattered with grime and spotted with oil-stains. Kuhl had never seen it any other way.

'All ready?' she asked.

'Primed for when the order comes,' Krujax replied, pulling off one of his gauntlets and shaking it. 'Throne, but it was hard to get the gangs in place.'

Kuhl smiled dryly. 'Always is, though.'

Around the two of them, tech-priests and mechanics shuffled from station to station. The floor underfoot was a mesh, exposing several levels below them, all crowded with robed attendants and menials. Plumes of steam hissed from safety valves as ranks of pressure gauges steadily ticked up. An atmosphere of nervous excitement permeated each level – priming the sacred warp drives was always a moment for anxiety, no matter how often it happened. To break the barrier between the real and the unreal was the most fundamental demonstration of the Omnissiah's power, enacted with regularity on every great ship of His realm, and yet it could still all go so very wrong.

'Any news from the Navigator?' asked Krujax, wiping a sweaty hand across his brow and doing nothing more than smear the grease more liberally.

'She'll be in touch.' Kuhl shook her head. 'If she can be bothered.'

No official injunction prevented Kuhl, Master of the Enginarium, from heading up to the upper decks and speaking to Santalina directly, but it never happened, any more than Santalina would ever deign to dirty her skirts down here. If the Imperium knew how to do anything, it was to maintain the silent boundaries, the vice-like grip of class and status, and on a Navy voidship those fetters weighed more heavily than anywhere.

But those were dangerous thoughts, even to intimate between close comrades. Kuhl shot a quick glance at Krujax to check he didn't disapprove. He was from the same stock as her, a good man, one she could rely on for most things, but you never really knew who you could trust.

He wasn't listening. He was fiddling with the catch on his other gauntlet, wheezing deeply as his gummed-up lungs struggled in the heat.

*Be more careful*, Kuhl thought to herself.

Then the first klaxons went off, followed by the chiming of great bells in the depths. A chorus of prayer-servitors started up, blaring out hymns of warding, and the tech-priests began the ritual chants.

Kuhl turned back to her instruments. The air prickled around her, making every surface sting with static. Five hundred yards away, buried deep amid layer upon layer of protective wards, the warp drives were blazing into life, their hidden innards pulsing with the eldritch energies necessary to rip a tear in the weft of realspace. No mortal ever gazed directly at those chambers, unless Santalina was somehow able to peer at them – only the effects were felt, the stomach-churning, mind-turning wrench that meant the warp was reaching out to swallow them.

'In we go, then,' said Krujax, making the sign of the aquila and gazing at the droning priests. Worms of electricity scampered over the instruments, and muffled booms echoed up from the pits below. Plasma lines were shutting down, immense thrusters were guttering out, but the true power drain was only just beginning.

Kuhl mouthed a prayer of her own, and briefly touched the skull-cog sigil at her breast, just out of superstition. Rumour was that a Sister of Battle had been taken on board, which made her a little happier – surely something like that would ease the passage. He wouldn't let harm come to one of those.

Then it happened – the snap, the flex, the readjustment of reality that made you blink and stare and wish fervently to vomit. Santalina had performed whatever strange magic she'd had to, and the routine miracle had taken place once again. Kuhl took in a breath and shook her head to clear her double vision. The priests carried on droning, the engines carried on churning.

'Course set,' she muttered. 'Now I have to climb some stairs.'

'Really? The king wants you for something?'

Kuhl rolled her eyes. 'The worst thing of all,' she said. 'Dinner.'

The chamber was grand, set high on the ship's spine with galleries of real-viewers giving spectacular vistas out into the infinite void. Except that now, since the ship was currently in the warp, every one of them was safely shuttered and locked. The high panes had been replaced with projections of starfields, making it possible, for a moment or two, to forget that the battle cruiser was plunging through the tides of hell.

Kiastros had fitted it out opulently. Part of this was natural piety – a voidship was His property, and hence had to be looked after – but it was also political. This was Kiastros' world, his domain, and visitors would expect him to behave much like a hive-city governor or Militarum general. So the decks were marble here, the columns fashioned from basalt, the shuttered windows lined with gold. The suspensors were fashioned into crystalline chandeliers, the atmosphere filters were faintly perfumed. Real candles, made of real wax, flickered on the long real-wood table. Goblets and decanters were all full, topped up by dozens of menials clad in pristine tabards whenever they looked in danger of being drained.

And then there was the food. The average hive-dweller in the Imperium subsisted on protein-sludge and the occasional carb-slab. Much of the ship's own worker cadres did the same. Up here, though, up in the spires and the domes of the command level, things were as refined as any noble-born's citadel. The meat was genuine, not vat-grown, taken from the breeding pens on the twentieth deck; the fruits and the vegetables were products of the long hydroponic trenches tended by over a hundred servitors. Other delicacies were imported whenever the ship was laid up in void-dock, then stored in heavy ice-lockers that drained almost as much raw power as an entire hab-cluster for the gunnery teams. The refectory staff knew what they were doing too, having mostly been poached from planet-bound institutions serving the gilded classes.

Kiastros sat at the head of the table. What he saw pleased him – a full table with his crew impeccably turned out. Avati on his left-hand side, the honoured Sister of Battle on his right. Ortuyo had come, wearing a typically florid gown, though Santalina was needed in her demesne and thus had not been able to attend.

Spleed and Boroja sat a little further down, muttering about something to one another in their conspiratorial way. Magda Kuhl, the Master of the Enginarium, had turned up a little late, still tugging at the tassels on her dress uniform. She looked almost as uncomfortable as Garrock, whose armsman battle plate was far rougher on the eye than the Naval uniforms around him. Other officers and Administratum adepts sat further down, each in the robes and uniforms of their many and varied cadres.

They were all eating. They were all drinking. The hum of conversation flowed just as he liked it to. He imagined himself then as the benevolent father of some large and unruly family, a family he was fond of even as it required constant attention and regular discipline. They would observe the proper decorum, recite the litanies, keep the standards high. That, after all, was the chief difference between the glorious Imperial Navy and the far more varied regiments of the Astra Militarum. Order. Regularity. Tradition.

He lifted his goblet, and a menial soundlessly glided forward to refill it. 'Comrades and guests,' he said, stilling the many conversations. 'Let us give thanks now for His beneficence.'

All bowed their heads while he recited the 14th Observation on Perpetual Abundance. As soon as he'd finished, a second course was brought in on silver salvers, and the clink of cutlery being taken up filled the chamber.

'I see that you enjoy your food, Sister,' Kiastros said, observing Isobel's enthusiastic engagement with what was placed before her.

The Hospitaller wiped her mouth, belched softly into a napkin, and nodded. 'Never seen the point in abstinence,' she said. 'A healthy body gives Him honour.'

'Indeed it does.' Kiastros speared a near-raw sliver of grox-meat and started to chew. 'But, if I may observe, some of your Sisters are not quite so... eager. At least in my experience.'

She lifted her goblet, took a generous swig, thumped it back on the table. 'No, they're not. Not all of them.' She leaned a little closer, cracked a broad smile. 'They can be insufferable, right? *Bloody insufferable*. But what is devotion, eh? Taking what is offered with both hands. That's devotion. When the moment comes, when the enemy is before you, your belly is full, your heart is joyous. That's the way to fight.'

Kiastros laughed. 'You're not what I expected.'

'Others have said that.' She shovelled the food in heartily. 'I care not. But this is a good spread, lord captain. A damned good spread. You keep a fine ship.'

'Honour is due to the purser,' Kiastros said, indicating a thin man named Trisk who sat four places down. 'Though I endeavour to maintain the proper traditions. We're gratified you came to join us for the passage, rather than remain with your Sisters.'

Isobel looked at him sidelong. 'The pleasure is mine, believe me.'

'Honoured Sister, our battle reports have been compiled now,' interjected Avati from the opposite place, looking a little flushed. Kiastros noted that she had not touched her drink. 'That shot you made, on the Archenemy vessel – it was a fine delivery, made at extreme range.'

'Nothing to do with me,' said Isobel with a shrug. 'The captain took a risk, and it paid off. Glory to the Throne.'

'Glory indeed,' said Kiastros.

'Do you anticipate more Adepta Sororitas vessels at the muster, then?' asked Avati. 'That level of firepower is always helpful.'

'I've not been told,' said Isobel. 'I'd guess so. Every convent has been placed on alert, every warrior mobilised. That's true of everyone, though, isn't it?'

'The Age of Crusade,' said Kiastros. 'A wondrous time to be alive. Tell me – I'd be most interested – what is your appraisal of the strategic situation?'

whole thing? The whole crusade?'

'We all prosecute our own little wars. Each fleet, each battle group, each task force. We hear so little from outside, another perspective is always welcome.'

She put down her fork, frowned. 'You ask a question. I'm only a stitcher of bodies.' Then she shrugged. 'Though I'm old enough to remember other crusades. Smaller ones, of course. The primarch wasn't leading them. I remember the high hopes, though. I remember the speeches. Like the ones we get now, from some of the same mouths. Doesn't mean it won't work this time. Doesn't mean it isn't different now, or necessary. But do we still have the ships for what he demands? Do we still have the numbers?'

Kiastros looked at her, intrigued. Getting such candour from a member of an order known chiefly for their zealotry was another unexpected thing. 'I believe that faith makes the difference,' he said. 'The fact that His servant is among us again.'

'Ah, but he's not here, though, is he? I mean, not on this ship, or even this fleet.' Isobel spread her hands. 'No disrespect intended. He's a man. Or something like a man. How many billions fight for us? How many billions does the enemy have? It only takes a single shot.'

'The primarch is more than a man,' said Avati, looking a little stung.

'Surely,' said Isobel. 'And I'm more than a woman, but you might still end me, on a good day. I saw the way you put away that amasec, so I could believe it.' She snorted a laugh. 'So it makes a difference. It does. But there were once nine primarchs, and they were not enough then. The enemy who comes for us now was alive in those days too. That's what they say, anyway. So there you are.'

'Then,' said Kiastros, carefully conscious that others at the table were listening now, 'do you doubt our endeavours?'

Isobel shook her head. 'Not at all. Not at all. We make to the Eye's edge, I'll be in the front line with my Sisters. What choice do we have? Duty is all there is, and I relish it.' Then she started to eat again. 'But be a realist. Fleet Quintus was becalmed, they tell me, though maybe they're moving again now. Tertius had to take up the slack, but who knows what it did to them. And Primus – that great first push – did they ever recover from Gathalamor? Maybe. Must have been several years now, but it all takes its toll. And us? Secundus? They want us to head to the *Eye*. Ha! Just that. Nothing more, nothing less. And nothing about it will be easy.'

'It can be done,' said Avati firmly. Kiastros found himself proud of his second – that was the spirit.

'We haven't yet moved beyond the Anaxian Line,' he interposed, anxious to keep the mood light. 'Not in numbers. Doing so now is only the first step.'

Isobel nodded. 'Quite right. I'm getting ahead of myself.'

'Though – praise Him – the day now moves closer.'

'The order will come, then?'

'I believe so. Hence the muster at U-93. The great concentration of force, the bringing together of our sundered formations. It will be a decisive moment – the first step on the long road.'

'So will the whole fleet be present?'

'The greater part of it. Lord Admiral Samil will be in ultimate command. Battle Group Dominus – our group – will be commanded by Jovanjiar. Other groups will join us, and I anticipate more than seven hundred hulls in all – a major encounter.'

'Seven hundred.' Isobel pursed her lips. 'Major encounter indeed.'

'But you will wish to rejoin your own ship by then,' offered Avati hopefully.

'Not unless I'm summoned.' Isobel glanced at Kiastros. 'And not unless I'd be in the way. I haven't seen your apothecarion yet – perhaps you could use an extra pair of hands.'

Kiastros smiled broadly at her. 'By all means. This is a hospitable ship. Perhaps you would find it interesting to witness a line voidship at war. Not the greatest ship in the fleet, this one, but far from the weakest either.'

Isobel nodded. 'I'd like that,' she said.

Kiastros looked over at Avati pointedly. 'Then let us make it happen,' he said. 'Because, whatever else is uncertain, one thing is not – we shall be in combat again very soon.'

'And praise His name for that,' said Isobel.

'Quite so,' said Kiastros, raising his glass to her. He had made his determination – he liked this Sister, was glad she wished to stay, and Avati would just have to get used to it. 'May it give glory to His eternal reign.'

# Chapter Five

**THE GREAT PIT**

**ARRIVAL**

**IRON SHADES**

She could see everything. The truth of things. The way the universe was internally structured from its hidden depths to its ineffable zenith, its cruelty and its wonder, its infinitude and its complexity. That was the joy of opening the Seeing Eye – the ability to peer behind the curtain of creation and bask in the raw stuff of being.

The practice took its toll, of course. The warp was no place for mortals, not even mutants heavily conditioned to gaze into its eddies and gyres. Strict procedures needed to be followed, ancient rites learned through trial and painful error over millennia by the sundered Navigator Houses. Look too deeply, and you'd go mad. Fail to pay attention and the ship could founder. No greater shame existed for a Navigator than to lose a ship – the ignominy of it could last generations, plaguing the employment prospects of painstakingly prepared descendants.

But Santalina was getting old. She couldn't be as scared of failure as she had once been, all of five centuries ago, learning her trade on system runners and escort vessels and dreaming of a proper voidship to guide. She'd never piloted a vessel awry, not once, and so now the ether felt almost comfortably familiar to her, like slipping into a warm perfumed bath, albeit one with poisons swirling around in the dregs. The immense mass of the *Judgement of the Void* extended around her physical form, vast and solid, an affront to the skitter of psychic forces continually washing up against it. Five more vessel profiles glimmered close by in the jewel-like ether – the flotilla coming along with them, ploughing through the turbulence like cetaceans through surf. Santalina could sense the other Navigators on those other vessels, just as they could no doubt sense her. Hers was a lonely occupation, for the most part – locked away in psychically inert chambers heavily shielded against any possible interference – but it was always some comfort to know that others of her kind were out there, doing the same things, the same duties, keeping the sacred vessels safe from destruction for just a little longer.

And now she was tired. The warp was vicious here, and becoming more vicious with every hour they spent in it. The Great Rift, that abominable tear in the fabric of the universe, was still far off, but each warp-stage brought them closer to it. Its proximity had begun to make her sick. Would Kiastros actually order them into it, when the time came? If so, she might have to swallow her pride and seek extra help. Many of her brothers and sisters in the Navigator houses had done the same thing already, or were contemplating it. The barrier was virtually impossible to cross. A mature Navigator, one at the very apex of health and power, might conceivably do it, at enormous cost, but her, ageing and infirm... It made her battered old heart quail.

Still, that test was a long way away. They might never get that far. Secundus had been engaged in heavy fighting all throughout its long push out from Terra, and that would continue whatever hopes the strategos had for further conquest. Alone of all the crusade fleets, Secundus was going directly up against the vanguard of the Despoiler's many armies. Perhaps Guilliman truly expected them to bludgeon their way right to the heart of darkness and stymie any further incursions out of its toxic depths, or perhaps the fleet was merely being used as a lightning rod to draw the enemy towards them as others ground out the real conquests. It didn't matter either way – they would follow orders and go wherever they were sent. Duty unto death, after all – it had to come at some stage, and better to find it in service than in some sickbed somewhere.

But the Eye. The Great Pit. The Hole in the Void through which light drained away and only madness radiated back. For as long as Santalina could remember, that singular place had commanded almost mythical status, the fulcrum around which all hopes and all despairs had circled. Now it was merely a component of the greater Rift, and a demonstration, if any had ever been needed, of the malign powers of the elder gods.

Yes, *elder*. Navigators, perhaps alone of all the Imperium's ancient institutions, preserved some scraps of the forgotten past, before the Imperium, before the Emperor, before Heresy and Faith, to a time when the voidships of long-dead human realms struggled alone without the faltering light of an Astronomican. Fractured legends were still half understood, rumours of curses sent against – or, *whisper it*, prayers offered up to – the four primordial Powers of the Dark. The Powers had always been there. They had never gone away. And now their might had only grown, their malice increased, their thirst for souls grown stronger. Santalina could close her mortal eyes, she could even sleep, and still she would hear their voices on the far side of the warp-tides, louder than ever, more urgent than ever, never still, never quiet.

So that was the price of it all. The enormous privilege, the fantastical visions and glimpses of the truly divine, it all had to be paid for. Insanity would always drag at her, pulling at her eyelids, puckering at the edge of her mouth, making her unsteady and off-centre.

Resist. Endure. She had done for centuries, and had plenty more endurance within her. As long as Kiastros trusted her, as long as the Rift remained on the horizon only, she was equal to the demands of her duty. The greatest tests could be reserved for another day.

She adjusted position in her throne, feeling the psychically charged stone prickle under her fingertips. The moment was upon them – the optimal moment, the place to strike. She uttered no word, gave no command, but the harmonics immediately changed, the atmosphere around her quickened. Points of hard light materialised ahead of her, hundreds of them. Those were not in the ether, but in realspace, just echoes of physical presences. Somewhere up in the command bridge Kiastros would be giving the orders now, shutting down the warp drives and preparing to tear back into the true void.

Santalina took a moment to gauge the scale of what lay ahead. Hundreds of warships, some of them true leviathans, battleships and grand cruisers, all bristling with weapons and stuffed full with warriors. Each was surrounded by constellations of support vessels, scout-craft, fighter wings. Tenders and personnel shuttles buzzed between the looming shadows, followed closely by supply barges and fuel tankers. It was like a wasp's nest in the abyss, humming angrily, consumed with the industry of warfare and preparation. She could sense the many hundred souls of her own kind, as well as the thousands of astropaths and sanctioned psykers all at work. You could let your focus drift, zoom out a little, and imagine a single colossal organism, a mind, an intelligence, one that acted as one, swarmed and swirled, before striking out en masse.

The warp began to fall away around her, its colours fading, its brilliance draining out. She switched her attention to physical wavelengths, and began to make sense of the sensor data streaming into her input jacks. The muster at U-93 was in standard defensive formation – a hard core of battleships with their long broadsides rotated out from the centre. Each position was exact, each profile carefully calculated. It was required to be – massed macrocannon fire had to be directed outward with no risk of hitting a friendly hull, and that took geometric precision. The core was protected by several layers of support ships – destroyers, frigates, gunboats – all equally carefully placed to avoid weak points in the sphere. The key to Naval combat, an arena in which there were rarely physical constraints on movement, was preparation. Expert force multiplication, layers of redundancy, elimination of defensive flaws. Once a formation was broken, its organisation destroyed, then the game was up. Naval captains spoke of the *Shell*, the invisible hard edge of force projection, the one maintained by constantly adjusted ship positioning, that needed to be ceaselessly maintained and renewed lest an enemy crack it open. Once order was dissolved, then the great advantage of force multiplication was lost and each ship was on its own. The Archenemy, whose vessels had strange gifts and powers, thrived in such loose conditions, and so the imperative thing was to deny them the chance. Keep them at range, outgun them, hold the Shell intact, respond to anarchy with cold, unyielding, merciless discipline.

The last of the warp-dream rippled away, and she reached for the bandana to cover up her Seeing Eye. The voices that had plagued her, the screams and the yammers of the long warp-stage, also echoed into nothing. She began to receive messages from all over the ship, most of them the standard reel of requests and confirmations from the enginarium and astrogation.

Kiastros had made contact, of course. He always did so punctually, one of the many aspects of his character she admired. She opened an audex channel.

'*Deftly done, Mistress Navigator,*' he said, sounding satisfied. '*We begin our approach to the muster now. How do you feel?*'

'Perfectly well,' Santalina lied. 'I find myself looking forward to the next commission.'

Kiastros laughed. '*Very good. Though do not expect another staging for a few cycles – they tell me it'll be a while until everything's assembled.*'

Santalina felt a brief surge of relief, swiftly quelled. That was welcome news, although she wondered if it was properly safe to linger here for so long. Groupmaster Jovanjiar no doubt knew his business. 'I shall enjoy a brief period of recuperation, then,' she said. 'Though I suspect you will not have such luxury – an Adeptus Astartes strike cruiser has broken formation to intercept our approach.'

'*Yes, as arranged. All line voidships are to carry Astartes contingents for ongoing actions. We are to be honoured by the presence of the Iron Shades.*'

Santalina's nose wrinkled. Space Marines were brutes, for all they had their uses. 'Then keep them out of my little place, if you please. The tapestries have been freshly cleaned.'

'*If they deign to listen to me. You should be pleased, Mergaux – it makes us just a little stronger.*'

'We're fine the way we are.' She began to feel light-headed – as much as she tried to hide it, these successive warp-stages were taking their toll. 'Perhaps, when all arrangements have been made, we might dine again soon? I feel the need for some decent refreshment.'

'*By all means,*' said Kiastros. '*Send me word when you are restored – I shall look forward to it.*'

He closed the link. Santalina slumped in her throne, ignoring the rest of the queued-up requests for audiences. She needed to sleep.

The Thunderhawk gunship angled slightly as it powered towards the open hangar doors, fired retros, then came down hard on the apron amid clouds of fire-flecked smoke. Garrock watched it the whole time, admiring the skill of the pilot. It had come in fast, burning across the short gulf between vessels – the spiked and rangy profile of the strike cruiser hanging a mile or two under the vaster shadow of the *Judgement of the Void*.

'Steady now,' he muttered, speaking to himself as much as the squad around him. They were arranged on the apron's edge, just under the high arch leading further inside the ship.

He'd encountered Space Marines before. Never fought alongside them – they'd just been passengers on the ship, ferried from one warzone to the next. The experiences had taught him that each of their Chapters was like a world of its own, as far removed from one another in doctrine and personality as the Navy was from the Militarum. Some had been terrifying, looking like they wanted to tear the ship apart and barely responding to any attempts at communication. Others had been courteous but taciturn, slotting in well enough to the other military cadres on board and deferring to Kiastros. They'd never hung around long, so first impressions were all he had.

He didn't worship them. Not like a hive-rat or a gun-deck grunt might do, despite everything the clerics told him. They were soldiers just like he was, not angels, but with bigger guns and better armour, though he'd never have voiced that opinion out loud. Whenever the Adeptus Astartes were blessed during the daily rites in the ship's many chapels, he just mumbled along with the congregation – dangerous to do anything else.

Now the ramps were coming down, the flight crew were emerging, the deck-servitors were starting their work. Smoke was everywhere, spilling across the rockcrete and sinking into the out-take grilles. Through it all came five giants, black against the turbulent gloom, fully armoured and armed, their helm lenses glowing a pale blue.

For all his cynicism, it was still hard not to react to that – to tense up, to reach for a sidearm, to bolt in terror. Every time it had been the same – that instinctive lurch of fear, the recognition that here was something very wrong, something that had no business standing in front of you unless it was about to kill you. It annoyed Garrock. He ought to be better than that by now. He ought to be able to resist it. Whoever had built these things had done a damned good job.

The lead warrior clanked up to him. His armour was jet-black, with a midnight-blue trim across the rims of the enormous shoulder guards. The surfaces were only dully reflective, in near-pristine condition and smelling of ritual oils. The reactor unit at the warrior's back rumbled. Garrock knew the Chapter designation only from his briefing – the Iron Shades – so the livery and sigils were new to him. He caught a glimpse of the device on the warrior's pauldron, what looked like a shrouded skull bisected by a sword picked out in bone white. Most of the other markings on the armour were incomprehensible – some scrawls in glyphs he didn't recognise – but he knew enough to mark him as a sergeant, which meant the four who came along with him were his squad.

'My lord Astartes,' Garrock said, making the sign of the aquila across his armoured chest. 'You honour us with your presence.'

The warrior nodded. 'Tuo Maizad,' he said. His voice was low, quiet, a little sibilant and with a thick accent. 'Akaida Squad, the Iron Shades.'

Garrock already found himself wondering what their story was – where they came from, what rituals they practised, what had prompted them to clad themselves in almost total darkness.

He doubted he'd ever find out. The chances were that they would cloister themselves away in their reserved chambers and spend the brief time before the engagement in relentless training. Still, you could always speculate.

'I have been ordered to show you to your quarters,' Garrock said. 'And to extend the invitation of the ship's captain for an audience at your convenience.'

Maizad briefly looked at one of his battle-brothers. He was wearing his helm, so the expression was hidden, but Garrock got the distinct impression he'd found that amusing.

'In time, captain,' Maizad said. 'For now, you have your garrison close, no?'

It wasn't just the accent – the use of Low Gothic was also a little eccentric. 'I do, lord.'

'No *lord*. Sergeant, like my brothers call me.' No mistaking it now – Maizad sounded amused, not mocking, just agreeable. 'I wish to see it. Your troops. I think it will be fine, if you are any guide.'

Garrock was taken aback. None of them had ever asked for this before. Half of his complement were on rest-rotation, and many of the remainder were on guard duty or lower-deck suppression patrols. How many could he rustle up? What state could he get them into?

'It will be done,' he said uncertainly. 'Though, do you mean–'

'Now? Yes, I mean now.' Maizad beckoned for his squad to come with him. 'I will find this interesting.'

Garrock led them out of the hangar and down the corridors towards the arming chambers. They strode alongside him in almost total silence, a low grinding thrum the only sound emitted by their immense armour.

'Forgive me,' Garrock ventured as they walked, deciding to risk the attempt. 'I've never served with your order before.'

'Few have.' Maizad looked directly ahead as he walked, back

straight, perfectly poised the whole time. 'We are not a First Founding. Not numerous. And we do best in the shadows.'

'Then... your fortress?'

'Shoba. A world of darkness. I would not recommend a visit.'

One of his warriors laughed – a rumble of gentle amusement. For all the projection of terror – which they managed perfectly well – they appeared more amenable than others of their kind.

They reached the elevator shafts, and began to descend. Somewhat to Garrock's surprise, Maizad remained happy to talk.

'So we are content in the void,' the sergeant told him. 'Not much change for us. Not much difference. Perhaps you miss the sunlight on your face. We only ever knew stars.'

'All the time?'

'Yes. And emptiness. And cold. And the ruins of another age to remind us of our hubris.' Maizad chuckled. 'But it made us strong. That is the only reason the Imperium cares for Shoba. It is an anvil of warriors. Ones beaten into strength for its wars. We can become more perfect, out here now. Not just freeze, scavenge, tell stories of ghosts in the dark. So we are grateful.'

Grateful. For the escape from such bleakness, or because it had made them what they were? He sounded genuine about it, either way.

Garrock stole more glances at them as they strode. They did seem perfectly attuned to the ship's signature gravity already, its many movements and idiosyncrasies, as if they had been extensively conditioned for it. As the lumens reflected from their dark armour, he could make out subtle patterning on the ceramite surface – complex, geometrical, almost invisible. There was an art to that – something hidden in plain sight, a paradoxical kind of reserved self-confidence. You had to get close to them to see it, otherwise all was darkness.

'You have fought often in the crusade?' Garrock said, as if it were really a question.

'From its beginning. And before that, in the defence of the Gate. The defeat, and then the victory.' He snorted – cynicism? Or maybe something else. 'Now much has changed. We have our new armour, our new weapons. But underneath? Still the same. The stars still watch the living and the dead.'

The words were morose, but the delivery wasn't. If they appeared to be a mournful Chapter, these Iron Shades, then it was tempered with some self-awareness.

'And we are the same too,' Maizad said. 'Your people, my people. Void-taken, knowing no world for long. Unnatural, is it not? We should have earth under our feet, not metal. But we like it better this way, all the same. Perhaps you do, too.'

'I never really thought about it,' said Garrock.

'Just so. This is your home.'

'Hah. Yes. For my many sins.'

They reached the entrance to the main garrison chamber. From within, Garrock could hear the sounds of someone laughing, the steady murmur of talking. He paused at the doorway. He ought to warn them, really.

'They'll be surprised to see you down here,' he told Maizad. 'Maybe a little rough around the edges. But they're good fighters.'

Maizad looked down at him. 'If you trained them, then they will be. And battle will be joined soon. Maybe we will fight together – then we will find out.'

Fight together. The thought was almost unimaginable.

'It would be the greatest honour,' Garrock said, just as he had at the start. But this time, much to his surprise, he actually meant it.

# Chapter Six

**FIRST GREAT PUSH**
*GORGON*
**SOMEONE SLIPPED**

Kiastros adjusted position on his throne. The seat was uncomfortable – polished stone with only a thin cushion on top – and not something he'd have chosen to use for a long tactical session. The strategium chamber itself was similarly austere, all bare granite and heavy pilasters, which offended his aesthetic sense. After this campaign he'd have to see if he could get some of the artisans up here – a few gilded aquilas, some cherubs, candelabras, maybe a portrait or two. The long council table running down its length could do with some embellishment too – the ship was his palace, after all, and had to look the part.

If the immediate surroundings were disappointingly drab, the view from the high windows was not. The chamber was set high on the *Judgement of the Void*'s spine, and gave a clear view of the long run down to the prow. Comms towers and lance housings rose up along the structure, lit by flood-lumen banks against the dark of the void. Beyond those lay the massed fleet, static and immense, a cluster of ships that seemed to go on forever. He recognised the profile of most of the big vessels – the *Glorious Contempt*, the *Zeal in His Service*, the fine lines of the new-build *Excelsis Imperator Nostrum*. Somewhere out of view lurked Dominus' flagship itself, the truly colossal Adjudicator-class battleship *Flail of Judgement*. The smaller vessels flitted between those unmoving nodes like coracles between islets, hundreds of thousands of them, a diffuse light dance that sent the shadows flickering across the many gilded and crenellated hulls.

Only one profile eluded easy identification. Kiastros had gazed at it for a while as the others had filtered into the strategium. It wasn't Imperial Navy, he could see at once – no visible fleet idents, and in any case it wasn't big enough to run unaccompanied. It wasn't Astartes or Sororitas either, and certainly not part of the Basilikon Astra. Kiastros' guess was that it was Inquisition. It certainly looked the part – dark and unadorned flanks, banks of weaponry he couldn't easily identify, a strange and intense glow from the few exposed viewports.

He shuddered a little. It was too close for comfort. The pious part of him was grateful for the diligent agents of the Emperor's Holy Orders. Of course he was. But you never wanted to get into proximity with one, even if your conscience was entirely clear. His ship, after all, had a complement of tens of thousands, if you included the waifs and strays in the depths. Would all of them be pure of heart and deed? Despite the vigorous efforts of the onboard clerics and enforcers, you could never be sure.

Kiastros looked away. No point dwelling on it – he'd never be told why that ship was there, so he'd just have to accept its presence and hope that once the action started, it found itself moving well away from him.

'Well then,' he said, placing his gloved hands together on the tabletop. 'Are we prepared?'

His senior command staff looked back at him from their places around the table – Avati, Boroja, Spleed, Kuhl and their respective adjutants. All of them had data-slates in front of them, and the adjutants carried auto-quills and lexrecorders. A couple of mute servo-skulls hovered overhead, each one stuffed with augur-jamming filaments and scan-bafflers. Chatak, his own adjutant, sat just behind him, poised to replenish his goblet if it looked likely to run low.

Before any answers came in, the hololith projector in the centre of the table crackled into life. The image skittered, slewed, then stabilised, showing the ghostly monocled profile of Commodore Hekaon, master of the Acertus Squadron within Battle Group Dominus to which they had been assigned.

*'In His Service,'* came Hekaon's machine-filtered voice.

'For eternity,' replied Kiastros, bowing slightly. 'Good to see you again, commodore.'

*'And you, Iannis. That little escort-retrieval has been noted in the logs.'*

Kiastros felt a small twinge of satisfaction – a few more notices like that, a few more observations of diligent tactics, and a battleship command edged just a little closer. 'And now for the real thing,' he said.

*'Indeed,'* said Hekaon. *'Orders have been received from Groupmaster Jovanjiar. Dominus will mobilise for the warp at chronomark fifty-six-forty-eight-one. Ship positions as in standard attack deployment quintus-A. Enemy counter-movements have been tracked to the Yeoqa System, where our first action will be conducted.'*

As the commodore spoke, adjutants took careful notes. These instructions would not be given a second time, and there would be no means of checking them again later unless the plans changed. Avati in particular was listening intently – her astrogation would be critical in ensuring the *Judgement of the Void* emerged into realspace in precisely the correct position.

'Very good,' said Kiastros, listening to Chatak's auto-quill scratch its way across the slate. 'Any more indication of what to expect on the far side?'

'*More of what we saw at Ghoja,*' said Hekaon. '*Maybe some stragglers from the spinward clean-up operations too. Our supremacy will be two-to-one, according to Jovanjiar's strategos – the enemy no longer has the capacity to muster more than half our tally this far out.*'

Kiastros nodded. That was similar to what his own staff had calculated. The last few months of combat had been grinding, but they all knew the enemy's resources in this subsector had been worn thinner. 'The first great push beyond the Line.'

'*By His will. Garrison systems have been prepared for support waves, prior to reorganisation towards Objective Prime.*'

Objective Prime. The location few of them ever willingly named. It had always felt such a long way off, but suddenly now it felt almost close.

'*Dominus will fight in standard assault patterns,*' said Hekaon. '*You have your Shell coordinates and idents, and there's no change to those. Save one.*'

Kiastros felt he already knew what was coming up.

'*The Emperor's Holy Orders of the Inquisition ship* Gorgon *stands three points off your prow. We are commanded to ward it. The battle cruiser* Hammerfall *has prime command in this – you will follow its lead. Under no circumstances is it to come to harm. This supersedes, if necessary, any other standing orders.*'

'Understood,' said Kiastros. 'And I assume you can tell me nothing about why it's there.'

'*You assume correctly. This comes from Jovanjiar himself.*'

Again, that little pulse of excitement – do this right, and the man himself would know the names involved. 'Am I to make contact with the Inquisition ship?'

'*Negative.* Hammerfall *will make contact in due course. Shadow both on the crossing, after which the* Gorgon *will be escorted to*

'Very good. Then I think we have everything we need.'

*'I think you do.'* A thin smile, flickering with hololith motes.
*'I wish you fortune. This has been a hard campaign, and we've
lost many hulls. I wish to be doing this with you again very soon,
with the objective in our scopes. Just one more fight, eh?'*

'All our hopes,' agreed Kiastros.

*'Oh, one final thing – the primarch has spoken with Jovanjiar
and the admiral. He sends his respects to us all in the fleet, knowing
what we do for the crusade. The darkest road.'*

'He said that?'

*'Reportedly. The road of martyrs, the hardest task he set. We
are in his thoughts.'*

'Then I shall pass that on to the crew. It will fortify them,
knowing that we are in the primarch's thoughts.'

*'Nothing matters as much as this. Nothing. While we engage
the Despoiler's forces on the direct path to Holy Terra, other fleets
are able to take back systems beyond number. While we threaten
the heart of the traitor's foul kingdom, a hundred battlefronts are
spared greater predation. We are the linchpin, the spear-thrust
into the darkest night. I truly believe, when victory is achieved,
the name of Secundus will be spoken with the highest honour.'*

Hekaon never said very much, but when he did, it was heart-
felt enough. 'Well spoken,' said Kiastros. 'Then we shall observe
the chronomark, and relish the moment to come. May He protect you, commodore, and keep your aim sure.'

*'As with you, Iannis. We'll speak again on the other side.'*

The hololith rippled away, and the lumens on the tabletop
faded back to black. Kiastros sat back, hands on his throne's
armrests, and looked at Avati. 'So what did you make of that?'

'They are moving sooner than expected,' she said. 'They must
have gathered up the rearguard quickly. But nursemaiding an

Inquisition ship...' She gave him a sour expression, as if she'd just sipped at spoiled milk. 'It'll complicate things.'

Kiastros regarded her carefully. Santalina had always warned him about Avati, saying she was too ambitious, too eager to leap over him to get where she wanted to go. He'd never seen it, himself. She was ambitious, yes, but that was something he admired. Was she sometimes less than properly respectful? Of the Church, of the Navy hierarchy? Yes, she was, and he'd reprimanded her for it more than once. But she was good at what she did. Perhaps Santalina was merely jealous, seeing youth and energy and remembering, ruefully, what it was to have those things.

'It will complicate things,' Kiastros said. 'But these are our orders, and you can thank the Throne we do not have to speak to them in person.' He turned to Boroja. 'If the *Gorgon* hails us, at any point, send it to me with priority override. I want a channel-station monitoring them the whole time, just in case.'

'It will be done,' said Boroja, looking as enthusiastic about it as Avati had been.

'Master of Engines,' said Kiastros, turning to Kuhl. 'What's our status for movement?'

'All repairs complete, all stocks replenished,' said Kuhl, who looked suddenly very pale. 'When the order comes, we shall be ready.'

'Are you quite well?' Kiastros asked, struck by her appearance.

'Yes I am.'

'You're sure?'

'Very much sure, lord captain.'

He stared at her for a moment longer.

'Very well then,' he said, reaching for his adjutant's data-slate to sign off the record of the discussion. 'We are resolved, we are prepared. The time will come swiftly now.' He scanned across the chamber, watching them watching him. Save for Kuhl's uncharacteristic weakness, they all looked ready. 'The numbers have been calculated, and this shall be a great victory. One for the annals. For so long, we have been building, constructing the defence in depth, fighting merely to hold ground. Now we push on. Remember this moment. Remember the primarch's words. We are instruments of his divine plan. He is the son of the Emperor, and is the perfect embodiment of His genius. As such, be confident we will prevail. We must prevail.'

They looked satisfied with that. He felt satisfied with it. He was rested, well fed, fully prepared. The ship was poised, its gun-halls full and its silos brimming. He stood, and his staff stood with him.

'So go now to make your final preparations,' he said, making the aquila. 'When we next convene, it will be for battle.'

Avati headed down from the council chamber alone. She'd considered saying something to Kuhl, whom she liked well enough, because the pallor of her skin was quite alarming, but in the end it was easier just to get on with things. She'd always been independent-spirited – you had to be, working down in those furnaces – and might have bristled at any intimation of weakness.

Besides, she had plenty to get on with. The timing was tighter than she'd expected, and despite what Kuhl had told Kiastros there was plenty still to do before the ship was ready for the warp again. Some of the hits they'd taken out at Jophra had caused some knock-on structural issues, and ideally they'd all be wrapped up with the engineering teams well before the plasma drives were kindled again.

As she walked through the crowded corridors, brushing past the many ratings, who all saluted her as they passed, she ran through the state of preparation for the warp. The Space Marines had been taken on safely, and were now working with Garrock to gain familiarity with the upper decks. Isobel was up in the principal apothecarion with Jep, either studying his instruments or rooting through the cabinets looking for amasec. Boroja had gone back up to the command bridge with Spleed to finalise the jump sequence, and the Navigator and astropaths were safely locked away ready for the voyage. The battle cruiser's escorts were all in position and standing close for orders, the gun-crews and enginarium clades had been handed their rotations.

She should have felt that old familiar rush, the pleasurable tension of the pre-action phase. Combat was what she lived for – it was what they all lived for. You never wanted an extended period away from it, not a line voidship like the *Judgement of the Void*. And yet, for some reason she felt a nagging anxiety eating away at her – a gnawing sense that something had been left undone. It didn't matter how many times she went over the rosters, the schedules, the tactical schematics, nothing showed up. Nothing had been left out. Just reviewing the data reassured her of that – she'd presided over a hundred major actions, and she knew what to look out for.

In truth, what was there to be concerned about? The ship was vast and old. It had been through tremendous clashes and emerged to tell the tale. To lose a battle cruiser-class ship entirely was relatively rare, even in significant actions – the Mars-built structures were incredibly hard to destroy, and a prudent captain knew when to retire from an engagement and seek the safety of the warp. Unlike the more fanatical elements of the Militarum, who were happy to throw expendable resources into wars of annihilation, the Navy husbanded its priceless artefacts, its sacred fortresses, its beloved temples. These were worlds entire, the ancestral homes of those who served within them, the beginning and the end of their whole existence.

In the current case, the addition of a squad of Space Marines gave an extra layer of formidable protection over and above Garrock's well-drilled forces. And if all that somehow went wrong, if the warp core was breached or a major boarding action was successful, then they would all die as they had lived – in glorious service. She did not fear that. None of them did. No member of the Imperial Navy died of old age, nor expected to – they would all go out, one way or another, with the decks on fire around them and the hiss of an escaping atmosphere.

So what did she fear? Not that. Maybe failure. Maybe the prospect of a career stalling as Kiastros held her back. Maybe, or maybe...

None of those things. Perhaps it was an aimless fear, something that snagged at her when her mind wandered.

*Discipline, then*, she thought to herself angrily. *Do not let it wander.*

She decided to visit the command level's strategium complex. She headed straight up to it, ignoring for the moment the many other demands on her limited time. Nodding to the guards stationed at the heavy doors, she pushed inside the main space – a large domed chamber with lozenge-patterned columns and a transparent roof onto the void. A few dozen scholiasts and scribes shuffled around the margins, but the wide circular floor was mostly empty. Overhead hung a vast, translucent schematic of the various battle groups' deployment, glistening like an orrery in points of light. It was updated in real time from the constant sensor-feed, showing hundreds of ship positions together with runic idents and squadron markers. The ship locations were overlaid with movement vectors, formation boundaries, chain-of-command indicators.

Avati came to a halt before it, peering up into the schematic's formidable complexity. Kiastros was right – this was a very big engagement. She narrowed her eyes, trying to get her bearings amid the gently rotating constellations of illumination.

'You sense it too?' came a voice from the shadows.

Avati turned to see Boroja shuffling towards her. The Master of Signals looked hunched, tired, as if he'd been on shift for too long.

'I don't know what you mean,' Avati told him, looking back up at the tactical display.

'That there's an issue here, and you can't put your finger on it,' said Boroja, standing next to her. 'Or at least, one that's been bothering me. I've been staring at these for a while. Before the king's little pep-talk. Nothing's wrong.'

He was right, at least as far as she could see from her initial look. She found the *Judgement of the Void*'s locator towards the edge of Dominus' defensive Shell. She picked out the *Gorgon* standing close, a few dozen frigate-class vessels in standard guard positions. It was like staring into a galaxy, watching as the starfields spread and clustered – ship after ship, each one armed to the limit and poised for action.

It should have filled her with confidence. Enthusiasm, even.

'So why do you do it?' Avati asked, continuing to survey the lattices.

'I don't know.' Boroja laughed. 'I don't know. No reason at all. I just... feel it.'

'Then you should report something to the captain.'

'If I had anything to tell him, I would.' Boroja shot her a wry look. 'How do you think he'd take it? A *feeling*?'

She couldn't see anything either. No problems, no weaknesses. The entire structure looked ideal.

'Maybe I just want it all to start,' she said, half to him, half to herself. 'You know what I mean?'

'The real thing.'

'The real thing. The Prime Objective. I truly wish to see it,

If the stars glow with the colours of madness. Then I want to
see it burn. All of it.'

Boroja chuckled. 'Santalina could tell you already. She looks
into strange places.'

'She loves me, you know that?'

'Does she now?'

'If she could only admit it to herself.'

'We all feel the same way, to be fair.'

'Oh, I know you do.'

The chrono was ticking. She could hear it, faintly, tracking
the strategium's updates, a soft tap as the metal cylinders slid
back and forth.

'What's the range on this thing?' she asked idly.

'Thirty v-u.'

'Can it go out further?'

Boroja shrugged. 'Maybe. Why?'

'Just ask them.'

Boroja beckoned to one of the adepts, who scurried off to the
projector controls. A moment later, the constellations shrank
down as the scale was altered. Detail was lost, runes became
too small to read. A large expanse of emptiness opened up all
around the diminishing sphere.

'What are you looking for?' he asked.

'I don't know,' she mused, watching the display pan and
shrink. 'Maybe just a broader view. But then... what's that?'

Boroja held up a hand, and the movement halted. An inde-
terminate pattern of interference ran around the extreme edge
of the projection.

'Warp distortions?' Avati asked warily.

'Can't be. Far too big. Anyway, the outer pickets would have–'

He stopped talking just as the tactical hololith showed the
fleet's outer layer of scout-class sensor-pickets abruptly start

to contract back to the first line of destroyers. Avati watched him tense up – she could faintly hear a hiss from his implanted comm-loops, which meant that he was suddenly getting a lot of urgent demands. She looked up at the display, and saw the hard perimeter of the fleet muster start to move – to curl up on itself, to adopt tighter defensive structures.

'No, that can't be,' she said weakly, glancing back towards the interference zones. 'It can't be.'

Boroja started moving. 'We need to get back to the bridge,' he snapped. 'Kiastros' been informed.'

She didn't move straight away. She just stared at the extent of the distortion as it curled around the sphere of the muster. 'They said the sector had been cleared,' she muttered, going after Boroja at last, her shock giving way to a disbelieving anger. 'They all did. I saw the figures.'

'Then someone slipped,' said Boroja, his jawline tight. 'Maybe even the damned precious primarch, who we're always told is so infallible. Doesn't matter. This is going be a shitshow. A *shitshow*.'

It was. Just a glance at the rapidly evolving constellations told her that, and she wasn't half as proficient at reading the signals as Boroja.

The doors slid open ahead of them, exposing a corridor already busy with running crew members. Avati's heart rate started to pick up. Her training and conditioning kicked in. She started to process what she had to do, in what order, and how quickly. That helped a little. She was doing. She was acting.

'Emperor preserve us,' she breathed to herself, breaking into a run of her own to reach the elevator station to the bridge. 'Throne of Light, may He preserve us all.'

# Chapter Seven

**THE SHELL**

**NOVA CANNON**

**TAKE THEM TOGETHER**

If a single voidship departing the warp to enter realspace was an arresting sight, then the departure of hundreds was unforgettable. Instead of a single rupture in the fabric of the void, an entire series of puncture wounds were stitched together in a rolling set of silent explosions that ploughed up the endless black into a roiling storm of unreal, over-vivid pigments. Lightning forks the length of comet trails snapped and writhed across the perforations in reality, snapping around a host of ink-dark hulls surging up through the maelstrom. For anyone foolish enough to stare directly for too long, sickening glimpses of the world beyond were plainly visible, like muscle glistening under peeled-back skin. Not that the ships themselves were much easier to look at – they were twisted mockeries of their Imperial counterparts, stretched and bloated and flensed and corrupted, trailing spores and backlit smog-trails from vents shaped like agonised mouths.

And they kept on coming. Squadron after squadron, formation

after formation, crashing into reality in waves of ether-glistening metal. The sizes, classes and armour patterns were bewildering in their variety – some hulls looking not very different from a standard Imperial ship, save for the desecration of their icons and livery; some looking nothing like a voidship at all, with straggling tentacles or burning spike-fields. They had little in the way of spatial organisation, spilling out of the breach like barbarians surging up to a gatehouse, but they had numbers, and they had weapons. The long-range scopes picked them out in pitiless detail – gaping cannon maws cast in bronze, ranks of rusting torpedo launchers drenched in ritual bloodstains, colossal guns of unknown provenance glimmering with eldritch energies. Fighters spilled from angry red launch bays, accelerating up to attack speed in whining swarms. Escorts streaked ahead, their forward weapons arrays already cranking up to fire, while the giants wallowed after them, one after the other, vast and obese with killing potential.

The geometry was well chosen. They spread out rapidly, trusting in their numbers, cutting off obvious escape routes back towards optimal warp-exits, forcing the Imperial cluster to stage a defence. They moved with the decisive speed of an operation long planned, a careful accumulation that had now been unleashed.

Kiastros raced up to the command bridge, clicking the last of the buttons on his collar into place, his pulse racing. He could hear alarms going off all around him, overhead and underfoot, rousing every deck to instant combat footing. Ratings jostled with armsmen and officers, all of them hurrying to their stations ahead of time, some looking like they'd just completed a long shift, others bleary-eyed from being woken by the sirens.

How had this happened? How had no warning come?

It didn't matter, not right now, but it was hard not to dwell on it all the same. He'd seen the reports. He'd seen the numbers. There should have been no significant concentrations of enemy power between here and Yeoqa, and those they expected to meet there were merely a tithe of what was now racing towards them. How could the strategos have got it so wrong? Mere incompetence? Treachery, even?

He reached the armoured doors to the bridge, shoved his way through them. He had to get rid of his fury, his baffled outrage. Stay calm. Remember his own words to the rest of the crew: *We are instruments of his divine plan.*

'Status,' he snapped, jogging up the steps to his throne.

'Hostiles to fire-range in ten minutes,' Boroja reported. He looked very sweaty after sprinting to get to his station. 'Fighter wings running ahead, escort-wave impacts in less than five.'

'Commence nova cannon power sequence,' Kiastros ordered. 'Secondary power to forward lances. We'll get one shot before it'll be over to broadsides.'

Aides scurried to comply, and the bridge rang with shouted orders.

'Any word from Hekaon?'

'Negative, lord captain, save for general order to engage and repel.'

Engage and repel. How in the name of Holy Terra was that supposed to work? Kiastros didn't need to study the scopes in depth to see that the entire muster was already outgunned, and the warp rift was yet to close. By the time it did, Dominus and the other groups would be outnumbered by at least the same ratio they'd expected to have in their favour at Yeoqa. Their current formation was purely defensive, as per regulation – shifting to an aggressive posture would eat up all the time they had before the first enemy escorts got into fire-range.

'Priority signal to all escorts – move into defensive close-shell and follow our lead. Signal the *Hammerfall* and request coordinates for shadow. Move out one point and hold for axis-change. Astrogation – do you have a target?'

Avati never looked up, keeping her head buried among the tactical lenses. 'Target acquired, aye,' she replied, her voice muffled by the sleeve of a viewfinder funnel. 'Shunting coordinates now, your confirmation requested prior to orders for Gunnery.'

Kiastros blink-clicked to her feed, and his throne briefly shimmered with a hololith projection from her station. It was centred on a monster of a ship – something that might have once been a Desolator battleship, a vessel class that heavily outranked the *Judgement of the Void* in size and capability, and had clearly been heavily modified over the long centuries of service in the Eye. Its hide was black-red, disfigured with erratic stripes and blotches, and its many viewports glowed intense crimson. It seemed overstuffed, somehow, as if its belly were ripe to burst – the ribbed vaults and substructure were bowed and splayed, bolted back down by haphazard plates and bracing beams. Its movements were halting, and long gouts of soot and smuts trailed from its overworked plasma drives. Fighters were streaming out of its hangars like blowflies, and in its wake came more than twenty support vessels, each so heavily modified and extended that the original typology was virtually lost.

'Target confirmed,' Kiastros ordered. 'Gunnery – fire when able. Astrogation, route nova cannon power to main drives once discharge complete – we'll need to be able to shift on demand.'

The deck started to hum more forcefully than usual, a deep throb that told Kiastros the ship's immense feeder-coils were diverting power to the nova cannon. Firing even once from the singular weapon absorbed ludicrous amounts of energy – in the cavernous loading halls, hundreds of gunnery crew would now be hard at work under the lash, straining on chain-pulls and attitude wheels in order to deliver the ammunition from the conveyers to the breech chamber.

'Astrogation, your discretion to bring us into firing position,' said Kiastros, dissolving the hololith and bringing up a wide-angle tactical projection in its place. 'Gunnery, ready starboard cannons for targets. Response from the *Hammerfall*?'

'Negative, lord captain,' said Boroja, breathing heavily as he worked to filter the deluge of incoming signals. 'They're moving to starboard, barrels-out and primed to fire. *Gorgon* in shadow position.'

Kiastros swore under his breath. This would be a problem. 'Stay on it. We'll see how it looks once the cannon's spat.'

*'Loaded and ready, lord captain,'* Spleed announced over the comm.

'Then do it, Gunnery,' said Kiastros, an edge of spite in his voice. 'Do it now.'

He could almost hear the bulkheads slamming closed, the shield doors grinding into place, the final locks thunking tight on the breech chamber's entry maw. He could almost feel the heavy crash of the lone shell being secured by the accelerant-claws before the motive fields got their teeth into it.

The launch couldn't come soon enough. Everywhere he looked on the tactical displays, ships were racing towards him. The non-augmented real-viewers across the command bridge's dome were alight with what looked like stars but would soon clarify into the grotesque panoply of Archenemy warships. Standard augur displays were already giving close-up views of the decayed and corrupted hulls and spires, thundering closer with every passing moment. The Imperial battleships had loosed their long-range weapons – torpedoes streaking out into the void, tracking out towards the oncoming enemy, backed up by wings of scrambled attack craft. A few lances had fired from some of the larger ships, but the las-beams would come into their own at closer range. The few vessels with nova cannons were all doing the same as them – getting their shells away while the enemy were not yet among them, knowing the tremendous damage done over wide blast areas and the potential for indiscriminate blowback.

The bridge shook, rumbling heavily and making the chandeliers shiver. Alert runes flashed red as the enginarium compensated to recoil, and the nova cannon finally loosed its deadly contents.

'Power back to plasma drives,' ordered Kiastros, switching his own scope to a narrower focus. 'Prepare for cannons and prime both lance arrays.'

The single shell blazed off into the void, streaking at near lightspeed, untrackable, impossible to evade. A tiny fraction of a second later and it had found its target, exploding on contact with the Desolator halfway along its distended flank. The explosion was catastrophic, visible through even unaugmented viewers as a blaze of silver light radiating out from the impact zone. The augurs gave a more detailed picture – Kiastros zoomed in on a slowly spiralling zone of blown-clear metalwork, a mini-nebula of spinning dust and secondary ignitions. Several of the Desolator's escorts had been destroyed entirely, caught up in the wide blast radius and blown into atoms. Some of the neighbouring voidships had also been badly damaged, with their prows driven in or their backs cracked apart amid plumes of gas and flame. The principal target, struck directly by the shell, had absorbed the brunt of the impact. If its shields had not been fully operational, it might have been completely annihilated, but even given the coverage of working voids the impact had been ruinous. The Desolator's forward sections were in tatters, ripped open and crackling with electric sparks. Fragments of decks could be glimpsed through the spinning wreckage, glowing red from the internal lumens and rapidly spreading fires. Eerie witchlight ghosted across the devastation, perhaps some after-effect of the explosion, perhaps something less explicable.

'Fighters incoming bearing four-five-one,' Boroja intoned flatly, busy with the thousands of other signals reports. '*Hammerfall* moving ahead of formation, other escorts in standard position. Major incoming enemy signals.'

'Hail them again,' said Kiastros, irritated. 'Impress on them the need to remain under the cover of our guns.'

He was painfully aware of Hekaon's instructions regarding the *Gorgon*: *Under no circumstances is it to come to harm.* What was he supposed to do if the *Hammerfall*'s captain lost Shell discipline? Were they even working to the same set of orders?

Time was running out to react. The two fleets were hurtling towards one another, racing into effective lance range at gathering speed. The Imperials had not remained static – that was the worst of options, presenting yourself as a steady target while trying to hit an enemy moving at speed. Each of Dominus' squadrons was now ramping up to full acceleration, all of them holding their three-dimensional deployment patterns and maintaining the overlapping fire-lane discipline. Few fighters had been launched yet – Jovanjiar's preference had always been to commence initial massed gunnery before sending the attack wings into close assault. The first torpedoes were streaking into contact, though, corkscrewing and diving in close enough to get a proximity lock.

It was only a few seconds, the interval before full engagement, but it was strangely muted. Kiastros felt himself go a little numb, a little dislocated. He saw the two great spreads of ship locators as they charged into one another, he dimly heard the shouts across the bridge as the crew struggled to adjust, he felt the muffled thunder of the plasma drives keying back up to full speed. It was like taking a short breath before the hammer fell, a brief snatch of oxygen before it would all be a whirl of fear and anger. It was the very last chance to ask himself how this could have happened – how no intelligence had come in from the Inquisition or the web of clandestine agents, how no warning had been received from astropathic relays or far-sighted Navigator stations. And that was the worst anxiety of all, the chance that their plans were known, had always been known, and some traitor within the ranks had spilled the data. Or perhaps just carelessness, like at Jophra XI – some stray comms being picked up, pored over by enemy strategos, used to unpick all Samil's careful preparation.

*We have failed here,* he thought to himself miserably. *We were on the cusp of achieving it all, of taking our step towards the final horizon, and we have failed.*

'Multiple barrages incoming!' Boroja shouted, shunting the schematics to Kiastros' display. 'Range to first targets four v-u and closing.'

Kiastros snapped out of it, and turned his attention to the morass of hololithic signals on his spectral tactical sphere. 'Instruct the *Gladiax* and *Impeccable Hate* to move on those fighters,' he said, back into his accustomed world of calm, precise delivery and ready to organise the *Judgement of the Void*'s response. 'Push the *Contempt for Freedom* and *Holy Will* two points ahead for screening action. Bring us alongside the *Gorgon* at chronomark-plus-six, assuming it has not yet turned by then. Lances to fire on my word, followed by starboard barrage on isolated targets four, five and eight.'

The storm hit. The action was still highly dispersed in comparison to terrestrial combat – each ship being tens of thousands of miles distant from the closest enemy – but the volume of shells and las-beams swiftly became ferocious. Picter lenses on the augur terminals zoomed in close, picking out the detail of the incoming ships – fighter wings angling and diving through massed shell-fire, followed by the swiftest escorts, then backed up by the lumbering profiles of line voidships. The ranged screens were filled with grainy, jumping images of tortured adamantine and flames burning in defiance of the vacuum, of spined ventral towers and acid-wet thruster maws, of death's-head prow lines and serrated cannon barrels.

'*Lances ready on your word, lord captain!*' shouted Spleed.

'Moving to attack position, aye, lord captain!' shouted Avati.

'*Hammerfall* moving further ahead, lord captain!' added Boroja, before shunting him more salient tactical vectors.

He replied to them all. He gave them what they needed. They responded smoothly, competently, even as the volume of space around them dissolved into a hell of ordnance and energy beams.

But he couldn't shake it off, not even once combat became all-consuming.

*We have failed.*

After the garrison, Garrock had taken Maizad down to the series of ancillary chambers used by his squads and support detachments – the armouries, the training halls, the refectoria. He'd shown him the records of recent engagements, the patrol patterns they used, the various duties they undertook for Kiastros. Maizad had shown particular interest in the weapons, and had taken up a lasgun to study it.

'Looks like Accatran,' he had said. 'But some difference, I think.'

Maizad's Gothic was curious to listen to – fluid enough, but with a very thick accent and occasional dropped words.

'Standard Achilles-seven,' Garrock had said, showing him the forge world marks. 'Short form – easier to handle in confined space. Extended power pack life, lower-power beam, but you don't want to be slicing into the scenery anyway, not on a ship, so the trade's worth it. I've used an M-Galaxy Short plenty, and I prefer this. At least in here. Most of my troops use the Navy shotguns, for the same reasons, but I prefer a lasgun.'

The sidearm, which felt cumbersome when Garrock used it, had looked like a toy in the Space Marine's armoured hands. He might even have had trouble pulling the trigger on it. Still, Maizad had listened to what he was being told, asking highly informed questions from time to time, never belittling or mocking their equipment and doctrines.

It had become clear that whatever Shoba was like, it wasn't remotely like the Imperium Garrock knew. Perhaps that was why the Space Marine was so open with him – maybe the stifling social conventions and endless laws didn't work there in the same way. Or perhaps they did, but a member of the Adeptus Astartes could choose to rise above them.

In any case, they weren't there to exchange pleasantries. Garrock had taken him through the deck rosters and the standing defence plans, all of which Maizad had absorbed with a single glance, merely nodding here and there, or murmuring something in his own language to his second-in-command. It had become disconcerting, so Garrock eventually asked him outright whether he approved of the arrangements.

Maizad had chuckled. 'Approve? I am not your captain. We are guests here. We will adjust to you.'

No, Garrock had never worshipped the Angels of Death. Not even when he'd been required to by the priests. But, strangest of the strange, he found that it was possible to like them. At least these ones.

If there had been more time, Maizad had wanted to see a training drill. He'd wanted to see a large-scale mobilisation of the armsmen corps across multiple decks, mostly, as far as Garrock could tell, out of professional interest. That would have been some labour to arrange, given the need to rework the shift patterns following an action, but the garrison was in good shape so it would be possible to work something up.

In the event, though, there hadn't been more time, not even

to fully install the Astartes squad into their own chambers and begin preparations for the next warp-stage. The alarms had gone off across all decks, and Garrock had known instantly what they meant.

Maizad had turned to him sharply. 'Drill signal?'

'Negative.' Garrock had reached for his helm. All around him, his squad were going for their breacher shields and shotguns. 'Something's wrong.'

After that the comm-bursts and battle orders had flooded in. He'd started shouting his own orders, opening up the garrison-wide channels and rousing the entire detachment. Those on rest duty were pulled from their bunks, those in the mess halls summoned immediately to the armouries. The Space Marines silently drew their bolters and sealed up their armour.

The plans were well established. Squads would be deployed to strategic chambers studded throughout the ship, across all deck levels and inside all major systems – the bridge complex, the enginarium, life support, comms and gunnery decks. None of those chambers were located near the edge of the external hull, for the task of the squads was to survive a first breach, even a catastrophic one, then respond as quickly as possible. The nodes were positioned at the junction of fast-access mag-train tubes and heavily armoured mainline access corridors so that the troops could move swiftly to where the contagion had occurred and, like white cells in the blood, staunch the worst of the infection until more help arrived.

That was the theory, at any rate. It all depended on what kind of thing was trying to break in. An assault boat full of cultist fighters, blundering their way through to the interior – that could be fought off. A torpedo strike setting off an incendiary chain reaction – that could often be contained by slamming down the bulkheads and jettisoning the worst deck segments. But if something worse struck – a critical explosion taking out a big component, a boarding action in numbers, or something truly horrific like Traitor Astartes getting on board – then none of them were under any illusions about what fate awaited the first response squads.

By then he was running along the corridor, snapping orders down the comm-lines and pulling up tactical data to his helm display. He didn't need Avati's updates to know that the ship was now at war – he'd felt the plasma drives roar into combat speed, and after that the echoing clang of impacts on the shields and hull plates told him the first strikes had landed.

'We'll move to the main forward station,' he told Maizad. The rest of his squad was with him, and Hobes had now taken over the bulk of the comms-work. He was already looking ahead to how this would go – just twenty troopers with them, the remainder distributed across the rest of the ship. Having the Space Marines with him made all the difference, and freed up hundreds for other areas.

It was always a strange time, the first moments of combat. Aside from the distant noises and occasional deck-shudders, nothing much had changed. The lumens were on, the grav was functional, a few of the menials hadn't even had time to don void gear. And yet, you knew, right in the pit of your stomach, that your enclosed community's existence was under assault. Right now, less than a mile away, colossal forces were being unleashed across the stiffening void shields. Soon the noise would become a cacophony, a ceaseless smash and thunder that could leave you in no doubt what was going on just on the edge of the metal world that enclosed and protected you all.

Maizad had access to all the same tactical data that he did, sent tumbling in a constant stream from the command bridge sensor banks, though he probably had all sorts of other signals that Garrock wouldn't have known what to do with. So far he hadn't issued any orders of his own – the Iron Shades had come along with them like any other members of his squad, only twice the size and with bootfalls that made the deck shake.

They reached the forward station – a circular chamber set near the heart of the *Judgement of the Void*'s prow section. In the tangle of capillary tunnels ahead lay the torpedo loading halls, the prow weapons complexes, accommodation for several hundred ratings, secondary power generators and a host of other minor systems. Aside from the long launching tubes, much of the area was given over to heavy shielding and shock absorbers – in the rare event of a ramming action, the entire region had to absorb truly immense pressures.

Garrock went over to a control column and activated the combat screens. Maizad came to stand beside him. The lenses filled with a swarm of signals.

'Throne of Terra,' Garrock swore, despite himself.

'Indeed,' said Maizad. 'A sight to witness.'

Garrock had fought in a hundred actions, and had never seen anywhere close to the number of ship-idents crowding through the near-volume battlesphere. This was not like the majority of void engagements – a ranged game of cat-and-mouse, movements and counter-movements, feints and misdirections. This almost had a look of a terrestrial battle out of the old legends, with thousands of warriors streaming across the battlefield to crash into hand-to-hand combat. The fact that it was taking place across three dimensions and at distances of thousands of miles made no real difference – in void-combat terms, this was up close and claustrophobic, a crashing together of colossal armies into a broad and interlocked scrum. He'd never been privy to the full extent of Kiastros' intelligence, but he knew very well that this must have come out of nowhere – it was an ambush, one of unimaginable scale and secrecy, and the fact that the enemy had struck completely out of the black meant that someone somewhere had made a terrible mistake.

Damage reports started to come in swiftly, transmitted from the external augurs and translated into screeds on the picter lenses.

'Already taking some hits,' Garrock said bleakly. 'And getting worse.'

The chamber around them began to shudder, just tiny movements of the deck, but still detectable as the violence of the assault ramped up. The void shields were intact still, but the kinetic force of the impacts had begun to radiate through the ship's internal structure. Thunderous roars, muffled by distance, rose up from the levels below, and the lumens flickered in their swaying mounts.

'They will board soon,' said Maizad dispassionately, looking at the pattern of incoming ships.

Garrock grunted an agreement. 'Only a matter of time.'

It would be happening all over the fleet – assault boats let loose flanked by fighter wings, torpedoes stuffed with power-armoured troops. At this stage in the battle, void shield coverage would be near universal at high levels, but the energy fields were designed to repel kinetic shocks – though it was risky, slower-moving objects could be threaded through. Most would be destroyed in the attempt, at least until the rain of shells reduced the shields' effectiveness, but the loss of a hundred would still be worth it if even a single battleship were crippled by a successful breach.

Garrock felt his heart rate picking up as he checked his weapon's power pack. He went through the spares at his belt, pulled at the straps on his armour. All around him, his squad were doing the same thing, getting ready, knowing the call would come at any moment. As they did so, the impacts increased in frequency and strength, and the lumens buzzed and flickered. The Space Marines stood silently throughout, unmoving, as if lost in some pre-combat trance state.

Maizad was the one to speak first. 'Here it comes – enginarium zone tertius.'

Garrock got the confirmation just a moment later. 'Confirmed. All hands, zone tertius – we have a breach.' He turned
to Maizad. 'You wish to lead us?'

The Iron Shade chuckled, hefting his enormous bolter. 'We
will take them together,' he said. 'Your warriors and mine –
may the Emperor's wrath sustain us all.'

# Chapter Eight

**DO WE MOVE?**

**SPIRE-SILENCE**

**ON THE EDGE**

'Fighters away!' Avati shouted, having to work to make herself heard over the constant clamour.

Three wings had been loosed, each one composed of Fury interceptors. Kiastros had held them back until the offensive formation had been established, trusting to the escorts to pick off enemy frontrunners, but now the volume of incoming hulls was so dense that he'd had to act. Only one wing remained in reserve, poised to be loosed in the event of massed close assaults.

'Tell them to focus on assault boats,' Kiastros said, constantly swivelling to process the overload of data from his picter lenses. 'We have one confirmed breach, more to come.'

'Armsmen moving to intercept,' Avati reported. 'Enginarium level, one impact under voids, no reports of further damage yet.'

It was possible the assault boat had been destroyed trying to break the void-barrier, or that it had smashed against the outer hull before clamping tight. Sensor readings from the suspected impact site were scrambled now, no doubt due to the damage, so the next they would hear was when Garrock made contact. Avati found herself glad that they had Space Marines with them – they would counteract whatever had been landed, and there was plenty else going on to worry her.

Spleed was now furiously working the gun levels, setting punishing fire rates for both the cannon ranks and the lances. Boroja was feeding him targets as quickly as he could, but more kept coming. The escorts were working for themselves now, each one surrounded by clouds of enemy void craft and buckling under the ranged impacts. Both Imperial and enemy line battleships were in fire-range now, and every so often a mile-long energy beam or high-payload macro shell would scream across the contact zone and into its target.

Information was now the critical factor. The sheer number of signals coming at them meant that not everything could possibly be attended to. The key was discrimination – filtering out what was merely important to concentrate on what was essential. Avati's staff were yelling down their comm-tubes the whole time, ordering the destroyers to close in or fan wide, to target an enemy capital ship or flush out interceptor squadrons. Hekaon's people were doing the same across a larger scale, desperately trying to hold the line as the big beasts crashed into range and opened up. You could get lost in the detail, overwhelmed by it, your mind scrambled and your senses addled, but that was the trap. You had to stay calm, stay on top of it, find the sliver of weakness in an enemy's defence and exploit it while remaining in formation.

'*Gladiax* falling two points too low,' warned Kiastros disapprovingly.

'They've taken a hit,' replied Avati. 'Instructed to raise prow.'

'Second assault boat sighted!' Boroja shouted.

'Squadron Secundus are on it,' Avati countered, irritated

ahead as ordered.'

Her arms were aching, her head was hammering, and still the lumens on her console flashed with alerts and the command tubes rattled hard into the receiving racks. The big Desolator they had smashed open with their nova cannon was still just about alive and had swum closer looking for revenge, only to be disabled entirely by a combined salvo from the Imperial grand cruiser *Cataclysm* and Overlord-class battle cruiser *Immortal Retribution*. That was exactly how it was supposed to work – overlapping fire from all points. Now, though, the discipline was under severe stress as the enemy probed and swarmed and pushed.

Her biggest problem remained the Inquisition ship. It had still not responded to hails, but had pushed ahead and out of formation, following the *Hammerfall*'s lead. That made the squadron perilously exposed, and going after it would compromise the shield arrangement the *Judgement of the Void* had with its own escorts and Shell counterparts.

She turned in her throne to face Kiastros. 'We have to make the call now, lord captain,' she said, knowing that only he had the authority to break Hekaon's standing orders. '*Hammerfall* will be out of protection range within minutes.'

Even as she spoke, the *Gorgon* opened fire. Throne only knew what esoteric weapons it carried – Avati had never seen anything like them. Neon-blue energy beams crackled out from its prow-mounted lances, spearing into the fiery battlesphere and punching through an incoming enemy cruiser. The effect was startling – something ruptured in the cruiser's midsection, setting off a chain reaction, and a few seconds later the entire ship imploded as if sucked back into the warp itself. The *Hammerfall* opened fire immediately afterwards, coordinating a massive strike from its escorts to bludgeon a path ahead through the mass of enemy ships. The volume of fire was impressive, but it surely couldn't be sustained for long.

'Damn them,' hissed Kiastros. 'Who's commanding that ship? Why don't they respond?'

Avati shared his irritation. The position matrix was loose now, and it felt as if every enemy voidship within range was swooping in to take advantage.

'Four more line-class hostiles moving to intercept,' Boroja helpfully supplied. 'Will be in range within three minutes.'

Avati twisted around to get a look at the tactical augurs. 'Major enemy cluster moving up from below-sphere to target us,' she said. This was getting difficult – wherever you looked, threats were multiplying. 'Do we move?'

She could see the indecision on Kiastros' face. He wasn't an indecisive commander – far from it – but this was asking him to choose between the safety of the entire battle group and the survival of the Inquisition ship, one that was being pushed further and further out of the protective lattice.

Kiastros turned to Boroja. 'Anything from Jovanjiar?'

Avati knew what he was fishing for – the order to break for the warp. They were already heavily outgunned, and it was only getting worse. U-93 was no strategic priority, whereas keeping Dominus from being battered into scrap was. It all depended on whether the groupmaster thought he could do some damage and clear a space for an orderly withdrawal, or if he somehow thought a miracle was likely and he could drag a victory out from nowhere.

'Nothing yet,' Boroja said ruefully. 'Nor from supreme fleet command. Orders remain to engage and repel.'

Kiastros drew in a long breath. He glanced at his scopes. He gazed out at the labouring bridge crew. He looked over at the augur lens showing the *Gorgon* letting loose its energy beam again and slicing the enginarium out from a scuttling enemy frigate. Holy hells – that thing was lethal. Avati knew well enough what Hekaon had ordered. She also knew how much Kiastros cared about Navy discipline, and about the ship he had devoted his life to. He could be a stiff-necked man, a pain in the arse concerning regulations and religious observances, but he could never have been accused of not caring.

His expression clarified. His eyes narrowed, his jawline set.

'Astrogation, plot a course to overwatch the *Gorgon*,' he commanded wearily. 'Do what you can to bring the escorts with us, get a damned comm-line to the *Hammerfall* to find out what in the hells they're playing at, but the priority is that target. Gunnery, line up lances for counter-fire on marked hostiles.'

Then he sat back in his throne, looking mightily annoyed.

'And the blessed Throne be with us all,' he muttered.

The engine was labouring, coughing and wheezing, its tubes and converters and grilles seething. Some of the preparations had not been made. Why would they have been? No orders had been expected for many hours. Now, though, every sinew was straining, every muscle was overloaded. The *Judgement of the Void* was not and had never been a nimble ship, and the things being asked of it were pushing it hard.

Kuhl had been asleep, catching a short break before her next long shift, and so had emerged bleary-eyed into the heart of the storm. The king's orders had come down without warning, making the enginseers scramble to their stations and causing a stampede of menials in the under-halls. Krujax had done his best, but it needed her hand at the tiller, so she'd donned her full voidsuit and clambered down the shafts and into the furnace.

For a while, she'd stabilised things. The panicking Martians had been coaxed and wheedled into doing their jobs, the rites had been hurriedly performed, whole censers of sacred oils had been flung over the hissing control nodes before anyone dared to crank up the irascible machine spirits. Enforcers had been sent running down into the depths to ensure the rabble were rustled up and the main drive-trains and transformers were at full capacity.

Now it was all rattling along, the conduits thundering with promethium and all the plasma chambers blazing. Kuhl had hardly stopped since the first orders had come down from above, striding from chamber to chamber as the work-gangs strained under the electro-lash amid hissing palls of steam and smoke.

'That's all we can give him,' Krujax told her, coming up to her observation platform on an elevator shaft and leaping free of the swaying cage. 'We're on the edge as it is.'

Kuhl glanced up at him, then went back to her data-slates. She was surrounded by pipework, some of it very big indeed, and there were strange noises coming from the metal. 'The ship will respond,' she muttered, smacking the valve in front of her with a closed fist until the readings lurched a little closer to where they should be. 'It always does.'

Krujax stomped over to the edge of the platform and peered over the railing. A hundred yards down, half lost in firelit shadow, a team of heavy loaders was attempting to insert a refitted component into a major power converter. Krujax sniffed as the chains went taut and the macro-lifters started to rumble into life. 'I saw some of the tactical read-outs from up above. Hells, it's all kicked off.'

The entire place was shaking around them. So many warning lumens had been lit that every smog-choked space looked to be on fire. Some of that was natural movement, some of it the result of hits from outside making their presence known.

'Forget about it,' said Kuhl. 'Not our business.'

That was quite right. It wasn't. They were buried deep, away from all possible command decisions, toiling in their under-world of heat and darkness so that the inhabitants of the high spires could conduct their games with weapons.

'But we're being moved out of position,' said Krujax, ignoring the warning signs. 'You know that? We're out of the Shell, moving up on our own.'

'I don't care.'

'They say there's an Inquisition ship out there. One we're following.'

'I really don't care.'

'But it's insane!' Krujax laughed. 'The bloody Inquisition! Imagine, if we catch it, what are we–'

'Shut up!' Kuhl shouted. 'Just shitting shut your shitting mouth!'

Krujax stared at her, open-mouthed behind his helm visor. Kuhl put her data-slate down, took a breath.

'Sorry. I just need... Do you have the output figures from the secondary thrusters?'

Krujax swallowed, looked briefly angry, then nonplussed. 'What did I–'

'Nothing. Look, do you have the figures?'

He blinked, reached for a data-slug, handed it over. 'Like I say, we're on the edge.'

Kuhl plugged in the slug, took a quick look at the runes. Then she handed it back, grabbed his arm. 'We'll be fine. We just need to keep our eye on the prize. Forget about what you got from the lenses, and forget about a ship we'll never see. You're a good second, Krujax, and I'll need you to get us out of here alive. You hear me? I'll need you.'

That cheered him up. 'Glad to hear it.'

'We'll give them all the power they need,' said Kuhl, dis-tracted again. So much to do. 'But I don't want the engines risked by anything stupid. They'll come to their senses. Halt this pursuit and get us back into the Shell – when they do, you let me know right away, see?'

Krujax nodded. 'Will do.'

Then he was off again, back into the elevator cage and clattering down to the furnace levels.

Kuhl leaned against the pipework, her heart beating hard. She had so much to do, so many duties that required her immediately, but she had to take a moment. To remember.

Then she roused herself. She was being foolish. Nothing would come of it – as she had told Krujax, this was a ship they would never lay eyes on, and there were hundreds more in closer proximity.

She got back to work. But her hands didn't stop shaking.

In such circumstances, Santalina almost missed the warp. At least there she could divine secrets that other eyes missed. It was a place of horror, to be sure, but it also had a seductive quality to it. It could come, in a strange way, to feel like home.

Now, though, she was as blind as every other human on the ship, locked tight within the giant sarcophagus as the enemy strikes began to tell. Deprived of the military scopes used by Kiastros and the bridge crew, she could only imagine the spectacle outside the hull – the void shields flexing and buckling, the lance strikes peeling the protection back, the ordnance and fighter strikes gradually getting through and tearing at the hard armour plates.

She headed back to her chambers as fast as she could, her skirts swirling as she hurried. Attendants scurried with her, bowing and scraping even as they struggled to put everything in order for the jump. She hadn't expected to be summoned for hours, possibly days, but all of a sudden the need to be ready for transition was acute. The sacred chants had already started up in her outer chambers, the fluids were bubbling through the pipes, the inner sanctum was pungent with prescribed unguents.

Her Seeing Eye twitched under the bandana, as if eager to open of its own accord.

'Any reply yet?' she snapped to her adjutant, a wiry man named Xinarola who had to trot to keep up with her.

'None yet, lady,' he replied. He was bald, and the rear section of his scalp was a collection of metal plates and comms-wiring. 'I am trying again.'

It was a worry, not to be able to get through to Ortuyo. Why didn't the comm-lines connect? Had something important been destroyed in the relay systems? Not likely – she could still make contact with her own people, with the majority of the upper-decks crew.

'Any damage reports from the astropathic spire?' she asked.

'None, none,' said Xinarola, but he looked unhappy. 'Though, with all the many problems, the many issues...'

Yes, yes. It was always difficult to tell, when a ship was under such sustained assault. You could think that all was entirely well, only to find out that an entire section had been blown into the void hours ago and the oxygen was on the verge of running out. That was the nerve-testing thing – they were all ignorant, really, save those with their eyes in the augur lenses, locked away and subject to the whims of fate.

No, not fate. The *captain*. There was a difference. Kiastros would steer them through it.

'Keep trying,' Santalina said. 'I wish to speak to him before the doors close. This is very odd.'

It was indeed. She'd had unsettling dreams. Not an unusual event, of course, given her nature and duties, but something that she'd ideally have been able to discuss with Ortuyo, to see if he'd had similar. And there was the strangest aspect of them – that he'd been in them. She didn't usually dream about crewmates, and had no special affection for him beyond a certain collegiality and shared status as tolerated mutants.

But nothing had come back. Perhaps the astropath's spire had been damaged. Perhaps they'd been pulled out of it for some reason, or were busy on some errand from Kiastros. You never knew – it was all a damned bloody mess, and one that spoke very poorly of Jovanjiar's vaunted strategic talents.

So now they were already preparing for veilbreak again – too soon, too hasty. It was always dangerous making the jump unscheduled, all the more so when battle raged around them. Ideally you'd never even try it – all manner of things could go wrong as the ship's energies focused on the immense transition, so the chances of being outright destroyed rose exponentially. Santalina didn't even have coordinates to use – it would be an emergency haul-out, a scramble for temporary safety, and there was no guarantee the order would ever come. Kiastros would hate to bail on a fight, even one he was bound to lose – it was shameful, a stain on a captain's honour, and that probably outweighed any metric of danger.

The irony was not lost on her. Such a short time ago she'd been raising her glass to the prospect of an advance on the Eye itself. Now Dominus was on its uppers, being hammered by enemy ships no one had known were anywhere close. Such were the vagaries of void war, a grand game based as much on the fever dreams of scryers as the considered plans of strategos.

They reached the doors to her inner chambers, and she smelled the oils – something to be both loved and hated. The great engines had started up to power the wards against corruption and feed the mechanisms of her arcane throne.

At the threshold, though, she paused. A sudden fear assailed her, like a warning, as if by crossing now she would never come out again. She hadn't felt that since she'd been a young woman at the very dawn of her career, subject to all the energies and terrors of inexperience.

'Lady?' pressed Xinarola nervously. The chronos were ticking, the order tubes were ready.

'Alert me if you hear from Ortuyo,' she said, going inside. 'Something is odd here. Very odd indeed.'

Then the doors closed behind her with a heavy clang, shutting her off from the echoing corridors outside.

# Chapter Nine

**MACHINES**
**GOING IN**
**THEY GOT IT**

Garrock dropped down behind the bulkhead, aimed and fired. His las-beam speared into the burning gloom, followed by solid rounds as his squad found their targets. He saw Refad edge forward on the left flank, going warily in the dark and relying on his helm's scanners as much as sight.

The squad had dropped down a dozen levels, running hard towards the sounds of mayhem. It became evident very quickly that whatever had landed was serious – the lumens were down, the power was down, bodies were everywhere and the sound of machine tools was deafening. Maizad had brought his entire squad with them, though they had opted to take a different path towards the enemy.

'We will take this route,' he'd said to Garrock as they'd pushed down the corridors and elevator shafts. 'Head directly for ingress site – we shall aid you.'

Garrock had nodded – what else was he going to do? – and watched the Space Marines tear off into the murk. It wasn't obvious how they knew the path down, given the myriad ways through the ship's innards, but their equipment was no doubt capable of opening things up. His own squad had run on with him, guided as much by the noise as by their helm's sensors. Something very big and very destructive had carved its way inside the hull, and they were heading right for it.

Enginarium zone tertius was buried in the substructure of the ship's prow sector. It wasn't home to the truly essential systems – the plasma drives, the warp drive, the fuel tanks and the core manoeuvring mechanisms – but instead housed a number of the backup and redundancy complexes, as well as the prow thruster arrays and the generators for the main shock absorbers. Losing it would be a major issue, affecting the ship's ability to control its attitude and firing angles, so the incursion had to be shut down as soon as possible.

First signs weren't good. Garrock didn't have any real idea what he was facing for a long time, and was guided more by the growing volume than anything else. It sounded like industrial drills and turbo-hammers had been landed, and the shriek of metal being torn apart made his teeth itch. Soon his squad isolated the source and prepared to engage – heat sources were identified, grenades on short timers were tossed down the shafts, and then they plunged down after them to meet the enemy. They found the first intruders in a wide transit corridor, eight yards across with a high arched roof, as they cut and scraped their way into the ship's interior. The space was already burning, the lumens out, smoke spilling from ruptured panels.

Initial glimpses, twenty yards off, half-caught amid the smoke from the grenades, showed only horrific fragments – fighters like the denizens of Mars, but twisted and distorted into even more grotesque intersections of the human and the machine. Garrock opened fire immediately, as did all those around him, and the las-flares and bullet impacts pierced a shrouded scene of snaking metallic tentacles and wildly spinning rotary blades. He saw multiple eyes swivel towards them through the smog, blood-red and unblinking. Something scuttled out of the gloom, fast as a real spider, a scatter of steel limbs and flailing spikes that scrabbled madly until the volume of return fire blew something up inside it and the whole monstrous contraption imploded with a machine-wail.

Then the real enemy caught up – skitarii, or debased versions of them, misshapen horrors of branded iron and torn flesh, sliding and cantering under the weight of absurd mechanical outgrowths. Garrock's scopes picked out fleeting visions of exposed cranial folds, flayed skin bubbling over superheated vents, empty ribcages glowing internally with the fires of unearthly generators.

The creatures swarmed closer, filling the corridor with energy beams. One of Garrock's troops took a hit in her slammed-down shield and the beam passed straight through it, throwing her against the wall with a sick thud and a stink of cooking muscle.

'Fall back to holding chamber,' Garrock ordered, firing all the while, going for the intersections between the creatures' jointed limbs to disable them before they got close. The rest of his squad kept up the barrage while retreating, shields raised and shots latticing the width of the corridor. They reached the chamber's main entrance and hunkered down behind a series of bulkheads and ledges. Refad reached for another grenade and hurled it straight at the incoming gaggle, though that didn't do much to halt them. An ear-splitting whine broke out from somewhere, and the drills became visible at last, hefted by quadrupedal walkers that swelled up out of the flames and sparks. The creatures chewed up the terrain as they came, ripping out metal plating and tearing up thickets of exposed wiring.

'Hold here,' Garrock grunted, switching his aim and firing into the cowled maw of something with a vox-emitter for a jawline. 'Hold them here, then–'

A huge explosion erupted from behind the throng of false skitarii, blowing out an entire wall section and crushing several of them. Figures leapt through the gap – two, maybe three –all in dark power armour. The ear-piercing drumbeat of bolt-rounds cracked out, close-range and lethal, shredding the skitarii into flecks of spinning metal as the reactive shells exploded.

'Keep firing!' ordered Garrock, edging forward again and picking his target. 'Support the Angels.'

The Space Marines were already getting down to work, silent as ghouls save for the grind of their battle plate and the echoing hammer-strikes of their bolters. Garrock saw one of them take on a big drill-construct, smashing up its bulbous chest-section before yanking out a cluster of cabling from its neck and severing the joint. The skitarii swarmed back at them, fearless, shrieking in their weird machine-cant. It was all close-packed, hemmed in, a stink of blood and oil that splattered up against the cracked wall sections.

Garrock's squad inched ahead, still pressed up against the corridor's edge, burning through power packs as they kept up the tight volume of fire. The Space Marines had ploughed straight into the heart of the enemy horde and had moved almost out of view among the swirls of iron and tentacles. That had pushed the enemy back in on itself, forcing the lead fighters to turn and face the real threat and allowing the armsmen to take shots at them in retreat.

The scale of violence was startling. The enemy wielded a daunting array of close-combat weapons – claws, beam-guns, crackling electro-staves. They lashed and they screamed, far wilder in style than the Space Marines but effective nonetheless. Garrock saw an Iron Shade thrown back by the kinetic force of some electric field, nearly disabled, before he managed to scramble back up and plunge a gladius into the creature's midriff.

Still, they were outnumbered. Garrock pressed the advance,

keeping the intensity of las-fire high, hoping to take a few down at least. Just as it looked like the momentum might swing back against them, a second panel blew clear, this time overhead, and two more Space Marines dropped down from the level above. The precision of the strike was impeccable – without impeding their battle-brothers, they immediately slammed into knots of the enemy and started slaying, punching out with short power-blades and bolt pistols.

One of them was Maizad. Garrock was sure of it, despite the dark and the smoke and the rapid flurry of movement around him. Amid a close scrum of formidable fighters, he was a step above – controlled, brutal, lethal. Caught in a pincer, the skitarii broke at last, forced back the way they had come.

'Stay close!' ordered Garrock, pushing forward with the rest of the squad and maintaining the barrage of fire. He'd be out of power packs if the intensity lasted much longer, but the ferocity of the slaughter made him think it would all be over soon anyway.

The gaggle of skitarii were pushed back into a chamber beyond, one that had been comprehensively wrecked already. The bodies of Navy ratings were all over the place, hacked into chunks and bleeding out across a metal-mesh deck. The entire left wall was missing, a gaping maw of tangled struts and rebar, red-hot and steaming from where the incursion had begun. This was closer to the ingress point now, coming right up against the inner edge of the hull, and Garrock felt the steady buffet of escaping atmosphere – clearly some of the emergency seals hadn't come down or had been destroyed.

He felt sick. The chamber was full – *completely* full – and seething with augmented bodies and bizarre amalgams. How in the name of the Throne had so many been landed? There were far, far more than he had ever imagined, and surely even the Space Marines would struggle against such numbers.

'Reinforcements!' he snarled over the comm, having no idea whether the signal would get through. 'Priority to zone tertius – all forces respond.'

The creatures looked to be building something – a towering construct at the heart of the chamber, bulbous and armoured, glinting with lumens and glowing a violent red at its heart. It was as ramshackle as the warriors who protected it, a piled mess of linked boxes and grilles and coils, festooned with bloodstains and brass death's-heads and scraps of still-quivering flesh. Cables splayed out from it, snaked up against the ship's own systems and hastily bolted into them. A keening whine came from its myriad ports, like a turbine working its way to full speed, and the entire chamber shook from the resonance.

'Destroy it,' came Maizad's calm voice over the comm. It was so hard to square that placid voice with the evidence of Garrock's senses – the astonishing way he and his squad launched into combat again. They were moving faster now, incredibly so, far too rapid for something as heavy as they were. They fired as they leapt, punched as they landed, pivoted and gouged, twisted away from one outstretched claw only to blast apart the next. It was balletic, choreographed, spectacular, and all conducted in their habitual eerie silence even as the chamber screamed at them from every angle.

Garrock fired, his squad fired, adding las-bolts and hard projectiles to the cacophony, and it made a difference, though not a big one. The Space Marines were superlative, tying up the enemy warriors so that none of them had the space or time to even think about taking on the armsmen.

*Iron Shades.* They looked like them, then: blackened-metal ghosts, sleek and shadowy, spectres of the void loosed on the gaggle of grotesques before them. Where the false skitarii were flamboyant in their horror, a gruesome fusion of the worst of humanity and the vilest excesses of a twisted machine cult, the

Space Marines were a purer kind of weapon, pale-edged, keen, pitiless and without compromise.

'Picking up elevated energy levels!' shouted Hobes over the squad comm. She was a few yards away, hunkered down behind two shield-bearers and firing steadily through the gap with her shotgun. 'That thing's about to... do whatever it's going to do.'

'Hold fast,' grunted Garrock, damned if he was going to withdraw while the Space Marines were still fighting.

Maizad was almost at the device already, battling hard through the knots of monstrous constructs. The rest of his squad were just behind him. Static danced across every exposed surface, and whips of lightning started to curl at the edifice's bloated base. His battle-brothers changed formation, pulling together and pushing hard to catch up. With a pang of recognition, Garrock suddenly saw how their seemingly random formation had actually been incredibly complex – they had been fighting like a miniature Shell, overlapping one another so that no weak point remained, all coordinated through what seemed like instinct but was more likely ruthless training. Now they had abandoned that, going for the target and exposing themselves to greater danger. Time was clearly critical.

'What in the hells *is* it?' Refad asked.

Garrock squinted through the storm of las-bolts and boiling steam. Scrapcode injector? Some kind of system-corruptor? He had no real idea, but if this army of invaders had gone to such trouble to install it, rather than simply rampage through the decks in order to destroy a few subsystems, then it was obviously very nasty.

Maizad fought on, but he was surrounded by skitarii dragging him back. His battle-brothers pushed close behind, but the fighting was by then absolutely ferocious – one of the Iron Shades was brought down at last, strangled and dragged under by five or more stave-wielding creatures with compound eyes and steel-jointed hands. It was a horrific shock to see that.

The whine grew louder. Lumens flashed into life along the construct's jerry-built flanks. The cables twitched, as if power had been jerkily pushed down them.

They were running out of time. Garrock took a quick look at his squad – eighteen-strong still, all hunkered down, many using their blast shields for cover, all offering supporting fire. It wouldn't be enough.

He cleared his throat.

'Prepare for close combat,' he told them, drawing his blade and signalling the move towards Maizad. 'We're going in.'

Kiastros felt like screaming. He didn't, of course, because that would be a shameful display of emotion, but he felt like it all the same. It would be a stifled scream, a suppressed cry of intense frustration accompanied by slamming impotent fists on the armrests of his command throne.

'Maintain current pursuit line, Astrogation,' he said instead, his voice as calm as an oil slick in the fuel tanks. 'Signals, press for something concrete at the commodore's earliest convenience.'

Convenience. An inappropriate word, when all the hells were breaking out around them, when ships were burning and falling out of position, when the enemy was still coming at them surrounded by ragged fighter escorts and the numbers were only barely being thinned.

It was sloppy. It was careless. A round of executions when this was over was the only proper consequence.

'Incoming barrage to port-nadir! Brace, brace!' cried one of his officers – he couldn't even see which one.

*'Losing primary plasma conduction, down ten points!'* came a shunt from Kuhl over the comm, who was clearly struggling down there.

Avati had been working furiously in impossible conditions. He had to hand it to her – she might be an ambitious little snake, but she was a competent one.

'Now well outside overlap conditions,' she reported bleakly. 'Incoming fire on all flanks. Attempting to move below current plane and roll to port batteries.'

'Do it,' said Kiastros smoothly, reaching up to his forehead to flick a single bead of sweat from his brow. 'Signals, what can you give me?'

The bridge shook again. Every viewer was alive with fire – from the hammered void shields and their kaleidoscopic stress patterns, from the explosions as escorts and assault craft were destroyed, from the immense energy weapons now being deployed by the lumbering battleships closing in around them.

'No response from the *Hammerfall* or *Gorgon*,' Boroja reported. 'Two hull breaches reported, attempting to lock down reports of a third. No internal signals from astropaths, intermittent from prow zone. Minoris augur arrays down, majoris array close to failure.'

'How soon until we go dark?'

Boroja shot him a despairing look. 'At this rate? Minutes. And not many of them.'

The scream welled up again – the scream of absolute, all-consuming frustration. Jovanjiar had still not given the order. The groupmaster's ships were taking a ferocious beating, the flagship included, but still he hadn't ordered the pull-out. Hekaon had stayed loyally in position too, holding on to what he had, albeit only barely. Everyone was obeying orders, even as it was getting them flayed. That was the glory of the Navy, its one great and irreplaceable weapon – discipline – but it had two edges to it.

'Gunnery, report,' he said, voice still unruffled.

*'I can give you a few more from the port side,'* came Spleed's

harassed voice over the comm. *'Lance-fire operational. But not much'* – the link fizzed with static as a hit came in and scrambled the feed – *'getting mauled on the counter. Too much! Too much!'*

Kiastros cut the link. Spleed was getting emotional, and that couldn't be tolerated. The crew were holding on – just – but soon something would break. Once you lost the augurs, the game was up – you were blind and unable to triangulate, and the enemy would spot it soon enough.

He shut out the cacophony of shouted reports for a moment and stared into the close tactical display. The *Gorgon* had been damaged now but had taken out four capital ships already. That was astonishing – its strange guns certainly drilled through hull plates well enough. The *Hammerfall* appeared to be pushing ahead of it, soaking up tremendous punishment and going for an exit vector. Its run, plus the heavy barrages from the *Judgement of the Void* that had smashed and pummelled everything within two v-u bigger than an interceptor, was all that was keeping the Inquisition ship protected, but the cost had been more than heavy – the *Gladiax* destroyed, the *Impeccable Hate* disabled and drifting, soon to be picked apart. He couldn't do anything for them, not with the remaining two escorts under intense bombardment and the battle cruiser itself surrounded by a permanent corona of fire.

The enemy was too numerous here, too swift and too powerful, and they just kept coming. It was all so concentrated – were they deliberately swarming the Inquisition vessel? The *Gorgon*'s move had drawn them out of covering range from Hekaon's formations, which were now so far back that they couldn't intervene even if they wanted to.

What was the *Hammerfall* doing? Trying to break out for the warp? Trying to destroy as much as it could? It was madness, either way – the heavy battle cruiser was venting badly, rolling across hits that would soon knock it out. Perhaps it was sacrificial, smashing its way into harm in order to give the *Gorgon* a way out, but that wouldn't be enough, surely – the volume of incoming fire was just too great.

'Astrogation,' Kiastros said, beckoning to Avati. 'A word in private.'

Avati glanced up at him, then unplugged herself from her station and came up to the throne. Kiastros overlaid an audex screen over the two of them, muffling for a moment the ongoing crashes as the void combat went on.

'They do not respond to hails, they break our formation,' he told her, voice low, speaking swiftly but softly. 'Hekaon tells me the *Gorgon* must be preserved, I assume because they carry persons or items of value to the crusade. *Hammerfall*'s current course will see them destroyed, along with us. So I propose an interpretation of our orders.'

Avati looked wary. 'An... interpretation?'

'We have some lance capacity. We target the *Gorgon*'s engines, bring it to a halt. Once it is static, we come alongside and take its crew in a hangar transfer. Then we break for the warp on Jovanjiar's word. Or before that word, if destruction is imminent, since both he and Samil appear to have taken leave of their senses. Damn the *Hammerfall*. Your comment?'

Avati looked shocked, as well she might, but forced herself to consider it. 'They are the Inquisition, lord captain,' she said. 'It will damn us.'

'We are damned already. I see no other course. Get them on board, and we save their lives. If we make it into the warp, we can deal with the consequences then. I am mindful of Hekaon's insistence.'

Avati looked unconvinced.

'Your counsel would be valued,' said Kiastros, 'but I need it now.'

She was about to speak, and from her expression it wasn't

obvious what she would say. Whatever it was, it was rendered instantly null by a truly immense explosion, one that sent the near-volume scopes white and blew out another precious augur relay.

Kiastros snapped the audex screen down and pulled up a picter lens. Wreckage was spiralling everywhere, tumbling like chaff from a hopper, and a flotilla of ugly-looking enemy cruisers was blasting its way through the scraps. He whirled to face Boroja, who looked like he'd just ingested poison.

'The *Gorgon*,' he said weakly. 'They got it. It's gone.'

# Chapter Ten

**BLOODWORK**
**IN CLOSE**
**ANGEL DOWN**

Blood. The stink of it, the stain of it, slippery, sticky, on every surface. You cleaned it off, more came. You wiped it from your face, more splattered up.

Some of Isobel's Sisters liked blood. It had a symbolic purpose for them, a significance that went beyond its obvious physical importance. Many of the Orders Hospitaller revelled in the names they gave themselves – the Bloodied Blade, the Keepers of His Sacred Blood. Even as the rest of the Imperium venerated the symbols of death, the Sororitas revelled in the symbols of life – its suffering, its sacrifice, its pain and its wounds.

She couldn't blame them, and she understood the role it played, but neither did she share the obsession. Blood was just another liquid – less agreeable than amasec, less useful than water. You only really wanted to keep it where it belonged – under wraps – and once it started getting out, well then, you knew things had gone wrong.

Now she worked her way through it, her surgical gloves sopping, her plastek apron smeared with it. The rest of the apothecarion staff were busy too, but they deferred to her. They tiptoed around in a kind of awe, which she quite enjoyed. No doubt they didn't get out much, locked away in the medicae chambers with their vials and suture packs, and so to have a real-life Sister of Battle come among them, one who deigned to talk with them, listen to them, and – imagine it – *laugh* with them... No wonder they were starstruck.

The time for laughing was gone now, though. The requests for assistance had come in to her chamber, far earlier than she'd expected. She could have armed up, gone to the command bridge and taken over a squad of armsmen, but she'd already promised the first lieutenant she'd take a look at the apothecarion, and in truth that was where her real talents lay. She might take out a few enemy boarders if needed, but she could save the lives of many more crew over the same period, and that had the greater value.

It was a gift. An intuition. The canoness had told her so herself. 'He has blessed you in this, Miriam,' she'd told her, decades ago, back when she'd still wanted to join the full Chambers Militant and take the war to the hated enemy.

'I wish to hold a blade,' she'd insisted, her cheeks flushed with shame and anger.

'You presume greater wisdom than the one who made you? There's a place in the Repentia for that kind of thinking.' Then the old woman had smiled at her. 'You'll hold a blade, child. Just another kind.'

So she did now – a long scalpel, her own private instrument, the finest surgical steel anywhere in the Imperium and engraved with purity sigils by the artisans of the best convents. She took sutures, she doled out antivenin and adrenaline. She'd helped set the cots up before the first strikes had come in, and now watched them fill with the wounded.

These were all senior ratings, officers, armsmen. The bilge-rats and gun-grunts would have other places to go, but getting the senior ranks patched up quickly was the priority. A single macrocannon had hundreds of crew to pull it into place, whereas the loss of a lone sensor attendant might spell disaster for an entire hull sector. You had to staunch the flow, drain out the poison, fill them with stimms, get them back on their feet and into the fight again. If they were too far gone for service, then you had to administer the Emperor's Peace, quickly and without hesitation, because more would already be waiting for the cot. It was rapid, it was brutal, but it was also expert and conducted without rancour or favour.

So Isobel worked hard, moving from body to corpse to body, her helm sensors whirring as the servitors proffered up the specialist tools she needed. Slavo Jep, the old medicae, was decent enough, but he couldn't do what she could. He couldn't stop the rot and counter the infection, spot the hidden trauma and rebuild the necessary tissue, not in the time they had. More importantly, he couldn't inspire them like she could. An armsman with his leg blown to sinews, a deck-commander with her forearm mangled, they looked at Isobel and saw a fragment of the Emperor's divine will made manifest. They gazed up at her, their expressions taut with pain, and their eyes shone. They believed. They endured the pain, they sucked up the potions and transfusions and the nerve-caps, and then they hobbled off the cots in their shackles and their flesh-supports and went right back to their stations.

All the while Isobel just kept working, knowing that most of what they thought about her was nonsense, and feeling like she'd really enjoy a lho-stick right now, or a rare slab of grox-steak on a platter, and they'd never know any of that, because all that mattered was the belief, the power of the miracle, the service only she could provide and that Jep, for all his undoubted skill, never could. You couldn't get hung up on it, you had to just accept it. That was her philosophy, at any rate, and it seemed to work out pretty well.

'They just keep coming,' she murmured, pulling some sutures tight and reaching for the skin-glue.

'More armsmen on their way,' Jep told her, sounding apologetic about it.

'Really? Where from now?'

'They never tell me.' Jep leaned a little closer. 'More than three incursions. Four decks cut off, they say. All stretched thin, getting cut down quickly.'

Isobel snorted. 'You've got Space Marines. It'll be fine.'

'I trust so.' He didn't sound convinced. 'Nothing from the astropaths. Nothing from the Navigator.'

Isobel turned on him. 'I care not – they bring the bodies down, we send them back up. Trust in the lord captain, trust in the Throne.'

Jep looked startled. 'Of course, Sister. I meant no–'

Isobel didn't listen. She had work to do – the blood would flow, one way or the other, and someone had to mop it all up.

Garrock felt no fear, only a rush of adrenaline, a hit of fury that made him sprint. His troops came with him, shields hefted now as weapons, guns firing and blades glowing with energy fields.

He shouldn't have done it, he knew. It went against his combat doctrine, and there was nothing much an armsman could do that a Space Marine couldn't, so they would likely die before making much of an impact at all. But it was *something*, a charge to the aid of those who had treated him with respect. If the device was going to do whatever it had been brought over to do, well, better to die in the thick of it than merely watching from the sidelines.

He smacked hard into contact, slashing his powered blade across the back of a mechanical horror. Refad crashed into the one next to him, bolstered by a shield-carrier, using it like a bludgeon. Garrock could hear his troops shouting wildly, more for themselves than the enemy, mustering up courage, knowing this would be bloody and rapid.

The skitarii turned. Red oculus clusters, flayed faces studded with brass pins, segmented limbs daubed with foul runes. They lashed back, swinging their electro-glaives and flesh-slicing beam-guns.

Garrock roared out loud. 'Get back!' he screamed. 'Get back to the pits that spawned you!'

He felt no fear at all. Nothing like it. Just anger, desperate anger, a savage energy that propelled his limbs far harder than ever before. He shot one-handed, at point-blank range, and shattered a protective neck plate. He slashed with his crackling blade, a good sword that cut through the tangles of steel and brass. He heard his people dying – screams of sudden pain – and it only fuelled him further. He heard the clang of the heavy breacher shields, massive slabs that could do serious damage when wielded by trained hands. He smelled the sharp tang of blood, and knew that some belonged to the enemy.

They still bled, then. They hadn't lost touch entirely with what they had once been. That was good. Make them bleed some more.

Maizad reacted immediately. The fractional lifting of pressure enabled the Space Marines to push on towards the construct. Garrock could only detect two of them by then, Maizad included, a beleaguered pair of armoured figures blasting and hacking their way through the scrum of augmented horrors. They were silent still, utterly indifferent to the shrieks and chatters around them, fighting like charred-metal revenants.

But he never got more than glimpses, just snatches as the enemy blocked his view. They slashed at him with frenzied mechanical precision, their hands turned into industrial slicers and grinders. Refad went down under their onslaught, his armour penetrated by another one of those foul energy beams. More and more fell, and the sound of drills being turned on the shields made the air scream and shimmer. Garrock panted hard now, arms burning, feeling the pressure, the intense pressure, pushing on, determined at all costs not to lose ground.

When it happened, it was staggeringly quick. Maizad had got closer than Garrock had thought possible, right under the device's piled-up foundations. He'd stowed his blade and bolter and now held a whole clutch of krak charges. The Space Marine leapt up high, propelled as if by a catapult, rising through a storm of las-bolts and projectiles. His armour looked half-blasted, carrying rents and gouges and crackling with unleashed electric sparks, but he made it up to the construct's first stage and clamped the charges to its thundering power core. The false skitarii screamed even louder for a split second, as if they intended to surge up after him, but then the charges went off, blasting the entire level of the device apart. Secondary explosions went off immediately. The cables cut free, lashing like flails.

Kicked back by the blast wave, Garrock skittered crazily across the deck, feeling the hot blast roar around and over him. Even in his armour he felt the intense heat, the rush and boom, tumbling him over and dragging him along the rupturing deck. He saw bodies flying – limbs, armour pieces, struts and power lines, all flung wildly across the chamber amid the racing flames.

He skidded to a halt, scrambled back up, staggered, desperately shoving aside the battered bodies around him. His ears were ringing, he couldn't hear anything, he could feel hot blood run down the inside of his helm. He twisted around, tried to get a fix on what had happened, and saw a huge hole blasted into the chamber's roof and far wall. The construct itself was gone, a tattered skeleton over an ongoing inferno, its external units popping like firecrackers as the chain reaction gnawed its way through the remains. Everything smelled of promethium and boiled flesh. The chamber's structure had been critically damaged – as Garrock's hearing returned he could make out muffled klaxons indicating rapid depressurisation, so whatever precautions the invaders had taken to keep the atmosphere intact had been smashed away by the blast.

He staggered to his knees, trying to spy the rest of his unit amid the searing flame and smoke. He couldn't see any of them, just wreckage and corpses. He voxed Hobes – nothing.

His hearing came back in snatches. The deck beneath him shook, flexing like a drumskin being beaten. His head jerked up, and he saw one of the skitarii lurching towards him. The creature was half-destroyed, its flesh stripped clean from a glistening metal shell. The stripped-skull face chattered madly. It carried a burned-out electro-stave in its ravaged claws.

Garrock shot at it, then shot again, and the las-bolts blasted chunks out of its carcass. Still it came. He swayed into its path and slashed with his blade, severing a metallic tendon and making it stagger, but still it came – it was looming over him now, stave poised to crunch down.

The blow never fell – something huge and dark and lumbering crashed into the monster from behind, breaking it open, running it down, grinding it into the shivering deck. Garrock limped clear, relieved to see Maizad return, only to find himself staring up at a ruined demigod.

The fighting at the centre must have been ferocious beyond imagining. The Iron Shade's armour was cut to pieces, hanging in severed chunks from exposed grey skin. Blood was everywhere, semi-clotted, caked over the joints, dripping thickly onto the deck below. Maizad's head lolled – he looked barely sensate. He was alone – none of his battle-brothers had returned from the wreckage, though in his wake were great heaps of slain skitarii, twitching and sparking.

'Sergeant!' Garrock shouted, trying to catch his swinging forearm, to guide him away from the disintegrating chamber.

He gripped the Space Marine's gauntlet, felt the enormous weight there, far too heavy for him to lift or even to guide. He glanced back again, willing for help to emerge out of the heaps of bodies – from his own detachment, from Maizad's – but nothing came. Was it really just the two of them, now? Had *four* Space Marines been killed by those monsters?

Maizad stumbled, dropping to one knee. Parts of his breastplate looked to be steaming, as if superheated by some strange process, but Garrock had no idea how to remove whatever was causing it. Blood was welling up between helm and armour seal, thick and black and viscous.

'We have to move,' Garrock urged him, looking nervously at the piles of bodies again. Some of them appeared to be getting back up, all of them with mechanical stiffness.

Maizad slurred something, and blood spotted at his vox-grille. Garrock grabbed his gauntlet again, trying to guide him at least. The huge Space Marine took the direction, shambling along as Garrock hauled as hard as he could. As they went, the deck bounced savagely, and cracks shot up the walls around them. A huge snap sounded over the wreckage of the ruined device, and the entire structure around it started to sag.

'Faster!' Garrock grunted, wedging himself under Maizad's elbow and hauling with all his might.

He made very little difference – the Space Marine was astonishingly heavy for something that had just been moving so fast. The deck plates started to crumble under them, the walls to disintegrate as the panels crumpled inward.

'*Faster*,' Garrock implored, putting everything into shoving the Space Marine towards the nearest bulkhead. The heat grew around them – the inferno was erratic now, starved of oxygen as the breach in the hull widened, but something somewhere was still fuelling it.

Maizad made it to the chamber exit at last and toppled through the gap. Garrock unthreaded himself from the Space Marine's stiffening arm and staggered over to hit the lock panel. He hesitated at the last moment, poised on the threshold, checking one final time to see if any other survivors were coming.

He saw a site of total desolation – a tottering mess of power lines and burning modules collapsing in on itself and dragging the entire chamber down with it. A few skitarii were limping towards him, or dragging themselves back towards the great gash in the chamber's far end, but they wouldn't get far – more explosions were coming.

He hit the lever, and the bulkhead's blast doors slammed shut. The cacophony abruptly ceased, locked away behind heavy adamantine void-panels designed to withstand huge pressures. He'd need to get further back now, quarantine the whole deck, summon reinforcements in case any stragglers somehow managed to worm their way out of the disintegrating hull section.

'Level command,' he voxed, feeling the pain of his wounds rushing into focus. 'Immediate reinforcement to level–'

A huge crash made him start, and he whirled around to see Maizad collapsed on the deck, a pool of blood spreading out from under his prone body.

He crouched down next to him, wondered how on earth he might go about looking for a pulse, or getting the helm off, or staunching the bleeding.

'Medicae detail to enginarium, zone tertius, level twelve, sector thirty-four,' he voxed, unable to keep the note of panic out of his voice. 'Lone surviving Astartes is down. Repeat – Astartes is down.'

# Chapter Eleven

**SURVIVOR**

**RACE FOR THE DOORS**

**THE SCREAM**

Avati stared at the wreckage for a moment, hoping against hope that some mistake had been made. Boroja shunted the secondary data over quickly, and it became apparent that there was no mistake – the *Gorgon* was nothing more than a twisting gyre of hull plates now, a mini solar system of scrap around its destroyed core. Beyond it, the *Hammerfall* was falling away from the battleplane too, every surface burning, sucking up fresh impacts even in its ruin. Whatever desperate gamble it had been pushing had come to its end – it was doomed now, isolated and ripe for the killing blow.

'All engines, full reverse,' Kiastros ordered, snapping quickly back into command. 'Withdraw to protective position – Gunnery, I'll need that spread broadside now.'

He was doing what he had to – the *Hammerfall* had destroyed itself, had destroyed the *Gorgon* too, thus rendering Hekaon's orders null. If the *Judgement of the Void* could extract itself from the immediate firestorm and gain a measure of protection from

Jovanjiar's surviving formations, then they'd all live for an hour or so longer.

'Survivor detected!' Boroja shouted, hands darting over his console as he zoomed through the wreckage. 'The *Gorgon* launched something. Yes, yes, getting it. System-runner class, bearing ahead four-five-one.'

Avati cursed. 'Too far out,' she warned, cross-referencing the coordinates. Even as she did so, more impacts made the bridge shake. 'Multiple reports of further boarding actions, lord captain – we *must* withdraw.'

Kiastros would know that. He'd be fully aware of what sounded like a huge disaster on the enginarium decks, of the total signal-absence from the astropaths' spire, of a third incursion site in the under-decks that had sent an entire squad of armsmen packing. The void shields were a minute or two from total collapse, the plasma drives were under strain from constant manoeuvring, and their single remaining escort would be pounded into atoms within moments. They were exposed, wounded, and running into a whole constellation of fresh pain.

'How far out is the runner?' Kiastros demanded.

'Zero point one v-u,' Boroja replied. 'Turning towards us and picking up speed.'

Once again, a flicker of indecision on his face. That was the closest he got to ordering the retreat, but as soon as she saw the expression Avati knew it was only temporary. An order was an order, and Kiastros was a creature of his training.

'Come about to receive it,' he said. 'Order any fighters we still have to bring it in, then dock. Main hangar, open doors on my mark. Belay previous course and alignment – bring us two points ahead, dead slow. Emergency power to the voids, but warn Kuhl we'll need to push everything to the plasma drives momentarily.'

They all scurried to obey. They knew it would likely kill them, but they never hesitated. Boroja hailed the Inquisition craft and cascaded the commands to the surviving fighters. Spleed cancelled the full broadside and shifted to lances to shepherd the incoming ship. Avati executed the turn and course correction and made sure Kuhl knew what was coming. The *Judgement of the Void* turned ponderously on its axis, its void shields now a halo of incoming las-fire, and moved out towards the incoming system runner.

Avati zoomed in to get a better look at it. It was a strange thing, crow-like, black and angled, much like its mothership. Its running lumens were a pale green, as sinister as anything she'd ever seen, and it travelled with a crabbed, jerky motion, no doubt to evade the waves of ordnance that were more than capable of smashing it out of the void entirely.

She instantly hated it. She hated what they were doing on its behalf, and she hated that it was even here. No one had told her why an Inquisition ship was present, why it was so valu-able, why it had to be protected at the cost of everything and everyone else. She would never say a word, though. No one would. Even having such thoughts made her palms sweat a little more, made her want to look over her shoulder.

They couldn't spy on your thoughts, though. They couldn't. No one could. Surely?

'Enemy battle cruisers moving from *Hammerfall* to intercept us,' she reported calmly, as if none of that were going through her mind. 'They're targeting.'

'Turn prow full into barrage,' Kiastros ordered. 'Stay on course.'

The system runner hurtled closer, burning its engines to make the sanctuary of the *Judgement of the Void*'s hangar. Avati sent the turn order, and watched as the heavily armoured prow came about. The closing enemy battle cruisers opened fire immedi-ately, sending a phalanx of torpedoes shrieking straight at them. Avati watched them track into contact, unable to launch eva-sive manoeuvres, unable to do anything at all.

'Impact in five seconds!' she warned, gripping the sides of her throne as if that instinctive gesture would do anything at all. 'Brace, brace!'

The torpedoes hit – three of them, one after the other, slamming into the overlaid void shields and dousing them in riotous explosions. One shield section failed in a blaze of ions, letting a fourth torpedo in to crash directly against the hull. If that strike had hit amidships, it would have burrowed deep inside and set off a catastrophic chain of explosions; as it was, the ram-proof prow absorbed the worst of it and the results were only horrifically painful – the whole battle cruiser buckled, slid as if kicked, its near-volume thrusters blown apart as they struggled to compensate, its power grid interrupted and its energy drain doubled.

'Status, Signals,' Kiastros demanded, a note of strain in his voice.

'Hull cohesion compromised across prow-zone,' Boroja intoned grimly. 'One more of those, and–'

'Understood. Astrogation?'

Avati smacked the side of her picter lens to regain the picture. Something solid the size of her head crashed to the deck just a yard away, a cogitator station blew up in the pit below. The bridge was coming apart.

'System runner ready to dock – coming in hard,' she reported. 'Enemy battle cruisers angling for broadsides – no counter-strike possible from allied hulls.'

Of course there wasn't – *Hammerfall* was breaking up now, and they were too far out of position for any possible assistance, even in such a crowded battlesphere with so many ships jostling for precedence. Jovanjiar's main formations were under siege and totally removed, bracketed by a rampant enemy and still making no sign of breaking for the warp. This was carnage.

'Signal engines for immediate full-stop and drop to nadir two points as soon as the runner's in,' ordered Kiastros, turning to her. 'Can the ship take that?'

It was a standard move, a sound one, but the damage levels they'd already taken made it difficult.

'It'll have to,' said Avati, projecting more confidence than she felt. 'I'll prime Kuhl.'

'Do that.' Kiastros switched back to Boroja. 'How soon before those broadsides?'

The Master of Signals scanned his picter lenses. 'Estimated fifty seconds.'

'And the runner?'

'Sixty seconds out, lord captain.'

Kiastros swore. 'Tell them to flay their engines. Come in red-hot – we'll handle it.' He switched to the comm. 'Gunnery – we need some time. Can you muster a lance strike? Split between those cruisers?'

*'It won't stop them,'* Spleed replied over the comm.

'It doesn't have to. Just hold them up, play havoc with their cannons – anything. You have discretion.'

*'By your will.'*

Kiastros cut the link, looked over at Avati. Fine dust was raining down over all of them now, a sign that the overhead structure was badly compromised. Half the bridge stations were fizzing with static, the lumens were blinking erratically, everything shook and rattled and creaked.

He smiled at her. 'Enjoying yourself, Astrogation?' he asked dryly.

'Very much so, lord captain,' Avati replied, busy with the order package for Kuhl. 'Enginarium primed, thruster-gangs primed – we can move on your word.'

'Do not wait for that, lieutenant. Soon as the runner's in, you make the move.' He smiled again. Why was he smiling so much? 'I have full faith in you.'

'*Lances away!*' came Spleed's voice in her earpiece.

The *Judgement of the Void* shuddered as all of its turrets fired at once, sending high-energy spears out into the black. The sudden power drain made all the lumens shut down, throwing the entire bridge into total darkness, before serried blazes in the distance told them some strikes at least had hit home.

The power flickered back on, and Avati looked up to see Kiastros craning for the results.

'Hits registered,' Boroja reported. 'Minor damage – they are still shifting position to fire.'

'Runner has entered the hangar!' Avati shouted, punching the codes to Kuhl.

The *Judgement of the Void* immediately crunched to a halt. The manoeuvring thrusters swung round in their housings and pushed the entire ship down to nadir, a sudden wrench that sent out echoing shrieks and booms throughout every deck. The inertial field generators whined up to compensate, and red alerts flashed all across Avati's console indicating heavy damage somewhere down in Kuhl's sprawling kingdom.

The enemy fired a second later, spewing two broadsides of macrocannon shells directly at them. The *Judgement of the Void* continued to descend, faster as the momentum built. Avati found that she was gripping her throne supports too tightly – she'd drawn blood under her gauntlets – but couldn't let go.

The barrage hit. Avati's sudden position change meant they evaded the worst of it, and a whole swathe of shells whistled over the tops of their spires and into the void beyond, but there had never been enough time to escape entirely. Dozens of shells smacked into the port flanks, crunching through brittle and underpowered void shields. Explosions smashed along every deck, rippling from stern to prow and cascading up the already damaged levels. The main augur array blinked and went out, extinguishing half the bridge's picter lenses.

'Void shields down on all faces!' Boroja yelled. 'Only second-tier sensors left – we can't see far.'

*'Follow-up broadside ready,'* Spleed offered – his comm-feed was thick with the tinny sound of distant explosions.

'Negative,' ordered Kiastros, his jawline tight and his eyes shining. 'Barrels-in and seal every bulkhead – your part is played.'

He turned to Avati. 'Get us out of here, Astrogation.'

'But, the admiral...'

'I had the signal – the fleet's breaking for the warp.' He fixed her with a rock-steady look. 'Now get us away before those ships fire again, or we'll never see any of them again.'

The Navigator's demesne was not spared. Every time the ship took a serious hit, even though her little realm was heavily shielded and surrounded by inertial suppressors, the whole place shook. Vases were smashed, glasses broke; one of the paintings now hung at an angle and would need to be remounted.

All deeply tedious, but it would only get worse. Santalina had completed the preparations by then, had changed into her cere-monial robes, entered the spherical inner sanctum and plugged the cables into the input nodes of her arms, spine and neck. She drank deeply from the ritual bowls and felt the narcotics enter her bloodstream. Then she settled into her throne, activated the external comms and watched the carnage unfold.

She wasn't a member of the Navy – neither an engineer nor an officer – but she didn't need to be to see how desperate things were. The augurs were down; they were shouting over the vox-lines, which was deadly serious. The hull had at least three breaches – suspected landings from enemy troops, no word yet on whether they'd been beaten back. The Space Marines who'd been deployed to guard against that very purpose had gone dark; even the Captain of Armsmen couldn't be reached, on the channels she had access to at any rate. The void shields were collapsing, the plasma drives were close to burn-out; the entire structure of the hull, all three miles of it, was now creaking and cracking itself apart – a few more major strikes and it might disintegrate entirely.

Had it ever been this bad? Not that she could remember. She'd expected to die a few times, got very close to it a few times more, and yet they'd always scraped through. She trusted the captain, but this wasn't his fight. Something had gone wrong at the fleet level, and now they were all paying the price.

She shifted in her throne, adjusted one of the uncomfortable cables in her forearm, switched over to one of the sphere's internal viewfinders. It was a tactical display, not something she was adept at reading, but one that nevertheless gave her an overview of the situation. And it was shocking – ships everywhere, marked as dead, marked as dying, marked as incoming, marked as drifting. No formation left, as far as she could see, just squadrons breaking from the firestorm and haring for the void. Jovanjiar's massive formations, built to assault the Eye of Terror itself, were turning now, breaking out of engagements and trying to disentangle from the cat's-cradle of las-fire and shell impacts.

'You have left it late, Iannis,' she breathed to herself, wondering if he was panicking now. Probably not. Captains didn't panic – they'd had all that knocked out of them decades ago.

'*Mistress Navigator!*' came Avati's voice over the comm.

Santalina stiffened. Even now, even given what was going on, she disliked hearing that voice. No finesse, no style. 'Aye, lieutenant,' she replied.

'*Extraction course set, drives engaged. We are primed for veilbreak – are you prepared?*'

Throne, the insolence of it. Of course she was prepared. She was always prepared.

'I am,' she said coolly. 'But can we survive the move?'

She knew a little about the mechanics of realspace position-ing, and knew how hard it would be. You couldn't just power up the warp drives anywhere – if you were surrounded by close-run hulls, or bracketed with too much las-fire, or going too fast or too slow or at the wrong angle, the whole thing could smash the ship into spars and drag the asphyxiating survi-vors into undiluted hell. You had to break clear, do what you could to shake off the worst enemy attention, claw out a slice of breathing space and hope for the best.

*'I have no idea,'* Avati replied, and that shocked her.

The link cut, and Santalina felt the entire ship keel over, a toppling dive that the damaged inertial controls could clearly not compensate for. She watched her monitors as Avati steered them out of the worst congestion. The lieutenant had sent their lone surviving escort right into the teeth of the oncoming enemy. That was cold, a deliberate suicide run, but it bought them a few seconds. The situation was tight, all the same – a narrowing gap between oncoming giants, a hard burn towards relative space.

Santalina tensed, readying her body for what was to come. It would hurt. It always did, of course, but the transition would be jarring now. She could almost feel the warp coalescing around her, spinning out of nothing, stiffening the air and making the lenses frost over.

The ship shuddered as the engines roared. The alerts kept coming. Another hull breach – how had they managed that? Another torpedo strike. Throne, the hull was coming apart now. She heard screaming. Was that real? A foretaste of what was to come when they jumped?

She reached up for her bandana, peeled it off, folded the fabric neatly. Now she was all-seeing, caught like a swimmer knee-deep in surf, strung out between the worlds. She felt the souls on the ship, tens of thousands, all scared, all stressed, many dying in pain and crossing the boundary between realities and seeing, for the first time and for a split second, what she always saw on her journeys.

'Translation imminent!' came the familiar warning, and the lumens in her sphere dropped to a dull red. Slivers of witch-lightning kindled on the bare steel, her heart rate quickened. She could sense it, like a coming electric storm, curdling the atmosphere, wrapping around her body like a cloak.

'Protect us,' she whispered, more out of habit than anything else. 'Send your light to guide us.'

Her stomach lurched, her blood pressure shot up. She detected the sudden switch – the move from plasma to warp drives. The veil tore in two, and she stared into the living Seethe again.

She screamed.

Then she stopped. Why had she screamed? She hadn't seen anything untoward. The open wound in the universe beckoned, flecked with lightning, boiling like molten tar.

She was sweating, she was shaking. Why was she doing that?

The threshold beckoned, the maw into oblivion, and she didn't want to cross it. She wanted to screw her Seeing Eye closed and force the ship to remain in the universe. That would destroy them, but she wanted to do it.

Santalina clenched her fists, focused hard, caught the first glimpse of the beacon's clean light. The *Judgement of the Void*, bleeding and burning, hurtled towards it.

*Do not go in.*

This was insanity. This was madness. She pushed towards the light. Always, always, push towards the light.

Avati's voice came again, insistent, urgent, like a gadfly at her neck.

*'Are we in?'* she asked. *'Are we safe?'*

Santalina didn't reply for a moment. Her heart was hammering so hard she thought it might burst. The warp was all around her, howling at her, trying to get in, just like it always did.

Why had she screamed?

'We are in the warp, lieutenant,' she replied, forcing her voice to remain level. 'We are safe.'

# Chapter Twelve

**SON OF THE EMPEROR**
**A BLOODY MESS**
**UNWELCOME GUESTS**

Isobel looked up as the doors slammed open. She'd told Jep to keep them closed – the apothecarion was overloaded, the cots were full, and she badly needed to rest for just a moment. Her mind felt sluggish – she'd patched up so many bodies that she could barely focus. Combat was easier – you could ride on the fury of it, use the anger to keep you sharp, but this kind of fleshwork, it was unremitting. The deck was swimming in blood and spilled fluids. The menials were on their knees, even the servitors were hanging back, jaws slack, drool looped under exhausted chins.

But then they brought him in, the Space Marine, the one she'd heard about but not had time to meet. Five of them had come on board, they'd told her, part of a squadron-wide distribution, something Hekaon had set up once he'd got the resources. Not *ordered*, mind – set up. You never did anything with Astartes without asking nicely, so they'd have had to agree to it.

She looked around her. Jep was nowhere to be found – back

in some other chamber working the bone-drills or something – but the man leading him in was in an armsman's livery. He'd taken his helm off and had blood all over his face, matted in his beard. He started when he saw her – had he known she was even on board?

'Honoured Sister,' he said, bowing.

'I can't help him,' she said flatly. 'His own people can.'

The Space Marine was lying prone. They'd brought him in on an ammo hauler, a heavy slab of metal used for dragging gun-supplies around. It took four menials to pull it under normal circumstances – twelve of them had been needed for the current payload.

'He's the last one left,' said the armsman.

She stared at him. 'The last one?'

'The last one.'

She shook her head in disbelief. 'What happened?'

'I don't know. Something like... I don't know. Lots of them landed. An army.'

She looked over at the Space Marine. She looked back at the cot – would it even take the weight? 'What's your name?'

'Garrock. Captain of Armsmen.'

'Clear the cot. Get him onto the slab. I'll need you here with me while we move him.'

It was hard work. Even in her power armour, it was hard work. She cut as much of the Space Marine's own armour free as she could, but ceramite was designed to be tough, and some plates were fused together. In the end, the whole team of them had to do it, with servitor support, dragging the ruined body over onto the surgical cot, which then bowed and creaked under the weight. She added supports, hauled across a higher-powered lumen stand.

At first glance, she thought he was dead. She ran a scan and picked up a faint pulse, almost undetectable, a shallow breath in those huge, ravaged lungs.

Everything she saw was destroyed. Skin flayed, muscle torn,

bones broken. It was hard to imagine that any blood still lingered somewhere inside, given how much had leaked out. She ordered an immediate line, and struggled to get the needle into the vein – Throne, the skin was like mesh-metal.

'Can you save him?' asked Garrock, hovering nearby.

She looked at him. He appeared to be only a little better off himself, leaning heavily on a blood-speckled gurney. 'You need to tell me what happened.'

'Martians. Twisted versions of them.'

'*More* twisted.'

He didn't laugh. He didn't look like he was able to. 'They had... weapons, things I've never seen before. They killed four of the Space Marines, all of my squad, a few hundred armed crew before we even got there. They must have landed more than one assault craft.'

She turned back to the body. Glancing down at the wounds daunted her. She had never done more than trivial work on one of the Astartes. They had their own surgeons, their bodies were designed to self-heal. They had two hearts, entirely reconstructed skeletons, organs implanted everywhere – they were virtually xenos, the gulf was so wide. And she had no idea what forces had been unleashed on him – nerve damage, maybe. The Fallen Mechanicus had devices that could shred a body from the inside out, melt its armour and burst its vitals. They must have unloaded everything they had at this one, and it had almost been enough.

'I'll do what I can,' she said, beckoning more servitors over and sending Jep an immediate summons.

Garrock reached across, put his hand on her arm. It wasn't impertinent – it was desperate. 'Save him.'

She nodded, respecting the piety.

'He is a Son of the Emperor,' she said. 'If He wishes it, then I will.'

\* \* \*

Avati hurried down to the main hangar. She should have been relieved – they were out of the battle at last – but she felt anything but. Her chest was tight, her temples throbbing. A bitter taste had emerged at the back of her mouth and she couldn't shift it.

Perhaps it was the warp. Everyone was sick in the warp. Or maybe just the shock of it all.

The decks below the bridge level were in turmoil. Several life-support systems seemed to have failed, so everyone was still in full void armour. Lumens shut off, then shuddered back on. Panels would suddenly blow, revealing snakes' nests of cabling within, and menials would scurry over to try to stuff it all back in. Under it all, the warp drives growled, sounding intermittent and unhealthy.

She wanted to go to Kuhl. That was what she should have been doing – speaking to engineers, identifying where the core problems were, moving to staunch the damage. Instead, she was going to the hangars, sent by Kiastros to find out just what they'd taken on board. She only had an escort of four – all guards taken from the bridge detail – since every single member of Garrock's garrison was either dead or still trying to put out the many fires.

A bloody mess. They were alive, at least, but that alone meant very little. The fleet had failed, utterly failed, and running under her adrenaline high was the shame that was already beginning to bear her down. They had all been so proud, so eager to complete the muster and then head off to the main objective. Could Jovanjiar even survive this? Could Samil? Groupmasters had been court-martialled and executed for less. Maybe admirals too. Maybe all of them were destined for the firing squad now – the Imperium was remorseless when it came to punishing failure.

She remembered the look Kiastros had given her, just before they made the break for the warp.

*I had the signal.*

The captain was an honest man. Painfully so, and he venerated the chain of command almost as much as the sacred pantheon of the primarchs.

And yet. She hadn't seen that order. There was no record of it on the bridge console. If Kiastros had *run*, if he'd fled from combat without authorisation...

Dangerous to even think it. The Inquisition was on board. The bloody Inquisition!

She swallowed as she marched. The newcomers were likely as battered as they were, knocked about by the destruction of their voidship. A system runner could only house a few dozen souls, plus a small cargo-hold – what could they do against a crew of thousands? What was there to fear?

*Everything*, her inner voice told her, born of a lifetime's schooling in the ways of the decaying empire she served. *There is everything to fear.*

She reached the hangar's inner doors, and one of her guards activated the release. As the heavy panels ground upward, she did what she could to calm down.

On the far side, the enormous hangar stretched away from her, capable of housing a dozen large void-going vessels. Now it was almost empty, the Inquisition system runner the only occupant of the wide apron. It was steaming, heavily damaged, its matt-black profile looking even stranger up close than it had on the scopes. Something made her think of a wounded crow, an animal many of the crew would never have seen in life. The flight crews hadn't gone near it, hanging back with their refuelling trucks and maintenance gurneys and looking like they would rather be back in the void battle. Avati stood them down as she marched past – if their guests had need of assistance, they could ask for it.

As she approached the ship, a lozenge on its hull cracked open and a ramp extended. A dozen figures came down to meet her – half were soldiers in black armour and full-face helms, the rest were what she guessed were the Inquisitorial retinue. They were a bizarre-looking group, with lace-trimmed facemasks and wide-brimmed hats and semi-reflective breastplates. One of them was obese, another had jewels for eyes.

They all hung back around a single figure, the one she guessed was the inquisitor himself. He was tall, very tall, almost unnaturally so, and stick-thin. He had a long dark-grey face with pronounced bone structure, eyes set in deep wells. His fingers were slender, his robes drawn tightly around him. He wore a purple sash across his waist, which looked as if it was concealing a weapons belt, though not very effectively. His head was bare, displaying a tattoo of the Imperial aquila in blood red.

His physical presentation was intimidating enough, but the truly unsettling thing about him was the way he moved, the expression on his face, the curl of his thick lips. Everything radiated contempt, a desire to take apart, to pull to pieces, to rearrange. It was almost surgical, like the worst medic you could ever hope to come before, one who had your interests absolutely not to heart, but only a kind of sadistic interest in seeing what stuff you were made of.

'Be welcome aboard, lord inquisitor,' she said, coming before him and making the aquila. 'Captain Iannis Kiastros sends his regards, and expresses thanks to the Emperor that we were able to preserve you. I am First Lieutenant Leroa Avati. Do you require any additional assistance?'

The grey-skinned face regarded her coolly. When he spoke, the voice was just as frightful as she'd expected – a vile whisper that sounded more snake-like than human.

'I am not the inquisitor,' he said. 'Lord Gertruda was killed in service, and her soul is now one with the Throne. I am her interrogator, Hastin il-Moro. I now command the retinue. My authority is absolute.'

A strange thing to say. Of course it was. Avati regarded him carefully. Maybe he wasn't quite as all-powerful as he wanted to appear. Maybe even members of the Inquisition had to boost themselves from time to time.

'My commiserations for your loss,' she said respectfully. 'Our priests shall be instructed to remember your master in their rituals.' She glanced over his shoulder at the smouldering mass of his ship. 'Do you require any assistance for repairs? I can command our Master of Engines to assign you a lexmechanic detail, if you–'

'No.' Il-Moro's tone was final. 'No assistance required in any way. This hangar is to be placed off-limits to your crew, even the servitor class. I shall require unfalsifiable proof that the space is protected from hostile scans, and a guard placed on the outer doors. Communication between me and your captain will be by remote link only. We will need supplies for our crew of thirty-nine souls to be delivered at a schedule I shall outline in due course.'

Despite everything, Avati found herself bristling a little. They had risked everything for these people. 'I understand,' she said, keeping any sign of that irritation out of her voice. 'I shall communicate that to the captain.'

Il-Moro drew a little closer to her, demonstrating just how much taller he was. If it was an attempt to further intimidate, it was clumsy.

'Another thing. This ship must survive. It must run ahead of any pursuing enemy craft, exit the empyrean without further combat, and make arrangements for rendezvous with my people. I shall require the use of your astropathic choir soon, and a dossier will be supplied to them with further details.'

Avati hesitated. 'The choir is currently out of contact with the bridge. We suspect significant damage to the spire, and have not yet been able to speak to them.'

Il-Moro frowned. 'Destroyed?'

'Unknown at this stage – teams are being sent to investigate.'

'I shall require immediate notification, once their status is known.'

She could have told him plenty more then, if she'd been inclined. Like how the warp drives were believed to be within a hair's breadth of failing, and how the augur arrays were shot beyond repair, and that if they were forced to drop back into realspace then they'd likely be shot to shrapnel by anything capable of tracking them. It was all almost comically awful, a cluster of terrible news that just kept getting worse.

In the face of that, even the terror of the Inquisition lessened just a little bit. They might well be dead within a few hours, or plunged straight back into a battle they couldn't win. How could this Hastin il-Moro, with all his dead-eyed theatrics, make that very much worse?

Careful, though. Careful. It was that kind of thinking that got people locked up in the examination chambers with their eyes and fingers missing.

'I shall make sure that is done, interrogator,' she said. 'And if there is anything else you require, please do not hesitate to contact me again.'

# Chapter Thirteen

**OLD FEARS**

**NO LOOSE THREADS**

**TAKING STOCK**

She had to get out. She couldn't get out. Perhaps she could hide. Somewhere down in the deeps, where only the blind gangs scratched around amid pools of ancient oil. Would that save her? No, it wouldn't. A tentacle would find its way down, creeping through the gearboxes and axles, coming after her until it gripped her ankle and never let go.

Kuhl woke up, covered in sweat. She was still standing, propped up against a shaft-housing. It hadn't been proper sleep – just a few moments of exhaustion that had sunk into a dream-filled doze. She had to sleep soon, or she might go properly mad, and yet there was no time, no time at all, everything needed attending to, the great machines needed her...

She rubbed her eyes, pressed her knuckles into her cheeks, slapped herself a few times. This was no time to lose her composure. Destruction had been averted – just – but perils awaited. The plasma drives were half shot, and might be called into action at any time. The warp drives were suffering too, for reasons she didn't yet understand – it was possible damage sustained in combat had fed back into the main chambers, compromising the arcane internals. She would have to look into it, but held out little hope of finding a proper solution. Warp drives were as much sorcery as they were mechanics, and properly required servicing in dedicated Geller-shielded Mechanicus void-docks. Sending menials into the core sections was as likely to kill them as anything, or bring them back with their skin hanging off in sheets.

But that wasn't what scared her. She replayed the message from Avati in her mind, over and over again.

*Inquisition party has been landed. Dispatch servitors to attend to system runner.*

That order had since been countermanded – the Inquisition had decided, apparently, that they didn't need any help with their damaged craft. That was a mercy, but still. They were here. On her ship.

No escape. In a real city, somewhere planet-bound, you might stand a chance of getting away, but here, while in the warp, alone – impossible.

Something like this had always been likely. The *Judgement of the Void* was a serious warship, and had hosted ambassadors and Space Marine captains and Astra Militarum generals. The clandestine orders were always bound to have boarded at some stage or other. The fact it had been over twenty years without such an incident had probably been more than lucky.

More than twenty years it was since she'd been a master of engineers on the industrial world of Oolenta, eking out a living that had been as grinding as any in the Imperium. She'd had her family, her husband, three children, long shifts, little coin, frequent scarcity of food. It was impossible to look back on those years without mixed feelings. There had been laughter in the little hab they all shared, some tenderness, a kind of practical love and mutual tolerance. But it had been so hard, so hard. Others had gone under, driven into sickness by the endless demands, the punishing shifts, the toxins in the air and the water. So was it any wonder that some stopped listening to the priests, and took up darker pursuits? If your children had died of the wasting-pox in your arms while your overseer was shouting at you to get straight back to the production lines, would you, too, not have found yourself thinking a little harder about the strange pamphlet you'd been handed a few weeks ago but hadn't looked at yet? Would you have wondered why you hadn't destroyed it straight away, but had kept it safe and secret, just in case? And once you'd read the unsettling words within it, would you not have been tempted to ask more questions, to go back to the fellow worker who'd given it to you, maybe even visit them in their hab?

She hadn't done any of those things. She had just understood why others might have been tempted. She hadn't even *known* about the pamphlets, not really, nor the little meetings that took place by candlelight, nor the spreading rumours of something coming to Oolenta, something wonderful that would free them all from the grind of their impoverishment forever. Although you did hear things, and you might have guessed close to the truth, and wondered if you ought to make some kind of report.

And then something *had* come to Oolenta, but it hadn't been what the little groups had expected. It turned out that not all the pamphlet writers had been quite as committed as they had seemed. Some were agents of the local enforcers, who were in the pay of the city governor, who in turn had contacts of a far more powerful nature. The ships landed at night with no warning, black ships with strange running lumens, and after that the purges had started.

Kuhl shuddered to remember it. Barely a night had passed since when she hadn't suffered memories of that time – children taken from parents, workers dragged from the manufactorum floor, denunciations and weeping denials in the public tribunals. They burned the ringleaders – or those, at any rate, whom they thought had been the ringleaders. Under the instruments, people would confess to anything, just to stop the agony. And you never forgot the stink of burned flesh, the way it was like grox-strips but worse, because it had the smell of human in it and mingled with the memory of those agonised, mad-with-fear wails.

Most of all, she remembered the one who had come for her. She'd had kind eyes, that woman. A soft face, a gentle manner, but Kuhl hadn't been fooled. She'd taken her away, bundled her into a transport and thrown her in a cell. Kuhl had been so terrified she'd soiled herself, but they'd never given her replacement clothes. No food, little water, just night after night listening to the screams in the cells down the corridor.

She'd prayed so hard, on her knees mired in her own filth, over and over.

*Divine Emperor, Master of Mankind, protect your servant. Make them see! Make them understand!*

And maybe those prayers had worked, and she had been spared for a reason. Or maybe the investigators had found everything they wanted, and gone off in search of other targets. Or perhaps it had all just been an oversight, some mistake made by some scribe who'd mixed up some names.

After they released her – no explanation, no apology – she'd limped back to her hab, stinking and dishevelled. They'd all gone, husband and children, moved to another site. She never found out where they'd been taken, if they'd moved themselves or had been forcibly pushed out. Another family unit had replaced them in her old home, and they'd stared at her with hostile fear.

Life had become impossible after that. She had been numb

with shock, pale with grief, and had the mark of the pariah on her. Her supervisor got her removed from the manufactorum, her old friends wanted nothing to do with her. She would have starved, if she'd stayed. Or frozen, with no one willing to house her even as the winter gales boomed down the narrow streets. Getting off-world was the only hope, and she knew they didn't ask too many questions in the domestic ports. She used the last of her coin to get hold of some new idents, hoping and praying that it would be enough.

It had been. She'd never looked back since, working her way up from under-deck rating to her current lofty position. Once you'd been a few years away from home, out in the black, your past had a way of disappearing, of blurring into nothing. It was an old superstition on the big voidships – no questions about any life before the decks. Too many of the non-voidborn had something to hide, perhaps, or maybe it was just easier to try to forget the old web of loyalties, of family, of relations and friends and pretend that this iron-enclosed world was all there was.

One official had guessed the truth, though. Right at the end, as Kuhl had been preparing to board the lifter that would take her from Oolenta forever. The purges were still a raw memory then, and he'd looked at her papers long and hard before giving her clearance for orbit.

'They'll come for you,' he'd told her. 'They do not leave loose threads.'

She'd laughed, pretending not to understand what he'd meant. Then he'd shrugged bleakly, and waved her through. And ever since, on every ship she'd ever served on, those words had snagged at her mind.

*They do not leave loose threads.*

She'd done nothing. A little loose gossip, maybe, some impieties whispered when the priest looked the other way. Who hadn't? Who hadn't dared to dream, in their private solitude, of a world free from pain, from back-bending labour, just for a moment or two? Was that truly a crime, even to entertain some idle blasphemy? Would they *know* those things, though? Would they have records of it? Would they take one look at her, and run some checks, and realise that an interrogation docket from twenty years ago was still outstanding? Or would they have a quiet word with Kiastros, or Avati, and casually destroy everything she'd built here? That might even be worse than the cells again.

It made her sick. She couldn't think, couldn't function, and there was so much to do. It was as if all the fear from those terrible few days on Oolenta had rushed straight back, crossing time and space to revisit her again, just as vivid, just as terrible.

'*Master of Engines,*' came Avati's voice over the comm, jarring her out of her thoughts. '*Report, if you please.*'

Kuhl collected herself.

'Holding steady,' she reported, mostly truthfully. 'Reconstruction teams dispatched to all damaged sites. Warp drives functional for the moment, though under-strength. I will know more within the hour.'

'*Fine. Keep working. Though the captain has ordered a senior council, high deck. Your presence is expected.*'

Kuhl had been waiting for the summons. 'Understood. So, will our guests be present?' she asked, keeping her voice as flat as possible.

'*The Inquisition? No, thank the Throne. Why do you ask?*'

'No reason. I'll be there as soon as I can.'

'*See that you are.*'

The link cut out.

Kuhl leaned back against the plastek housing. Her palms were sweaty, her breathing shallow. She'd have to make herself look a little less shocking before going up the elevator tubes to the high deck. At least the bastards wouldn't be in the chamber with her. Maybe they'd never emerge at all. Maybe this could all somehow be managed.

*They do not leave loose threads.*

She sighed shakily, pushed herself from the shaft-housing, and wearily began her preparations.

The same room. The same bare granite and heavy pilasters, the same long table, the same lack of suitably ornate lighting and decoration. The throne was just as uncomfortable as before, though now the walls were also cracked and the thrum of the engines felt staccato and uncertain.

Kiastros looked out at his senior crew. Avati, Spleed, Boroja, Kuhl, Santalina and Garrock all looked back at him. They had each attempted to look the part – their uniforms brushed down, their rebreathers removed – but the shabbiness couldn't be hidden. They had been in a proper beating. It had been humiliating. Degrading. The kind of thing that could haunt a career forever.

Still, no use dwelling on it now. They were all in danger, and the prospect of being plunged back into combat again was very real. They needed to plan, work on a recovery, attempt to retrieve something from the confluence of disaster before it overtook them for good.

'So,' he said heavily. 'This is the situation. The fleet has dispersed under heavy assault. The last communication I received indicated that Jovanjiar's own squadrons were intact and leading a break for the warp. I could not raise Hekaon again before we made translation. They will head, those that survive, to the designated muster point at Taleda. The enemy may seek to pursue them, or may rest content with the damage they have already done and move elsewhere. Supporting systems in the Anaxian Line may now come under attack, and the medium-term priority will be to divert additional forces to bolster them, if any can be found.' He smiled grimly. 'Though that is for another day. First comes survival. Lieutenant, your report, if you please.'

Avati cleared her throat. 'We are alive. The Geller field is intact, the warp drives function. Most life support is operative, and all core decks are powered.' She locked her fingers together. 'That ends the good news. On the other side of the ledger, we have lost almost all our augurs. Signals reports less than ten per cent of the arrays are operative, making us blind in the void. Our plasma drives took heavy damage, and their functionality is unknown ahead of full investigation. Main broadside capacity is at twenty per cent, estimated, lances at thirty. We cannot fire the nova cannon unless power levels rise significantly. We have no fighters, no escorts. Hull integrity is rated critical, with over a hundred catalogued open wounds requiring reconstruction. Our void-shield coverage is null, rising to twenty per cent over a cycle subject to successful repairs. Four major hull breaches were recorded, one of which accounted for most of our attached Space Marine squad. The survivor of the encounter, the sergeant, is in the apothecarion. Though the precise objective of the boarding party remains uncertain, it seems likely from Captain Garrock's report that the Space Marines saved the ship from major damage, possibly destruction. If Sergeant Maizad recovers, we may learn more.'

It was grim listening. Kiastros knew most of it, but getting Avati to summarise was useful to fill in blanks for the others. If nothing else, they all needed to know how severely damaged they had been.

'We have lost all contact with the ship's astropathic choir. A second hull breach is suspected at their location, but we are unable to reach the affected decks – all access routes are destroyed and backed up with debris. It may be that the spire has been destroyed, though sensor readings indicate something is intact. Further investigation will be difficult within the warp.

A third, smaller landing was repelled by the garrison. The fourth has yet to be locked down, so we may yet have active hostiles on board – our remaining armsmen's current priority is to isolate and destroy. The ability to scry for near-void hostiles is limited, but we believe at least one vessel is following us. Other hunters may be stationed beyond our weakened sensor range. We are in uncharted regions, and no clear path back to Taleda can be plotted at this time – for that, we may need to exit the empyrean and triangulate in realspace. The Inquisition system runner is secured on board, but no access to its crew or contents has been granted. We still do not know what their mission or orders are, though they have indicated that they expect us to rendezvous with their own people as soon as we are able.'

Avati sat back, grim-faced. No one else spoke.

'Signals, how soon can we get some augur range back?' Kiastros asked.

'We are working on ascertaining, lord captain,' Boroja replied. 'Two cycles at least, for the wide-scan arrays. The finer-grained sensors have been burned beyond repair, according to early surveys, though we shall keep at it.'

'What of the guns?'

'All current work is concentrated on the lances,' said Spleed. 'I have a target of forty per cent capacity within a cycle. Replenishing ammunition for the cannon ranks will take time, and the forges have their work cut out for other tasks.'

Kiastros nodded, making notes as they spoke. 'But we can maintain our position in the warp?'

'We can,' said Santalina. 'And that would be, I would think, our most prudent strategy for the moment.'

'Though we're being followed.'

'We are. I shall work with my people to establish more details, but something is clearly coming after us.'

'Then we need access to the Inquisition ship,' Kiastros said.

'We're blind and crippled, and Throne alone knows what equipment they have on board that thing. It might be helpful – it can hardly be harmful.'

'They have told us nothing about what they carry,' said Avati. 'Nothing at all. I wonder whether they even understand it fully themselves – their inquisitor was killed, they say, and the interrogator is now in command. Perhaps he was never briefed, and is working from incomplete information. He looked nervous, when he spoke to me.'

'Nervous?' asked Kuhl warily.

'He was at pains to let me know he was in charge. Which immediately made me think he wasn't.'

'They've already hijacked our whole engagement,' Kiastros said darkly. 'We threw away our position to keep them alive, so they owe us more than stonewalling. But who's going to go down and demand they open their doors? Any volunteers?'

Garrock snorted. 'If we still had the Space Marines,' he mused, 'they'd have done it.'

'Another reason to hope that Sister Isobel is able to revive the one we have left.' Kiastros shook his head. 'I never would have thought it. Angels of Death, an entire squad, and yet...'

'They ended the threat,' Garrock said, looking offended on their behalf. 'It was a major landing.'

'No doubt,' Kiastros sighed. He had no wish to criticise the conduct of those who had fought. It was simply hard to believe. 'Though the danger from the incursions is not yet over.'

'Every armsmen still able to stand is deployed to the lower decks,' said Garrock. 'Soon as we're done here, I'll head down myself. We have the intersections around the ingress site secured already – whatever's down there, we'll find it.'

That didn't fill Kiastros with much optimism. The best case was that it was a false alarm – a torpedo hit that registered as a landing. Next best was a containable gang of enemy crew,

sion in the forward enginarium decks had taken out a whole
squad of Astartes, then it didn't look good. What if something
similar was active in the bilges, even now, lumbering its way
upward, deck by deck?

'Very good,' was all he said, hoping his uneasiness was well
masked. 'Emperor-willing, we'll cut out the rot swiftly.'

'Lord captain,' interjected Avati, 'if I may, the lack of astropaths is my greatest concern. We are far out of comms range
of whatever remains of the fleet, so Ortuyo is our only hope
of locating reinforcements. We must find a means of getting
through to him.'

Kiastros turned to Kuhl. 'Can it be done?'

The Master of Engines looked pensive. 'It looks like the whole
sector's collapsed. It'd need a survey, and bringing some heavy
drills up. Not easy. Drop out of the warp, though, and I could
push a drone out to take a look from voidward.'

'We're not leaving the warp,' said Kiastros. 'Not with no augurs
and our guns barely working.'

'There's something registering on the scans of the impact
site,' said Boroja. 'Maybe just a heat source, maybe something
trying to get a signal out. Hard to tell – the whole place has
melted together.'

Kuhl looked thoughtful. 'Very well. I'll pull out a heavy engin-
seer cadre. We'll need to tunnel up from the base, rebuilding
as we go. The spire foundations are old up there, and the hull's
already been hammered. It might take days.'

'But possible?' Kiastros asked.

'Possible.'

'Then I concur with my first lieutenant – it must be attempted.
We get through to Ortuyo, we have a chance at making contact
with whatever remains of the fleet.'

Kuhl nodded. She looked almost relieved. 'I shall give it my personal attention. Krujax can oversee the plasma-core restoration – he is perfectly capable.'

'Then we are resolved,' said Kiastros, sitting back in his throne and addressing them all. 'We are wounded, we are hunted, but we still draw breath. Faith is the thing now – faith in the Emperor, faith in our training. We will rebuild. Priests will be deployed to every sector to bolster the spirits of the crew, extra rations are authorised during the next cycle. Cleave to your orders. We purge the ship of invaders, we rebuild our stocks, we repair the damage. When the time comes, we turn on those pursuing us, and deliver the vengeance of the just.'

He had to work to make himself believe the words. Important, now, that they kept things together.

'The Eye still lies ahead of us,' he told them firmly. 'Glory awaits those who fight there, and we must yet be among them.'

# Chapter Fourteen

**AMBITION**

**GETTING HOTTER**

**INTRUDER**

Kiastros caught up with Avati as she headed back to the bridge. She looked preoccupied, as well she might – all of the crew would be feverishly making calculations now, deciding which systems and order-chains to prioritise and which to leave to the Emperor's grace for the time being. He would need to enforce rest periods soon, or they would all burn themselves out. Soon. Not yet – too much to do.

'Astrogation,' he said, bringing her to a halt.

'Lord captain,' she replied.

'You didn't say much in there.'

She looked taken aback. 'Did you wish me to?'

'Only if you had something to contribute.' He attempted a smile. 'You performed well during the action. Very well. I wanted you to know that.'

'My thanks,' she said. 'It was... frustrating. To be placed in that position.'

'Agreed, though we are out of it now at least.' He felt a little warm just then, the faintest of hot flushes on his skin. Maybe he was more tired than he thought, or maybe the atmosphere controllers had been damaged. 'And our guests concern me. This is my realm, and they are interlopers here.'

'They are the Inq–'

'I know it.' He rolled his eyes. 'Throne, I know it. But still. A king must rule, or he is no longer a king.' He drew a little closer, lowered his voice. 'We will need them, I judge. We have no escorts, we are barely capable of firing a las-beam. Their system runner – it looked very well armed.'

'It was. I mean, from what I could tell. Lascannons, I'd say, though powerful.'

'Or maybe something more exotic – we all saw what its mother-ship did. I'll speak to them.'

'Do you wish me to accompany you?'

'I believe I can handle it, lieutenant.' And then, in case that had been a little abrupt, 'But I will need you to attend to our other pressing matter – the ships in pursuit. At present we only have Santalina's warp visions to guide us, and that won't be enough if they close. I wish to know as much as possible, as soon as possible – if we are required to leave the warp then we must be able to defend ourselves.'

'As you will it.'

'Spleed is a decent gunner, but I'll need someone on him,' Kiastros went on. 'He feels the pressure, and it will only build. Keep an eye on him, enforce the rate of repair. Lances is one thing, but the glory of a voidship is its batteries, no?'

'Just so – it will be done.'

'Good. And, last of all, think of it – this is a great chance. These are the moments, the times when a soul destined for greatness can make a mark. I wish to get back to the fleet, keep whatever the Inquisition have brought us intact, demon-strate the prowess of the crew. There will be empty places in the hierarchy now. There will have to be, after this disgrace. You, in particular, can gain what you have always wished for. A command.'

Her eyes narrowed. 'If you think that is what I care about now, then–'

'Of course not. But you are human, are you not? You joined the service with ambitions, like all of us. You should not be ashamed of it. The Throne guards the brave, the ones who forge their own path.'

Avati looked uncomfortable. 'So. If there is nothing else...'

'Nothing else.' Kiastros drew back, raised his voice again. 'Send reports to me at regular intervals. I shall require tactical scenarios for engaging our pursuers, once we know more of them. Factor in the presence of the Inquisition runner, if you please.'

Avati bowed, then hurried off. Kiastros watched her go with some amusement. For a supposedly astute operator, she'd never hidden her burning desire to rise up the ladder. Having it made explicit seemed to irritate her, but the time for secrets was surely passed now. Crises such as these had a way of bringing all sorts of semi-hidden truths out into the open, and he found it refreshing. Perhaps he should speak to Boroja too about his overuse of stimms, or Garrock about the too-enthusiastic enjoyment he took in meting out broken limbs down in the bilge-decks.

He'd known, or guessed, about such things for a long time, of course. A captain's job was to know his crew. Only now did he find himself strangely eager to pick at the scabs. Why was that?

He felt hot again. He'd have to speak to Kuhl about the atmosphere controls.

Before he set off for the lower levels, Garrock managed to pull Kuhl over.

'You alright?' he asked.

The corridor was emptying, crew heading off to stations, an air of subdued panic making the atmosphere thick. Kuhl looked briefly confused, as if her mind was a long way away.

'Fine,' she said, shrugging his hand from her elbow. 'Feeling fine. You?'

Garrock turned and spat on the deck. He felt lousy, like he'd got stomach gripes that wouldn't resolve into anything. Most of the wounds he'd taken during the firefight had been dressed and treated, but everything still flared with pain. And then there were the dead, some of whom he'd served with for years. You didn't think too hard about them – there was a job to do, and he'd seen plenty of death in his time – but it had only been just a moment ago. No time to take a breath, make sure the bodies were retrieved, to pay the proper respect.

'Something's strange about all this,' he muttered. 'You think so?'

'Don't know what you mean.'

Garrock shook his head, reached for a lho-stick. 'I don't like being blind. I don't like thinking about it. An enemy we can't see.' He lit up, took a drag. 'You're heading up to the top decks.'

'It'll take a while yet. Getting the gear lifted will be the hells.'

'You think you'll find something?'

'We'll run a survey.'

Garrock grinned at her, not very humorously. 'They're all dead, though. You know it. The king knows it. It's just a pile of molten plasteel up there now.'

Kuhl's face flashed with anger. 'You've seen the scans, then? You were down in the prow with your invincible Angels, weren't you, getting your arses kicked? How do you know that?'

Garrock clenched his fist, getting ready for a snarled reply, then held back, surprised at his reaction. Why was she so angry? Why was *he* so angry? He liked Kuhl. Always had. The best of the officers, the only one who spent any time among the grease and the filth to keep the ship running.

He was exhausted. It was too clammy, for some reason. Everyone was teetering on the edge.

'Hey,' he said, relaxing, trying to relax her too. 'Nothing meant by it. Just a view.' He took another long breath in, feeling the hot smoke in his lungs. 'Though be careful up there. It could all come down on your head. And astropaths, well...' He coughed up a laugh. 'You find them alive, you keep your distance. Never liked a mutant.'

Kuhl laughed too, then – nervous, he thought. 'Yeah. Foul bastards.' Then she looked over her shoulder, as if worried Santalina might still be hanging around. She looked back at him, clapped him on his armour. 'Be careful *down* there.'

He snorted. 'It's my home. Prefer it down there to up here.'

Kuhl hurried off. Garrock finished his lho-stick, then he was moving too, heading down to the elevator shafts, to the mag-train running aft, to the low-runs into the deep levels.

He wasn't sure he really meant that. The population of the lower decks were more to his liking, that was true. But the place itself stank. It was noisy, it was dangerous. And that was at the best of times – right now was, most emphatically, not the best of times.

His first call was at the forward security station, plumb in the centre of the ship's core and staffed by a few dozen armsmen. They were all armoured and waiting, half of them with shields. They looked like they'd been in a few fights themselves – he could see bruising and bandages across exposed flesh, heavy scorching across the breacher shields and breastplates.

A burly man got up when he entered, made the aquila. 'Lieutenant Herj, captain,' he announced, then pointed out his squad. 'Kevem on comms, Iolan heavy support. We've sent two squads on ahead to reinforce the first intersection.'

Garrock found himself thinking of Refad, Hobes, the rest of them. The casualty tallies were still coming in – Throne only knew how many had been lost.

'Good,' he grunted, checking them over. 'Anything new to report?'

'We found where they got in. Thought you'd want to take a look.'

'Good. Lead on.'

He suited up, snapped a fresh power pack into his lasgun, took a long swig of water from a canister followed by a short one from the flask at his belt. The squad clattered out of the station and into the corridors running down and aft. The helm lights flickered on, spreading pools of weak light into the gloom ahead. These places were never easy to negotiate – with the power down across so many sectors, they were like pits into the void itself.

The engine noise was oppressive. Garrock adjusted the dampeners on his helm, but the throb still made his jaw itch. Every surface – dirty metal grilles, rusty panels, grime-clogged intakes – seemed to vibrate with it, jarring his bones. A ship had a feel to it, a kind of nebulous sense of health. When all was as it should be, it felt tight, taut, every rivet hammered in close. When it was wounded it felt loose, as if the great spars were moments away from coming apart at the joints. That was how it felt now, the enormous skeleton creaking and rattling, a bag of bones and nails, ready to spill out into nothingness.

'Any positive sightings yet?' he asked, trying to snap out of his increasingly morbid imaginings.

'Not yet,' said Herj. 'Whatever they are, they're not moving fast. Maybe hunkered down somewhere. Reckon they've got wounded – you'll see the way they came in.'

A few more decks, becoming steadily more decrepit in the dark, and Garrock saw what he meant. They passed through the perimeter guards, headed further down and out towards the ship's edge, then reached the ingress site, a hundred yards or more from the hull exterior. Twenty or so armsmen stood guard around the area, guns drawn, looking twitchy.

The place was like a cavern, gloomy and dank and carved out of the bedrock by some catastrophic explosion. The walls were blown in, the supports twisted like straws, the low roof gouged to ribbons. A big water pipe had been ruptured somewhere, resulting in a steady rain from above that spat and dribbled over the still-cooling metal. Cables twisted like torn cobwebs, grazing the anti-flamm foam that had been sprayed over every surface. Further back, down the long tunnel that led eventually to the void, sparks danced in the gloom. Even further back, just on the edge of vision, Garrock could make out the gauzy shimmer of atmosphere barriers – temporary forcefields strung across the breach prior to physical repairs.

Herj squatted down, reaching for a handheld auspex and gesturing down the long tunnel. 'Not much left of the transport. It was small, came in fast. Maybe a torpedo of some kind. We've got pieces of it everywhere, but a lot was melted.' He sniffed. 'Can't have been intended. There's blood down there too, plenty of it.'

'Just one transport?' asked Garrock.

'Think so. If we were in the void, I'd send a drone out, check the damage from there, but we're stuck where we are.' He reached out for a piece of shrapnel, held it up, looked at it thoughtfully. 'I'd say this was one of a squadron. Maybe we shot the rest down, or they blew up on impact. This one got through – just. Whatever came with it got mauled, crawled out, maybe to die, maybe to get better. It's no more than a squad – can't be more than that.'

Garrock edged forward, his boots crunching through the debris. He felt vaguely sick, like an attack of vertigo. The warp was out there, a few hundred yards off, churning away on the far edge of the Geller bubble. Too close. Even shielded, with extra barriers strung up by the field-generators, it was too close. You wanted solid iron between you and that place, all the time, no exceptions.

'No bodies?' he asked.

'Not yet.'

He looked over his shoulder. The destruction petered out a few yards ahead, resolving into the hard edges of the corridor they'd come down. It branched out after that, running both up and down, then spreading like capillaries in a body. 'You've run scans,' he said.

'Where we could. We were fighting a lot of fires.'

'Aye. That we were.' He stalked back up across the ruins, treading carefully. 'Might just have been a squad. Maybe less than that – a single fighter. I'd like that less.'

Herj laughed, coming after him. 'I'd like that plenty.'

Garrock turned on him. 'No you wouldn't. Because only one kind of fighter comes in on a torpedo alone.' He wondered if Maizad was recovered yet. Or if he'd died. Would be good to know, either way. 'Get someone looking harder for bodies, blood trails, anything. I want to know the instant they find something.'

'By your will.'

Garrock edged further up, away from the worst of the damage. 'We'll form up below the galleries. That's where they'd go – they'd have to. String up sensors across the gangways, prime the bilge-rats to shout out – they'll be scared enough to do it, if we tell them what's got in here.'

'By your will.'

'They can be useful. Put out the word, all broadcast channels. Tell them to attack anything – *anything* – that doesn't belong here. No hesitation. I've seen it before. They're like animals when they're scared, and there's lots of them – it just might save us some work.'

'They'll be slaughtered.'

'You care about that?'

Garrock halted. He sniffed. Just for a moment, he thought he

caught the scent of something familiar. Like it had been in the
enginarium, among the stinks of fyceline and blood.

He couldn't get a hold of it. Maybe his imagination.

'Tell your people to stay sharp, though,' he grunted, walking again. 'Chances are, we'll be in the firing line one way or another. Pray that when the time comes, it's something we can handle.'

# Chapter Fifteen

**USEFUL SERVICE**

**MATERIAL THINGS**

**SOMETHING GOT IN**

In truth, what a thing of wonder it was. What a marvel, what a construction. The ship around her was a marvel of its own, of course, a piece of engineering splendour so immense and complex that she could barely get her head around it, but this, *this* – perhaps it was even greater, even more singular, than anything she had ever witnessed.

Isobel leaned back against the wall. Her hands were sticky with more blood. Strange blood it was – it seemed to curdle and thicken the instant it left Maizad's body, as if it knew it was no longer needed and could therefore degrade into something baser.

The Space Marine lived. She didn't know how much of that was due to her art and how much was the Emperor's grace. It was a strange kind of life, though – a suspended state, a deep sleep in which his incredible physiology was steadily knitting itself back together. She knew the rough terms and parameters from her old studies at the convent – the hibernator implant, the membrane implanted over the subject's brain that enabled voluntary coma, after which the body entered a period of structural recovery. She'd watched the scans herself, fascinated by the results. At times it had seemed as if Maizad was simply rebuilding himself, cell by cell. She had assisted as best she could, of course – injections, transfusions, stimulants and antisep compounds. Perhaps, at some level, he was aware of that. Perhaps his unconscious mind knew that he was in the hands of an ally, and thus let his body slip into its phenomenal regenerative fugue, greatly boosting everything she did.

Whatever. It bolstered her faith just to witness it – this was a creation of the Emperor, here, under her instruments, demonstrating with every hormone spike and tissue rejuvenation what divine genius was capable of. To be sure, Maizad's body was not especially lovely on the outside – a dark-grey slab of scarred muscle, over-bulked and laid thick atop a monstrous skeleton – but on the *inside*, when you witnessed what sorcery it could perform, that was enough to renew all your old vows, to make you grateful for the merest glimpse of it.

*How are such things possible?* she found herself breathing. *How can such arts ever have been known?*

It was good for her. All the old frustrations at not serving on the front line with her Sisters – pious and insufferable as they were – melted away in the presence of such magic. This was service. This was *useful* service. She was recreating a weapon here, as much as a master forger might hammer a sword into shape. In time – a few days, maybe a few weeks – the weapon would be wielded again, one more precious blade in the Emperor's service.

She reached for her cup and took a long draught – just water, sadly, but you had to stay alert in this work. The ship had been falling apart around her for hours, every missile impact sending the apothecarion deck skidding and the instruments clattering across the tiles, but she'd kept at it throughout, stitching and draining.

Now that things had calmed down, Jep could handle the rest of the intake. This was her project now.

'Honoured Sister,' came a voice from the far side of the chamber.

She turned to see the ship's captain standing in the doorway. The last time she'd laid eyes on him had been at the dinner, and it was striking to see the change in him over such a short period. He looked drained, his skin pallid and sweaty, though he was still standing tall, spine-straight like all the Navy officers did.

'Captain,' she said, putting her cup down. 'I'd presumed you were busy. How stands the ship?'

Kiastros glanced over at Maizad. 'Much the same as him, I reckon.' Then he looked up at her, as if concerned he'd caused offence. 'But both shall live, I trust. Both shall fight again.'

'If He wills it.' She took up her instruments, moved over to an ewer and started to wash them clean. 'I'd begun to wonder whether I'd made the right choice of transport. Jep couldn't tell me much, but I've been in void battles before. We lost, didn't we?'

'Badly. A pre-emptive strike, a huge one, launched hours before we were due to make for the warp. Our intelligence was wildly wrong – they'll be busy with the gallows up at command.'

'So what next?'

'We're on our own. No tidings from outside – our astropaths are cut off by damage, our augurs out of action. We're running, for the time being, trying to patch things up. We think ships have come after us, but we can't see them and have no guns left even if we could. Boarders are suspected to have landed. Oh, and the Inquisition is sitting in one of my hangars, refusing to talk to us. I was on my way to speak to them.'

Isobel chuckled. 'That good, eh? Well, I'm sure you'll charm them.' She rinsed down the last scalpel, dunked it in some anti-sep solution.

'I have no idea what they want,' Kiastros said ruefully. 'They may not know themselves. We may all be in the dark. Figuratively speaking.'

She folded her arms. 'It could be helpful. They have a ship?'

'A small one. I wish to... borrow it.'

She laughed. 'Ah. Good luck with that.'

'We'll need every tool we can lay our hands on.' Kiastros glanced back at the Space Marine. 'We could use him too. How long until–'

'I don't know. I've been doing what I can, but I really don't know. A week?'

'Too long. Hours.'

Isobel sucked her teeth. 'I don't even know how to wake him up. And if I did, whether it would kill him.'

'Every tool. And that includes you, if I may be so bold.' He looked nervous. 'We're on the edge. Fortune has given us two of the Emperor's finest servants. That might just be enough to keep us from going over.'

Isobel suppressed a smile. He was like a bashful young suitor on a first negotiation with a potential breeding partner. Or, at least, how she imagined one of those might be.

'Be at peace – you have my service, captain,' she said. 'The least I could do after such excellent hospitality. But do not take too much comfort from that – I can't do much about the ships coming after us.'

'No, you can leave those to us. But there's plenty on board that worries me.' He looked around, checking they weren't being overheard. 'We need to get back to the squadrons, somehow. We need to stay alive for the next cycle, find a way to destroy those tracking us, get the astropaths back. Nothing else matters, whatever our guests tell me.'

'We have to strike back, now. Isn't that the way this works? They blood us, we blood them back.'

'Something like that.' He sighed, pulled his jerkin tight, made

He's running down rumours of unwanted visitors in the bilges.
If – *when* – you can restore our sergeant here to health, he
should be the first to know.'

'Understood. I'll do what I can.'

'I know you will. If there's any way, any way at all, that doesn't
risk killing him... Well, I'd be grateful.'

He was stalling now, she could tell. Couldn't blame him –
who wanted to talk to the Inquisition?

'Would you like me to accompany you, captain? Might be
helpful, to have me with you.'

Kiastros laughed. 'You too? These offers are more generous
than I deserve.' He drew in a weary breath. 'No, it's my task
to perform. And you have yours here. With fortune, we'll succeed at both.'

'Not fortune,' Isobel said, reaching for some reinforced steel
suture wire. 'But success will come – just look at what glories
we have to work with.'

Had it been this bad before? Avati tried to recall. She'd served
on a destroyer once, right at the start of her career, that had
come horrifically close to rupturing its warp core during a firefight. She'd been in transit on another warship that had run
into an ambush from xenos corsairs, and survival had looked
pretty bleak for a few cycles until an Astartes strike cruiser had
finally intervened.

But no, not in all truth. Neither of those close scrapes had
been as bad. This was the worst disaster she'd been part of –
the ship had almost been destroyed outright, and the odds were
still that the enemy's task would be completed soon. For a battle
cruiser-class vessel to be properly annihilated was rare, but successful boarding actions following a void-mauling were less so.
Hulls were so precious to both the Imperial and traitor sides

that getting hold of something with intact warp drives and some functioning weapons was eagerly pursued by the enemy whenever it could. Avati had never heard tell of such things from the other side – an Imperial capture of a traitor ship – but she'd often wondered if it ever happened. You'd have to cleanse it, of course – get the priests to fully exorcise it, scrub out the worst of the filth and blood, whatever else the degenerates who crewed those things spewed across the decks. Was that even possible? Not officially, perhaps. But it was a big galaxy, with hundreds of fleets. Maybe some ships had shadier pasts than the manifests made obvious.

Best not to think about that. Best not to think about any of the possibilities ahead, save the one Kiastros was aiming for. For all she knew, Traitor Astartes were currently burning their way up to the bridge in teams. Or the pursuing voidships were getting ready to unleash fresh punishment on the *Judgement of the Void*'s ravaged defences. Or the plasma chambers were about to implode and send them all spinning into an icy grave.

Those were always the risks. It wasn't as bad for her as it was for the hull-born, the vast majority of the crew who had been birthed and raised on board. Destroy this place, and everything was gone – ancestors, descendants, a discrete culture unique in the galaxy. She, on the other hand, had seen other worlds, served on them, and planned to depart for a bigger ship as soon as the order came. This was just survival for her, the chance to get clear of the current mess and plot a course beyond it.

Kiastros could go on as much as he wished to about duty, piety, observing the minutiae of the Imperial Cult. He really believed all that stuff. She never had. Of course, she believed in the godhood of the Emperor – who didn't? But the rest of it – the rituals, the superstitions, the priests and their ignorance – she could leave most of that behind. The Imperium ran on material things: guns, blades, engines. Navigators and star-speakers were regrettable necessities, but everything else useful was either human or mechanical. Nuts and bolts, energy coils and thruster-trains. That's what won wars.

Sadly, you couldn't ignore the mystical entirely, especially when you had orders to seek it out. She paused before the threshold of the Navigator's little kingdom, collecting herself. Maybe Kiastros knew how much she disliked Santalina, and had sent her as a test of some kind. More likely, he'd never really noticed – the two of them had worked together for a very long time, and probably stopped noticing each other's character quirks.

The guardians at the gate – two armed warriors decked in the gloomy livery of the Navigator house – took their time unlocking the heavy doorway. Once inside, Avati was shown into an ostentatious antechamber. It smelled faintly of mould, and the carpets were thick. Precious objects stood under glass, most of them looking like they needed a polish. Maybe Santalina's human eyes were no longer what they had been.

The Navigator came in a little later, bustling through a double door set in the far wall. She was in the robes she'd been wearing to make the initial translation, and smelled of sweat and incense.

'Lieutenant,' Santalina said breathlessly, adjusting her bandana to make sure it was properly in place. 'I can give you a few moments before I will be required to guide us again. Will you take a seat?'

Avati settled into a musty armchair facing Santalina's more elaborate throne.

'You want to know about the ships in the warp,' Santalina said.

'Anything you can tell me,' Avati replied, trying not to stare at a thin line of blood running slowly down Santalina's forehead. 'We're still working to restore the augurs.'

'They wouldn't help you. Not in here. Ortuyo might, but then he's out of commission, isn't he?'

Santalina's tone was polite enough, if frosty. Avati had never really got to the bottom of what her problem with her was.

'The captain said you detected two signatures.'

'It doesn't work like that. Not precisely.' Santalina reached up with a finger, absently wiped away the blood. 'It's like the astropath's visions. I see things at a distance, but nothing clear. A soul-warmth, or a phosphor trail in the Seethe. At times they're like shadows, just under the surface, a little darkness against the colour.'

So tedious. Avati didn't care much for what the experience was like, only what it could tell them.

'How close?'

'Distance is hard to gauge. In fact, *distance* doesn't mean the same thing in there – you're not really moving within it. It moves around you. And them.'

'All I really need to know is–'

'Yes, they can track us,' Santalina said. 'If they have a skilled Navigator. Or one of their foul magicians, they could spy us more clearly than we can spy them. We can't outrun them, not in our current state. If I were to be drawn on it, I'd say they're getting closer. Inch by inch, hour by hour.'

'Can they engage us within the warp?'

That was rare. Almost all engagements took place in real-space, and no sane commander would volunteer to do otherwise unless they had to. You would have to have the services of whole teams of psykers to orchestrate warp-bound combat, be very sure of your Geller field power levels, and even then it would be like trying to fight inside a bad dream.

'Maybe. Not yet. They're coming as close as they can, I think. Maybe they think they can force us to engage. I would not recommend it.'

Avati leaned forward, elbows on knees, thinking. 'I don't know how long we can maintain our trajectory. Kuhl tells me the warp drives are as damaged as everything else – we'll have to power them down sooner or later.'

'And what of the weapon systems?'

'Shot. Spleed has his teams working all hours, but they have a lot to do.'

Santalina gave her a look that might almost have been sympathetic. 'Tricky. Look, I can't tell you how close they are with any precision, only that they're gaining. You want my best guess? Hours. A cycle, maybe two. They'll be able to track us far more accurately than I can track them.'

'When the moment comes, we'll need to drop out quickly. At a moment's notice.'

'Yes, I assumed as much. It can be done.'

'You need anything? Supplies? Your comm-feeds are working?'

'We took a little damage, like everyone else. We will be fine.'

'I'll need regular reports then, direct to the command bridge. The captain will want to know the moment they move in.'

'I'll give you what I can.' Santalina folded her hands in her lap. 'Though you're cross with him, aren't you?'

Avati looked up sharply. 'What do you mean?'

'You think he ran. Right at the end. Counter to orders.'

'Nonsense.'

'I was listening in on some of the comm-lines. And I know something about how to read things. There's no record of an order from Hekaon, is there?'

'That is nothing to do with you. Even if there wasn't–'

'You have to let it go, lieutenant, or it will eat away at you. Trust him. He's a good man.'

What in the hells was this? Why was she presuming to advise her about anything?

Avati got up. 'Thank you, Navigator. I think that will be all.'

Santalina smiled at her. 'I've offended you.'

'No, not at all.' Avati looked at her with a steady gaze. 'Though you should remember your function. You guide us in the warp. Nothing else.'

Something about Santalina looked odd to her just then, as if her face had been somehow subtly changed. Avati felt a sudden urge to strike her, to see her sprawled on the deck. Maybe rip that accursed bandana free and see what all the fuss was about.

Damn mutants. Damn, filthy mutants.

'Ah, so you feel it,' Santalina said, looking unperturbed. 'I sense it too. Something got in. I don't know if Garrock can root it out, but it'll make the crew hard to manage. They'll get angry.'

'It's just the warp. We'll cope.'

'Don't be complacent. The hull's full of holes. Things can slip inside.' Her eyes briefly lost focus. 'I keep hearing Ortuyo, even now. I think he's alive.'

Avati found her irritation turning into contempt. The woman was too old, she was too tired. The chance should have been taken to replace her when they were last in void-dock – Kiastros had let it go for too long, blinded by loyalty.

'The Master of Engines is cutting into the astropath spire – if any still live in there, we'll know soon enough. Until then, speculation is pointless. You should get some rest while you can.'

Santalina laughed. 'Because I'm an old witch, eh? Too dried up and withered to be useful? Hah. I feel sorry for you. So much ambition, so eager to claw your way out. No one's going to come out of this well. Not you, not even poor Iannis. He deserves better. You... I don't know.'

Before she had even realised it, Avati's hand had slipped to her service laspistol. It wouldn't take much – one shot, right into that grinning face.

Throne, what was making her so jumpy? And what was making *her* so antagonistic? Avati forced herself to relax – again – and took a step away from the Navigator. Warp travel was hellish, and Santalina was probably right – their wards against it were no doubt depleted. They'd have to drop out soon, or things would become much worse.

'Regular reports,' Avati said crisply, turning to walk out. 'Right up to the bridge. And keep them to the point – you worry about your addled dreams, and I'll worry about the ship.'

# Chapter Sixteen

**DRILLS**

**PROGENY**

**CARGO**

The spire foundations were a wreck, far worse than Kuhl had imagined. The core structure of a voidship was incredibly strong, so it took a lot to mangle it completely. She leaned against a heap of melted metalwork, still tangibly hot even through her environment suit.

'Sector complete?' she asked her tech-priest companion.

'Complete, affirmative,' came the muffled voice of Arfo-5, whose cowl hung so low Kuhl only got a shadowed glimpse of a rusty metal chin. His ironwork fingers scratched over a pair of wrist-linked data-slates. 'Full analysis as follows. Segment immediately ahead, integrity five per cent, access impaired across all subsidiary–'

Kuhl listened as the Mechanicus adept itemised the damage. It was as thorough a survey as they could have performed in the circumstances – a few dozen servo-skull clades, three hundred menials transferred from the engine decks, heavy lifters, some remote augur-rigs. Even approaching the site was hard work, creeping along half-collapsed corridors, constantly pausing to erect braces and supports, trying to gauge how secure the decks were underfoot, or the likelihood of the roofs collapsing and burying them all under hundreds of tons of compressed adamantine.

Kuhl could feel the sweat pooling inside her suit as she crouched. It was far too hot. Some of that was residual radiation from the heart of the impact site, but it felt unlikely that was the only source. She badly wanted to pull her helm off, get a rag and wipe the grime off her brow, but the conditions were too toxic for that – coolant pipes had been severed, generator boxes had been ruptured, spilled chems were everywhere.

'Your assessment?' Kuhl asked, once Arfo-5 had completed his run-down.

'Optimal,' he replied.

*Optimal.* Not the word she'd have used. *Best of a bad lot* might have been better.

At least she had a clearer idea of what had happened. Something very big, or possibly a series of very big things, had hit the base of the astropaths' spire, just at the juncture where it plunged deep into the hull's edge. The spire itself was gone, she was sure – blown clear of the long expanse of core plating and sent spinning into the void. Most of the debris from that had bumped and gyrated its way through the ravaged void shields and was now lost. The astropathic choir, though, did most of its work below the spire's base, in the warren of chambers and halls sunk properly under the heavy layers of hull structure. Many of the menials at least could well have been in those sections, perhaps even the members of the choir itself. The problem was that the remaining labyrinth was collapsed and fused in an unholy mess of melded metal. The impacts had been so ferocious that an entire deck segment looked to have been forced inward, pushed down several levels and compressed into a concertina pattern of destruction.

Anything alive in those chambers would have been crushed, surely. Her limited readings had picked up plenty of trace feedback indicating corpses in the rubble. But it was possible something was still alive in there – some of the major elements were incredibly strongly reinforced, ringed and studded with structural as well as psychic guards. Certainly, the augurs gave her some kind of registration from the epicentre of the impact site – an intermittent hiss on the audex channels, possibly just interference, but maybe something deliberate. It repeated semi-regularly, like a failing heartbeat. An attempt to communicate? Possibly. Or maybe residual readings from a cluster of survivors. If mutants were among them, ones who could commit to receiving messages from the fleet, however vague, then it gave them a chance. If not, if they were simply menials huddling in the dark, then the colossal efforts in digging through to them would be wholly wasted. Everything depended on finding star-speakers.

Kuhl shuddered. 'It'll support the weight?' she asked.

'Affirmative – potentially. Sixty-eight per cent certainty.'

Two-thirds. Not great odds.

'We have little choice. Send the order.'

Arfo-5 turned away and started to chatter things in binharic. Kuhl withdrew down the corridor, picking her way carefully through the web of tortured steel bars and imploded panels. She couldn't stand straight, and went hunched the whole way, her back aching and her thighs burning. Further down the twisting corridor, towards the point where it intersected with less heavily damaged zones, she could already see the crew mobilising – the skulls flocking about with their eye-mounted lumens flaring, the work-gangs limping into position for the big haul.

Further down, lodged in the darkness, was the hulk of the main excavator, the monster they'd dragged up from the heavy elevator shaft-entry. It was already steaming as the power units revved up, filling the narrow chamber with sooty blackness.

Kuhl clambered down further, taking a closer look at it. The drill's maw was five yards in diameter, a huge and glinting morass of interlinked rotary grinders. The intake at the centre was gaping, allowing the twenty-yard-long machine to suck in chewed-up debris and pull it inside, passing the compressed matter down its gullet before incinerating it and expelling the residue from apertures at the rear. It was a beast, an ancient thing created when the ship was first forged, one of over twenty such heavy gougers that mostly lay dormant in their lightless pens. Breaking it out for use was rarely done, partly because of the enormous power requirements, partly because merely moving it around was a logistical nightmare. Multiple haul-gangs, each a hundred strong, were required to manhandle the huge lengths of the chain. Pathfinder teams had to clear out transit hauls, demolish entire platforms to create a route to the target site. The machine itself, flanked by cadres of Mechanicus workers, crawled and hissed its way through the internal mazes leaving trails of inch-deep oil in its wake. Support braces had to be drilled in place on the levels below to stop it crashing through weakened deck plates.

Now it was powering up fully, its furnaces kindled, its drives booming towards their full deafening cacophony. The preparations had been made, everything that could be shored up had been shored up. Kuhl finally reached a point where she could stand up straight. The last of the haul-gangs scurried away, their rags blackened and exposed skin glistening. The machine's many claws clanged down, biting hard into the damaged landscape, poised to haul it forward when the moment came. Its lateral grilles glowed a furious red, lighting up the otherwise pitch-dark surroundings. Hoister arms mounted on its rear quarters activated their cantilevers, each one capable of ramming in struts to keep the ruined hull segments from collapsing as it plunged its way in. The engineering gangs would do the rest, hurrying in once the flames had died out to make good the tunnel their beast had created. That work was ludicrously dangerous, with a serious risk of partial collapses or ruptured power lines, so Kuhl's team of enforcers went with them too, electro-staves at the ready. Ideally, she'd have had a squad or two of armsmen, but they had all been pulled into counter-boarding actions at Garrock's command, so some of Arfo-5's motley collection of gun-servitors and tech-thralls stood guard instead.

Soon the tech-priest came down to join her, his multiple eyes glimmering in the ochre gloom. The gangmasters were look-ing at her expectantly, even a few of the menials cast nervous glances in her direction.

The moment had come. They all awaited the order, anxious to get on with it now.

Kuhl gazed back the way she'd just come, up the tortuous and twisting tunnel to where the first clumps of fused and molten iron glinted darkly. It looked like a fissure into some ill-favoured mountain, the kind of place that could only harbour foul spirits.

She checked the augur readings one last time. Just a hiss of static, no pattern to the signals. Why was she hesitating? The first, back-breaking stages had been completed – all that was needed now was to set the drill moving. The sooner it was begun, the sooner they'd know what was inside.

She was sweating harder. The heat was becoming unbearable. Something about the fissure was hard to look at.

'Advance,' she said, forcing the words out.

The drill's systems snorted, growled, kicked out smoke, and it ground into motion.

Time was running short. Kiastros could feel it in every bone of his body. The ship had a rhythm, a way of telling you what it needed and how healthy it was. Now that rhythm was broken up, uncertain, its steady drumbeat replaced with a thousand unfamiliar creaks and groans. The vibrations rose up from his boots as he walked, betraying the compromises in the enormous curves of its long hull.

They needed to get the guns back in action. Then they needed to drop out of the warp – give the powerful drives some space to recover and refit, attempt some kind of course triangulation, deal with whatever was following them. None of that could happen right now – Spleed was a long way from getting the lances into any kind of shape, and the lack of escorts and functioning shields made them fearfully vulnerable.

Another captain might have doubled down, aimed to play things safe. Stay in the warp for as long as physically possible, hope that the enemy lost interest in the pursuit and turned to other prey. A tempting proposition, maybe, were it not for the absolutely catastrophic prospect of overloaded warp drives malfunctioning. Some things were worse than death, and being sucked into a live warp breach was certainly one of them. In any case, running from combat without some kind of plan to turn things around was not the way he had been trained. You had to take the fight back to the enemy at some stage – best to do it as soon as you could. This opponent was neither stupid nor merciful – the only way to fight them was to get them off balance, act as decisively as you could, never do the expected, hit back first.

So best not to think about everything that had gone wrong, far less all the things that were about to go wrong. Think about what you had in your pocket, what an adversary might overlook, the kind of fractional gain that could turn a scenario your way.

He reached the hangar doors. Closed and guarded, just as had been requested by its new occupants. The two armsmen saluted and stood aside as he approached.

Impossible not to feel a pang of fear just then. Avati probably had, too, though she might have been better at hiding it. Every living soul in the Imperium had been schooled to fear them. Amid all the tangle of overlapping jurisdictions in the Imperium's immense military machine, the inquisitors cut straight through, beholden to no one but themselves and their interpretation of the Emperor's will. What did that do to a human soul, that much power? Were they all sadists and butchers, as their reputation made them out to be? Did the burden of command drive them mad, or make them insensible to simple human emotions?

Throne knew the endless war made them all less empathetic than they ought to have been. As for himself, Kiastros knew he'd hardly escaped unscathed. You couldn't stay truly human, not when the running of a ship entailed the ruthless suppression of thousands of lives on a daily basis. They were all part of the same machine, the one that ground them up and spat them out in the cause of the war that they all knew, in their most honest and private moments, would never end. So much lost. He'd never even laid eyes on his eight children, conceived with a woman he'd only met three times and who was in all likelihood, due to the temporal consequences of regular warp travel, long dead. The whole process had been conducted through genetic matching under the auspices of the Navy hierarchy, who took care to ensure a plentiful supply of officers via the administrative husbanding of suitable command potential. If they lived, all would have passed through the Schola Progenium themselves by now, undergoing the same harsh training he'd undertaken. In due course, if they succeeded in rising to commander level, their genetic material would be harvested and matched too, ready for the next cohort to be trained. None of them would ever meet, in all likelihood – the galaxy was just too vast, the demands of the fleets too all-encompassing.

He'd been honoured to do it, of course. It gave him some pleasure, knowing that the Kiastros lineage would be well repre-sented in voidships of the future. All the same, when you spent any time with the hull-born, saw how they actually *knew* their progeny, even lived in the same cramped quarters, ate together, shared their crude laughter with one another, you couldn't help but think that some systems were more unnatural than others. It had to have an effect. The hollow sensation in the pit of his stomach, when he saw a child of one of the bilge-rats scamper across a corridor, that sudden wrench, the realisation that he'd been denied all of that, and this ship, this bloody ship with all its filth and its splendour and endless demands, was all he had...

Hells, his mind was really wandering. It was strangely hard to keep focused, and the need for it had never been greater. He flicked the door controls, and entered the hangar.

The interrogator, Hastin il-Moro, was waiting for him on the far side. Some way off, the system runner lay on the apron. Pre-sumably the retinue and crew were all on board, cloistered away safely. The craft looked almost powered-down, though presu-mably they had fully operational life support at least.

Avati had been right – it was a fearsome-looking creation, one that projected an uncanny aura of threat. At a glance, it was hard to make out what kind of weaponry it carried, though the nozzles slung under its prow looked far larger and more capable than the lascannons his own escorts had used.

'Lord interrogator,' Kiastros said, making the aquila and bowing. 'Please accept my apologies that I could not come in person to greet you earlier. As you will appreciate, I had many other matters to attend to.'

'Your lieutenant explained.'

'Do you have everything you require? Supplies?'

'For the moment.'

'My offer of hospitality still stands.' Kiastros attempted to smile. 'We're running a little ragged at the moment, but if you would join me at my table, I could–'

'We shall remain here. Your only task is to bring us safely to rendezvous with my people.'

Kiastros spread his hands. 'I wish I could guarantee it. As my first officer explained, I think, we are running blind, badly damaged, and have no certainty of surviving long enough to discover where your people are.'

'That is not my concern.'

Throne, he was stupid as well as arrogant. His mistress, surely, must have been more acute. Then again, the *Gorgon* had been destroyed, so perhaps she hadn't been.

'Well, it is, at least insofar as we need to be intact in order to carry you. And defend your... cargo. Can I take it that you are unable to tell me anything of it?'

'No information shall be disclosed.'

Avati, as usual, was probably right about this one – he hadn't been fully briefed. He knew he had something powerful, something dangerous or important, but he'd never been told exactly why. That was what made him so defensive, so prickly – he was on uncertain ground, and the only way he could survive it was to get out somehow. You could almost feel sorry for someone placed in that position.

Almost.

'I understand. However, we have already been somewhat hampered by lack of mission disclosure. The *Hammerfall*, your prime protector, did not explain its movements during the action. We never even made contact with it.'

'Did you not? Perhaps you were not given clearance for comms. My understanding is that arrangements for our defence were still being finalised when the attack came.'

That sounded plausible – a bureaucratic snarl-up over pass-words and clearances, with everyone involved too terrified to break regulations even when the las-bolts were sizzling. So stupid, though. So very stupid.

'I did not comprehend their strategy, if I'm honest,' Kiastros said. 'You were made vulnerable by their positioning, which confused me. Were they trying to break early for the warp?'

Il-Moro looked irritated. 'I was not in tactical command, captain,' he said. 'My only responsibility was for the shepherding of what we carried. If the *Hammerfall* erred, then their souls will already be in damnation. My mistress cannot have been at fault.'

That might have been true, it might not have been – impossible for Kiastros to tell now.

'Surely,' he said soothingly. 'Though if there is anything – anything at all – that you can tell me, then–'

'Do you know the name "Rostov", captain?' il-Moro asked.

'No, I do not believe so.'

'And you have had no firm communication with other crusade fleets, nor other members of the Holy Orders? No involvement in the actions at Gathalamor and its aftermath, nor Srinagar?'

'No, not really. Secundus was always the isolated one, I think. The hardest road.'

Il-Moro nodded. 'That is good. Ignorance is the greatest shield. I recommend you cleave to it.'

Kiastros smiled grimly to himself. The man was really not going to open up.

'Very well – I shall do so. Your cargo, however. The thing you have brought here. I have one question that I must ask – can you move it from your ship?'

Il-Moro blinked. 'Move it?'

'Temporarily. All under your control, of course. We have psy-shielded bunkers specifically created for the safe storage of difficult material. It would be more secure there than on your ship. You would, of course, move it yourself, and maintain full mastery of the process at all stages.'

The interrogator looked confused. 'Why, though?' he asked. 'Why would I even consider it?'

Here it came.

'Because I need your ship.'

For a moment, il-Moro looked stunned. Then he laughed. 'You are jesting with me.'

'No, I'm perfectly serious.' Kiastros hoped he looked suitably commanding – inside, it felt like his guts were dissolving. 'We believe at least two enemy ships are pursuing us. They will catch up soon, and we cannot remain hidden from them for long. We will have to fight. At present, we would lose, however hard we make it for them. I have very few guns left, I have no proper sensors, our shields are compromised. I need every scrap of advantage I can possibly find. One such advantage is your ship.'

'It is merely a shuttle.'

'A shuttle does not carry weapons like those I can see here. I saw what your mothership did, and I suspect your own craft can handle itself very effectively. I could use it.'

'It is not yours to use, captain.'

'I'd need your permission. That of your crew, too.' Throne, this was hard work. 'Believe me, I would never dream of asking were the situation not so desperate. Consider it – as things stand, we are all going to die. Very soon. Your cargo will be destroyed or taken, and whatever importance it has will be lost. The only way to preserve it – and us – is to allow the use of your ship. I am entirely certain of this. If you do not accept my judgement, which is your prerogative, then all is already lost.'

Il-Moro said nothing. That, possibly, was a good sign. Maybe he was thinking it through. Maybe he wasn't as stupid as he looked.

'I will need tactical data,' il-Moro said eventually. 'Comprehensive reports on the state of your weaponry and drives. Every piece of information you possess on the supposed pursuers. Then I will confer. Then you will have your answer.'

Kiastros cursed him silently. That would take time, and time was what he didn't have. Pushing things too hard might well be disastrous, though – the man's ego was evidently fragile. He would need to save face, assuming he could be persuaded, be made to demonstrate to his people that he'd not been negotiated into things but had come to the decision himself.

'It will be done, interrogator,' Kiastros said, trying to strike a balance between ingratiation and courtesy. 'All records can be made available. But, if I may, I would respectfully impress upon you the need for some haste – I do not know how long we can maintain our current status, and we may have to exit the warp without warning.'

Il-Moro gave him a chilly glare. 'I will let you know when I have completed my scrutiny. This vessel is the property of the Holy Ordos, and may not be employed for the purposes of any other soul without full consideration of all factors.'

That was better than nothing, Kiastros thought. He'd have to hope a decision came quickly.

'You have my thanks, interrogator,' he said.

Il-Moro made to return to his ship, but then paused. 'I am curious, though. From what you say, we will be heavily out-gunned even if I make the runner available. What are your intentions?'

Kiastros couldn't help a sliver of a smile then. Despite every-thing, despite the prospect of imminent destruction and the ruin of all their hopes, a tactical puzzle still made life worth living. An audience for his proposals was even better.

'It'll be hard, very hard, but possible,' he said. 'Listen – this is what I have in mind.'

# Chapter Seventeen

**THE DREGS**

**MATERNAL DEBTS**

**ONE MORE BARRAGE**

Now he was deep in the underworld, the lightless kingdom that underpinned the ship.

Garrock occasionally dreamed of the place. He wasn't an imaginative man, and never spoke about it, but the dreams had been coming, on and off, for years. The warp did it, they said – made your unconscious visions more vivid and frequent, kept you from the deep sleep you craved and needed. That was in fact what warp travel was, he'd been told once – a long communal dream, provoked by the strange minds of psykers, a nightmarish skip across the tortuous face of the abyss.

Who knew. He only ever dreamed of one thing, at least as far as he remembered: the ship, in cross-section, murmuring and whispering with its crammed multitudes. He saw the officers at the summit gliding around in relative comfort, the ratings on the gun-decks all rammed up close together, then down, down, through the titanic engine chambers and into the dark places, the voids at the very base – old storage halls, redundant mechanical stations mothballed after refits, surplus chem-tanks. Nothing was ever lit up down there, and the denizens scampered around like rodents, half blind, their pale grey fingers flickering across the surfaces to make their way. He saw them stare at him, famished, terrified, before darting deeper into the all-consuming blackness.

On the relatively few occasions he'd ventured right down to the base of the ship in real, waking life, he'd found it much the same as his imagination. You never went down without a fully armed squad at your back. The constant dark was oppressive. The rebreathers clogged up, the narrow pathways were cramped and dangerous. Everything stank, and the heat was punishing. All the excess energy from the drive-trains and the plasma coils ended up down here before being shunted out through the vents and into the void, and when those vents were shut the entire place became hellish.

It was a miracle that so many souls lived down there. No one knew where they came from – deserters from the gun-crews or the mid-deck ratings, or stowaways picked up during void-dock stays most likely, though the numbers were replenished over time by those born in the vaults. It was even less clear how any of them survived, given the conditions and the lack of supplies, but they did somehow. Stories abounded of abandoned food-processor units being maintained in secret, or raids on the lesser refectories, even collusion with the less scrupulous set of ratings. Garrock had always assumed that deals must be struck between the fugitive population and the official crew. Exchanges must have been made for food, med-supplies, blankets for the wretches, though best not to speculate what the ratings demanded in return. Every so often, captains would order purges, fuelled by the delusion that they could cleanse their ships entirely once and for all. After the blood had dried and the screaming had echoed away, the dregs would creep back, year on year, until you were back where you started.

They even had their uses. Tales were common of boarding parties punching their way into the base of Imperial ships, only to be torn apart by feral packs of defenders perfectly attuned to the blind mazes. There was a part of Garrock that hoped this was exactly what had taken place here and now – a small unit of enemy troops, bereft of support, isolated in the bilges and ready to be swamped by the packs that waited for them in the shafts and crawlways.

He'd set relatively few patrols around the ingress site, preferring to keep the squads big and in places where they could put up a fight. He'd assembled a team of twenty to be led by himself, and headed down further than any of the others. Herj was still with him, together with his team. A decent fighter, Garrock reckoned, as were his people. Most were decked out with the standard shotgun and armour combo, though three of them carried breacher shields and two troopers carried las-volleys. They went down into the deep corridors warily, crossing from the shabby-but-maintained realm of the lower decks into the perpetual twilight of the dream kingdom.

The main challenge was space – they all had to stoop, twist their bulky bodies around exposed pipework. Garrock felt his breathing become ragged: he was still recovering from the fight up at the forward enginarium, and going hunched made it worse. Armour edges snagged on protrusions, boots sank into thick pools of spilled oil. The deep thrum of the engines was everywhere here, making every surface hum irritatingly. At times it felt as if their entire surroundings were shaking, ready to suddenly break apart and remake themselves into something worse.

They pressed on. For a long time, they saw nothing untoward. They uncovered evidence of habitation – abandoned piles of rags, used ration-packs, makeshift latrines. The stink of it all was acrid even through their rebreathers. The tactical scanners picked up occasional movement far ahead or behind or below – most likely gangs scurrying off. Occasionally they'd reach one of the really big shafts, the ones running down and down all the way to the monolithic base of the hull where the old grav-generators hummed and crackled, and see makeshift bridges swaying in the hot turbulence.

Soon after that, they came across the blood. At first, it looked just like more oil swilling over the decks, but a brief analysis showed it was organic. Long trails of it, fresh and glistening under the flare of their helm lights.

'I'll head up,' Garrock said, shuffling through it and feeling it stick against the soles of his boots. 'Stay close.'

It didn't take long to find bodies. They were of the population – tiny, stunted and emaciated, with pale skin and sore-encrusted limbs. They had all been killed with some kind of bladed weapon rather than projectiles. As Garrock stooped to take a look at the wounds, a cold sensation kindled in the pit of his stomach. The blows had been tremendous – limbs had been lopped clean off, torsos bisected. These weren't the strikes of a cultist or a conventional enemy warrior. They were far too destructive, far too powerful.

His proximity sensor suddenly pinged.

'With me,' he growled, hastening to his feet.

They ran. It was hard going, skidding and slipping on the greasy decks, ducking under bulkheads and twisting around narrow corners. The helm lights slid across the grime-encrusted landscape, a narrow world that seemed to close in further with every twist of the maze. Garrock's sensors picked up signals – heat sources, dozens of them, running ahead of them. They weren't his own troops, so they were either an enemy or more of the underworld population.

'Close them off – dead-end coming up.'

Herj split off down a narrow rat-run, taking four troopers

with him. Garrock led the rest down an only slightly wider capillary, pushing on rapidly, their armour clanking from the overhangs.

Eventually they burst into a larger chamber, roughly spherical, some kind of nexus of piping and control cables. Refuse littered the meshed circular deck, and fluid leaked from the cluttered roof in steady lines. About twenty of the population cowered against the far wall, cut off from escape by Herj coming from the other side. They averted their eyes from the helm lights, dazzled and squealing.

Garrock ran a scan over them – they weren't armed with much, and looked in terrible shape. A few carried poorly bandaged wounds, all were terrified.

'What happened here?' he demanded, singling out the closest one – a woman marginally older than the others with a dirty eye-patch and carrying a turbo-drill.

She struggled to focus on him, and he turned down his helm light.

'We got the message,' she muttered, clearly in some kind of shock. 'We did our duty. Faithful, we are. Always faithful.'

'You tracked down an intruder?' Garrock asked. 'You attacked it?'

'We did – took it by surprise.' The woman looked disgusted. 'And it killed us. All of us. We never even laid a blade on it.'

'You saw it yourself? Tell me everything.'

She did, haltingly, looking at him warily throughout as though he was the enemy. Garrock couldn't really blame her – the only time the regular crew made any contact with the bilge-levels was either to purge the population or corral them into some kind of dangerous action. Still, she told him what she knew. They were loyal, her people, in their own way. What else could they be? Where else could they go?

What she told him didn't make him feel any better, though.

After a few more questions, he let them go. They slunk off, grateful to slip back into the dark, their bare feet soundless against the tarnished metal.

Garrock sank down onto his haunches. He felt light-headed, and badly needed a lho-stick. Herj came over to join him. 'That bad, eh?' he said.

Garrock grinned. 'That bad.'

There could be no mistaking it. The woman hadn't really known what she was describing, but Garrock did. The heavy crimson-and-brass armour, the glowing helm, the horrific ease with which it had killed her kind. At least there was only one of them active, so far as she knew.

'It must have moved slowly,' said Herj.

'Wounded. Maybe badly. If it wasn't, it'd be well into the upper decks by now.' He remembered the state of the boarding torpedo ingress point, the heavy damage around it. 'Not all of this blood is the crew's, we know that.'

Herj nodded. 'They get better quick, though.'

'They do. So we have a problem.'

'We also have our own Astartes. Time to make the call?'

Garrock had been putting it off. Hoping the incursion would be something he could handle. A part of him still hoped for that – a Traitor Marine, badly damaged and moving slowly, could possibly be taken out. If they got lucky, made the right calls, they could overwhelm it before it moved up into dangerous areas. This whole sector was a labyrinth, and if the traitor's systems were damaged it might take it a while to find its route out. They had some advantages, then – detailed schematics, a trail to follow, numbers.

It wouldn't be enough.

'We'll regroup up at the next hall,' he said, getting to his feet. 'Tell Kevem to pull the squads together – we'll hunt it in numbers. But you're right – we can't do it alone.'

Herj turned to relay the orders, while Garrock activated his comm-link to the apothecarion.

'My sincere apologies, honoured Sister,' he said, hating that he had to do it. 'I must beg for your indulgence.'

No time to rest, no time even to pause. Avati had gone back to the bridge to confer with Boroja. The Master of Signals had been morose.

'We can't see a damn thing,' he'd said, punching his console in frustration. 'Blind as the soul-bound. I can't get the systems to register, let alone function.'

'What, all of them?' Avati had asked.

Boroja had sighed miserably. 'We've got some life at the extreme edge – the long-range arrays. The rest, the ones we need for combat – all malfunctioning.'

It had been bad. She'd commiserated, assigned some of her own people to his restoration teams, but the prognosis was weak. Kiastros wanted to be in fighting shape within the hour, and that clearly wasn't going to be possible.

She hadn't been able to stay to help out more, and in any case Boroja didn't look like he wanted her around. He was normally so amenable, even under pressure, but the fractured atmosphere had clearly got to him too. So she'd delegated a few junior officers to attend to her bridge duties, sent out some order dockets, and hurried down to the elevators.

Once inside the cage, she leaned heavily against the metal, breathing deeply. At least she was busy. Doing. Far worse to be becalmed and waiting for circumstances to change. They were all pushing hard, all frantically shoring up, fixing, welding, battening down. That was better. Better to keep moving, to stay on the front foot.

That had always been her way, ever since joining the service. She could remember her mother giving her the advice, long ago in another world. Avati only had faulty memories of her now – a grey face, lined with care, thin hair almost falling out, threadbare clothes. They hadn't got on. Avati had found her pathetic, contemptible even, stuck in her dead-end role as a minor functionary on a drab world of parchment stacks and petty ledger filing. She had wanted to get away the whole time, to claw a route out of the tiny hab she shared. They would have screaming matches with one another. On one occasion Avati had even thrown a heavy metal vid-box at her, something thick enough to have cracked her skull had it connected. Only much later had she realised that her mother had destroyed herself – her health, her potential – solely to give her daughter the chances she'd never had herself. She'd gone without food to pay for the specialist tuition from the retired old Chartist crew member who lived a few habs along the corridor, she'd let her robes fall to pieces so she could give Avati the nutrition she needed to avoid conscription into the production-line classes and make her eligible for military service. All of it, the fighting, the screaming, it was because they were the same, the two of them, animals that couldn't bear to be caged. And that faded old woman, alone, bitter, curled up with suppressed rage, had done what she had to in order to let Avati escape.

'Keep moving,' her mother had told her, as they'd embraced tightly after yet another tumultuous row. She'd smoothed her daughter's hair down, stroked her cheek, looked at her with those worn-out eyes. 'Never let them pin you down. You can stay ahead of them. You stay still, they'll lock you into their chains.'

The message had been clear: *Don't be like me*. But now, with the benefit of space and time, Avati saw what miracles that exhausted woman had worked, what impossible tasks she'd performed, all to get her daughter out of the slough that had swallowed her up. The tuition had paid off, the physical conditioning had done its job. She'd escaped, got out, headed off into the glorious black. And at the time she'd barely given a second thought for the one who'd made it possible, instead just overcome with relief that she'd never become as washed-up and withered-out.

Now she wished she could go back. She wished she could give her mother a last hug and this time hold on tight. Impossible, of course. Once you boarded the ships, you never came back. And even if you tried it, by the time you'd arrived, the entire world would have changed beyond recognition, and no one would even remember the grey-haired woman with the non-descript hab and the empty, sad expression. So all that was left was to honour the memory of the sacrifice, to keep her words in mind, to think better of her than she had done when the two of them had been together. If that made Santalina think she was an over-ambitious chancer, then so be it. If it made Kiastros doubt her commitment to the cause, then that couldn't be helped. It was her legacy, her last gift. It was all she had left.

*Keep moving.*

The elevator crashed to a halt, jarring her shoulders where the cage rattled. Avati pushed her way out, hauling the heavy doors open in the absence of working pistons for release.

She walked straight out into one of the wonders of the ship. It didn't matter how many times you found yourself in the big gun-halls, you still had that little lurch of disorientation as you adjusted to the scale. From the tight-packed web of corridors and chambers, you suddenly found yourself in a soaring nave that would have done honour to any macro-cathedral of a major hive city. One side had the look of a vast manufactorum – stacked ranks of lifter claws, heavy cranes, blast doors guarding conveyer racks, gangs of servitors crawling across it like insects. On the other side were the gun-ports – immense windows decorated with intricate statuary and gilded flourishes.

They were shuttered for the moment against the warp, but when in use they gave some of the most impressive views onto the void anywhere on the ship, glimmering with atmosphere fields and void shields. In between those two flanks were the guns themselves, rank after rank of them, each one a titanic angled cylinder of dark iron encrusted with valves and purity wards and targeting cog-wheels and turntables. Plumes of superheated steam shot out from all angles, hissing down the long galleries and turning the entire place into a hazy, echoing miasma of ceaseless industry.

Gun-crews were everywhere, flanked by hordes of servitors and servo-skulls, hauling the mighty shells to the waiting maws of the main breeches, tightening chain-pulls, delivering fuel cells to the reactors thrumming at the cannons' bases. The vox-enhanced shouts of the gangmasters resounded down the long galleries, vying with the boom of the machinery and the whine of a thousand straining servos. Nearly as numerous were the repair details, some of them in Martian red, others in Navy blue, milling around cracked coolant runs or smashed armour plates. For all their superficial splendour, more than half the cannons looked to be out of service, their gun-ports cracked and their tracking rails buckled. Every part of the enormous gallery had come under heavy assault, and the effects were visible everywhere, from ruptured decking to collapsed hull sections. Scaffolding was being erected even as she watched, accompanied by the relentless banging of turbo-hammers and drill-rigs.

It didn't take her long to locate Spleed, who had ascended halfway up the inside wall on an observation platform to get a better view of the works. He was surrounded by a tight crowd of gangmasters, tech-priests and junior officers, looking just as harassed and frantic as Kiastros had warned her. She found an elevator plate and ascended to join him, and as soon as he caught sight of her coming he bustled over to the edge of the platform, dismissing the hangers-on around him.

'A bloody mess,' he said, gesturing out to the vista below.

Avati stepped from the elevator plate. 'But you've been busy.'

'Of course we've been busy. Damn you. Damn it all.'

Spleed's eyes were shining brightly. He had a sheen of sweat on his brow, and his hands trembled slightly.

'We'll need one macrocannon barrage,' Avati said flatly, not trying to sugarcoat it.

'Hells! What does he think we're—'

'Just one. But it'll need to be the full complement, concentrated tightly, fired at short notice.'

Spleed looked at her disbelievingly. For a moment, Avati thought he might lose it entirely, go mad, attempt to throw her off the platform. Everyone was suffering, but he was the worst she'd seen – almost manic.

'Tell him to go to the hells,' Spleed snarled.

That was too far. That was insubordination, the very worst crime an officer could be capable of. Perhaps Spleed had picked up on the tensions between her and Kiastros, thought that he could use them somehow. If so, he was a fool.

She closed in on him, straightening up, fixing him with a heavy-lidded stare. 'One word from me, and you'll be up before the procurator, and you can kiss all this, and your miserable career, goodbye. Do you want that? Is that what you're aiming for?'

Panic replaced defiance. He suddenly looked incredibly fragile, as if he'd break apart under the merest pressure.

'N–no,' he stammered, backing down. 'No, it's just…' He looked up at her, almost pleading. 'We're in terrible shape. Terrible. Half the gangs are mutinous, I've had to pull every enforcer out I have, and it's still not…' He stopped in mid-flow, shook his head as if to clear it, then looked appalled at himself. 'So what's going on? Why am I… like this?'

'We need one barrage. That's all. Heaviest shells you can forge, tight-pattern, close to full complement as you can get.'

'We can't target,' Spleed protested. 'You understand that? We're blind down here, all the links gone, no augurs, nothing. What good will it do?'

'Did I ask you to take care of any of that? Did the captain?' He was close to the edge, but they still needed him. She'd have to return to the bridge before long, and only Spleed understood the ways of the gun-decks – their culture, their flashpoints, the little techniques you needed to get them working at maximum efficiency. 'Get the barrage keyed-up, and register the gun-ports within twenty minutes. After that we'll need intensive lance-fire. It'll need to be fast, it'll need to be effective, just as if we had all systems at full pitch. Succeed, and we stay alive for a few more hours. Fail, and we die.'

That seemed to get through to him. He nodded. His gaze flickered away, falling out of focus as he concentrated furiously.

'Maybe, if we... But then the core lines will be... But I could–'

'I'll leave you to it,' Avati said, walking back to the elevator. 'Do not disappoint me – as ever, it's all about the guns.'

# Chapter Eighteen

**VOICES**

**THE PRUDENT CHOICE**

**AWAKENING**

The order would come imminently. Santalina had been plugged in for a long time, waiting. She was in the inner sanctum again, enthroned, the roar of the engines subdued by the thick layers of shielding around the core sphere.

Normally, she would be feeling a level of relief to be leaving the Seethe behind. Exits could be botched, but in general they were safer than entries, and once you were safely back into the black then the worst of the sickness would ebb. It felt particularly bad this time, and the closer she came to the point of departure, the worse it seemed to get.

She let her mind lose focus, enter the Rites of Disengagement. She had to preserve herself this time, keep a little energy for the trials ahead. Kiastros would want a sudden exit, a drop without warning or preparation. After that, the fight would be brief, and if they prevailed he would no doubt want a sudden return as soon as the warp drives were up to it. That was the way of these hunts – rapid switches from one state to the other, all in the cause of keeping the enemy guessing.

She gripped the armrests of her throne, tensing for the impending command. The exposed eye in the centre of her forehead wept a little, still prone to bleeding from the last time. Avati, the little bitch, had noticed it but said nothing, probably appalled at the reminder that the woman she was talking to was a foul mutant. Ah, the hypocrisies they all indulged in, happy enough to make use of her services, all the while pretending ignorance over how she did it. Was Kiastros any better? Probably not. He was polite enough, a result of all that officer-class conditioning, but when he left her chambers he probably went for a pulse-shower afterwards. Only the fellow mutants really treated her as an equal, which was why she missed Ortuyo.

She closed her natural eyes, beginning the process that would see her pull down out of the unreal waves of the empyrean. Just as she did so, she heard the astropath's voice croaking in her ear.

*The... pain...*

Santalina's eyes snapped open again. 'Garg?' she said out loud, staring at the interior of her sphere.

Nothing. No echoes, just the lingering suggestion in her mind. It had been his voice alright, only twisted with agony. He was gifted enough to have sent her a vision, particularly while the ship swam in the warp and such things were easier, but it didn't sound like he'd meant to communicate. It was barely his voice at all, more like a parody of it, though perhaps his evident anguish had disguised the sonic signature.

She checked the chrono built into her throne, reviewed the brass-lined order panel below it. Nothing from Kiastros yet.

'Xinarola,' she voxed, relaying the signal through the sphere's outer casing and into the antechambers where her staff waited. 'Any word from the captain on the star-speakers?'

'*None, lord,*' came the response.

'The Master of Engines oversees the work, correct?'

*'I understand so, lord.'*

'Can you make contact with her?'

*'Please wait – I shall try.'*

Santalina looked around the interior of her cell again. The dark metal gleamed dully, perfectly clean, reverently polished. The tiny inscriptions carved into its surface were just as they had always been, and yet just then, staring at them, she found she could barely read the screeds. She blinked hard, concentrating on a passage just ahead of her, but the sigils swam before her eyes, blurred and illegible.

*'I have her, lord,'* came Xinarola's voice, interrupting her steadily rising alarm. *'You have a link open now.'*

The comm-bead in her ear fizzed for a moment, then clarified into a clogged channel filled with bangs and whines.

'Lieutenant Kuhl?' Santalina asked, wincing at the noise. 'Can you hear me?'

A long hiss of white noise, then something clicked into place.

*'Just about, honoured Navigator. I do not have long – what do you require?'*

'Your status, if you please. I gather you are attempting to break into the spire.'

Something short and sharp barked down the line – a laugh, maybe. *'That was the intention. It's slow – we're not even into the foundations yet.'*

'Have you uncovered anything? Anyone?'

*'No bodies. The lower chambers are all fused – we'd not see them even if they were there. It'll be hours, at this rate, before we can hope to break into the primary halls.'*

*The... pain...*

Santalina shivered. The residue of human suffering in those echoes was chilling. 'You have not witnessed anything untoward? No phenomena that have given you cause for concern?'

*'Like what, Navigator?'*

She didn't want to give her any ideas. An astropathic conclave was an esoteric place at the best of times, and it was bold of them to even consider tunnelling into it.

'I merely wished to enquire after your safety. Yours is a dangerous business.'

A long pause. *'Thank you, Navigator. So, will there be anything else? I have much to–'*

'No. Nothing at all. Emperor be with you.'

She cut the link. She sat back. She tried to get Ortuyo's voice out of her head. The sigils around her blurred even more, seeming to dance in front of her like ghosts. A signal blinked red on the console before her, indicating communication from the bridge.

The tunnelling would go on. They would drive right into the heart of it. Would they find Ortuyo alive? If they did, would he be lucid? Deranged? That was uncomfortable to think about. A damaged astropath was a very dangerous thing.

'Xinarola,' she voxed. 'Contact Sister Miriam Isobel. She is currently resident at the apothecarion. Impress on her a request that she makes her way to Lieutenant Kuhl's position as soon as she is able. Having someone with her... gifts present in the event of something unfortunate occurring would be prudent. It is her choice, of course. But I believe, given the circumstances, she will concur.'

*'By your will.'*

As soon as he'd said it, the priority link to the bridge opened up.

*'Honoured Navigator,'* came Kiastros' voice – calm, but with a familiar undertow of eagerness. *'It is time – if you please, bring us back into the void.'*

As soon as he opened his eyes, she saw that her prognosis had been correct. They were sightless. He blinked, once, twice, and no focus returned.

hoarse whisper.

'In the apothecarion of the *Judgement of the Void*,' Isobel told
him.

'My brothers?'

'Dead,' she said. Then, as if to soften the news slightly, 'Honour-
ably, in combat.'

A brief expression of pain, swiftly erased. The Space Marine's
features were crusted with a web of scabs and scars, some still
glistening where the blood refused to coagulate.

'The ship?' he asked.

'Under pursuit. We've taken heavy damage. Garrock – the one
you fought with – he's hunting boarders down in the bilges.'

Maizad tried to rise, sliding tube-filled forearms up and attempting to push from the cot. He failed.

'Not yet,' Isobel warned, checking over elevated life signs.
'I brought you back sooner than I'd have liked. Can you see
anything yet?'

Maizad blinked again. 'A little.'

'You've been damaged with some weapons I don't understand. I think your vision will return – I can give you something
to accelerate the healing, but there's nerve damage. It will take
time.'

He tried to rise again, and succeeded this time. One by one,
he started to pull out the tubes. 'You are of the Sororitas,' he
said. 'They told me one was aboard.'

Isobel laughed. 'What, you can smell me?'

'I have fought with your kind many times.'

'I'm sure. What did you think of them?'

'Fine warriors. Very fine.' He winced, trying out his muscles
in turn. 'So I was in the Dream.'

'A state of accelerated healing. I found it fascinating. I only
wish I could leave you in it for longer.'

He looked up at her, his gaze uncannily meeting hers. Perhaps he had some blurry visual impressions, or perhaps he was merely adept at negotiating his surroundings through sound.

'I must join the armsmen again,' he said. 'The things that were landed... they were formidable.'

'We don't know what remains on the lower decks. I don't think it's what you fought up in the prow. Captain Garrock believes it may be a Heretic Astartes. Hence his request to bring you back so soon.'

Maizad pondered that. Then his ruined face creased in a misshapen grin. 'And what use will I be against that, do you think?' He chuckled. 'I assume it can see.'

'Maybe. Garrock thinks it's damaged too. It would be have to be, otherwise it would already be up into the main decks and raising the hells. It might be as near death as you are.'

'Still a danger.'

'Indeed. Can you stand?'

He drew in a breath, then tried. He almost collapsed, but steadied himself, holding on to the cot's edge for a moment before letting go.

Even in his ruin, he was magnificent. Though criss-crossed with surgical wire and mottled with deep bruising, his body was still a vision of the Emperor's genius. The exposed skin was grey, stretched tight over the ridges and slabs of the absurdly defined musculature. It wasn't a conventionally attractive physique – far too over-bulked and distorted by the subdermal armour interface – but in its very ugliness it somehow conveyed the purity of the Emperor's unmatched vision. Nothing wasted, nothing extraneous, a perfectly efficient extension of human physical violence. It might have been her imagination, but the wounds looked almost like they were healing even as she watched.

'My armour,' Maizad said.

'We kept it. It is in poor condition.'

'It will have to do. Show me.'

She led him from the medicae bay and into the antechamber where her menials had reverently arranged the armour elements. It was similar to the plate she wore, only far heavier. He reached out to run his fingers over it, taking up the worst pieces to examine the damage by touch.

'I am impressed you are able to remove it,' he said.

'Not so different from my own plate,' she replied. 'How much is usable?'

'I shall attempt to judge. I require servitors, any menials you are able to spare.'

'They're yours.'

She was about to leave him to it, when he turned to her. For a moment it looked like his eyes focused properly, but then his gaze shifted a little to the side. Not yet.

'If Garrock is correct, this enemy may be beyond me,' he said. 'You are a Daughter of the Emperor. Will you fight with us?'

She was taken aback. It wasn't a cry for help, nor an admission of weakness, just a statement of the facts and a suggestion for their remedy. Hard not to be flattered, all the same.

'Oh, I'm no warrior,' she said. 'Not like the rest of my Sisters. I'd fight with you readily though, if I were not needed elsewhere. There's more than one problem on this ship.'

'Which is?'

'The astropaths are cut off. Maybe dead, maybe trapped. The retrieval teams will need protection when they break in, given that the armsmen are otherwise engaged.'

Maizad gave her a strange look, as if he thought that an unworthy task for one of her station.

'There are... worries,' Isobel added. 'About what they might find on the other side.'

Maizad nodded. 'I understand. Then you must go, and may the Emperor guide you.'

She almost changed her mind then. To don her helm, take up her blade, follow this blind warrior down into the depths suddenly seemed the greater path of virtue. The kind of thing she had always imagined her calling would lead her to, had it not been for the demands of healing.

But then she had given her word, which was never offered up lightly, and in any case something in the Navigator's relayed plea had rung true with her. This ship didn't *feel* right, even as they prepared to return to realspace after their short spell in the warp, and it wasn't just the physical damage. The atmosphere felt curdled, running with a kind of static charge, and tempers were shorter than they should have been. They needed the star-speakers back in action if they were to have any chance of getting back to some kind of safety, but such creatures were best dealt with from a position of strength. You never knew with mutants, particularly if they'd been wounded or had panicked.

'Captain Garrock has mobilised the entire garrison,' she said, as if that constituted some kind of apology. 'When you are restored–'

'I am ready now,' Maizad said. 'I will arm myself, return to the hunt.'

She could have questioned that – his pupils were still clouded, and every movement he made looked freighted with pain – but the way he said it brooked no disagreement. He was an Astartes, one of the Emperor's Angels, and he had spoken.

'Then I shall aid you, while I can,' she said, sending a summons to the servitors in the chamber beyond. 'I know a little of power armour, and I can at least ensure you head into combat with your battle plate in order.'

Maizad bowed, and turned to begin the process of assembling the cracked and dented pieces. 'I am indebted to you, Sister,' he said. 'This will not take long.'

Before she did anything else, she reached for a syringe at her belt, and then for a vial. 'A last gift,' she said, smiling forcedly. 'Your constitution is remarkable, but a little more will help.'

As he offered his arm up, she felt a pang of misgiving.

A Traitor Astartes, they said. One working its way through the bowels of the ship like a cancer gnawing through bone. The most terrible of all the enemy's servants, and all they had to send against it was a blinded, wounded casualty in cracked armour. Garrock struck her as a capable fighter, but could it possibly be enough?

'May you find the strength you need,' she murmured, depressing the plunger and sending a cocktail of stimms into the Space Marine's system.

*For you will need it*, she thought.

# Chapter Nineteen

**FIGHTING BLIND**

**IN CLOSE**

**YOU MUST FLINCH FIRST**

Kiastros took up position in the bridge's command throne just as Santalina set the translation in motion. He surveyed his kingdom for a moment, quickly trying to take in the mood of his subjects. Half of the cogitator stations down in the pits were out of action, some still fizzing with live current. The columns above the trenches were bowed, cracking under the weight of the badly damaged roof. Some bridge crew were still hurrying to their positions from previous assignments, all looking distracted and on edge. Debris littered the decks – no one had had the time or energy to clear it away.

Shabby, he thought. Ragged.

He turned to his Master of Signals. 'Prepared?'

Boroja looked like he wanted to be sick. 'Prepared, aye, lord captain.'

Then Avati. 'Astrogation?'

His first lieutenant was weathering the storm better, though still looked tense. She glanced back at him, and for a moment he thought she might protest the plan, place a formal query in the log. She'd never done so before. No officer of his had ever done it, but these were unique circumstances, and something febrile was in the air.

'All is made ready, lord captain,' she said, voice firm, as though she was trying to talk herself into confidence.

Next he got a shaky-sounding response from the enginarium's second-string crew. Kuhl was still busy, and Kiastros had never been entirely sure about her deputy, Krujax. Nothing he could do about it now – the man would have to prove his spurs.

The shutters in the high windows began to rattle. Great booms rang out from down below, followed by the sclerotic grind of plasma drives keying up. Kiastros fancied he heard a wild howling from outside the walls, as if the wails of banshees were scraping down the long flanks of his ship as it plummeted out of their eerie realm. He swiftly put such foolish notions out of his mind.

'My final injunction to you!' he called out, aware that the vox would be sent cascading to all departments. 'You all know that we are blind now in close. If the enemy comes within ram-range, we will be undone. We keep them at distance, we have a chance. A dangerous one – our long-sensors are in poor shape too – but enough to risk the action. So keep us nimble! Keep us moving! We strike them at distance, and Emperor willing we shall leave them spinning in the void.'

Even as he spoke, he felt the desperation of the situation. They knew very little of the enemy – its displacement, its weapons, its condition. A battleship coming at them would end the game. Cruisers would be easier, but still risky. A battle cruiser would pose a tantalising challenge – if it carried its own wounds, they might put up a fight; if it was in pristine shape, the odds were against them.

Santalina hadn't been able to give him a clear picture, only some mumbling about strange overlaps in the warp wakes, or something. She'd said there were two distinct profiles, then only one, then two again. Throne only knew what the truth was – they'd find out soon enough.

'Terra demands we perform this duty,' he went on, hoping that he could rouse some last morsel of resolve from them. 'We survive this, and we push on for reunion with the fleet. Glory still awaits us – the chance to fight within the Eye itself. I have this conviction. I believe without the slightest question that we shall yet make it there. So do not let us slip here! No mistakes, no slacking, no weakness!'

That was it. Some murmurs of assent, some averted faces.

Then the deck started to vibrate. A picter lens cracked, sending slivers of glass bouncing across the metal floor. Kiastros knew that if he tuned into the right channels, he would hear the roars of the gangmasters on the gun-decks hauling their cannons into position, the shouts of engine hands over the thunder of the furnaces, the frantic cries of errand ratings as the flurries of orders came in.

He turned back to Avati. 'Hangar doors primed?'

'Hangar doors primed, aye, lord captain.'

It would have to happen as soon as the empyrean was ripped clean away. The very split second that the true void surrounded them, the doors would have to slide down, spilling the oxygen pocket out and venting continually to look like a wound. It wouldn't fool a close inspection, but he didn't plan to let the enemy get close enough for that. It would need to happen so, so quickly. Just like everything else.

'Gunnery, all primed?'

*'Initial volley in place for your command, lord captain,'* came Spleed's wheezy voice. *'Angled and targeted for exit-trap, shifted to your specifications.'*

*Exit-trap.* One of the orthodox responses in a situation such as this – the pursued craft loosing a wide-spread barrage immediately on exit from the warp, aimed rearwards towards the location where its pursuer must break into realspace after them. It was hard for the following ship to avoid, given that they had no accurate near-space astrogation until they found themselves back in the world of reliable physics. Equally, it was little more than guesswork for the gunners – a hit-and-hope, relying on the slow recovery of augurs and scanner arcs to get a decisive strike in before the enemy crews got their full bearings and the shields had crackled up to maximum power.

There was an art to it, all the same. You got a hunch, once you'd been in command for long enough. Kiastros prided himself on his mastery of the manoeuvre – he'd successfully run the trap a dozen times, on three occasions triggering a hull-disable from the barrage itself. It might have been luck. It might have been something more profound. Either way, the crew had come to respect his judgement, and he and Spleed had developed a close understanding of the geometries involved.

This volley might hit. It was possible, but unlikely, because this time Kiastros had put in a large offset shift from where he expected the enemy to emerge. According to the best predictions, then, the spread of heavy shells would sail a long way past their target. A waste, it might be thought, of scarce ammunition. But no one had questioned it. No one ever did.

'All hands to stations for re-entry,' he ordered, watching the lenses avidly to check the order cascades. The alarms started up, the prayers were droned, the engine key rose a further notch.

'Entering translation nexus,' reported Avati, working hard to control the ship's veilbreak attitude and velocity.

'All hands, brace,' ordered Kiastros.

'Brace, brace!' echoed the station commanders all the way down the long bridge, their voices now half drowned by the clamour of the alert chimes.

Kiastros felt his heart rate pick up. His palms were slick against the stone of his throne. Normally this was a moment to savour – the ride into the unknown, the enacting of carefully prepared tactics. Even when the ship had been in danger before, he'd enjoyed the thrill of the imminent contest.

Not now. Much of the sweat that coated him wasn't from tension – it was from the damned heat, the heat that persisted no matter how far down the environmental controls went. The nausea wasn't from the warp, and the banging headache behind his eyes wasn't from lack of sleep. Everywhere he looked, the visions were *wrong*, not in a way that he could pin down, just... out of sync. It engendered doubt, that most fatal of emotions, the one that allowed error to creep in. What had he forgotten? What was staring him in the face that he couldn't see?

Nothing. Nothing was wrong. He had to get a grip, retain control. This would work. It would work this time just as it had worked every time before.

'Veilbreak!' shouted Avati, sounding almost panicked by it.

'Hangars open,' Kiastros commanded, switching back into full focus. 'Gunnery – let fly in twenty seconds precisely, marks as defined.'

*'Marks as defined, aye, lord captain,'* Spleed replied.

'Signals, lord captain!' Boroja reported. 'One emergent translation nexus, two point one v-u, bearing four-one-zero.'

Very close to where he'd guessed. Kiastros felt a faint glow of satisfaction. 'Status, Astrogation?'

'Hangars open, cargo away,' Avati replied. 'Angling for gunnery on requested vector.'

He needed a glass of wine. Why didn't he have a glass of wine? It helped him concentrate.

'Commence venting,' Kiastros ordered. 'Prepare power transfer to lances on my word.'

*'Firing, aye,'* reported Spleed. *'Solution conveyed and locked.'*

The ship bucked from the massed recoil, far harder than it

should have done. The inertial controls were clearly out of kilter, and the entire bridge swayed drunkenly.

'Broadside away,' said Boroja, struggling with his faulty controls. 'Out of augur sight, but trajectory confirmed. Translation nexus isolated and mature – one mass incoming.'

One. Just one. That was something – maybe Santalina had made a mistake. But how big would the ship be?

'Full power to plasma drives,' Kiastros ordered, deeply missing the weight of a goblet in his hand. 'Astrogation – keep us over two v-u from that thing if it's the only thing you do. How stand the lances?'

'*Working on it, lord captain!*' Spleed wheezed. '*Notification to be given when complete!*'

They were picking up speed. Everything vibrated, the noise in the bridge gallery ramped up. So few sensors were working at all, it felt strangely numb, bereft of the constant stream of data that enabled him to act. The real-viewers were empty – just a screen of stars and void – so you could almost imagine the ship was alone, running from a phantasm, all the sound and fury for nothing more than a fevered imagination.

'Signals,' he snapped. 'I need a little more, please.'

Boroja was working as hard as he could, coaxing the sole battery of long-range augurs to give him something he could use. 'One translated mass confirmed, lord captain,' he said, struggling to bring a haze of phosphor into clarity. 'Powering up to pursuit speed, void shield activation detected. No clear designation yet. My guess – battle cruiser class.'

Kiastros' mouth twitched in an ironic smile. Evenly matched, then. Though they had no idea how damaged their hunter was.

'Have they responded to our broadside?' he asked.

'Negative, lord captain,' said Avati, also struggling with the paucity of signals coming in. 'Volley trajectory well to starboard of target. They have ignored.'

'Good. Maintain speed. And inform our guests their moment has come.'

Coming out of the warp played havoc with a ship's systems. Whatever captain was on that ship might normally have paid close attention to a spread of macrocannon shells even if it had been sent spinning well clear of his or her prow, but it was tricky when everything was crackling into faulty life and you had to negotiate all the perils of translation with your half-functional augurs while attempting to zero in on genuine threats. So, seeing that the standard exit-trap barrage had been sent well wide of the target, it was entirely understandable that no one paid it very much attention and instead focused their efforts on the pursuit ahead of them. That did mean, though, that they missed the sleek and diminutive system runner sent shooting along amid the spread-pattern of heavy shells, its running lights doused and its weapon mounts inactive. Very few craft could have kept pace with a loosed broadside, even with a barrage modified to run at reduced speed from the cannons' mouths, but then this particular ship was a craft of many surprises.

Il-Moro hadn't divulged many of its secrets, of course, but he had given a minimal indication – perhaps out of pride – of its impressive capabilities. Sensor-baffling hull plates, exceptionally quiet running, beam weapons of highly secret classification. It was fragile, he said, but it packed a fearsome punch, and had been designed to run fast and hit hard. Not so very useful, perhaps, in a crowded fleet engagement surrounded by looming titans of destruction, but very handy to have deployable in a simpler scenario where you might control the parameters.

'Runner is active,' Avati reported. 'Weapon systems now active and turning for attack run.'

'Do you have live contact with the crew?' Kiastros asked.

'Negative. Poor comm-link over the distance, all sensors scrambled – will attempt to improve.'

That issue had been anticipated, but it was a difficulty all the same. The Inquisition's pilots would have to operate remotely, out of contact and largely out of sight. Il-Moro hadn't been happy about that, especially since the system runner had poor augur capacities of its own, being designed to work with a functional capital ship. He'd be brooding over it still, no doubt, down in the hangar with whatever cargo he'd taken off the ship, maybe already regretting his decision to lend a hand.

There hadn't been any choice, though. This was the one gambit they had, the one chance they had to land a punch.

'Lances?' Kiastros asked again.

'*A few seconds, lord captain!*' Spleed replied. '*Almost there!*'

Now the system runner turned. It had travelled with the cannon barrage to the far side of the enemy ship, coasting silently past its flanks and only moving once it was positioned ready to open fire. It shifted trajectory rapidly, powering up far faster than Kiastros had thought possible, activating twin beam weapons and swivelling in for the attack run.

'Now, Gunnery!' Kiastros shouted. 'I need them now!'

Spleed did what he could. The dorsal lances, starved of power until then and carrying heavy damage from the earlier engagement, finally opened up, hurling their long, shimmering beams out into the void. This time the targeting matrices had been calculated with no offset, and zeroed in to the oncoming enemy vessel.

'No clear sight of enemy, no augur improvement,' Boroja reported dolefully. 'Initial estimate stands – battle cruiser class, matching our speed, preparing to fire.'

Even as he spoke, the system runner engaged, loosing a pattern of its own energy beams against the distant cruiser's far flank. All they knew of it on the bridge came from the scraps of data blinking onto the lenses – Kiastros had to imagine the visual effects, the same eerie energies unleashed by the Inquisition warship, capable of gnawing through void shields and slicing up hull plating. A fraction of a second later, his own lance-beams struck the cruiser's near face, capturing it in a pincer between the two assaults.

'Hits?' Kiastros asked.

'Unknown,' Boroja replied. 'Too far out.'

'Enemy course altering,' Avati said. 'Adjusting to match – distance maintained.'

'Good, Astrogation. Gunnery – another barrage when you can.'

*'Power coils recharging, lord captain!'* Spleed's voice crackled over the comm. *'We're struggling to–'*

Kiastros muted the rest. The man's protest grew tedious. 'Void shields?'

'Half-power,' Avati said. 'Nothing left in the reserves – they'll have to do now.'

The system runner opened fire again, darting in close to unload another strike before angling away once more. At least, that was what Kiastros thought was happening – it was so hard to make sense of the data. Radiation and electromagnetic readings betrayed some major energy releases, but it was impossible to pinpoint where exactly they were coming from.

*'Secondary barrage resolved, lord captain!'* came Spleed's triumphant bark, and the lances fired again.

They were getting their angles, calculating from Boroja's vague sensor readings with impressive improvisation.

'Hits registered!' Boroja said confidently. And then, in a lower voice, 'I think.'

The rad-counters suddenly spiked, followed by proximity runes flashing up on Kiastros' personal console.

'Incoming!' he shouted, gripping the stone. 'All hands, brace for–'

The macrocannon shells struck hard and fast, raking along

the rear starboard hull in a hard-edged sequence of impacts. No close-augurs meant no warning – the entire vessel slewed over, tilting along its axis like an ancient galleon wallowing in the swell.

'Shields reduced!' Avati shouted, grappling to keep her position. 'One more of those–'

'Maintain speed, maintain lance-fire,' Kiastros ordered, clinging tightly to his juddering throne. 'Gunnery – as soon as you can.'

'Inquisition craft priming for third run,' said Boroja. 'They're firing again.'

The energy signatures from the system runner were insane – far more potent than anything that size had any right to be. The enemy battle cruiser fired again, a full broadside from its distant flank this time, and somehow the runner evaded the shells. Had it skipped past them all? Taken a hit? Something that small surely couldn't survive more than a couple of impacts, however cunningly made it was.

'Enemy course changed,' Boroja reported. 'Velocity increased, moving prow-ahead.'

So the pursuit had begun in earnest. That was encouraging – the enemy captain had clearly been unable to keep the pace while maintaining a tight angle for broadsides. It was down to lances now, torpedoes if it had any, maybe fighters, though those would struggle to remain in close contact once the plasma drives had pushed up to full momentum. Did it have something nastier up its sleeve? No sign of it yet.

'Keep us aligned, Astrogation,' Kiastros said. 'Minimal profile. Distance maintained?'

'It's gaining,' Avati replied, looking concerned. 'And we can't go faster.'

'Find a way,' said Kiastros, looking back at the tactical data. Already the scant blips showing relative position were fading, becoming blurrier as the ship's long-range augurs struggled to pinpoint its position.

Spleed fired again, a reduced volume; the lances were over-heating quickly. The noises of strain and unit-failure – clangs and cracks – rose in frequency, a chorus of impending collapse.

'Fourth attack run,' Boroja reported. 'It's... Hells, it's...'

Kiastros switched to the ranged augur, only to see nothing on the scopes. 'Energy readings?' he demanded. 'Comm-bursts?'

'I've got something on my terminal!' Avati shouted. 'No chronomark – could be a delayed signal.'

Boroja, though, shook his head. 'They got it, lord captain. The runner. Total destruction.'

Kiastros swore under his breath. The system runner had done well to last so long, but he'd hoped for a few more hits, some-thing critical struck, a void-shield array knocked out.

'Enemy ship within hail range, lord captain,' Avati reported. 'Vox-bursts incoming.'

'Mute all channels,' Kiastros told her. Standard practice – the enemy's hails were maddening things, full of unholy screams and whoops that could send a terminal staffer insane. 'Clamp down on all decks.' He switched to the enginarium. 'I need more power – what can you give me?'

A storm of static was the immediate response, followed by a squawk of metallic interference. *'All systems running beyond red, lord captain!'* came Krujax's strangled vox-feed. *'We're trying to push the secondary furnaces harder, but no promises it'll come good! Throne willing, we'll–'*

Kiastros shut him off. Kuhl would just have delivered the bad news. 'I'll need another lance volley imminently, Gunnery,' he said. 'Flog the crews to death if you need to – just get me one.' Then back to Astrogation. 'Hangar venting still active?'

'Still active, aye, lord captain.'

'Depressurise the whole deck, but keep it coming.'

'Incoming!' yelled Boroja, catching it late again.

This time the impact was ferocious, a far tighter smash of

shells that overloaded the outer void shields and slammed directly against the hull slabs. Did it have prow-facing batteries, then? Or had it fired before making the run in close? Either way, it was causing havoc. Enemy captains had a reputation for erratic aims – they made up for the lack of discipline in other ways – but this one could clearly run the angles.

The *Judgement of the Void* careened madly on its axis, plunged into darkness as the lumens gave out and the power coils screamed. The plasma drives howled in protest, caught by the sudden lurch and the jolt to their momentum. Crimson alerts flashed up everywhere, screams rose up from the terminal pits where something big and bone-crushing had just given way.

'Damage,' Kiastros said, trying hard to stay calm amid the swirl of disorder.

'Volley aimed aft, targeted at hangar,' Avati reported breath-lessly. 'They went for it.'

That was something. The venting was an obvious enough ploy, but there was no reason a captain wouldn't aim for weakness. At range, it would look like pre-existing damage, maybe even an engine-casing breach, though in truth the area was non-critical and about as heavily fortified as anywhere else on the ship. They could afford to take some pain there, whereas a major impact in the already fragile prow sectors might cripple them at a stroke.

'*Lance strike away!*' reported Spleed, somewhat desperately.

'Give me some good news,' said Kiastros grimly.

Boroja took a moment to collate the sparse data. 'Hits, lord captain,' he said, almost disbelievingly. 'Detecting void shield failure across forward sections.' But then it got worse. 'No reduction in pursuit speed. They will pass into blind-range within five seconds. Energy spike detected for incoming lance-fire.'

Time was running out. Once it closed, got in near, they'd be properly unsighted, bereft of tactical advantage and ripe for the killing blow.

'Turn us around,' he ordered.

Avati looked up disbelievingly. 'Turn us around?'

'We have a nova cannon,' said Kiastros.

'It will not function.'

'They do not know that.'

She looked appalled. Boroja appeared as if he was going to vomit.

'I do not–'

'Enough,' Kiastros snapped. 'That is the order. Turn to angle nova cannon, offset zero point two points, immediate course-change. Do it now.'

There was no time to explain his rationale, no chance to make the case for the desperate change of course.

It hadn't been enough. The system runner gambit had clearly done some damage, the lances had made their mark, but it hadn't been enough – they couldn't maintain distance. The *Judgement of the Void* was two, maybe three good hits away from being disabled, and after that the game was up. All that remained was a lurch into improbability – a switch around so audacious that it would give their hunters just a moment's pause, a moment's indecision, the kind of volte-face that could force a mistake. At the speeds both ships were travelling at, everything would move very fast now.

'Coming about!' Avati shouted, sounding almost furious with herself for complying. 'Prow angle direct to enemy, offset zero point two points, velocity maintained.'

The inertial controls were askew, so the manoeuvre was hellish. The whole ship yowled like a canid caught in a spike-vice, spars shuddering so violently it felt as though the super-structure would fly apart. Menials went skidding across the steepling decks, grabbing on to rails and crunching into cogitator housings. Kiastros himself was thrown hard over, nearly losing his position in the throne.

'Full power, Engines!' he roared, knowing the instinct would be to throttle back now, to try to blunt the worst of the carnage. They couldn't. It had to be fast, decisive, overwhelming.

'Incoming!' Boroja shouted.

Lance-flares scythed into them, deeper and more ruinous across their exposed nearside flank. The explosions shook the entire ship, audible from many decks down, the telltale hard crack of hull plates being shivered. Warning runes signalling depressurisation flashed up in droves, staining the picter lenses crimson.

'Where did they get us?' he demanded. 'Enginarium?'

'Negative, lord captain,' Avati replied, flustered and still busy with the manoeuvre. 'I think... the astropath spire.'

He shot her a sharp look. A mistake? Misfire? 'Damage?'

'Unknown.' She was beginning to lose composure, her hands scrabbling across her controls, her ears no doubt full of dozens of overlapping vox-streams. 'Heading achieved, speed maintained, intercept with enemy vessel at chronomark forty-five-one.'

'Enemy ship off ranged augurs!' Boroja reported. 'Now running fully blind.'

Kiastros felt his heart thumping. It was estimates now. Hunches, based on long experience. He knew the other ship had been mauled too. Badly, he had to hope, thanks to the Inquisition's eerie weaponry. They were closing for the kill, staking everything on a close run. If they could muster something concentrated at short range, a major prow-launch, then this would all be over very quickly.

But they'd be nervous of the nova cannon. Nervous enough, he hoped, to flinch at just the right moment.

'Gunnery,' he voxed. 'One last volley. Everything you have. Lances, cannons, scrap-jettisons. I mean everything. Blow out the last of your galleries, leave them in ruins, but give me one blast to remember.'

'*Aye, lord captain!*' came Spleed's almost crazed reply. '*But... trajectory?*'

Kiastros was already working on it, triangulating, calculating, his fingers dancing across the tactical geometry console. 'On its way now,' he said, before another incoming salvo smashed into the racing ship. He could feel the spires being ripped from their roots, the adamantine panels being shredded, the plascrete mouldings melting. Armaglass shattered overhead, showering the bridge with crystals. The deck was not so much vibrating as rattling, throwing everything about in a drumbeat of impending destruction.

He could see nothing. Just the material implosions around him. No enemy, no void-lines, no sensor blips. There was a kind of purity about it – just mental images, the knowledge of what his counterpart must do, what a thousand prior engagements had taught him about the probabilities, the angles, the necessities and the pitfalls.

'Lord captain,' came Boroja's voice tentatively. 'We are on a collision course.'

'As far as we know,' Kiastros replied calmly.

'But, I–'

'Silence! Astrogation – hold course and increase speed. Engines – direct excess heat into nova cannon's primary systems. Make it look powered.'

'Aye, lord captain!'

'*Aye, lord captain!*'

The shaking got worse. He heard screams from somewhere down in the pits – a collapsed platform? The engines sounded like strangled equines, punctuated by shrieks of shearing metal. Flying apart. It was all flying apart, flinging every component into the void in a final petulant roll of the dice.

*You must flinch first,* he thought, directing the sentiment to his opposite number, at last beginning to enjoy the abandon of it. *For I will not deviate. I will smash us both into shards before I slow down now, for my Emperor awaits me in paradise, and all you have before you is annihilation.*

'Incoming!' screamed Boroja.

The volley struck deeper, smashed and crashed harder, blew out subsystems, gouged out armour chunks, burrowed and gnawed its way through decks and into pristine chambers. He could almost hear the screams of those blown clear into the void before being fried alive amid the remnants of the void shields. He could almost hear the cries of those immolated in the backdraught from the overworked furnaces, the yowls of those caught under toppling supports and exploding bulkheads.

*I will fly us into the very maw of hell,* he thought deliciously. *I will not deviate.*

'Mass dead ahead!' screamed Boroja, who'd resorted to using crude void-displacement scans to get some idea of what was going on. 'Impact in–'

'No change!' shouted Kiastros. 'Full speed! Damn them all, and flay the engines!'

The ship was thundering now, ramping up to full straight-line velocity, a hurtling hunk of rapidly dissipating iron and flame. The distance between them was almost nothing, rapidly disappearing, shrinking down into the singularity that would destroy them both.

'Gunnery – your volley!' Kiastros shouted over the tumult in the bridge.

*'Prepared and ready!'* came Spleed's shriek.

'It's moved!' Boroja screamed. 'Immediate mass-shift to four-two-zero! It's moved!'

*You flinched!*

'Gunnery, on my mark!' Kiastros shouted. 'Everything you have!'

This was the hunch. The guess. The offering to fate. The

enemy had dodged the nova cannon's challenge, veering away before entering catastrophic range. Now it would sheer off, presenting its flanks for a brief moment as the ships passed one another. It would tumble to zenith or nadir too, if the captain had any nous, and that all had to be allowed for.

And Kiastros was certain. He was more certain, just then, than he'd ever been. He'd approached with a small offset, just a tiny deviation, but enough to plant the seed in the enemy's mind. He'd shown his damage, both real and faked, and knew where the enemy's worst hits had come. He had placed himself in the mind of his opponent, assessing what he would do were the positions reversed. There was only one response – a shift to starboard, upshift by two points, a pull round for the next pass. That kept the enemy's best remaining armour in harm's way, avoided the nova cannon's firing arc and gave the shortest route for the return approach.

Wait. *Wait.* Wait now – just a few seconds more...

'Mark!' he roared, rising up in his throne. 'Now, Gunnery! Empty the barrels!'

Spleed complied. The *Judgement of the Void* nearly blew itself part, vomiting out every last piece of ordnance in its remaining reserves. Lances burned, cannons recoiled, shells whistled out. The entire port flank erupted in flame and vapour, lighting up the void and overloading the real-viewers. The ship keeled over again, wilder this time, thrown off its central axis and sent reeling drunkenly. Huge explosions echoed up from deep below, roaring booms that spoke of horrendous destruction, but it was still drowned out by the thunder of the big guns, the slams of the recoil rails, the creak and snap of the structural beams under colossal pressure.

'Hits detected, lord captain!' Boroja reported, now in close enough to use the real-viewers themselves. 'By the Throne, immense hits – visual destruction registered across all hull-faces.'

'Pull away!' Kiastros commanded. This was dangerous now. 'Ventral turn, steep angle. Get us clear.'

Avati complied immediately, already prepared. 'Steep turn, aye!' she shouted. 'Engines now close to burn-out!'

'Shut down the plasma cores,' Kiastros told her. 'Use our momentum to spin clear.'

She did what was necessary, the bridge filled with the clanking whine of the plasma lines guttering out. Now they were immobile as well as blind, thrown through the void only by their own enormous inertia.

Had it been enough? Had it done the job? The real-viewers were empty again, the near-augurs still down, but there were other ways to search for what he wanted.

'Radiation levels elevated,' Boroja duly reported. 'Accelerating readings, more coming in. Are we clear? Are we clear?'

Kiastros felt like laughing suddenly. 'Well clear, Signals,' he said. 'Can you confirm a kill?'

Boroja worked on it, hands shaking. The bridge was still shuddering, half-ruined, a mess of hanging cables and smashed lenses, menials struggling to regain their feet, fires flickering across half the pits.

The *Judgement of the Void* shifted again, shoved abruptly as if kicked. A few more lumens blew, a few more consoles went red. Boroja looked up at Kiastros' throne, his jaw hanging slack.

'Core breach detected at zero point one v-u aft,' he reported, as if he were having trouble believing it himself. 'It's dead in the void. It's gone.'

For a moment, only silence. Half the crew were still struggling to keep the ship from spinning out of control, the other half were nursing wounds or trying to activate damaged equipment. Avati didn't even look up – she was concentrating furiously on something at her terminal.

Even he didn't want to believe it so soon. He ran his own

tests, checked his own data. No more barrages came in. No more alerts were flagged. He was surrounded by fire, but had not yet been consumed by it. His ship was alive, if only barely. His enemy's was not.

He slumped back in his throne, utterly drained.

'Thank the Throne,' he murmured. 'Ship-kill. Thank the Immortal Throne.'

# Chapter Twenty

**STRIKE FROM THE VOID**

**COMING AROUND**

**WITCH-MARK**

The noise of the tunneller working had been so all-consuming that Kuhl had never even heard the first impacts from outside. It had snarled and hammered, chewed and spat, dragging itself like a famished ursine up and up, tearing apart its surroundings even as it lurched steadily higher.

The going had been slow, horribly so, hampered by the creaking terrain and the confined spaces. Every yard of ground gained had to be consolidated quickly, with servitors and tech-ratings darting up close to install fresh brace-beams and support pillars. Arfo-5's people scurried everywhere, frantically probing for weakness and calling up more build-gangs to keep the whole cavalcade on the move.

Every so often, progress would grind to a halt. The drills would hit something durable, or a void would be encountered that risked sending the machine tumbling. Kuhl would shout out the command to cease work, would wearily get to her feet and pick her way close to the excavator's head, panting heavily in the heat and the confinement. Surveying accurately was crushingly difficult in the conditions, and already there had been fatalities – supports had cracked, heavy gear had crushed limbs. No alternative, though – no choice but to keep slogging on, break the seals, get inside. The closer they inched, the stronger the readings became. It got harder once the void combat started, since Kiastros was throwing the ship around as hard as he could, and that all had consequences for stability. For as much as it felt good to be out of the damned warp, trying to maintain progress during all of that was not easy. She had thought about calling a halt to it all, but her orders had been clear – to keep going until they found something to report. So she'd stuck at it, pushing, pushing, driving herself as hard as any of the ratings, only ordering temporary shutdowns when absolutely necessary.

Arfo-5 had come up to her on the last reconnaissance haul, his spindly frame stalking across the broken terrain and his grime-spattered cloaks billowing. He'd coped better with the extreme environment than her – no surprise, perhaps, given the extensive replacements he'd inflicted on himself. The two of them had laboured past the steaming flanks of the excavator's main module, squeezing between the hot metal and the crumbling edges of the gnawed-through decking. The rest of the crews had stayed down below, more than thirty yards off, no doubt grateful of the respite from their back-breaking efforts.

She'd dropped to her haunches, close now to the immense drill-wheels at the very front. Her handheld augur chattered, ticking a range of readings into the lens.

'Fifty per cent complete,' said Arfo-5, turning his cowled head towards her in the dark. 'Estimate.'

Kuhl nodded, reaching up to wipe spots of grease free of her helm's visor. 'These are the roots,' she said. 'Three levels up, the base of the speakers' chambers.' She peered around her, running more scans on the molten plasteel. 'Still can't believe they demolished it all this deep down. What kind of weapon does that?'

Arfo-5's eyes – some of them, at any rate – blinked. 'Many weapons. A high-yield charge following a breakage in the void shields. Something that got under the crust. The enemy is resourceful, for all they are hateful.'

It still didn't feel right. A major explosion on the surface would have had a broader damage arc. This looked ferociously targeted, the kind of tight-focused deep ingress that was hard to pull off without some level of planning.

'I read Garrock's report,' she said. 'They landed troops elsewhere. They were building something inside the ship. Some kind of device. Maybe they did it twice.'

Arfo-5 considered that. 'Possible. But if they had succeeded, why are we still here? Would they not... detonate it?' He sniffed. 'And we do not detect high energy levels. So perhaps it is another failure. A misfire.'

'A good outcome. Which makes me believe it can't be right.'

'And yours is an emotional response. I remain optimistic. We may yet find survivors, we may yet restore the communication function.'

Kuhl almost laughed. Tech-priests could surprise you sometimes. They were like children mostly, with their stunted expressive range and awkward set of preoccupations, but there was something occasionally human in most of them still, albeit buried deep.

'So we must h–' she started, but was cut off by a sudden eruption of noise from above them – a heavy crash, then another, followed by a peal like breaking thunder. It ramped up so quickly that it felt as if the whole ship were being burned away over their heads. She screamed – or thought she did – clamping her hands over the audex intakes on her helm. The deck plates underfoot began to shake, and chunks of heavy masonry smashed down around her.

'Withdraw!' Arfo-5 bleated, trying to grab her as their surroundings melted into confusion. 'Strikes from the void!'

The two of them slid and slithered back the way they had come, pursued the whole time by the roar of destruction from above. Kuhl heard frantic shouting on her comm-channel, shouts of alarm from the gangs hunkered down behind the extractor, but the view ahead of her swiftly dissolved into a haze of dust. She lost her footing, plunged down faster, only held back from being dashed against a criss-cross thicket of broken ironwork by Arfo-5 pulling her towards him. The two of them finally emerged back where they had started – at the base of the extractor's main drive-unit where the lead work-gangs had been stationed. The space was almost as confined, a rubble-choked chamber scarcely wider than the tunnel they had bored. Kuhl tumbled across the deck, accompanied by a rain of debris. More explosions went off from far above, and the drive-unit shuddered on its tracks.

'Secure those lines!' she shouted, scrambling to her feet, seeing the long cables holding the extractor in place tremble like a spider's web in a gale. 'Lash it down, or it'll take us all down with it!'

The crews were slow to respond, stunned by the ongoing roar of disintegration, struggling to find their stations as plumes of smoke and dust rolled over them. Arfo-5 let go of Kuhl and limped ahead, screeds of binharic squawking from his vox-emitter. Kuhl found one of the gangmasters stumbling about, dazed, and gave him a hard smack on the side of his helm before pushing him into position.

'We need to lock it all down!' she thundered, getting her bearings, beginning to gauge the damage and plan a response.

The hits had come in from the void, part of the battle

Kiastros was conducting with whatever had followed them from the muster. Stray shots? Or had the enemy detected the existing damage and tried to make it worse? The good news was that things sounded worse than they actually were – at least according to her semi-scrambled augur readings. The decks above them, the ones the excavator was lodged halfway through, were holding up, shaken but not critically weakened yet. Most of the damage had come from cascade effects, the ripple of kinetic energy radiating out from the impact sites a hundred yards or more above them. The bad news was that this still risked sending the excavator plunging down through the weakened decks below, smashing the machine and causing Throne-knew-what havoc on its descent. It needed to be stabilised, and quickly.

'I'm coming down,' she voxed to the team on the level below, leaving Arfo-5 to do what he could with the lead drive-unit. She slid and tumbled down a great gouge previously cut between decks, using the ramps built by her teams. It was even darker down there, just a handful of functional lumens, more billowing smoke. She sought out the gangmaster and hauled her to her feet.

'More struts!' she shouted. 'Now!'

That seemed to register. The gangmaster roused all the workers she could find, plus some bewildered-looking haulage servitors and a lexmechanic. Bracing struts destined for higher decks were dragged up, hoisted into place, hastily riveted and welded where the ceiling was sagging alarmingly. The rearquarters of the excavator were visible just ahead, huge and cumbersome, already listing badly and kicking out smog. Ominous creaks sounded from the far side.

They were going to lose it. She grabbed two manual brace-jacks, dragged them across the deck to the excavator's side, wedged them into place and started on the auto-pumps. Even as she cranked them up, she heard the sound she dreaded most of all – the steady whine of the compensators overloading, the snap and clang of footings failing.

The enormous metal structure began to sink, as screams rang out from the level above. The deck rippled under her, flexing like fluid, and she staggered away.

Too slow. A big joist came loose overhead, knocked out of its moorings by the excavator's movement. It was solid iron, ten yards long, and as soon as she saw it come for her she knew she couldn't escape it. All she could do was watch it topple, swinging down in the dark like the hammer of vengeance. The memory of Oolenta suddenly flashed in front of her, all that guilt and anxiety cradled so carefully for so long, now pointlessly, because this was going to end her.

Except it didn't. Something interposed itself, something dark and glinting and armoured, surging up out of the shadow and dust to brace the toppling beam. Kuhl fell over backwards, upended by the quicksand-like deck, stupefied by what she was seeing – a figure, an armoured figure, holding up the roof. Its arms were bent upwards, pushing back against the weight of the imploding floor above, its knees straining to keep it all from falling apart.

'Struts!' Kuhl thundered, remembering herself. From somewhere, from out of the gloom and flame, ratings emerged, servitors lumbered, priests chattered. Finally, haphazardly, they started to shore it all up, working as fast as they could, swapping precision for a flurry of activity. All the while, the armoured figure remained static, the fulcrum of the entire operation, the only pillar guaranteed not to move or snap.

Only when the excavator finally slithered into rest, when the last of the temporary supports had been drilled into place, when the ceiling had stopped sagging, did it move. The arms fell, the body straightened. The armoured figure dropped down, hauling in deep, pained breaths.

Kuhl shuffled up closer, eyes wide, still unable to believe what she had witnessed. 'By the Throne of Light,' she murmured. 'Are you... alright?'

Sister Isobel looked up at her, her ruddy face hidden behind her battle helm, but giving the distinct impression that she was smiling crookedly inside it.

'What kind of damned shoddy operation are you running here, then?' she panted.

'Do you need medicae assistance?'

'Hells, no.' Isobel grunted, flexed an arm, then the other. Then she looked up, to where the vast carcass of the excavator lay semi-buried in the ruins of the decks it had bored its way through. 'You've made a mess, though.'

Kuhl snorted an exhausted laugh. 'Oh, it was like this when we got here.' She glanced at her augur, grimly surveyed the wreckage. 'That thing isn't going further. We've failed.'

Isobel clambered up to her feet, and the servos on her armour creaked. Something whined inside her helm – an ocular focusing, probably. She cast her gaze upward, through the broken decking and back to where Kuhl had been crouching just moments earlier.

'No, I think you did enough,' she said cautiously. 'I detect weakness ahead of where the drills stopped. A few heavy las-cutters, and we could still break in. What do you say? Or would you rather head back to the engines?'

Kuhl thought of the interrogator still hunkered down in the hangars, his presence infecting the ship like a bad smell. No, she would not rather head back down. However difficult it got, however perilous the path became, she would not head back down.

'It depends,' she said, wiping more smuts from her visor and squinting into the dark. 'You plan to help us out?'

Isobel laughed. 'Why I'm here. How quickly can you get all this mess made safe?'

'An hour or so, if we work at it,' Kuhl said, then looked upwards, past the wreck of the machine. 'And after that, we keep going up. Right to the very top.'

'So be it,' said Isobel, shaking herself down and making ready to help. 'The very top.'

Avati was still panting, still covered in sweat, her hands trembling. Her terminal station was almost completely non-functional, its casing cracked and its internal valves exposed. Everything was silent.

'Astrogation.'

She couldn't concentrate. Her mind felt scrambled. Where was she? On the bridge of the *Invincible* again? No, that was years ago. She looked up, wincing as the sparks flew from the open wounds in the metal. The bridge had been plunged into darkness, relieved only by the odd glow of combat lighting and the hard blaze of electrical fires. Servitors had been rustled up from somewhere, limping through the wreckage with anti-flamm canisters.

'Astrogation.'

It smelled awful. Scorched steel, ruptured coolant runs. Chemical smells, like she'd been buried alive in some refinery on an industrial world. Was that where she was? No, she was on a ship. The *Judgement of the Void*. She blinked. She ran her hands up to her mask, unclipped the seals.

'*Astrogation.*'

She heard it now. Avati started, looked up properly, turned to see Kiastros staring at her.

'Are you alright?'

Reality flooded back in, booming in her ears, swilling around her. She felt like vomiting.

'Quite alright, lord captain,' she replied, working hard to clear her head. 'Just processing the last of the tactical readings.'

A lie. There were no tactical readings, not any more. She could count the functional systems in her terminal on the fingers of one hand – normally, she'd have access to several hundred data-feeds.

'Come up. We need to speak.' Kiastros turned towards Boroja, who was looking similarly groggy. 'You too, Signals.'

Avati unplugged her input jacks, stowing the cables in their sockets. She deactivated the lone functional retinal overlay inside her command helm, and pushed her throne back from its gyro-clasps. Getting back to her feet was difficult – she was light-headed still, her thighs tight with cramp. Combat fatigue, no doubt, but worse than she'd ever known it. The brain fog was worse, a kind of dead weight that just didn't lift. Ever since the mass engagement at U-93. What was that? Why were they all suffering so badly from it?

Once the three of them were together, clustered around Kiastros' command throne, the audex screen came down again, masking for the time being the sounds of erratic reconstruction across the bridge's main chamber.

'We were lucky,' Kiastros said. He looked almost as bad as her, his forehead sticky with perspiration, his cheeks strangely hollowed out.

Boroja managed a dry chuckle. 'No, your judgement again,' he said. 'Artfully done, lord captain.'

'Not so much.' Kiastros looked oddly defeated, given that survival had just been bought. 'They must have been damaged already. Or poorly crewed.' His brow creased. 'They could have had us, I think. Better targeting. Were they hanging back? No. They came at us. But all the same...' He snapped out of it, rubbed his eyes, flexed his shoulders as if to get some blood flowing again. 'We are alive. That is all that matters now. We must decide how to prolong this state of affairs. How stands the ship?'

Boroja shot Avati a nervous look. 'From my perspective,' he said, 'we're barely a ship at all. Even the ranged augurs are now gone. I have almost nothing. Minimal life support, minimal power. I can't even tell you which way we're pointing, let alone if there's anything else out there coming for us.'

'Can you improve things?'

'Every one of my ratings still alive is down in the sensor pits. All the priests that could be spared, too. I don't know. No time soon, I fear.'

Kiastros turned to Avati. 'Anything to add?'

'Shields are ineffective. Plasma drives burned out – it'll be a while before we can do more than crawl. Spleed used up everything we had.' She struggled to find something useful to report. 'The warp drives are still in poor shape, though we might chance a translation soon, as long as the Navigator is strong enough. But I fear for the hull now – we're damned weak.'

Kiastros nodded grimly. 'We can't risk veilbreak. Not yet. Kuhl's people will have to shore up what they can – if we can get some minimal integrity readings, check out the core structures, the warp must now be safer.'

'Is it?' asked Boroja idly. 'Unless something else was tracking us, we're alone now. Drifting in the deep void. Perhaps that's where we need to be.'

Kiastros gave him a sour smile. 'For the time being, we have no choice. But it can't last. They sent a ship after us. More may be on their way. The enemy has powers of divination, and if our own Navigator can spy ghosts in the abyss, then do not doubt they can do so too.' He drew in a pained breath. 'It's the damned Inquisition. They've brought something onto my ship, and it has now damned us. A curse. Some witch-mark. Do you not feel it?' He shook his head. 'So damned hot. I can barely breathe.'

It wasn't hot. It was close to freezing – the environmental controls had long since been stuttering along at a fraction of their normal power. Avati glanced at Boroja, but the Master of Signals seemed to agree.

'His ship is gone now,' Boroja said. 'He has a handful of his acolytes with him. What power does he have, truly? We could... demand some answers.'

Kiastros seemed briefly startled, then he laughed humourlessly. 'They are the instrument of the Emperor,' he murmured. 'They make the demands, we scurry to comply.' He shook his head. 'But they are key to this, that is true. We must speak to him again. Perhaps their cargo can aid us. Perhaps they have some knowledge that could see us clear.'

'I got some signals,' said Avati cautiously. 'Not much, not anything I could understand. From the system runner, before it was destroyed. I could work on them, try to clean them up – the interrogator might appreciate more knowledge of their sacrifice.'

'He might. Or it might enrage him further. I had to plead for that ship, and now it's gone.' Kiastros placed his hands together, wringing them so hard that the leather of his gloves puckered. 'But do it, if you can. It might help a little. And then there's Kuhl – can we spare her still on the speakers' spire? She would do more than her deputy to get the plasma chambers back into order.'

'If you wish to pull her back, lord captain, we shall have to send ratings after her in person,' said Avati. 'The deck-comms are down across half the ship.'

Kiastros laughed again, and there was a wilder edge to it now. 'Ha!' he snorted. 'One more piece of joyous news. Anything else? A rupture in the warp core? Genestealers in the hold?'

'It's possible,' muttered Boroja.

'Captain Garrock hunts the signs of the intruder,' said Avati. 'If he finds it, he will end it.'

'I trust that is so,' said Kiastros grimly. 'Though whatever force he has with him, it will have to do – no more can be spared.'

He pulled himself together. The levity, febrile or not, disappeared, and the expression Avati was so familiar with – calm again, focused, determining the course ahead – returned.

'So here we are. We must make repairs as quickly as we can, stabilise the hull. Once we are strong enough for the translation, I will instruct the Navigator to take us back into the warp. She may be able to advise us then on whether any pursuers still linger in our wake. Not that there's much we can do about it now – we are defanged entirely, at least for a few cycles. Our priority must still be the astropaths, to hear something, anything, from the fleet. Failing that, we chart a course to the nearest safe haven. That will be challenging. Not Yeoqa, that is certain. I shall consult the charts – something will emerge, I am sure.'

He looked around him briefly, as if to check that the devastation of the enormous chamber was real and not some appalling dream.

'Signals, you have the bridge,' he said. 'Do what you can to restore functions. I will need full communication with the enginarium and the Navigator as soon as possible – everything else can wait until then.'

Boroja bowed. 'By your will.'

'Astrogation, with apologies, I must task you with shepherding our unwelcome guests.'

Avati's heart sank.

'When time allows, I will speak to him again, but my first duty is to the ship – the Navigator and I will confer. In the meantime, I wish him to be reassured – to be briefed on the destruction of his vessel, and for my gratitude to be conveyed. It saved us, that is certain, and he must be made aware of that. Inform him we are working on the audex from it.' Then his voice lowered.

'But their presence here drags us into the abyss. I wish to know what they carry. If he will not divulge the truth, we must prise it from him in other ways. We know the chambers they squat in. Assess their power, make a plan to take it from them, if we have to. Nothing is served by our destruction, and I have no faith that this interrogator is in full control of his situation.'

That was more like it. Having to be polite to a monster was a trial; being tasked with its removal was a challenge.

'By your will. Though you recall, I am sure, that we have the services of the honoured Sister as well.'

'Quite so. Though Santalina wanted her with Kuhl, and I will follow her judgement on that, at least for now. If Isobel, or even Maizad, prove necessary, we can call on them. They have their tasks before them, and we are stretched too thin to change much now.'

He attempted a smile.

'They have tried to end us twice now,' he said. 'Twice they have failed. Take it as a signal – we will find our way home, one way or another, and damned be any who seek to prevent us.'

## Chapter Twenty-One

**PATHFINDING**

**TOGETHER AGAIN**

**READING THE RUNES**

Other gangs had attacked the intruder. The story was the same every time they found them – scattered teams of the feral population, doing what they'd been told, launching themselves at the monster prowling through their twilight realm. All of them died. None of them laid a blade on it. The corpses began to mount up, a grim set of cairns along the twisting paths of the deeper decks. Did they even slow it down? Perhaps. The one thing they had in their favour, thought Garrock, was that the traitor was undoubtedly hampered in some way. More blood was found, and it wasn't baseline human. Perhaps the repeated attacks were at least getting in the way of its healing process, opening up wounds as it was forced to fight. That alone made it worth the cost in bodies.

The route it was taking was hard to pick out. At times it looked as if it was heading up, maybe towards the bridge, but then it would duck down again, making for the rear enginarium.

Garrock squatted down, reaching for yet another patch of

blood on the metal deck. Herj came to join him. Others of the troop edged forward, scanning ahead with their muzzles.

'Lost?' Herj asked.

Garrock grunted. 'Don't think they get lost.'

'It doesn't know the ship. It's clearly wounded.'

Garrock smiled wryly. 'Even so.' He rubbed his fingertips together, looked at the way the blood clotted thickly. Not so very different from the heavy oils that coated everything. 'Unless... No.'

'What?'

Difficult to know how to put it. 'Are you... finding it hard to fix your path?'

'What do you mean?'

'Don't know if it's lack of sleep. Probably. I just... The routes seem to shift.'

He expected Herj to laugh then, but he didn't. He said nothing for a moment. When he spoke, his voice was very low.

'I thought I was going mad,' Herj said. 'The cartoliths aren't reading true, are they? We go down transit routes, and get stuck in dead-ends. Are we still in the warp?'

That was a dangerous thought. Everyone knew the warp mixed things up, but it didn't rearrange the internal structure of the ship.

'No, not any more,' Garrock said grimly. 'Probably nothing. But this... thing. Somehow it's getting snarled up too.'

He really didn't know whether he believed that, or, if he did, what to make of it. A priest might have tried to persuade him it was the Emperor's will or something, a piece of divine providence amid all the destruction. Or maybe it was something more sinister, some effect or malaise picked up in the fighting. He thought back to the device, the one Maizad had destroyed. Had they cleared out every last bit of it? Had anyone checked?

He sighed, got to his feet. 'It must be ahead,' he said. 'On this deck, I reckon, hunkered down somewhere up there.' He checked his handheld augur. 'It can't get out – we've got squads at every exit point, sealed the down shafts. We just push on. This is where we run it down.'

It was impossible not to feel daunted by that, no matter how many actions he'd led. He had a sudden memory of chasing after claw-spiders on his birth world. It was the same mix of emotions – yearning to find them, to track them down so they could be squashed, but also desperate not to, because they were lethal things, the stuff of nightmares.

'Getting a reading, captain,' said Kevem, stationed a little up ahead. 'One deck up, making its way to our position.'

Garrock felt a cold twinge in his stomach. 'How close?'

'It's not the target. I think your call was answered.'

The relief at that was a physical thing, one that washed through him like water. 'Thank the Throne,' he said, holstering his weapon. 'Hold position with the squad. Lieutenant, with me.'

He and Herj made their way back down the corridor, found the crawlway up to the next deck, squeezed themselves through the gap and clunked along the next access tube.

He was waiting at the far end, a hulking presence in the gloom, his helm lenses glistening with the familiar pale-blue sheen.

'My lord Astartes,' said Garrock, making the aquila. 'You are restored.'

Maizad came a little closer, stepping into the weak pool of light cast by a grimy sodium lamp, and Garrock saw that that wasn't true – not entirely, anyway. The Space Marine's armour was a mess, still bearing the rents and gouges that had been inflicted up at the enginarium chamber. Some areas had clearly been welded back into place – the best the tech-priests could do, no doubt – but it was hasty work. The helm was the worst – one smashed lens, a ravaged vox-grille, part of the skull-cap missing. Maizad's breathing was a metallic lisp through the damaged rebreather unit, and he stood awkwardly, as if compensating for broken bones that had not yet healed.

'Somewhat,' came the rasping voice from the ruined helm. 'Have you located the enemy?'

'It is ahead – the next deck down, a few hundred yards.'

'Sighted?'

'No. Only reports from the bilge-rats.'

'You are sure of it? Its nature?'

'Nothing else it could be,' said Garrock. 'Nothing else kills like... one of you. If you'll pardon me for saying it.'

A hiss escaped from Maizad's helm. 'Not like me. Not any more.' He looked around him, as if assessing his surroundings, though Garrock got the distinct impression he wasn't really looking at it. 'Forgive me for not coming sooner. Finding the way was difficult.'

Not him, too, surely? Maizad's ability to map a route from memory had been perfect before, instant absorption of carto-lith data.

'Yes, something is strange down here,' Garrock agreed, wondering how much to divulge of his own issues with path-memory.

'Maybe so. But a greater problem remains.' Maizad reached up to his helm, unscrewed it, revealed a blotchy, bruised face latticed with scars and scabs. His eyes were clouded and pupil-less. 'My sight.' A thin smile. 'Just blurs, tactile sense, some assistance from my armour. It will return, the Sister tells me. Not rapidly.'

'So, how can you...?' Garrock didn't finish the sentence. How could he fight? How could he possibly go up against a Traitor Astartes in that condition? However badly injured the enemy was – and they had to hope it was severe – lack of sight surely made it impossible.

Maizad chuckled, drew his blade. The edge glowed with that

same soft pale light. 'I get in close,' he said. 'You get me there. Once in contact, sight less useful. It is dark down here anyway, yes?'

Garrock nodded, trying to mask his doubt. 'If you wish it, lord,' he said.

'I do.' Maizad sheathed the blade again, and it slid into the scabbard with a faint hiss. 'Now, gather your men together. We fight again, just as before. This time, the honour will be mine.'

Avati watched Kiastros leave. Then she looked over at Boroja. The Master of Signals seemed at a loss to know what to do. He stood for a moment or two, arms by his sides, listless. Then he shivered, shot her a weary smile.

'So that's it,' he said wearily. He looked like a man who'd been lost in a fever for a long time, now coming back to the surface, but drained by it all and ready to succumb again at any time.

She felt horribly vulnerable. Every moment they remained here, unshielded, virtually depowered, they were little more than prey. Anything coming out of the warp could pick them off with no trouble at all. They wouldn't even see it coming.

'Can you get our sight back?' she asked.

'Possibly. Some systems were close to being restored. If they're not shot through, now...' He trailed off, looking confused. 'So what do you think of him?'

'The captain?'

'Yes. The captain.'

What was this about, now?

'I don't know what you mean.'

Boroja drew closer to her. She saw the deep bags under his eyes, the dark-grey shadows in the hollows of his cheeks. 'Can he get us out of this? I want him to. I want him to get us out of this.' His hands were shaking, and he clamped them together.

'You seem to be unwell,' Avati said firmly. 'Speak not of such–'

'I am very scared.'

The worst of all things to admit. A career-ending, *life-ending* thing to admit. What was he playing at?

'I believe you are too. I believe we all are. Something is wrong. We have to *get out*.'

'Be silent.' She felt her fingers stray instinctively towards her sidearm. He'd be a loss, if she had to do it, but better that than a collapse of command on the bridge. 'No more such talk, or I'll call for the armsmen. What are you thinking?'

He suddenly looked horrified, blinked hard, and something like his old resolve returned. 'I don't know,' he mumbled, staring back at her. 'Throne, I don't know any more.' He tried to still the shaking. 'The augurs. Some of them, it seems like they're working, but then I see what they're showing us... Feedback effects, I guess. Strange ones. But we're not in the warp now, are we?'

Avati reached out with both hands, held him by his arms, not gently. 'You have to recover yourself. Now. I can't stay, the bridge must be commanded. You understand?'

He nodded.

'Do not look at the lenses,' she said. 'Get servitors to check the feeds. We can route them to the terminals when we're ready to move again.'

Again, a mute nod.

'The captain's right. We reach the star-speakers, we gauge our position. Failing that, we get the engines restored and strike out for the fleet. All we have to do is hold it together for a little longer. He's saved us twice – is that not enough for you?'

Even as the words left her mouth, the rogue thought entered her head. Did Kiastros really save the ship? Or had he got lucky? Did he run, back at the muster? Did he break before the order came? Perhaps there never was an order – maybe the fight at U-93 had lasted for hours longer than any one of them knew about. And if that was the case, did Kiastros even *want* to get the astropaths back? Was he just set on running now, out into the void, far enough away that he could escape Hekaon and Jovanjiar? Was *he* the one frustrating everything? Was he the poison?

'There are... things I can do,' said Boroja, looking chastened.

'Very good. See that you do them.'

He shuffled off. Her eyes followed him all the way back to his terminal. His deterioration was alarming. He might crack. Not something she would be able to check on – she had her own duties to attend to. It was hard enough to keep her own concentration, to keep her resolve. For all that she'd snapped at him, Boroja was right about one thing – a cold fear underpinned everything now, an unnatural sensation that couldn't just be explained by lack of sleep and sustained tension.

*We have to get out.*

That was true enough. They just needed to keep their heads down now, try to remember their courage. It was a shame the Sister was fully occupied – she found herself, quite against character, wishing to share a few words with her. Maybe even a prayer. Or a drink.

Hells, what was happening to them all?

She walked back to her terminal, pulled up her seat, plugged in the few operating jacks. Just one of her lenses was functional, and she cranked up the secondary power feed for it. Weak green light leaked out from the obsidian surface, and the control panel glowed into flickering life.

It took a while for her to locate the audex data – everything was sluggish. Even when she'd pulled up the right slot, the feed was just as it had been during the action – a nonsense of static, roaring, clicks and snaps. That was the distance working against them, the extreme range the system runner had been acting at, combined with the failure of the main augurs. She listened to a few more minutes, and felt her heart sink. Nothing much of use there. Whatever the pilots of the Inquisition craft had been trying to communicate, it hadn't got through. It sounded like they'd been trying hard, though – the logs were full of failed hails and repeat transmissions. None of them could be made sense of – they were just like the distorted images Boroja had seen on the scopes.

She cycled forward a little, right up against the moment when the craft was destroyed. Some limited astrogation data showed her that it had been running in close to the enemy's underside then, doing what it could to evade the hurricane of fire coming its way in order to train its own formidable guns where they would do most damage. She had to hand it to them – they had been ferociously brave and impeccably skilled. Not many of her crew could have pulled off those manoeuvres with a ship that size, nor inflicted the level of damage they had done during the short engagement.

The last few moments of intact audex were the worst of all, all but drowned out by the ambient noises of combat on the runner's bridge. She got snatches of human voices, then ear-shredding wails and the sound of something exploding. She was about to eject the cartridge and give it up when suddenly, out of the blue, the worst of the interference cleared. For a second or two, no longer, she got some speech. A man's voice, shouting over something else, angry, or maybe outraged, or maybe terrified.

The words weren't Gothic. They weren't any of the battle-cants she knew. Some private Inquisitorial dialect, maybe one they used all the time, maybe just employed during combat. They couldn't help themselves, she thought, wrapped up in their endless layers of secrets, engaging in such pointless security measures even as their ship was finally blown into fragments by the enemy. Nothing in her archives would be able to translate those words. Only one man on board could do so, and there was of course no guarantee that he would.

She unplugged herself, isolated the one intelligible fragment, shunted it onto a data-slug. Then she unclipped it and deactivated the console.

Would he help her? Would it accomplish anything, even if he did?

Nothing for it now, she thought, getting up with some trepidation. Kiastros had given her her orders – it was time to speak to il-Moro again.

## Chapter Twenty-Two

**UNWORTHY THOUGHTS**

**TICK, TOCK**

**THE AURA**

Kiastros walked the whole distance from the command bridge to the Navigator's demesne. Not something he did often – it took too long, and the private mag-train was quicker – but he no longer trusted the power supplies or the track integrity. Besides, walking the corridors of his kingdom allowed him to see the full state of things. The interiors were all dark now, a permanent gloom with all levels locked into an unchanging noctis-shift. The illumination, such as it was, came either from the still-flickering combat panels or from portable sulphur units rigged up by the work-gangs. The noises in those places had once been orderly, sequential, a tick-tock of shifts changing and maintenance being performed. Now it was haphazard, hampered by the conditions and the fatigue of the ratings. Many of them failed to recognise him as he passed by, sweltering over their labours, their sweaty faces lit up by arc welders or handheld augurs. You could be court-martialled for failing to make the aquila to a senior officer, but he had no intention of enforcing those precepts now. Those who did spot him hurried to salute, and he returned the gesture. Their faces were the worst of all to witness – harried, uncertain, exhausted.

Many had taken their jerkins off in the heat. Others, strangely enough, had put on more layers. He saw trembling hands, heard wheezing rebreathers, smelled sweat and blood in equal shares. Still, they were working. Out of a sense of duty, out of habit, they still obeyed the gangmasters, still put in the shifts. That was something. Mutiny was rare on an Imperial Navy vessel, as everyone knew the consequences of it, but it had been known to happen from time to time. The causes were always the same – military setbacks, long periods of privation, insufficient attention from the captain. This was a dangerous time. Once the immediate peril had passed, when they had weapons and shields again and functioning engines, he'd need to speak to Garrock, check that the lower decks weren't beginning to smoulder.

Still. You had to remain confident. Confident enough to walk without an escort, carrying only your ceremonial sidearm, walking like you owned the place – which you did, technically, under Naval ordinances, subject to the usual caveat that nothing in the Imperium was ever owned by anyone save the architect of it all who sat on the Throne.

And then the strangest thing of all was that it was hard to find the way. He'd been up and down those corridors a thousand times, knew them just as well as he knew all the upper decks, and yet the bulkheads seemed to have moved, or the intersections had the wrong number of doors, or the blank metal plates in the walls had an odd sheen to them that reflected his face back at him.

Just the faulty light, probably. Or his growing levels of heavy exhaustion. He found his way in the end, sticking to his memorised route, but it took longer than it should have done, and by the time he was up into Santalina's antechambers he was sweating even more, his shirt damp and his collar sticky. The ever-present grind of the engines reverberated in his ears, louder than it should have been, making it hard to think. Having some sleep would be good – it felt as though it had been far too long – but the prospect of that was now very distant indeed.

'What is happening here?' he asked Santalina, entering, sitting opposite her.

She looked a little better than he felt. Old, though. Old and worn down and as ready to crack as the ship's battered spine.

'Bad dreams,' she said. 'Everyone's having them. Including me. Tea?'

He nodded, reached out as she offered him a cup. The china – priceless – was chipped. He'd never noticed that before.

'I don't dream,' he said, cradling the saucer in a sweaty palm. 'Never have. Not got the imagination for it.'

Santalina smiled. 'You have plenty of imagination, Iannis. For void combat, if nothing else.'

That was probably true. A lifetime of trajectories and geometry, of logistics and cartolith readings. For so long, he'd not wanted anything else. No real aspirations for a greater command, whatever talk of battleships and flagships he'd let himself slip into, and certainly no desire to be shunted upward to fleet headquarters. Just to remain at the helm of a ship, a fighting ship, to see his time out in a progression of victories. Nothing worse than dying on the soil of a strange world, he'd always believed. Better to go out on the bridge, with flame and fury around you, beckoning the embrace of the frigid dark as you dealt vengeance to the enemy.

But it didn't seem enough, just then. He had the nagging feeling that if he stopped for too long now, if he took his eye off the hundreds of linked catastrophes that ran through the ship, the doubt would come flooding back. Not about survival – no one in service expected to live forever – just that it had all been, when all was said and done, a... waste.

He took a sip. These thoughts were unworthy, and he hated that he couldn't stop thinking them.

'I do not know where my mind is,' he said, shaking his head a little. 'I barely recognise myself in the mirror.'

Santalina leaned forward, reached out to touch his elbow. 'The ship is wounded,' she said earnestly. 'Something has got inside. It needs to be cut out.'

Kiastros looked at her. 'You mean the intruder? Every warrior I can spare is hunting it.'

'Maybe. Did we send a survey team to where the Space Marines were killed? Do we know what they were trying to do there?'

He'd meant to follow up on that. So many things to keep on top of, so much slippage. The place was still sealed off, as far as he knew. Depressurised, rad-stained, too dangerous to enter.

'The tech-priests were needed on the warp drive-trains,' he said, feeling as though it was an excuse. 'I have a preliminary report I need to read, but nothing conclusive.'

'They got on board, they started to build something. A weapon, I was told. But have you ever come across the like? A boarding party that needed to build its own weapon? Would they not, I don't know, simply have brought one with them?'

'Maybe it was something new,' Kiastros said, sitting further back into the armchair, letting the Navigator's hand fall away. 'Something we've not seen before. They're forever contriving new devilry.'

'Indeed so. But, when you can, I'd send some priests back to that site. I fear we've missed something.'

He felt the first flush of indignation. What did she expect him to do? The entire crew were stretched taut, all the priests, all the ratings, all running on fumes, all desperately trying to get the enginarium back into working order, the shield generators working, the augur arrays reconfigured. Every single soul was occupied, every servant of Mars buried up to their metallic neck in wiring and valve-casings, and still it wasn't enough to get them warp-ready again.

'It started with the Inquisition ship,' he muttered. 'That's what bent us off course. They have something with them. That's the poison.' He found himself wringing his hands together. 'But I can work on that. Avati will soften him up, I'll make the call. In the meantime, I need to know what you saw. Two ships, you said? In the warp. I killed one. Is there another?'

Santalina gave a delicate shrug. 'I don't know. And I won't until we get back into the Seethe.' She tapped her forehead. 'Out here, I only see what you wretches see. They're like dreams to me, my sessions in the sphere – hard to recall once they're over.'

'But you must have seen–'

'It's like I told your little helper – it's not cut and dried.'

'She's an officer of the–'

'They're just stories. Tales spun in the dark. You interpret them, you try to unpick past from future from present. I saw eddies in the empyrean. Ships? Possible. Some other entity? Maybe, and you should not ask me what such a thing might be. Perhaps you ended the thing I saw with your ingenuity. Perhaps I shall gaze back into the other realm in due course, and see *more* hunters coming for us.' She gave him a sympathetic smile. 'I say this not to alarm you. Just to tell you the truth. I can scry for you, but only in generalities. I can peer into the dark for you, but can only guess at what the visions mean.'

Kiastros felt his heart sink. It would have been good, for once, to get some confirmation of a solid victory in at least one area. 'And you still sense nothing from Ortuyo?'

'Nothing. Maybe that also waits for the warp – all things are amplified there.'

'We need him.'

'If he lives.'

'Something must be intact in there. Some transcribed documents, something we can use.'

'You think they were writing anything at all, when their spire was being melted down around them?'

Kiastros shrugged. 'We have to chance it.'

Santalina took a sip of her tea, and he noticed how her hands shook as she replaced the cup in the saucer. 'Chance it. Take the risk.' She smiled weakly, as if apologising for it, or maybe in scorn at her own frailty. 'But I fear the warp now, Iannis. Now, at last, I fear it. After a lifetime of plying its depths. So I'm definitely too old for this, too ruined. Even if you get your news of where to go, where to run to, you'll have to find someone else to pilot your ship, for I can no longer do it.'

He looked at her for a moment, shocked. She'd never spoken like that before, not even during the worst storms of the past, the ones that felt as if they might smash the ship apart and send them all whirling down into the hereafter. 'Just one more passage,' he said. 'As soon as we're strong enough. That's all I ask.'

'Oh, you'll get that. But then it's time for new blood. I can't afford to be afraid. None of us can, but me especially.'

He put his saucer down. 'What happened?'

'I looked into it. The Seethe. My true home. And I couldn't go in. Couldn't cross the boundary.' Her voice was soft, no trace of the sardonic assurance that was usually there. 'If there is a curse on us, then it's got to me too.'

'Nonsense. We all feel the strain.'

'No, this is different.'

She reached up to adjust her bandana, and for a horrible moment Kiastros thought she might take it off. Thankfully, all she did was adjust the trim, smoothing it over some new-looking scar tissue.

'I will not look into the deep Seethe, not now. I will not go to the Eye. I cannot. The fear is... too great.'

Santalina, like Ortuyo, was different. She had certain dispensations. The mutants were needed – both reviled and venerated, they were the essential components necessary for survival in the void. In any case, Kiastros couldn't summon up much animus. He felt much the same, if he was honest – a kind of churn of emotion that just wouldn't settle down. One moment he'd be angry, the next despairing. Everyone was the same now, afflicted by a sickness that fermented and bubbled beneath the skin.

'Make no hasty judgements,' he said, trying as best he could to sound reassuring. 'Something strange is aboard – when we clear the decks, cut it out, get back to the fleet, you will feel different.'

She smiled at him again, the kind of tolerant expression that indicated both gratitude and a clear certainty that he was entirely wrong. 'So you say.'

'One more journey. It will have to happen soon – as soon as the drives are operable. Can you do it? When I call on you?'

She laughed. It was a girlish sound, wild, as if she'd decided to throw everything away.

'For you, Iannis, I will do so. No one else. So work hard. Get us running again, cut out the sickness. I can smell death in the corridors, and the stench gets worse by the hour. Tick, tock. Restore the drives. We do not have much time.'

Now she alarmed him. She clearly needed to rest.

He got up. 'My thanks. We shall speak again soon – maybe attempt some sleep.'

'No time. No time. But thank you. Tick, tock.'

There was nothing much else to say. He turned on his heel, more perturbed than he had been when he'd entered. As he reached the door, he heard muffled noises from behind, but whether she was laughing or sobbing he could not tell. He didn't turn back, just kept on walking.

The elevator shafts weren't working. Avati punched the controls, and got nothing back but a crackle of shorted electrics. Strange – those shafts ran down the very centre of the ship, a long way from the damaged outer sections. The lumens strobed overhead, eerie noises echoed down the twisting corridors.

*Falling apart*, she thought grimly, heading instead to the deep stairwells and punching the entry code into the security doors. It was even darker inside the wells, and she turned on the lights at her helm seal. Everyone she'd passed was still in full void armour, despite the end of the action. No one trusted the integrity of the world around them any more, it seemed.

She trudged down the metal steps, keeping to the outer edge of the shaft. The stairs ran around the four edges, a long succession of plasteel stages hung from the bare rockcrete walls. The smell was appalling – more than the usual chem-stinks from the deeper levels, now a kind of rotten sludge, like overripe food. Something must have spilled, down in the storage hoppers, shaken loose during the combat, now filtering up through the airways.

She halted, hearing someone call out for her from above. She didn't make out the words, just a strangled cry of something or other. She looked up, her helm beams sweeping over the dirty rockcrete.

Nothing. No one there. She found herself feeling cold again, colder than she had on the bridge, and her heart thumped in her chest.

'Anyone there?' she called out firmly.

Silence, save for the low grind of the ship's life support humming away from the deeps. She smacked a hand against her helm's earpiece, checked for anything loose in the casing.

She turned back, going a little faster now, cursing herself for letting her imagination get the better of her. The ship was full of odd noises – it always had been. Spleed and Boroja had allowed themselves to crack under pressure – she would not. Still, as she passed down the long flights, she could hear her breathing in her helm, faster than it should have been.

Eventually she reached the hangar level, hit the exit controls. The doors didn't move, and a twinge of anxiety pulsed through her. She hit them again. This time the blast doors split apart, jerked open on their rails. The chamber on the far side was lit, at least, and smelled somewhat less bad. Despite herself, she felt a wave of relief crossing the threshold, seeing two ratings attending to some faulty system behind a wall panel, hearing the clunk of a servitor down the long corridor to her right. Things were still working, orders were still being followed. Why was she so damned jumpy?

It was a shorter walk to the hangars themselves. Normally the approaches would have been busy, full of engineering gangs attending to the shuttle crews and making sure the attack craft were fuelled and prepped. Now the antechambers were subdued, as gloomy as everywhere else, the staff stripped out and sent to attend the hundred crisis zones burning all across the ship. Most, she knew, had been seconded to the warp drive halls in a frantic effort to get the overloaded engines back into service. She didn't envy them that work – that was a realm governed entirely by the tech-priests, and they worked their serfs without pity in order to keep their sacred altars intact. What remained up here was a skeleton crew, kept running from task to task without pause. No wonder the electrics were failing, and no wonder the few glimpses she caught of their faces were so haunted and strung out. And they were, comparatively speaking, the lucky ones.

She approached the hangar doors, signalled to the armsmen

on guard, and they opened up and let her in. This time she wasn't heading for the ship-berths – the occupants of those were all gone now – but to the warren of isolation halls running alongside. These were all heavily secured and designed to act as quarantine zones when needed. Heavy blast panels encased the entire structure, as well as bio-screens and psy-wards, the same kind of extensive shielding that the astropaths' spire used. Normally the chambers were kept empty and under wraps, only opened up in extreme circumstances on the captain's orders. Their guests from the Inquisition had been happy enough to take up occupancy, though – they were no doubt used to such abodes.

The entrance to the first hall was gunmetal-grey and warded by a single doorway over ten yards high. Two of the Inquisition's black-armoured soldiers stood in front of it, weapons drawn. Between them stood the obese man Avati had noticed earlier. His skin was also black, almost purple, his eyes a livid pink. He wore dark robes that pooled liquidly over the folds of his body. When he spoke, he exposed a dry tongue flickering across thin lips.

'You are here to tell us our ship has been destroyed,' the man said.

'As was always possible,' Avati said. 'I wish to speak to the interrogator.'

'What purpose will that serve? He knew the chances.'

'The captain wished to pass on his thanks for the assistance, and convey all we know of the vessel's final movements.'

'I can pass that on.'

'He was insistent that I speak to the interrogator in person.'

The obese man thought about that. Perhaps he had some clandestine comms – it looked like his right eyelid twitched a little. Throne, they were all so paranoid. This went far beyond the usual dislike of strangers, the usual security precautions. They were scared. They were isolated, locked in, and they had no means of getting out. Her first impressions were reinforced, if anything – these people were stranded, without a plan, attempt-ing to hold things together until they could find a safe harbour. When they did so, when they made contact with others of their order, that was when the danger really began. A true inquisitor could command that a ship be destroyed without a thought, and the fleet would never make a fuss. Or the officers might all be taken away for interrogation, or mind-wiped, or...

'Very well,' said the man. 'You will come with me.'

The doors to the isolation hall creaked open and the man beckoned for her to enter. Avati went inside, conscious that the soldiers were shadowing her with their lasguns. It was like being taken hostage. The doors slid closed behind her.

Once inside the hall, it became clear that the retinue had taken a large amount of material from their ship – high piles of supply crates, ration boxes, weapon racks and power supplies. Heavy machinery stood up against the far wall, whole banks of it, all linked together with cabling and gently ticking over. There was furniture, too – ornate and expensive, wildly out of place among the survival gear and rough-cut surroundings of the chamber. More soldiers stood on guard amongst it all, blank visors totally unreflective, blunt-muzzled guns held ready for use. Other members of the retinue sat idly on the armchairs, or made adjustments to the dials on the machines, or stood in pairs further down the long hall, murmuring softly to themselves.

Avati took it all in, assessing numbers, assessing positions. The troops were clearly superior to Garrock's armsmen in equipment, and most likely in training too. At least eight of them were present – two outside the door, six in this chamber, likely more further in. The obese man didn't look particularly powerful, but you could never tell – he might be a psyker or some kind of esoteric weapons specialist. Five of the others looked potentially dangerous – the woman with jewels for eyes who wore sophisticated-looking body armour under a diaphanous outer garment, a squat man with a bristling beard who had a pair of nasty-looking laspistols at his belt, a heavily armoured figure almost as imposing as the Battle Sister, and two lithe killers who had the look of death-cult assassins. Some of them looked at her as she entered, some didn't. They looked listless, bored by their self-imposed confinement, eager to stretch their muscles properly. Some of that, Avati knew, was due to the psy-dampeners built into every wall of the section – they tended to muffle everything, emotions, passions, all the human stuff. Someone – maybe Kuhl? – had once warned her not to spend more than a day or two in the isolation chambers, lest she end up morbidly depressed. Did the retinue know the danger? Had anyone briefed them?

The obese man led her through another door that led to a smaller room beyond. This one was also packed with material taken from the system runner. In the centre of the heaps of crates and storage units stood the interrogator. He looked up from some device he'd been studying and gave her a sour-edged smile.

'He sent you running down here again, then, did he?'

'The captain sends his apologies – he is detained with urgent matters.'

'Of course he is. So what did he wish to convey? His apologies for the destruction of my ship?'

The aggression was, just as before, tedious. But the interrogator seemed more assured this time, perhaps simply due to running out of choices to make. They had no choice but to remain in position, guarding the last fragment of territory they controlled, keeping whatever secrets they had brought on board with them.

'No apologies, interrogator. Only gratitude, and explanations.

The captain thought you might appreciate a debrief on the action.'

Il-Moro's eyes narrowed. 'A debrief.'

'Your pilots performed exceptionally. Without their sacrifice, we would not be speaking here now.'

'They did their duty, no doubt. But I still hear no sign of the warp drives being kindled again. We are becalmed, are we not?'

'We have been very badly damaged – the result of two major actions.'

'We must move again.'

'We shall, just as soon as the engines are capable of it. You will recall, I am sure, that we do not have astropaths. If we cannot remedy that, the captain will have to plot a course without direction from the fleet. He is making preparations for that, among many other tasks. It is not straightforward.'

Il-Moro gave an irritated sigh. 'Very well. Inform us of the heroism of our pilots. Tell us all we need to know.'

She did so. The limited augur records prevented her from showing him just how expertly the system runner had weaved through close-packed shell-fire before launching pinpoint strikes at key locations on the enemy ship. Post-engagement analysis had underscored the step change in capability between the Inquisitorial weapon systems and the standard Navy equipment, giving them the slender advantage they had relied on to finish the enemy off.

As Avati spoke, she surreptitiously studied her surroundings further. There was only one way into the chamber, though multiple doorways led off further inside. The retinue didn't seem to have altered the interior arrangements at all, save for filling the space up with the gear they'd taken off their ship. Individually, the interrogator's people were no doubt fearsome, but there were not many of them. They were vulnerable, if Kiastros was serious about applying pressure.

Il-Moro said little. Every so often, his attention seemed to wander. His heavy eyes would flicker over to another doorway, as if there was something inside it that he feared but also couldn't stop thinking about. That door was open by a crack, and a soft golden light bled around its edges. That light didn't look like something the ship's lumen banks would emit – more like candlelight. The strangest thing was that, the longer she went on, the more Avati wanted to look at it too. For the first time in a long time, she didn't feel chilled to the bone. For the first time in a long time, her levels of anxiety seemed to ease slightly.

Strange. Everything was strange.

'Tell your captain I thank him for this information,' il-Moro said eventually. 'But now, unless there is anything else...'

'It is in there, isn't it?' Avati murmured, the words slipping out unbidden.

The interrogator stiffened. 'That has nothing to do with you.'

But it did. It had everything to do with her. The entire ship was creaking and flexing with eerie energies. Men and women were seeing things, being driven to sickness. And now, here, she felt the warmth of it, like some primordial campfire – hidden, powerful.

'You must tell him what it is,' she said, looking il-Moro directly in the eye. 'If you even know. You cannot endanger everything, not without at least–'

'Enough! Dare not make such demands again, lieutenant, or you shall discover just what I can do, and with impunity.' He controlled himself. 'For there is nothing else to say. We must stick to the course, return to the fleet when we can. That is all.'

The fool. He had no idea what danger he was in. In normal times, perhaps, no one would dare question his authority – he would have been perfectly safe even if he had no weapons and no retainers. But the air was charged, electric with a kind of febrile fatigue, so these were far from normal times.

Avati didn't protest, though, but took the data-slug from her uniform jacket. 'This is the audex we got from your ship. A small intelligible fragment only – the rest is just noise. The speech is in some kind of dialect. It would be greatly appreciated if you would inform us of what was being said.'

'It was internal speech. Private for a reason.'

'There is much we don't know. They were out of comms range for the entire action, and our augurs were blind. We still have no concrete data on the ship we destroyed – its origin, its allegiance. More vessels may come for us, so even small pieces of data can be useful.'

Il-Moro looked at the slug distastefully. In truth, Avati didn't really hold out much hope either – it wasn't clear what purpose any of it would serve now. Still, Kiastros had been insistent.

'Savant,' il-Moro said, beckoning the obese robed man over. 'Perhaps you can assist.'

The man waddled close, breathing heavily. He took up the slug, inserted it into a slot in his neck, twitched a flabby cheek. Avati heard the faint hiss of the audex playing, the shouted words.

Then the savant began to translate.

'No, I do not–' he began, affecting something of the original speaker's agitation in a truly unsettling manner. 'It can't be... Pull out! Cease fire! Oh, Holy Throne, it can't be! Hells! We have all been–'

That was it. The savant removed the data-slug with a wince, handed it back to Avati.

'Why were they so alarmed?' Avati asked, looking at il-Moro.

Despite himself, the interrogator looked perturbed. 'This was the last thing you picked up before their destruction?'

Avati looked at him steadily. Combat stress was always a factor. Members of the bridge crew on the *Judgement of the Void* had buckled under pressure. They all had.

But she couldn't get the terror in the man's voice out of her mind now. Now that she knew what the words meant, the wrongness of it was amplified.

'They were horrified,' she said carefully. 'Why might they have been horrified?'

The savant withdrew, giving il-Moro a significant look, and that seemed to pull the interrogator back into focus.

'It was a warship of the Great Enemy. They were at close quarters at the end. Perhaps you have never been so close to one of their ships, lieutenant, even in all your years of service. They are horrific machines.'

All true. But not enough. Not nearly enough.

'Just as you say,' Avati murmured, stowing the data-slug again. 'And I am sorry to have brought it for you to listen to – they were your crew. They fought bravely.'

Il-Moro barely responded. His surface disdain concealed something else now – more uncertainty, more doubt – and it was clear that the time had come for her to leave. That suited her fine. She had got what she had come for, knew where the cargo was stowed, had scoped out the retinue.

As she left the complex, though, passing back out past the guards and into the less stultifying air of the hangar beyond, it was hard to get the words out of her mind.

*It can't be... Pull out!*

Why had they been so appalled? What had they seen out there?

She began her long trek back to the bridge, and all she could hear was the panic. The terror.

*Hells! We have all been–*

What, though? What had they seen?

# Chapter Twenty-Three

**NOT AS A MACHINE**

**UNWORTHY THOUGHTS**

**CARTOGRAPHY**

Isobel felt the sweat under her armour. She could smell herself somehow, despite all the pungent aromas clustering around her. It was depressing, to be so filthy. No doubt her more overtly pious Sisters would have scorned the notion, believing as they did that the body was somehow beneath caring about, save as a weapon in the Emperor's service.

Still, for all the privation she was glad to be where she was, and not stuck on some Sororitas vessel. She liked most of her fellow warriors, deeply loved a few, but there was only so much time you could spend listening to homilies on the perfection of service, or the righteousness of combat, or the frustration of never being quite devoted enough. That was the way they were made, of course – psycho-conditioned and controlled and endlessly trained to the point where worship of the Throne was the only thing they ever thought about from dawn to dusk – but you could still regret it. You could wish that just a few of them might crack a smile from time to time, or think about reading a book that wasn't some kind of theological treatise, or light up a lho-stick and tell stories of past campaigns.

She often wondered why she wasn't quite cut from the same mould. She'd undergone all the same training – or most of it, at any rate. She'd passed all the trials, satisfied the rigorous examination of the canonesses and served with distinction. Rumour was that a full Battle Sister had never turned to the enemy, so powerful were the strictures placed on them all – even the Space Marines, who underwent similar levels of scrutiny, couldn't claim such a record. For some reason, though, her essential cast of mind had never changed. She'd continued to relish her food, to enjoy her drink, to crack a jest with the troops when she felt like it. Perhaps due to her vocation, she was never tempted by the more fanatical strains within the Sisterhood, and found the very existence of penitential machinery an embarrassing degree of overkill. You could maintain a devout species of faith without all that, she continued to believe. You could devote yourself to the Throne, not as a machine, but as a human. Surely, in the end, that was the point of it all. To preserve humanity, whatever the cost. And humans, whatever the upper echelons of the convents might choose to believe, had bodies. They laughed, they ate, they drank. And, right now, they sweated.

'Damned hard work,' she grunted, edging upwards a few inches, feeling her boots scrape on the ledge below.

The Master of Engines, Kuhl, came up close behind her. The two of them were wedged in tight, squeezing their way through a narrow gap between collapsed deck structures. It felt more like exploring some twisting cave system than negotiating a ship, inching precariously between colossal rock formations as ancient buried river courses tinkled and cascaded down into the deeps.

'That it is,' Kuhl panted, working hard to follow Isobel up. Although she was of smaller stature, her environment suit was far less flexible than Isobel's armour, and a few times she'd had to be physically hauled up through the narrowest of gaps.

Isobel finally managed to drag herself up through a serrated opening, twist her head around. Her helm lights exposed a narrow chamber, just a few yards across but with enough of a floor to make a suitable place to catch their breath. The walls and roof looked virtually organic where the metals had melted, and glistened in the complete darkness. As the twin beams flickered across the surfaces, the undulations seemed to twist and wriggle, which was an eerie effect to witness.

She pushed up, getting her body onto what had once been the chamber's main deck, and reached back to pull Kuhl through the gap. From deeper down, she could hear the clank and shuffle of the priests and ratings following them up. They were hauling heavier gear, so went more slowly – the two of them had a few moments before the climb would have to continue. Isobel reached for the flask at her belt, pulled her helm off, took a swig. She offered some to Kuhl, but she declined. Maybe too laborious to get her own rebreather out of the way.

Isobel looked around her, the view now unfiltered by her helm's ever-present targeting overlays. The impression of a natural subterranean environment was even stronger, though the swirls and stratification of the molten metal and plasteel were unsettling somehow.

She ran a check on her armour's locator. 'What deck are we on?'

Kuhl consulted her handheld scanner. Then checked again. 'That's impossible.' She looked up. 'Something's wrong with this thing. It says we're already up into the foundation halls. Right under the choir galleries.'

Isobel looked up at the roof. 'I can't tell where this is. Could it have fused together?'

'No, we're still in the unshielded sectors.' Kuhl drew an electro-knife from her belt, activated it, cut a long slash in the wall beside her. The blade sunk deep, whirring through the mass of material before she withdrew it again. 'Wouldn't be able to do that in the spire. All triple-shielded adamantine plating.'

Isobel looked at the impression she'd made. Something was oozing out of it. For a chilling moment, she thought the metal nodules around it were shivering. She blinked, and saw the trickle of oil glisten.

'My locator agrees with your scanner,' Isobel said warily. 'That we're higher up.' She looked around again. 'But we're clearly not.'

She clambered up a little further, using the irregular surface of the curved walls for footholds. A yard above her, a crevice opened up. It was large enough for her to pass through unimpeded, though the priests with their cutting gear might have work to do to follow. She donned her helm again, peered up into the gap. The reticules in her targeter struggled to lock on, cycling back and forth. Dimly, in the far distance, she picked up grainy impressions of something larger, some great dark structure still intact within the mess and the ruins. That was more than thirty yards up, the way choked with refuse and the tangle of twisted beams and struts.

It was hard to focus. Isobel blinked, tried again. The shadows crowded in closer, seeming to grow, to slither madly around the edge of her vision. She felt a hot flush, a sickening tingle that ran down her spine.

'Something's wrong here,' she muttered. She took some static picts, then dropped back down to where Kuhl waited. 'These readings make no sense. It's like... we're both too high and too low.'

'I'm getting very high rads,' said Kuhl. 'The equipment gets scrambled. You saw something up there?'

'The first intact structure. We can reach it, I think.'

But she felt no enthusiasm, only a strangely overpowering

sense of dread. She drew her own blade – a dark-metal sword forged by her own people bearing engraved wards of protection. The runes in the blade-face were dull, almost sullen. They had always been a comfort to her before; now they looked dead, burned-out.

'Though I do not think going further is wise,' she said.

'We have to,' Kuhl said.

'There's nothing left up there.'

The Master of Engines became agitated. 'But you can see a way up. To the base of the spire. It's intact.'

'It is. But you can feel it too, yes? This is all wrong. They were mutants. Psykers. If they were dead, there can be... effects. I don't think it's rads. I think it's something deeper.'

To withdraw felt like an abdication of duty, something she was loath to do. But equally her sense of wrongness rarely led her awry. The physical danger could be countered, but if something had gone haywire during the spire's destruction, if the mutants who dwelt in it were all dead, fused into the psy-reactive structure of their realm, then unpredictable effects could have been generated. The uncanniness of her current surroundings was sufficient reason to go carefully.

'We were given an order,' said Kuhl, still visibly uncomfortable at the prospect of pulling back. 'If Ortuyo lives–'

'With what you have seen here, in this place, do you really believe that? It was worth the attempt, but I do not see any value in pursuing this, not without proper reinforcement.'

'Then what do you counsel?'

'Seal it off. All of it. Report our failure to the captain, recommend he commissions an external survey when he can. We make use of the Space Marine, the rest of Captain Garrock's forces, once they are available.'

Kuhl pondered that. 'He won't like it. He won't agree to it.'

'Ask him anyway.'

Still she hesitated. It was true that the comms had been down for a long time, but some flickers of life had recently re-emerged on Isobel's own systems. It might be possible. It was worth a try.

Finally, grudgingly, Kuhl nodded, withdrew, activated her channel to the captain. Isobel remained where she was, giving her some space but listening all the same.

'That is correct, lord captain,' Kuhl was saying, after explaining the situation. 'The honoured Sister believes that withdrawal is the prudent course. Yes, withdrawal. I explained that. On grounds of unpredictable effects, the further we go. I did not ask her. Yes, I understand that. Yes, I said that. Yes. Very well. By your will, lord captain.'

She closed the link.

'You heard all that, I suppose?'

'What did he say?'

'That we're to press on. That restoring our astropathic capability is his highest priority. That if you wish to withdraw, then that is your decision, but that the drill-teams must break in.'

Isobel considered that for a moment. Kuhl's defiance and commitment to her orders was commendable, of course. In other circumstances, she'd have applauded it.

She looked up again. The crevice, with its tortured landscape of fluid metal, seemed to taunt her, to beckon her on and up. That was her imagination, of course. The strange effects that radiated throughout the entire ship, the ones that even the officers were beginning to acknowledge – the Inquisition, they said, bringing something on board that defied reality. Or the intruder, still alive and active as far as they knew, poisoning everything as it wormed closer to the bridge. Or the machine built by the boarding party, supposedly destroyed and sealed off but possibly active after all.

Or this place. This strange, tortured site. If the contagion came from here, it had to be cut out. Why was she even hesitating? Why did she stay her hand?

*I wish to hold a blade,* she'd always said.

'Of course we must not withdraw,' she told Kuhl. 'The captain is right – it must be addressed. My apologies. I don't know what I was thinking.'

She sheathed her blade again, unwilling to look on its dull and unresponsive surface any more.

'We should gather in force before we break into the spire, though,' she said firmly. 'We cut into a holding chamber, bring up all the priests and the armed ratings. The Martians will serve well if we encounter anything untoward, the shotguns can handle the rest.'

'Agreed,' said Kuhl, sounding oddly relieved for a woman who'd just committed herself to such a risky operation. 'I shall instruct Arfo-5 to accelerate the deployment of his teams.'

Isobel didn't look up again. She'd be climbing up the narrow shaft soon enough, and had no desire to look into its maw a third time. Nothing about this made her feel good, everything screamed at her to pull out, head back, send someone else to investigate.

It was temptation. The whispering voice of fear, the sly promise of safety at the expense of courage. Everything the Order had trained her against, and which the least of her Sisters would have quashed in an instant. Pious and dreary they might have been, but perhaps this was a reminder of why they had to be like that. And why, for all her bemusement at them, she had always failed to measure up.

You couldn't stay in the apothecarion forever – the Emperor's service involved more than stitching up wounds.

'When we are gathered ready, I shall be first in,' Isobel told Kuhl, pushing the seal down on her helm-gorget and making ready to climb again. 'A little faith. That is what we shall need.'

The charts no longer made sense to him. The more Kiastros stared at them, the more the symbols and the swirls of trajectory markers seemed to detach from the parchment and swim before his eyes.

He sat back, rubbed his knuckles into his eye sockets, then stretched his arms out wide. His head was hammering, his muscles tingled. He felt feverish – or was that just the heat? Why couldn't they do something about the damned heat?

He opened his eyes again. The long map table stretched away, just as before, covered in layers of heavy parchment and attended by the dozen or so scholiasts he'd summoned to assist him. The cartographic hall, with its high arches and shadowy aisles, sprawled off in all directions, a maze of vellum storage vaults and contemplation chapels. It was as much a cathedral as a chamber of business, which suited the kind of labour undertaken here. Mapping the stars wasn't remotely like mapping a terrestrial surface – there were no certain routes, borders or fixed points. Warp channels were marked more in hope than expectation, since a big storm could shift them from one side of a system to the other, or even many light years off course, a situation made much worse by the Cicatrix Maledictum. Every parchment surface was marked with revisions and corrections, all traced in spidery hands by the ship's scribes, overlapping and re-corrected and occasionally excised altogether. The business of collating all the relevant charts, cross-referencing them, attempting to plot a course using them – even in normal times, it was almost enough to drive a sane man mad.

He tried to focus again, to get some kind of a grip on where they were, where they might end up. They had fled the muster at U-93 in a tearing hurry, needing to get out and not worrying too much where they eventually emerged. That was always dangerous – Kiastros didn't understand the full lore of the warp, but knew well enough that intention and preparation were important. The Navigator needed to have a crystal-clear image in her mind of the destination and the insertion vector in order to get them even close to where they wanted to be. Will, desire, acuity of thought, these were all relevant factors in trying to pilot a ship through the empyrean.

Now that Santalina was losing her faculties under pressure, now that their ranged augurs were faulty and the engines themselves had been shut down for safety reasons, it was hard to even guess where they were, let alone plot a course out again. Having a functional astropathic spire would make things so much easier – they could at least find out where the remains of the fleet had headed, perhaps rendezvous with a surviving squadron and take on reinforcements. The ship needed to be cleansed, it needed to have its sickness purged from it, it needed to become... healthy again.

Kiastros stared at the parchment, took up the dividing callipers, reset the occult chronometers, signalled to the recording scribes that he was about to begin again.

'Holy Emperor of Mankind,' he muttered, just as he had done a dozen times already, 'Master of the Fleets, Compass of the Eternal Void, guide my hand and mind as I scry the deep.'

The symbols began to blur even before he'd finished. The callipers slipped, the chronometers skittered. He traced the paths given by the entabulation reference slate, running down the geometrical suggestions, trying to plot a course into calm space.

Everything took him back the way he'd come, spiralling around, shooting further out, until, with fearful inevitability, he sent the ship plunging into the Eye of Terror itself. He almost laughed out loud from the absurdity of it. That was where they'd always *wanted* to go, albeit in the company of several massed grand fleets, and now it felt like they couldn't escape it. He had a sudden image of a ball bearing rattling down a long channel, speeding up and speeding up until it plonked down the final funnel and into oblivion.

Will and intention. That was the key. He had to *want* to escape. So why couldn't he?

He scrapped the attempt, scratched out the notation on his data-slate, and wearily prepared to start again, but his comm-bead blinked.

'Avati,' he said heavily.

*'Lord captain,'* his lieutenant replied over the channel. *'Reporting back as instructed. The cargo has been transferred to the isolation halls in hangar three. I did not come into direct contact with it, but can pinpoint its location within the complex. It has some kind of aura around it – an energy field or similar – but I could not determine its size or nature.'*

Kiastros sat back in his chair, pursed his lips. 'No idea what it is?'

*'Nothing concrete. The interrogator guards it obsessively. The entire retinue seemed tense.'*

'I know the feeling. How heavily guarded?'

*'Eight Inquisitorial storm troopers, five members of the retinue with obvious combat training. They've taken equipment from their ship, but I couldn't determine what it all was. Nothing obvious in the way of major weaponry.'*

Kiastros allowed himself a weak smile. Of course there wasn't, but that didn't mean there wasn't plenty of the non-obvious kind. 'And how was he? With you, I mean?'

*'The same. On edge. But he listened to what I told him, and I briefed him on the action. He was able to decipher the battle-cant we retrieved.'*

'Anything in that?'

*'I don't know. Nothing specific. But they were badly upset by something.'*

'They were about to be destroyed.'

*'True. All the same. It wasn't nice listening.'*

Kiastros sighed. Nothing was going to be easy about this. 'Where are you now?'

'Good. Keep an eye on Boroja – I didn't like the look in his eyes. Keep the bridge together. As soon as I can plot a route out, we're going back into the warp.'

*'The engines will take it?'*

Was she pushing him? Being deliberately impertinent? Maybe it wasn't safe to send her back to the bridge. Maybe that would give her too much control. Boroja had looked almost as though he was having a breakdown, so maybe Avati saw her chance now. Santalina had tried to warn him.

Hells, it was hot. He pulled at his damp collar.

'They'll have to. Sooner we're out of realspace, the safer we'll be. Report back once all's ready.'

*'By your will.'*

He cut the link. He needed to concentrate now. He needed to get them safely away from here, pulling clear of the danger, back towards safety. He picked up the callipers again, prepared to make another set of calculations. The scholiasts picked up their auto-quills, and the rustle of parchment began.

Just as he was about to start, though, his comm-bead blinked again.

'Damn it!' he blurted, sending the callipers slipping over the marked vellum. 'What now?'

But it wasn't Avati. It was Kuhl, her transmission crackling and hard to pick up. For a few moments he could barely understand anything at all, then gradually realised she was requesting withdrawal from the astropath's spire in favour of an external survey.

Just a few hours ago, he'd have rejected such a request out of hand. Getting Ortuyo's assistance had felt essential, the first step on getting them back to safety. Now, though, events had moved on. He'd already begun the process of plotting a route into the warp, and the longer things went on without word from the spire, the less likely it became that anyone was alive in there. Perhaps it was best to leave the whole area alone.

'Sister Isobel wants to pull back?' he asked, just to be sure he was understanding. He'd liked her. Her judgement was probably sound.

*'That is correct, lord captain,'* came Kuhl's distorted voice. *'The honoured Sister believes that withdrawal is the prudent course.'*

'What, back below the fused levels?'

*'Yes, withdrawal.'*

'I gave the order to reach Ortuyo – you're saying you can't do that now?'

*'I explained that. On grounds of unpredictable effects, the further we go.'*

What in the hells was she talking about? How was that an answer to his question? He could barely make out a thing she was saying.

'What is your view?'

*'I did not ask her. Yes, I understand that. Yes, I said that.'*

This was gibberish. It was almost as though she were talking to herself.

'Listen – take her advice,' said Kiastros, giving up. 'I respect her judgement. Pull your people back, secure the area, and get down to the enginarium.'

*'Yes. Very well.'*

'Did you hear me? You have permission to stand down. The priority now is the engines, the Sister can report to me at her earliest convenience.'

*'By your will, lord captain.'*

The link cut out. For a moment, Kiastros just sat there, unable to make much sense of any of it. Then again, everything was difficult to process just then.

'Am I going mad?' he mumbled, before remembering that others were present. He looked up at the scribes, none of whom met his gaze.

This thing could be turned around. All challenges could be met, provided that sufficient faith remained. They just needed a little time, a stabilisation, a restoration of some key systems. Things had been bad before, combat had gone wrong before. It could always be fixed. They just needed a little time, a stabilisation, a restoration of...

His mind was racing. It was *so* hot.

He shook his head, tried to clear his thoughts. Then he looked at the charts again. A path would be found. The calculations would be made.

'We start again,' he said, straightening up, reaching for more instruments. 'One more hour. No longer. Throne be praised, and we will be back in the warp again soon.'

## Chapter Twenty-Four

**GHOSTS OF SHOBA**

**GETTING OUT**

**THE SECOND SHIP**

The world was a blur of darkness, a crowded visual field of soft-edged occlusion. Slowly, steadily, his sight was returning, but it wouldn't restore in time. He'd have to work with it, somehow overcome the burden and fight on regardless.

Maizad knew that Garrock doubted him. The captain was a good man, a good fighter, and had not questioned the decision, but Maizad didn't blame him for scepticism. His body was still ravaged, his senses dulled. Even his hearing was shot, resulting in a constant roar in his ears that was only getting worse. He felt rather like the ship itself – wounded, blinded, limping into combat with everything falling apart around him.

For all that, he was perfectly confident of success. The Iron Shades were all brought up on a world of perpetual night, a feral place where the populace eked out a perilous existence in trackless wastes and only ventured into the ruined cities when desperate for food and supplies. Those cities were haunted by an ancient evil, an echo of an old apocalypse, and spectres of it yet dwelt in the frigid shadows. You learned to go silently in the darkness, to use your sense of touch and taste as much as your eyesight and hearing. Even before his ascension into the Astartes, Maizad had been an accomplished killer in the dark, a shadow among shadows, learning to rely on instinct and muscle memory in places where opening your eyes could be a swift route to madness.

Those skills never left you. The Iron Shades Chapter had always recognised the value of them and had incorporated them in their combat doctrine. Even now, after many decades of service, he could still take himself back to the night-plains of Shoba, to the crumbling towers of jet-black and ice-blue, and sink into the trance-like state of total immersion. He could sense the change in the air that indicated a void or an obstacle ahead, feel the vibrations of incautious movement on the deck underfoot. The blurred images that crowded into his helm completed the picture, giving him just enough. It was sufficient. A way to fight, given the chance to get close, and that was all he'd ever needed.

Now he waited, hidden, his massive armour thrumming softly despite the heavy damage done to it. The sacred power packs and reactors had been painstakingly configured for stealth, just as always, and even now that gave him a slender advantage, something minor yet tangible.

He knew next to nothing of his enemy. Garrock had not yet laid eyes on it, only seen the trail of carnage it had gouged through the lower decks. Setting the bilge denizens on it had been a reasonable strategy, though it had resulted in fearful casualties. Maizad found himself admiring those who had launched themselves at the monster with such little hesitation. Most human troops would have run from such a horror. Maybe their miserable lives in this place, the endless damp and dark and confinement, bred the same kind of hardiness that he'd enjoyed on his home world. Something must have propelled them, made them race towards the danger rather than cower away from it.

And perhaps it had even done some good. Slowed it down a little, made it lose its way. Garrock had expressed surprise that it hadn't pushed up into the high decks by now, so maybe the combination of its wounds and the incessant attacks from the bilge-rats had played a useful part.

Or maybe there was something else. The way the corridors didn't seem to work properly, the way the sounds echoed uncannily up shafts that should not have been there. Maizad had been wounded himself, of course, and that hampered his own abilities, but either his memory had been affected or there *were* uncanny things going on in the bowels of the ship. The warp could have that effect, he knew – a breach in the Geller fields, passing through an anomaly – but they weren't in the warp at the moment. Some weaponry had psychic effects, and the Archenemy was skilled at employing it, but it wasn't clear where or how such a device could have been placed.

Whatever the cause, it was playing havoc. Captain Garrock looked to be coping reasonably, but many of his troops were not doing so well. Maizad had seen similar effects many times before, always when fighting the Archenemy. The loss of resolve, the heightened stress, moments of confusion or anger, all the weaknesses that proximity to corruption brought out. The monster they hunted was the cause, and it had to be ended. For as long as it existed, judgements would remain poor, discipline weak, tempers frayed.

Now, at least, it was cornered. Garrock's squads had run it down into a dead-end nestled between two enormous fuel tanks, a platform sunk deep into the entrails of a large and semi-derelict district of the under-engine realm. The squads of armsmen had taken up their positions at all exits, close by and in numbers. Blast doors had been lowered and welded shut, access tubes blocked up with rockcrete, crawlways demolished and cut into pieces. That funnelled the monster down towards Maizad's position, and the steady blip on his proximity scanner indicated that it had now taken the hint.

Could it detect him, waiting crouched behind an old bulkhead and poised to move? Possibly not – he'd deactivated all but his armour's essential systems, remained perfectly still, kept the disruptor on his blade doused. He would still have been emitting a heat signature, but down here, where the temperatures were all ferocious, it might be masked. And Garrock seemed sure that the monster's own equipment must have been damaged too, due to the evidence of its wounds.

Still. The enemy had many gifts, some of them completely unlinked to conventional technology. This was a fearful risk – the odds of success were poor. His entire body ached. He could feel fresh bleeding in his torso. The world was still a mass of ill-defined blotches. The roaring in his ears was, if anything, worse.

Maizad found himself smiling, his broken lips cracking. There was a purity about it. To go up against prey of unknown prowess where the balance of power could swing in either direction. All that remained was the play of fate, the way the wind blew, and cheating the spectres of their prize had always been the highest calling.

His helm display's alert pulsed briefly, silently, and that gave him the signal he needed. Garrock had seen something coming down the accessway towards his position. The captain would now be coming after it, keeping his distance, doing nothing to intervene but blocking any escape. He had about forty guns with him, which was just about enough to give him a fighting chance of holding off a determined effort to break back out. Just about.

Maizad's finger slipped onto the activation rune on his blade's hilt. It wouldn't come to that. The matter would be decided here.

Something stirred in the distance, twenty yards off, a heavy clunk on the deck. Maizad recalled his detailed survey, partly conducted by touch, of the terrain ahead. The immense horizontal curve of the two cylindrical fuel tanks enclosed an avenue just a couple of yards wide and fifty long. A broken-up and treacherous deck ran between the two sweeping walls, obstacles hanging overhead from the gantries. The room to manoeuvre was tight, the potential to become snarled up in the surrounding machinery significant. The enemy must come down the path. It would hug close to one or other of the tanks, going warily, weapon drawn. All indications were that it used a blade, not a bolter, which made sense given the surroundings and need for stealth.

Maizad inclined his head a fraction, trying to listen, to filter out the booming in his ears, judge the moment. He heard more muffled noises – more heavy clangs, the thud of ceramite on plasteel. He got the first tang of that familiar smell – armour servos, mixed in this instance with blood. He thought he picked up something else, a heavy breathing, like an animal's panting, slurred and liquid. It was going slowly, haltingly, as if dragging a damaged limb. Was it mutated? Perhaps. Or maybe just its wounds.

Judge the moment. Not too soon – the range would be too great. Not too late – if he were detected, he would be engaged before breaking cover.

More panting, closer and closer, an irregular rhythm to the creature's gait. Maizad caught another stink in his bloody nostrils, something unnatural and diseased, something foetid and otherworldly. He blinked once, twice, trying to clear the fog from his vision as much as he could. He stiffened in his crouch, preparing the muscles in his calves to push him out.

*Now.* He burst up and out from cover, whirling around in the dark and activating the disruptor on his blade. The blaze of light and energy briefly overloaded his senses, turning his world into a swinging, swaying kaleidoscope of painful starbursts. He heard his enemy roar back at him, an enraged bellow like that of a beast.

He swung blind, relying on his prediction of where it would come at him, and the two blades smashed together in a fresh explosion of plasma. Now he was close enough to respond to his enemy's mass, and the blows came in quicker, harder, propelled by his ravaged arms in fresh spurts of blood. He couldn't hold back, no matter what damage it did – this was it, the one chance, the brief window where he might prevail if he pushed the surprise.

He saw his opponent only in opaque snatches – a crimson swatch of ceramite, a dull flash of bronze. His enemy's blade was serrated and thick, its teeth wickedly curved. It stank and thundered, as if it were an amalgam of animal and machine. It came at him wildly, hurling the toothed blade in tight arcs, its movements strangely hampered, as if it had to fight within itself. Maizad could smell its blood, mingled with the various stinks of overworked power armour. It was slower than it should have been, but still powerful, still possessed of that unearthly Astartes physicality. They crashed together – he slammed its blade aside, went for its torso. At this range, his near blindness made little difference – it was about speed, about commitment.

The blow failed, parried at the last moment, then he was driven back in turn, a flurry of vicious strokes, aimed not to kill outright but to disable. The roaring grew louder, a crescendo of wild and desperate bellows. Was it trying to speak to him? Some vile blood-curse, dredged up from whatever debased religion it now followed? He wouldn't have listened even if he could have done, but the thunder in his ears, the crackle and blaze of the disruptors, it drowned it all out anyway.

And then Garrock was hailing him too, shouting something down the comm, something desperate, but that too could not be made out amid the roaring. Maizad was already in a universe of pain, his senses shredded and his body failing. The trickle of blood inside his armour became a torrent. Damaged sections of his battle plate were hacked off, knocked clear from their makeshift strapping. The enemy's blade was going faster now, whirring like a demented insect, shearing and slicing whenever it got past his guard.

Breathing became hard, then agonising. All that remained was spite – the determination that this thing *would not win*. Hatred surged up within him, a pure hatred like nothing he had ever sensed before. The enemy seemed to grow in stature, to morph and flex into a vast golem of flesh and iron that slammed and crunched into him, again and again, a fractured machine operating with demented speed and strength. The wrongness, the shifting corridors, the visions, the apparitions, they all amplified then, merging the little Maizad could still perceive of the real world into the stuff of visions and nightmares.

*It* was doing this. This creature. It was poisoning the ship. It was turning the real into the unreal. It had to be stopped *here*.

Garrock was screaming, it felt like, howling at him. Blood ran down his cracked visor – his own, the enemy's, he couldn't be sure. He remembered the ghost-cities, and all of a sudden he was back there, slashing his dagger at the spectres. You had to plunge the tip right into their gauzy hearts, end the threat at the source.

Timing was everything. Power was everything. He spun his blade around, a lightning-switch, taking the hilt two-handed. Then the movement, the single thrust, up, out, aimed high to catch the creature at its throat.

It left him exposed. It destroyed what remained of his guard. The whirring counter-blade at last bit deep, slashing into his chest, burrowing deeper, carving up the armour and sinking its teeth into his flesh.

It didn't matter. It couldn't stop his own thrust, propelled with every last element of his strength, pushed deep and deeper still until the enemy's head was near shoved clean from its neck.

They fell on top of one another, crunching to the deck, rolling across it like drunken brawlers, their blood mingled now and coating everything. Its blows became weaker; so did his. They were mirror images, caught up in a cycle of mutual destruction. It had stopped roaring – it was croaking, its throat cut out, its scarred face exposed under its broken helm. A foul helm, a helm forged on some dark world under the watchful eyes of ancient gods.

Maizad suddenly felt cold – a creeping numbness that spread from his extremities and up into his stomach. It was hard to keep focus, hard to stay conscious, but he had to. He had to keep pushing, keep tearing, keep hammering his enemy into the ground.

It was as weak as him now. They were killing each other, cut by cut, blow by blow. The roaring in Maizad's ears reached its apogee – an exultant sound, like a vast choir reaching some kind of musical climax. He couldn't hear Garrock any more, couldn't hear anything save that sound.

And then, suddenly, his vision cleared. Like a curtain being ripped away, the blurriness snapped into focus, the milky softness hardened.

His enemy was beneath him, a swamp of smashed armour pieces and bubbling blood-sloughs. One eye was intact, blinking through the mess of a destroyed helm visor. It couldn't breathe, it couldn't rise. The one eye stared at him, vivid with hatred and scorn.

*It is done*, thought Maizad, as the coldness swept up through his torso and into his shoulder. This was death coming for him, the last embrace of oblivion. In moments his body would be empty, his soul swept away to join the Emperor in the after-world, ready to fight again in the endless struggles that forever took place in the unseen realm. *It is done, the ship is secure.*

He leaned forward, still gripping the hilt of his blade, forcing it further into the cadaver below.

And amid the exultant shimmer of the choir, the glee and the shrieking that filled his ears, he heard the only words his dying enemy was capable of speaking – the very last, before death took him too.

'You... fool,' the warrior spat, outraged despite its ruin, cogent despite its wounds, suddenly speaking in unfiltered, standard Gothic. 'You... damned, blind *fool.*'

Even her chamber was changing now, flexing and pulsing like a heartbeat. She hadn't wanted to believe it at first, but now she couldn't ignore it. It wasn't stress, it wasn't sickness or exhaustion – it was madness, the rearrangement of the material world around her, just on the edge of vision. She would move her head and catch it – a tremor, a too-slow adjustment, like a faulty holocaster.

Santalina had taken a long time to move back into the sanctum. She feared it so much now, it felt like voluntarily entering a torture chamber again. She'd done everything she could to put it off – donning and shedding her robes, trying on every combination of ritual chasubles, dismissing her attendants before asking them back again. Her staff looked worse than her. At least, she hoped they did – she couldn't bear to look in a mirror.

Now there was no choice – the preliminary order had come in, the preparations had finally been completed, the incense was burning in the censers. She had to go back in. As she made her way to the throne, she couldn't stop her hands shaking. The walls around her seemed to shrink, hemming her in, locking her down, stopping her from getting away.

She remembered Kiastros' voice over the comm – changed now, though he didn't seem to recognise it.

*'We have a course,'* he'd told her. *'Study the vectors. Plot it for me. We have to move again. We have to get out.'*

Everyone kept saying that – *get out, get out* – but the warp was no escape. The warp was where the original contagion came from, the source of all the fear. It wasn't a place to hide in, no matter how vulnerable the ship might be in realspace. You went in for the shortest period of time you possibly could and stayed out for as long as you were able.

No point in protesting, though. Kiastros wanted them back into the Seethe, so back they would go. All they needed now was confirmation that the engines would take it, that the warp-chambers would hold together when the Geller fields went up. As soon as they got that, they'd be back inside, rolling around in the laps of malicious intelligences.

She inserted the cables into her jacks, smeared the sacred oils over her cheeks and forearms. She could half hear the chants from her attendants, the endlessly recycled prayers and supplications, but paid them no mind. She couldn't seem to concentrate on anything – her thoughts flitted from one thing to another. The captain, even in his current condition, wasn't oblivious to all this – he knew that damage had been taken, that half the crew were losing their minds, that reality was wobbling and throbbing like an overripe blister. He thought they could just power on through it, stick to their duties, say a few prayers and all would be well. That kind of determination had brought them unscathed through every difficult situation they'd found themselves in before, but this was different. This was something insidious, some mark placed on them at U-93.

Perhaps Avati might be better. Hateful as she was, perhaps she'd see the danger for what it was. Maybe she should–

*'Navigator, we have the confirmation.'*

Kiastros' voice in her ear was like a denunciation, as if he'd been listening to her private thoughts and now intervened to embarrass her.

'Lord captain,' she replied, trying to collect herself. 'The ship is ready to move?'

*'On your word, Mergaux. Our first step taken towards salvation.'*

He might be right about that. She still thought it doubtful.

'All is prepared here,' she told him. 'I shall effect the transition as soon as I can.'

*'And be comforted!'* His voice was so strange now, so over-animated. *'I know the source of the sickness now, and it shall be cut out soon. Once we are secure in the empyrean, I shall move.'*

'You know the source.' She hadn't meant to sound so sceptical, but he seemed oblivious.

*'The simplest explanations are the ones we overlook. The interrogator has something forbidden, and does not know how to use it. I shall take it from him, eject his cargo into the void, and all shall be well again.'*

'He is the Inqui–'

*'I know. I know. But what good does deference do, when the ship is being turned into madness? Eh? We must live, Mergaux. We must survive to reach the Eye. What other purpose is there?'*

He might be right about that too. She didn't know any more. All she could feel was the pain behind her eyes, the sickness fermenting in her stomach, the terrible, terrible fear that made her hands shake and her lips tremble.

'You must do what you think right,' she mumbled, not wanting to talk any more, dreading what was to come.

Kiastros, mercifully, shut down the link, and she made her final preparations. The attendants in the chambers outside scurried to complete their tasks; the outer doors were slammed shut, the runes illuminated.

She removed the bandana, opened her Seeing Eye, and was

immediately immersed into the crashing surf of the impending rip tide. For a moment, she was entirely overwhelmed by it, her voice frozen in another silent scream, her hands gripping the edge of her throne. It was worse than she remembered, a shifting curtain of howling, a bestial mass of half-formed fury that crashed and surged over the beleaguered ship.

Kiastros had only given her the vaguest sense of a course to plot – he just wanted to get out, to get anywhere, to escape the vulnerability of realspace for as long as he could. But that made things harder, of course. Stitching together the relations between the material universe and the snaking labyrinth of the warp was always helped by definite intentions on the part of those sailing.

Her sanctum shook violently. Everything rattled. Ornaments were dislodged from their clasps, and the tapestries flapped in false winds. It was hard to keep her Seeing Eye open, to stare into the maw that so badly wanted to devour them whole, but she did so.

She saw the abyss unfolding, the many-dimensional riot of pseudo-colour and fractional harmonics. As her viewpoint expanded she saw the stars dissolve into inky black points before finally disappearing altogether – the last vestige of conventional physical bodies dissolving within the world of ideas.

Now they were coasting along the splayed edge of dreams, speeding hard through the diaphanous layers of amalgamated consciousness. The yowls started up – the laughter, screams and bellows of the sentients that swam in that morass of despair. You could ignore them, for the most part, knowing that they were barred from entry by the ship's creaking protective fields – to listen to what they said, that was the great error, the one that caused hulls to founder on the shoals of madness.

She started to focus, to plot out the route, to try to trace a path through the deep even as it curved and bucked and

rearranged itself. The Great Beacon shimmered into view –
distant enough, dimmed by the turbulence, but still just about
there, a flickering fixed point around which all else swirled.

And then she saw it – almost the same as before, but dimin-
ished now, or maybe greater. So hard to tell until you got your
bearings.

A ship. Just one, this time, moving in and out of focus, then
disappearing altogether, then coming back again. It had been
two before, at least most of the time, but now just the single
shadow, like a fish glimpsed from below.

'It is closer...' she breathed, watching its wake in the empyrean. 'And gaining.'

Everything she had told Kiastros about predictions in the warp
had been true. You couldn't gauge spatial relationships there,
not with any reliability. There *was* no space in the warp, no true
dimensions or extension, only stories told by an infinite number
of tellers. The relations between bodies in there was more like
the relations between family members, or house bloodline ties,
or sanctioned histories and their theological interpretations.

Still, she could see it. Running behind them, a shadow against
the riot of gauze and plasma, a constant point, not slowing, nor
speeding up a great deal, just... *there*.

Another battle cruiser, like the one Kiastros had destroyed?
If so, why hadn't it dropped into realspace with the other one?
And how was it still tracking them, given that their ship had
been stationary for so long?

She stared at it for a while. You couldn't focus on it directly,
of course – if you tried, it blinked out of existence. Only when
you turned your gaze away did you see it again in the corner
of your eye, like a mote floating in the dazzle of a sunlit day.

She should tell the captain. But then he was busy, consumed
with his new obsession. He'd want to know how to counter it,
where it was going, and she wouldn't be able to tell him.

She'd wait. She'd pilot the ship deeper in. See if it followed. Though she knew already, deep in her soul, that it would.

'Ever closer,' she muttered, trying to still her shaking hands. 'Ever closer. But what *are* you?'

# Chapter Twenty-Five

**CORE FUNCTIONS**

**DUTY AND JOY**

**TO THE BRIDGE**

Avati shivered. It was perishing cold. She kept checking the environment readings, which were bang where they should have been, and still couldn't stop trembling.

She'd returned to the bridge as soon as she could but had been waylaid on the route up by the increasing dysfunction on all decks. Some work-gangs had abandoned their posts, others had been milling around aimlessly, a minority were obsessively pursuing their orders with what appeared to be an almost demented enthusiasm. Virtually none of them saluted her – they barely noticed her presence. When she'd accosted one, demanded that she make the aquila, relay what her duties were, she'd only received a bewildered stare back. The woman's expression had been somewhere between drugged and terrified, and she'd broken from Avati's grip and staggered off into the dark.

Things were collapsing now. Comms were erratic, and when they failed the vox-casters were filled with a metallic howling rather than silence. The lumens were either down or turned off and on with eerie regularity. The recycled air tasted of ashes, and every picter-lens station ran with unbroken static. It was a miracle that anything functioned at all, but the engines were still clearly powered, the life support still operational.

Somehow Kiastros had got them back into the warp again – she could feel the nausea in the pit of her stomach that signalled everything beyond the hull's edge was now an atomised stew of reality-chewing nightmares – and perhaps that was making it even worse.

She wanted to talk to Sister Isobel, but couldn't get through using her armour comms. She wanted to talk to Garrock – the same. It felt like everything was closing down, every last point of light and sound, until all that was left was to scurry around in the freezing dark, gradually starving, gradually running out of air...

Enough. *Enough.* She needed to keep her mind clear. Everyone else might be going mad or sinking into despondency, but she was the first lieutenant, Master of Astrogation and second-in-command of the entire ship. Someone had to hold things together.

She shunned the elevator tubes and jogged up the interminable stairways instead, hurried along the poorly lit corridors. Everything took longer than it should have, everything was harder. By the time she made it back to the command bridge she was sweating despite the frigid temperature, and her bodyglove was damp with it.

Boroja greeted her as she approached the throne dais.

'You're back!' he cried, pulling at his uniform agitatedly, his face twitching, his movements jerky. 'He's taken us back into the warp. You sense it? I told him not to. Not yet! But he's done it. The damned fool. That's where the *danger* is. We still can't see.'

Avati looked around her. The bridge was in a similar state of disarray to the rest of ship. Some crew members were at their stations, many were lying prone on the deck, or limping around aimlessly, or rocking back and forth in their seats.

'What has happened here?' she demanded, marching up to the throne itself. Boroja scampered after her.

'You don't *feel* it?' he said. 'We're not *ready*. There's too much to do.'

Avati took up position on the throne, activated the set of tactical lenses hung above it, started to scan the ship's vital statistics. 'There are order queues backed up,' she said, frowning at him. 'You've not restored the arrays. Why not?'

'He asks the impossible! Nothing *works!*'

Avati snapped the displays round, showed him the figures. 'You've got crew lying idle.'

Boroja crept up close, snatched at her uniform. 'No one answers,' he muttered miserably. 'No one can do anything. They tell me they're feverish, they tell me they're frozen, they tell me the vox-casters are filled with screaming–'

Avati sprang up, grabbed him, seized him with both hands.

'You're *weak*,' she hissed. 'Don't you feel it? The presence of the enemy? These are the moments when you must remain strong, when you must remember your training. We are getting out of this. We are purging the sickness and rejoining the fleet. You hear me?' She shoved him away, and he staggered backwards. She drew her laspistol, flicked off the safety and aimed it at his chest. 'Get the core functions back up and running. Do it now. Or, as the Throne is my judge, I will end you here and now.'

He stared at her for a moment, stupefied, then seemed to realise that she was serious. He whirled around, eyes wide, as if witnessing the disorder across the bridge for the very first time. He blinked hard a few times, rubbed his face, looked back at her with a mortified expression. He didn't say anything else, but hobbled back to the signals stations. His cracked voice soon rose, shouting out orders.

Avati holstered her weapon. Part of her had wanted to fire, very badly. She almost had. Keeping a lid on the always-simmering stew of madness felt harder and harder – something had to give, the cause had to be unearthed, or they would end up murdering one another before they got anywhere close to the fleet again.

She sat down again, tried to get a sense of how things stood. The reporting was, as she had come to expect, all over the place. Spleed had gone silent for hours, before sporadic bulletins had finally come in detailing insurrections across the gun-decks – he was kept busy with those, he said, trying to prevent a full-scale mutiny in the arming halls. That meant their offensive capability would not be fully restored for a while yet – Avati doubted that they could even loose a single broadside, which was no doubt why Kiastros was so keen to get them back into the warp. She saw order bursts that seemed to indicate a recall for Kuhl back to the enginarium, but for some reason that couldn't have reached her, because she was still sending progress reports on the excavation and preparing to strike at the spire's foundations. Garrock had sent a flurry of priority comm requests, but Boroja hadn't heard them, of if he had, he hadn't acted on any of them.

Avati tried to activate a link to the armsman, but got nothing back over her comm-bead. It was as if the ship were plunging through a mire of sonic interference: nothing but hard links seemed to work reliably, and Boroja was right – some of the feedback sounded a lot like human screaming.

But that was her imagination running wild. She concentrated on what she needed to do – restore command and control at the bridge, establish a link with Garrock, work with Spleed to lock the gun-decks down and prevent the disorder there from spreading. She did manage to speak to the Navigator over a crackling comm-line, but only briefly.

'So all is holding?' she asked.

'There's a ship,' Santalina replied, whispering conspiratorially. 'Another ship. Coming at us, closer, closer.'

She'd said that before – two had been in pursuit, only one had shown itself. Was the second still after them, then? Why hadn't it come out of the warp with its twin?

'You're sure, Navigator?' she asked. Kiastros would need to know. 'Absolutely sure?'

Then Santalina just started laughing, and the link cut.

So Avati recorded it, got to work on what she could do, what she could fix, and that was hard enough. Just as she was getting to the meat of it all, Kiastros suddenly burst in through the great doorway at the rear of the bridge and hurried up to the throne dais. As soon as she laid eyes on him, Avati saw that he was in almost as bad a way as Boroja. He'd taken his helm off, revealing a flushed face with too-bright eyes. His hair was matted and sweaty, his uniform blotched with stains. His movements were jerky, out of sync, and he nearly tripped twice as he made his way to Avati's position.

*Do I look like this, too?* she wondered. *Are we all going the same way, now?*

'The warp drives are holding?' the captain asked, giving her a hasty aquila.

'Holding, aye, lord captain,' said Avati, bringing up the schematics. 'Steady progress according to the Navigator, no breach of chamber integrity.'

'And the Geller fields?'

'Solid. But the Navigator said–'

Kiastros laughed. 'Then that's something! Something works! Praise to the Golden Throne, we shall escape this after all.'

'Yes, but–'

'No doubts in my mind, Astrogation. No doubts at all.'

Avati got down from the throne, but Kiastros did not assume his usual position.

'I've not come here to relieve you, Astrogation,' he said, grabbing a pivot-mounted lens and staring at the data on it. 'You'll need to run things a little longer – the time has come to take on our guests.'

So that was it.

'By your will. Do we have–'

'The force? Of course we do. We have hundreds. Thousands, if we need it. Why do we run so scared of them? They are human, like us. Flesh and blood. They bleed, I take it? Ha! Though it should not come to that.'

Hells, he was intoxicated. Or maybe delirious.

'My judgement, lord captain,' she ventured, going carefully, 'is that the interrogator will not cooperate. And he certainly won't hand over his cargo voluntarily. They are armed, they are prepared.'

'And there are only a few of them. As you discovered.' Kiastros grinned. 'We destroyed their ship! And they let us do it. They have nowhere to go, and they know it.'

Avati couldn't decide whether he was jesting.

'We are in the warp,' she said. 'The Navigator reports that we are still being followed. We can remain here for some time, but not forever. Perhaps, when Captain Garrock has reported back, he can assist.'

'He's busy, Astrogation.'

'Well, possibly – I haven't been able to–'

'He's busy with his Space Marine, just like Kuhl's busy with her Sister. All of them, running around my ship with their own concerns. Leave them to it.' He looked briefly confused. 'Though Kuhl said she was... Never mind it. But the engines are fine. Fine! And if something comes after us, we'll have the guns back up. We're back on track.'

He was sweating heavily now. His stiff uniform collar was soaking.

'So, what are your orders?' she asked.

'All the armsmen you can find. Two hundred should do it. Failing that, if they're all still skipping after Garrock, then drum up some ratings with guns. As many as you can. You have an hour.'

There were none left. They were all distributed across the decks, either hunting the intruder or suppressing riots on the gun-decks. The entire ship was teetering on the edge of anarchy, and he wanted a small army to go with him to the hangar level.

She could have protested. One look into his eyes told her that it would do no good – he'd be able to work around her, whatever she said. Would the troops even obey him now? Yes. Yes, they almost certainly would. Things were collapsing fast, but they weren't that badly gone. He would do it, one way or another.

And maybe he was even right. She'd felt the energy bleeding out of that chamber, the soft light that was somehow more disturbing than anything she'd encountered on this voyage of serried horror. It might be the source, the root of the problem. Better to take control of it, maybe destroy it. Ejecting the material out of an airlock might just send all the badness out with it, and they could worry about retribution from the Inquisition another day.

'You'll lead the force yourself, then?' she asked.

And at that, Kiastros looked positively ecstatic.

'I will take that privilege,' he said, beaming back at her with relish for what was to come. 'It shall be my duty, Astrogation, but also – be sure of this – my joy.'

She wanted to reply to that, but as she looked at his flushed cheeks, his ever-fidgeting fingers, his agitated and over-energised movements, she found she had nothing to say. All she could do was nod, before turning away to tend to her many duties.

Maybe it would work, she told herself. Maybe it would work.

\* \* \*

Garrock didn't want to believe it. He stared and stared, hoping that something was wrong, that his judgement was out. The alternative made him sick.

The two giant warriors lay side by side, lying on their backs, limbs outstretched. Just moving them had been a huge effort – each limb hauled back by four of his troops. They'd waited a very long time before moving in on them, crouching down in cover, fearful that one or both of them would get up at any moment.

But there was no doubt now. The scans had been run, the life signs double-checked. Maizad was dead. His opponent was dead. Two fighters of the Adeptus Astartes lay next to one another, twin studies of ruination. They were so similar. Their colossal armour was smashed and split, their blood was intermingled all across the deck. Even their weapons looked alike – two clean-bladed swords in a gladius styling. Maizad had told him to expect something more involved – a chainblade, or similar – so it was strange to see such a relatively conventional weapon in its place.

Not the strangest thing, of course. That was the slain warrior lying next to Maizad. His armour was crimson with bronze detailing. It was ferocious in aspect, as all battle plate of the Astartes was, but it bore no obvious signs of corruption. Garrock had approached it with trepidation, fearing what unholy things he would see, but the ravages across its body were of the standard kind – bloodstains, muscle gashes, broken bones. The livery was not one that he recognised, but then there were hundreds of Chapters, and the sigils on the warrior's armour were of a standard Imperial type. The few inscriptions were etched in Gothic characters, and read *Imperator Invictus* and *In aeternum servitium*. There were purity seals – just scraps now, mired in the slicks of gore – but recognisably Imperial in origin. The warrior's face was exposed where his helm had been smashed open.

It was ruined, its bone structure driven in and one eye missing, but it was not obviously twisted into mutation. It was of human origin, and any deviations from the species norm were, if anything, less than Maizad's.

He'd feared the truth just before the end. Just as Maizad's plan to entrap the monster was coming to its conclusion he'd got a report back from Cirroca, sergeant of one of the squads he'd sent on ahead to seal the escape routes. The sergeant had been animated, almost raving, screaming down the vox that he'd shot one of his own squad, a trooper who'd sworn blind that they had all been misled, that the monster was in reality one of the Emperor's own Angels, and that a madness of deception had overcome the entire ship, making them see an enemy where none existed and not see an enemy where they were truly active. Cirroca had been so disturbed, so furious with himself and his own trooper, and Garrock had suddenly felt a pang of fear. He'd reflected on how the ship itself seemed to be frustrating the monster's progress, how the blind masses in the bilges had launched themselves at it, how the internal labyrinth had seized up and changed and switched, and how none of them had raised the alarm over such astonishing effects, but had preferred to think that they were just exhausted, or mistaken, or that the warp was addling their minds.

And so when Garrock had tried to get in touch with Maizad over the comm, a last desperate attempt to stay his hand, to check whether some horrific error had taken place, it was little surprise that nothing intelligible had come back. For a moment, he'd thought that his transmission had somehow ended up going to some kind of animal – a canid, snarling and slavering – before he realised that Maizad was gone too, lost in a world of violence and insanity. Even he, even one of the Emperor's chosen, had been vulnerable to the madness.

Now the result was so blasphemous he could barely admit

it to himself. A loyal Space Marine had boarded the ship, had been making his way up towards the bridge, and they had killed him. They had set the bilge-rats on him, hunted him down, and eventually wasted their only other Astartes warrior in the cause of his destruction.

Why hadn't the intruder identified himself? Why hadn't he hailed the bridge? Looking at him now, Garrock could see the state of his armour, the broken helm and the wiring spilling out of its complex internal systems. The Space Marine had been badly damaged on hull-entry, so much so that he was already severely wounded even before attempting to move further inside. Perhaps he couldn't hail. Or perhaps he'd tried, and no one had listened. By the time he'd been tracked down, maybe no one could have understood what he was saying even if they had been paying attention.

'There is a curse on this ship,' Garrock muttered, feeling the truth of it in his bones. Everything was twisted, nothing was what it seemed. If Maizad himself had been deceived, then what hope did the rest of them have? Something deep and powerful was at work, a veil of madness that made them take the wrong course, over and over.

'What do we do?' asked Herj, looking jumpy and on edge.

The rest of the command squad hung back, standing or squatting, none of them wanting to get close to the corpses. None of them had fired a shot, but an air of deep anxiety hung over them all. Garrock couldn't be sure – it was so dark – but it looked like a few had run off, abandoned their stations, perhaps given in to the deep layer of fear that seemed to gnaw away at everything.

Garrock didn't know. His mind was so slow. Every time he tried to think, to formulate a plan, he just found himself staring at the two bodies, caught up in the madness and futility of it. The warp drives thrummed around them all, a low growl that

never went away, and you could imagine there were words
being whispered along with it.

*You will all die here you will all die here you will all–*

'Squads status?' he growled.

'Lost contact with Secundus and Quartus. Tertius is still at the zone exit. No idea about Sextus – just static on the comm.'

'We need to get them back. Send out the order – general muster at the forward barracks. Everyone. It's worse down here – we're too close to the warp drives.'

Herj nodded. Kevem should have jumped on that, started to bring up the squad comm-lines, but he was on his haunches, rocking slowly in the dark. Herj strode over to him, smacked him hard on the helm. Further back, hidden in the oppressive gloom, someone laughed.

It was everywhere. He felt like screaming. Who would be in control? Anyone?

'Can you raise a line to the bridge?' he asked.

Herj looked back at him. 'Nothing for over an hour. What we get back isn't... nice. You think there's anyone up there? You think they're even still alive?'

Throne, he hadn't even thought of that. Now it was all he could picture – the bridge emptied of life, the machines ticking over, the ship hurtling deeper and deeper into the warp...

'Stow that,' he snapped. 'We've got problems with the comms. Stay focused.' He shook his head, tried to clear it, tried to *think*. 'This has to be reported. The captain must be told.'

'I won't stay down here!' screamed a voice from a little way back. Garrock turned to see one of the younger troopers, a woman named Heija, taking off her helm. 'I won't stay here! They're still alive! They're both still–'

The tirade was silenced by Herj, taking two strides to her position and shoving his shotgun butt into her midriff. She doubled up, folding onto the deck. A few of the others, troopers who'd served with her for a long time, took a few ominous steps towards the lieutenant. Another shotgun was raised.

'Enough!' Garrock shouted. 'Stand down, all of you! No one's staying down here. No point. We've got to get back to barracks, get some working comms. This squad, though, we're going up. To the top. Back to the bridge. The captain must be told.'

He swept his gaze across the assembled armsmen. They looked very, very fragile. Ready to lash out, maybe even ready to rebel. He had to hold them together a little longer. Find out what was really going on.

'We stay close, within sight range, move together. You hear that? Push hard, we'll be up into the lit sections within the hour. Ignore any visions you get. Ignore any noises. It's your mind. It's the warp. Something's got broken, but we're going to get out of it, you hear? We're going to get out of it. If it's spreading, the captain will need guns. Our guns. So keep them charged, keep them working. Ave Imperator!'

They replied to that. They called out the words, though the response was ragged and fainter than it should have been.

Garrock marked the current location on his helm's tracker. He took a final look at Maizad's corpse, and felt a spike of remorse. The warrior should never have been pressed back into service so soon. If he hadn't been so hampered, he would surely have seen through the webs of deception. They had wasted their greatest weapon, and in doing so had killed another. It was a shambles, a debacle, the kind of thing that warranted execution when the truth came out.

He could keep it secret, though. All of them could. The level of confusion was such that no one would ever know, unless they reported faithfully.

He glanced at Herj, who was adjusting his armour and making ready to move out. He looked at Kevem, Heija, the others.

Maybe he'd have to get rid of them, just to be sure. Maybe

no one but him could be trusted with the knowledge. Just a
few shots, before they got up into the populated regions. No
one would ever–

Throne, what was *wrong* with him?

'Then we move out,' he grunted, starting to march. 'To the
bridge.'

## Chapter Twenty-Six

**BREAKING IN**

**THE WEB OF PAIN**

**RIGHT OF SEIZURE**

They were all lined up in the dark, crammed into the tight space no more than thirty yards across. Most were Arfo-5's people – enginseers, indentured labourers from the Martian levies, servitors with guns welded onto their shoulder blades. They were a grim-looking collection, all cowled and robed, their metallic extremities glinting darkly in the gloom. The remainder were Kuhl's crew, dressed in heavy enginarium boiler suits and carrying power tools that doubled up as weaponry when needed. A few had managed to haul some exo-suits up the narrow shafts, which towered over the assembled humans. The suits' powerful drills had already been at work, burrowing upward to carve a path towards the spire's foundations. Now the last set of barriers was strung with explosives, some forty yards off and up the steep slope graded by the engineers.

Isobel had drawn her blade again, and this time she kindled the energy field. Kuhl stood close by in the shadows, a lasrifle cradled awkwardly in her arms. Arfo-5 was next to her, his robes lit up by the crackling light of his electro-stave.

'Ready?' Kuhl asked her.

Isobel glanced up the slope. The charges were intricate things, rigged to blow their kinetic force up and out, pushing the damaged seat of the astropaths' lower halls in on itself and blasting a path inside. Kuhl had gone to enormous trouble to brace and secure the passage leading up to the site. Isobel had been seriously impressed by her diligence – she was absolutely determined to make this work. That, more than anything else, made her feel wretched for her earlier moment of doubt. She still felt it, if she was honest – the oppressive weight of raw dread, the sense that the ship had been badly corrupted and this corruption was now seeping out of every rivet and panel seal – but Kuhl had come up with the better response. Defiance. Raw, dogged defiance. That was supposed to have been *her* specialism, after all.

So she'd worked herself into the proper stance for what was to come. She'd mouthed the litanies, the catechisms, the injunctions to hate and to slay and to wreak vengeance. They'd never had much effect on her in the past, and they had even less now. Still, she had her basic training, the core level of physical fearlessness that the Sisterhood bred into all its warriors. Whatever lay on the other side of that barrier, she would meet it. If any souls yet lived, she would heal them. If all were dead, she would give their souls the Emperor's blessing. And if some weapon of the enemy had penetrated the hull and was still active in there, she would fight alongside Kuhl's crew to disable it.

'I am ready,' she said firmly.

Arfo-5 ran his final checks, the last of the build-crews retreated back down the slope and crouched at its base.

'You have your orders!' cried Kuhl, speaking to the assembled troops. 'We break in, we secure the entrance. If you locate any living souls, report at once to the honoured Sister and myself.

Do not approach! These are mutants. Any survivors will be transported to the apothecarion under Sister Isobel's watch.'

She drew in a shaky breath, looked up the long slope towards the charges.

'It will be difficult in there,' Kuhl told them. 'Hold to your training, work quickly, get it done. The captain is relying on this.'

Then she shot a brief glance at Arfo-5, steadied herself, and gave the signal to the build-crews.

They detonated the charges. Explosions erupted at the summit of the slope – a series of angry orange blasts that made both the chamber and tunnel shake. By then Isobel was already running, scrambling up the incline with her blade fizzing in her grip. The Martians were the only ones who could keep pace, and scampered alongside her as debris thumped and blew apart around them. The engine crew brought up the rear, struggling to drag the brace-beams and roof supports to make the breach good.

Once the explosions had blown themselves out, an eerie purplish light flooded down from the breach. Isobel heard a keening, wailing sound, one that cut right through her, and nearly lost her footing. She peered ahead, to the lip of the opening that was nearly upon her, and saw clouds of smoke pouring through it. It was hazy stuff, not the thick smog of an engine failing, but something almost... fragrant. It swelled up everywhere, tumbling and rolling across every surface and filling the narrow channel with a thick, turbid haze.

The Martians pressed on through it, their cowled faces lighting up as their night-sight visual systems compensated. Isobel remained at the forefront, cresting the jagged rise of twisted metal and masonry, clambering over the edge and pushing up and out into the expanse ahead. For a moment, the swirling fog obscured everything and she went almost blind, stumbling through the wreckage created by the linked charges. She heard the clunk and snap of rapid rebuilding behind her, the chatter of the tech-priest and his minions, the grunts and heavy panting of the engine crew struggling to keep up. It felt as if they'd all stumbled into some parallel dimension, weighed down by a fog that crept into every pore and erased the external world entirely, leaving only the sounds of frantic and hasty construction.

And then she burst through it, clambering up a ruined pile of burned-black plasteel until her head and shoulders at last punched out the other side. She crouched instinctively, her helm systems immediately overlaying the scene ahead with a welter of tactical data. Every alert suddenly pinged, and a riot of targeting reticules zeroed in – so many it was almost overwhelming.

She didn't pay any attention to those. They weren't needed. Her mortal senses gave her everything she needed, and that was more than enough.

She was staring, quite openly, into hell. The enormous astropathic choir chamber soared away from her, a grand dome that would have been the pride of any terrestrial basilica. Once it would have been mostly empty, a cavernous and echoing hemisphere in which the astropaths plied their murky trade. The polished floors would have glinted softly from the light of massed candles, the adepts would have shuffled from cell to cell, glancing from time to time up at the esoteric machinery hanging precariously from the dome's distant crown.

Now the crown was broken. A huge jagged hole had been gouged in its roof, gaping obscenely wide. With horror, Isobel realised that there was nothing above it – no remnants of the old spire, no broken hull plates piled up across the breach, no protective shutters, just the raw warp boiling and churning like a heavenly dome of variegated magma. This was the very edge of the extant hull, staring straight through the translucent screen of the Geller field into the unmediated stuff of Chaos.

'Do not look!' she cried, knowing the terrible danger. The Geller field warded the worst of the foulness, but not entirely – you could still perceive things moving on the far side, scratching at it, tearing at it, leering through it.

But that wasn't the greater abomination. Whatever had shattered the spire and smashed through the great astropathic dome below had wreaked more than physical damage. The grand array of empyreal lenses and augmenters still existed, but had been twisted and exploded into new and malevolent forms. Grotesque outgrowths spurted from the vents and the astrolabes, writhing in drifting seas of ectoplasm and luminous vapour. Colossal stringy organic fronds splayed out from the devastated crown all the way down to the dome's base perimeter, shivering like spiders' webs caught in the wind. Those fronds were intermingled with the skeins of cabling that burst like creepers from every destroyed piece of esoteric machinery, turning the entire space into a vast, dense lattice that twisted and shuddered as if alive. Everything stank – an over-pungent fug of sucrose and blood and musk that was enough on its own to make one want to scream. The entire inner surface of the enormous gulf glimmered with foul growths and coralline tumours, flexing and shuddering like a gigantic organ – a heart, maybe, or perhaps a shivering lung.

Amid that web hung polyps, pale as pigskin, wet and throbbing. Each polyp was far greater in size than a standard human – they were bulbous nodules, swollen and vile, linked together by yet more of those dense-woven strands of fibre. The nodules were clearly alive, writhing like insects stuck on glue, and in terrible pain. Only slowly did you realise what they truly were – the astropaths of the ship's choir, distended and mutated, their mouths gaping wide and stretching bloodily open. The rest of their agonised bodies had been transformed and split open and stretched into something like amplifiers – fleshy, gill-fronded, wobbling and wailing.

Right in the centre of it all, hung like a chandelier among the constellation of assorted grotesques, was the hapless master of this benighted realm, the one named Ortuyo. Isobel had never seen him in life, and now wished she'd never seen him in death either. Or perhaps he wasn't dead. Perhaps some part of Ortuyo still lingered, locked within the bizarre flaps and flutes of pulled skin, of gelatinous sinew spun out over yards, of absurdly swollen throat glands and exposed cerebellum. But the worst of it, by far, was the man's mouth, which had been pulled so wide that she could have walked down his throat without ducking. What vile sorcery had enabled his body to be so pulled apart without splitting in two was unknowable – he had been entirely transformed, folded out from a mortal man and yanked into some vast and occult instrument. The entire choir was a part of it – an orchestra of pain, bound up together in torment as the warp roiled ceaselessly above them.

Isobel was no scholar of forbidden magick, but it was clear enough what the purpose of all that suffering was. Every mouth was locked firmly open, frozen in a kind of perpetual scream. It wasn't audible, not operating on the standard sonic level, but was evidently doing something. And now, so close to it, she understood that something terrible had been happening to the ship. Madness, sickness and despair – it was all coming from *here*, broadcast across the entire structure by these poor altered wretches. Their strange aptitudes for dreams and visions had been turned against them, making them into conduits for the sanity-shredding stuff of the warp itself. They were quite literally mouthpieces, relays for the poison that churned in the abyss across which they skated. And they had been doing it ever since the hull had been ruptured at U-93 – something had got inside, smashed its way through during the confusion of the battle, and had been here ever since, growing and splitting and evolving like a cancer inside the body. If it was not excised now, everything would keep getting worse – the crew would sink into insanity, the corridors would keep shifting around and disappearing, the equipment would malfunction, and the drives would cease to operate. Eventually every part of the ship would be like this pain-chamber, a fused mass of flesh and metal, a perpetual hymn of torment to the false gods who forever lusted for the destruction of humankind.

Kuhl's teams could not fight this. Already Isobel could hear the ratings shouting with horror and alarm over the vox, unable to believe what they were seeing. Someone – was it Kuhl herself? – was screaming at them to keep moving up, but even she had to realise that they wouldn't be able to process such terror. The only hope lay with the Martians, purged of their capacity for disgust and able to keep marching, to secure the breach, to bring up proper weaponry and start to use it. And even they might not be enough, for they were not genuine warriors, not like the Space Marine she had treated and sent back into action. What she would have given to have had Maizad with her just then.

'With me!' Isobel roared, swinging her ignited blade around her, beckoning for the Martians to follow.

This had to be cut out. This abomination had to be destroyed. It didn't matter if they all died here in the attempt – if the contagion was allowed to continue, the fate of the ship was sealed.

Isobel fixed her gaze on the central monstrosity, the vast and bloated remnant of a man continually broadcasting psychic terror from its impossibly distended mouth, and prepared to climb up to meet it.

'You,' she breathed, angling her blade towards it. 'By all that remains sacred, I will end *you*.'

Kiastros surveyed his forces. Two hundred of them – a mix of ratings, a scattering of junior officers, some armsmen that

Garrock somehow hadn't swept up for his own operations, gun-crew and deck-hands. The officers and armsmen were well armed and armoured; the rest were not. Many looked surly and uncooperative, most looked very uncertain, with some uncomfortable murmuring rumbling away at the back of the hall. Avati had done well enough to rustle up so many in such a short time, but you couldn't be too confident about their quality. He didn't even recognise many of the faces.

Maybe he should have brought Avati down to the assembly chamber with him. But then someone needed to run the bridge, and he could hardly do both things at once. Had it been wise to give her so much control? Might she use it to take over entirely? She might. Perhaps he'd better see to that in due course. Once he'd dealt with il-Moro, he could keep these troops together, bring them back up to the bridge, clear out the rubbish if needed. It might even be handy to have some armed support with him at all times from now on – he had no idea where Garrock was, where the honoured Sister had gone, where that Space Marine was lurking. No one told him anything. He picked up nothing on the comm. It was too damned hot. He had trouble seeing straight, and he hadn't slept now for... He couldn't even remember.

'Something has poisoned the ship!' Kiastros cried, standing before them and attempting to quell the murmuring. The outnumbered armsmen spread out through the crowd, imposing order as they'd been commanded to. 'You can feel it. I can feel it. We were healthy until taking on our guests. Guests who have shown us scant respect for the granting of sanctuary. Guests who continue to withhold information on what it is they have with them. No more. I am the master of this ship, under the laws passed down by the Emperor Himself. The poison must be cut out. The cargo they have brought with them will be ejected. Sanity will be restored.'

The ranks of faces looked back at him blankly. Some of them

were sweating, just like him. Others looked sick. A few were twitching, as if their uniforms crawled with insects.

'I know what these people are,' he went on. 'I know what fear the name conjures. But they are only human! Like us, men and women, flesh and blood, in service to the Immortal Throne. They can err. They can fall from grace. When that happens, it is up to us, the most faithful of all His servants, to act. No one else will. Our actions shall justify us.'

He wasn't drumming up much enthusiasm. The murmuring broke out again.

'We must survive this,' he urged. 'We must preserve ourselves, for our destiny – *my* destiny – is to reach the Eye. Nothing else matters. Our oaths demand it. So put aside your doubts. Put aside your fears. You only fear because the sickness is aboard. March with me, drive it out, and we shall be restored again. The guns shall be reloaded, the engines relit, and we shall be a *warship* again, a blade in the Emperor's divine hand.'

A few scattered grunts of assent. They were wavering, their morale was poor, so the window for action was diminishing. Leave it for another hour or so and there was no guarantee he'd be able to marshal any kind of action at all.

'So you have your orders,' he told them. 'We move now, and get our ship back.'

The response was perfunctory, but at least they didn't look like backing out. He was still the captain, despite everything, so they picked up their shields, they snapped shut their helm visors, and they hoisted their shotguns.

Then there was the long march down to the hangars. He barely looked around as he went, instead concentrating on what he had to do, but every so often he'd glimpse his surroundings and it would be like seeing it in a dream – the corridors shifting in and out of focus, the symbols on the blast doors slipping and sliding. He glanced over at an elevator-shaft opening and for a moment it seemed like the doors were translucent, exposing the shaft within, which boiled and wriggled with overspilling tentacles and gristle nodes. When he blinked, the brushed metal was back, sealing it all in. He didn't even truly understand how he was seeing anything much at all – the lumens were all out of action, and he could hear the stumbles and curses of those following him. The darkness, the ever-present, all-consuming darkness, had become almost comforting, a blanket that wrapped itself around the increasingly changeable world of the ship's structure and hid all the unpleasantness away. He found that he didn't really want the lights to come back on – not yet, anyway. Better to get used to the new dispensation, to find better ways of getting around. The savings in power generation alone would make it worth it.

They reached their destination, and Kiastros barely even registered that the guards he'd ordered to maintain a vigil were gone. The doors were open, exposing the vast expanse of the empty apron beyond. The ships that should have clustered across it were all gone too – expended in the various battles they'd already had, thrown into the void like chaff into a hopper. The servitors were nowhere to be seen, the hangar-crew vehicles stood silent and inactive. A few clumps of refuse had been swept up against the raw rockcrete walls and left to moulder.

The guests were waiting for them. The doors to the isolation halls were open, affording a tantalising glimpse into their temporary realm, and they had lined up outside it. Il-Moro was there, plus his gaggle of hangers-on and mercenaries. They were tooled up, all weapons out, looking perfectly ready to fight. Had someone informed them? Or was it all so painfully obvious that they'd simply been biding their time?

An arrogant act, if so, to come outside. They could have hunkered down inside those heavily defended chambers and made this all very much more difficult.

'Interrogator!' Kiastros called out, coming to a halt a few

yards from them. His unruly followers spread out behind him, lowering their weapons and staring nervously at the much smaller band of Inquisitorial agents. 'Is there some problem with your accommodation? Have you become unhappy with the quarters we have given you? Perhaps you would like to leave. I can offer many alternative berths, should you desire it.'

Il-Moro ran his deep-set eyes across the crowd facing him. He looked rather more assured than he had done before, as if certain longstanding worries he'd had were now coming to a head, and so he could stop fretting about them and concentrate on what was to come.

'I see you've come here in force, captain,' il-Moro replied. 'Not really the action of a friendly host.'

'But we have been very friendly, interrogator. *More* than friendly. I have sacrificed everything for you – you must see that? There is a limit, though, beyond which I will not go.'

'And which you feel has been breached, I take it?'

'Look around you. You are not immune to its effects. Or perhaps you are. Perhaps you can rise above it somehow.'

'No one can rise above it.'

Kiastros laughed. 'Then you admit your guilt! No attempt to hide it. Throne, I knew you people were arrogant, but even so...'

Il-Moro gave him a heavy-lidded stare. 'You have no understanding of what is happening here. None at all. If you did, if you even guessed it, you would be ended by it, your entire crew mind-wiped. You are condemning yourself to death by this – do you not see it? All you had to do was bring me to safety and ask no questions.'

'I didn't ask. No questions at all. We did our duty, just as demanded. And now look. My crew are being dragged into mortal sickness. The ship itself is changing. I close my eyes for an instant, and I hear the world around me rearrange. This is not normal. This is corruption – and *you* have brought it here.'

'As I said, you have no conception of what you are dealing with. These are guesses, nothing more.'

'Then show us what you carry. Show us what you brought on board.'

'I cannot.'

Kiastros turned to those beside him. He could sense their fear – smell it, even. They wanted so very badly to run from this place, to scramble back into the tunnels behind them, but there was no hiding now. The moment was coming. The moment of crisis. He felt the same thrill he always felt before battle – the balance of risks, the real possibility of both victory and defeat, the horizon of determination.

'He *cannot*,' Kiastros told them. 'So he claims. Even though all he needs to do is keep the door open and let me go in.' He turned back to il-Moro. 'You should do that. It needs to be destroyed. It needs to be shunted out of the airlocks and sent as far away as possible. Then I need to train the remaining guns on it and blast it into atoms.'

'Doing that would not help you.'

'Because you cherish it, don't you? You worship it. You don't even know what it does, but you cannot let it go. Does that not *warn* you? Is that not the very epitome of the enemy's arts? You have been cut adrift, my friend, given something to hold that is both dangerous and unknowable, and your substandard mind cannot do otherwise than to nurse it, as if it were an infant to coddle.' He risked taking a step closer. 'But it is no infant. It is a device of the enemy, a sliver of its malice, cut loose and stuck here. You know the truth of it. In your better moments, you know that it is hateful, and that the only service you can do now for the Imperium is to destroy it. Do you have the strength, though? Do you have the power of will to go against your orders?'

'You cannot destroy it. I cannot destroy it. I will tell you one last time – your only task is to bring me to my masters, to whom it must be delivered. If you attempt to interfere with my mission, I shall not hesitate to render judgement.'

For the first time, Kiastros felt his resolve weaken. He looked into il-Moro's eyes, and saw the utter commitment there. The man would fight for his treasure. How powerful was he? Maybe very powerful indeed. A dozen or so of his trained killers might very well account for a hundred or so of Kiastros' rabble. But two hundred? Really? Maybe even the Space Marine would have struggled with that.

It was his duty. His only remaining duty. The cargo had corrupted the interrogator, just as it was corrupting the entire vessel. If he failed here, now, then everything failed.

'I am the captain,' Kiastros said, aiming his laspistol firmly at the interrogator's chest. 'Within this sacred hull, my word is law. And I command you now to relinquish the cargo, to hand it over to me and surrender your weapons. If you do so, you will not be harmed. If you resist, I shall destroy you.'

Il-Moro raised his own weapon – an ancient-looking pistol of some design Kiastros didn't recognise. The retinues on both sides did the same, and the atmosphere in the hangar became electric with tension.

'If you value your soul,' il-Moro told him, 'you will go back whence you came. You are forbidden from entering this place.'

Kiastros smiled. He couldn't help himself. He wanted to laugh out loud, to shriek with joy, and barely held it together for long enough to reply. He was *enjoying* this. Everything suddenly made sense to him. This was his destiny, his moment to shine. All the void battles of the past, all the long and patient commands he'd engaged in, they had all led up to this moment. He knew without a shadow of doubt that the cargo this man guarded was the most precious and dangerous thing he'd ever encountered. Ending it – and him – would be the greatest of his many accomplishments, the precursor of far greater things to come.

'You have miscalculated, interrogator,' he said. 'The fear you rely on has ceased to work. The game ends here.'

And then, via his helm's internal comm-channel to the mob behind him, he gave the order as he depressed the trigger on his laspistol.

'All hands, open fire!' he voxed with relish. 'And may the Emperor guide your aim!'

# Chapter Twenty-Seven

**IMPERIAL TACTICS**
**THE CHOIR**
**NEVER GOING BACK**

They were beginning to fall out of line, to leave their stations, to openly disobey Boroja's orders. Avati heard him screaming at them, reading them the litanies of punishment, but they didn't listen any more. Those who remained worked strangely at their stations, obsessively re-entering the same codes over and over, or just slumped in their seats staring at the warp-shutters above.

She should have helped Boroja out. She should have called up the remaining armsmen and tried to reimpose order. But it was so hard to concentrate, to remember what Kiastros had ordered and what the ship needed. Urgent messages were coming in from all decks now – desperate requests for reinforcements, declarations of mutiny, reports of machinery failure. She read some of them, ignored most. What did they expect her to do? She could pull the levers, but nothing was connected to them.

She tried to raise Kuhl many times. Getting her back was imperative – if the plasma drives could be brought into play, they could exit the warp safely. The ability to drop out of the empyrean felt like a priority, whatever Kiastros' views – the endless press of the immaterium was surely part of all this strangeness. Was Isobel still with her? It would be good to have her here too. She'd be able to restore control on the bridge. The officers and the ratings would listen to her.

No luck, though. All the channels were hissing now, sounding like open wells on to the ravenings of beasts, so she'd turned back to the data taken from the Inquisition ship, the last transmissions received before it was blown apart. The translation the interrogator had given her still rankled. She listened to everything again, filtering what she could, trying to discern from incomplete sensor data its last movements. Failing to discover much more than before, she moved to the logs of the enemy battle cruiser's movements. The data was incomplete here too, and what lingered on the lenses was vague. She studied its attack run as best she could, comparing its positional vectors to the known approaches of the system runner. Nothing stood out. If anything, it had been indecisive, fighting within itself for a long period before bringing its big guns to bear. And when it had gone for the *Judgement of the Void*, it had targeted the astropaths' spire, an area already in ruins and far from tactically useful. That might have been a misfire, of course – it was hard to target anything precisely when everything was in motion – but it still stuck out. The spire had been out of action from the very start, one of the first elements of the ship to be damaged. What was drawing so much attention there?

She re-ran the limited records of the engagement's final moments. The cruiser's approach had been orthodox, still displaying that strange lack of commitment that had puzzled her at the time. The enemy was not known for such restraint. Many were the times they had come undone due to overconfidence, blazing into contact with little regard for their own safety. The battle cruiser's tactics had, by contrast, been almost... Imperial.

'Lieutenant!' came a voice from behind her.

She looked up to see Garrock limping towards her. She rose quickly.

'Captain,' she said. 'We've had no report. Did you engage the intruder? Where is the Space Marine?'

Garrock didn't reply immediately. He twisted his helm off, revealing a grizzled face etched with horror. 'Can we speak in private?' he asked.

She nodded, ushered him up to the command throne, activated the audex screen.

'Some deception has been practised here,' Garrock muttered, looking disgusted with himself. 'Some sorcery. Our senses, the ship's senses... We've been blinded.'

'What do you mean?'

'Maizad is dead.'

Hells. Things just kept on getting worse.

'How?'

'He fought the intruder. Both killed the other – and they were wounded before they began.' He lowered his voice, struggled to find the words. 'But the intruder... He wasn't of the enemy. He was Astartes. Imperial Astartes.'

For a moment, she didn't know what to say.

'Can you be sure?'

'Damn you, of course I'm sure.'

He'd never have spoken to her like that before. Even he was feeling it, then.

'Why didn't Maizad detect it?' she asked.

'Because we're all under the curse,' Garrock said bitterly. 'Ever since the muster. No one sees anything straight. The decks are all seething, there's madness in every shadow.' He tried to calm down, to control himself. 'He was half blind. Just like all of us. The curse is everywhere now.'

She turned away from him, trying to concentrate. Even simple thoughts were hard to keep in sequence – half of her wanted to scream, or weep, or laugh.

'A loyal Astartes landed. Where was he trying to get to?'

'The bridge, I reckon. The ship stopped him. It kept him lost in mazes.'

'Why, though? Why land here at all?'

Garrock shrugged. 'It must have been during the battle at U-93, before we made for the warp. It couldn't have been easy – whoever it was sent them, they really wanted to land one.'

A terrible truth began to dawn on her. 'To warn us,' she murmured.

'To what?'

She looked back up at him. 'To warn us. That something else had landed on the ship. Something terrible. The battle cruiser was doing the same.'

'What battle cruiser?'

'The one we fought off before re-entering the warp. It was Imperial. It must have been. It was holding back, trying to target specific areas. Only at the end did it go for us – by then they must have despaired of making contact.' She felt nauseous. 'Kiastros was brilliant. He killed it. The runner's crew saw it too late – what we'd sent them to attack. That was why they were horrified.'

'What's doing it, then?' Garrock demanded. 'Why don't we see it? Why are my troops clawing their own rebreathers off?'

'The astropaths,' Avati said. 'It's the spire. Something's got inside.' She bunched her fists, tried to fight her way through the mental fog. 'The mutants. Could they have been turned, somehow? Damaged, maybe?'

'What of the Inquisition?'

'The captain thinks they're the source. He's gone to take over their cargo.'

'Can he do that?'

Avati shrugged. 'Maybe. Maybe not. Would it do any good, even if he could? I don't even know what it is.'

'And how... *was* he?'

She knew immediately what he meant. Was he mad? Had he succumbed to the fever that was drowning everyone else?

'Animated,' she admitted, even though that felt like a betrayal. 'Too animated. He was... hard to talk to.'

Garrock shook his head. 'Damn it. Then he's gone too. Every choice is cursed. We could use that interrogator. The Sister, too – where's she?'

'With Kuhl, drilling into the spire.'

'Let me guess – no contact.'

Avati nodded. 'Just static.'

'They're headed straight into the heart of something foul.'

'The honoured Sister must be equal to it. And Kuhl has hundreds of troops with her.'

'Not enough.' He rubbed his hand across his sweaty scalp. 'Not enough. We're losing the ship.'

'No,' Avati said. '*No*. We're not losing anything.' She blinked hard, relaxed and re-balled her fists. 'We still have time. We can pull this back.' She thought through the options, tried to put the priorities in order. 'The Navigator told me there's another ship in pursuit. There were two of them. We've been running, but that one must be Imperial too, right? They were in formation. So if we get back into realspace, knowing what we know, we can bring them over. They were targeting the spire – they will have seen it from the outside, they'll know what to do.'

'She's sure?'

'Of course not. She's half sunk into her nightmares, but she was right about it before. I'll go to her. The warp's making this worse anyway – we have to drop out again now. We have an ally right behind us.'

'And the captain?'

She drew in a long breath, looked him squarely in the eye. This was dangerous.

'He won't change course. He won't listen. But you've got your troops, yes? Still able to fight?'

Garrock nodded warily.

'Then take them. Go to the hangars. If he's got the cargo already, then that's one thing. Throne, maybe he's right – maybe it'll help. But if he's struggling, you can make the difference. It's either something we can use, or it's something we have to destroy. I don't trust him–'

She hesitated. It was so difficult to say the words.

'I don't trust him to make the right call now. So if we need to force his hand–'

Garrock nodded again – curt, this time, an understanding of the situation and of the order.

'By your will,' he said. 'I'll do what I can. And after that...'

'The spire. One way or another, that's where this is heading. I'll try to contact Kuhl again. And the Sister. But it might come to us – you know that.'

She looked around her. Beyond the translucent haze of the audex screen, the command bridge was still in disarray.

'If it's a weapon, we'll need it. If it's the problem, we destroy it. If he fails... it'll be you and me.'

Garrock shot her a grim smile. 'Always liked you better, anyway.'

'Go. Go fast, gather every armsman you can, get this done. I'll go to Santalina – can't rely on the comms. We get out of the warp, stop the rot. Keep moving.'

That was it. That had always been it. She'd wasted so much time, got caught up in the sloth and the despair. Keep moving on, moving up. Damn Kiastros. This was *her* ship. Her ship to save now.

'May He preserve you,' Garrock said, making the aquila.

She climbed, one hand hauling her up the long strands, the other free to use her blade. She went as swiftly as she was able, scrabbling for footholds as the web shivered around her, pushing up, up, ever higher.

Behind Isobel came the tech-priests and their rabble, swarming like insects across the fronds. They resisted the psychic horror almost as well as she did, and vigorously went after the physical extrusions. Circular saws whirred into the bizarre melange of organic and metal, drills were taken to the immense boles of the supporting stems. All the panoply of excavation was turned now towards pure destruction, and even the exo-suits lumbered into action, cutting and tearing the monstrosity down.

The creations – it was hard even to guess what to think of them as – did not wait impotently as their edifice was assaulted. They screamed back, both psychically and sonically, making the entire chamber resonate and howl. Cracks opened up across the decks and stacked terraces, disintegrating the very ground the Martians swarmed across. Slivers of etheric lightning, vivid as lance strikes, snaked and forked down from nodes on the lattice. Where those struck home, the Martians' inbuilt equipment shorted and burst open, leaving jerking corpses and flailing, out-of-control limbs.

Some of the embedded creations, the wretched scraps of flesh and pus that had once been mortal psykers, managed to detach themselves from their moorings, wrestling free in puffs of blood and torn flesh. They were still as blind as they had ever been, and their bodies had been stretched and contorted nearly beyond recognition, but the power that had created them imbued them with uncanny speed and strength. They swung down from the swaying lattice, mouths agape and spewing madness, fingers as long as forearms raking and tearing. Just to witness them move was to invite a kind of madness – it was as though they were swimming in a thick miasma, their obscenely stretched limbs raking and cartwheeling, their empty, agonised eyes weeping blood. Were they conscious of what they did? Did any remnant of humanity still reside in their pulverised brains? It didn't look like it. It looked like they were mere flesh-puppets now, marionettes strung up on their own psychic agony and propelled by external intelligences. Above them all, as they capered and plummeted, the orifice of the open warp turned and turned, fuelling and upholding the bacchanalia. When its creatures latched on to an unfortunate mortal, they enveloped it, stretched their scraps of skin around it, fused their fingers to its cranium and sucked the shrieking life out of it. Even the skitarii screamed when one of those things got them.

Isobel kept climbing. She couldn't see Kuhl. She couldn't see many of the engine crew – maybe none of them could tolerate the cauldron of madness. It mattered not. She was here, as if placed there by providence, the only one left on the ship capable of taking on such unbounded perversions. She could not falter. Not now, not here.

Her grip slipped, and she compensated, digging her heels into the yielding matter of the twisting frond. Another pull, and she was up higher still, surrounded by the dense fog that swirled and bloomed across the entire structure. The thing that had once been Ortuyo was bellowing, raging, thrashing against its bonds. It was so enormous now, splayed and extended and ripped apart, that it seemed as much a part of the vast structure as its unseen masters, and struggled to detach itself from the amplification matrix.

One of the lesser creatures managed to reach her. It swung across from a tangle of dripping fronds and threw itself at her. It was a scrawny thing, the hideous result of a skinny body being bent out of all proportion and contorted into a new, wild form, but that made it hard to strike at. Its spindly limbs flailed, its tortured eyes bulged. Its mouth was locked open, pulled ridiculously wide, the sinews yanked taut and exposed, screaming at her with an unbroken howl of anguish. More than that, though, it was still a voice within the choir, still part of that unholy transmitter of insanity, and she felt the waves of it crash across her. It was like a frigid wash, a shiver of primal fear, a sudden recollection of every failure and every weakness, all sent pumping into her body and surging up into her soul.

She never hesitated. Not for a moment. Her body kept moving, on and up, surging into the oncoming horror. She lashed out, a crossways strike with her blade, severing the thing's outstretched fingers and spraying them both with its boiling blood. She kicked out, shattering a kneecap, then twisted to punch out with her blade again, stabbing motions, fast and accurate, aimed into the open jawline to silence the maddening chorus.

It yowled at her, latching on to her shoulder with its lone remaining hand, and she felt an appalling sensation of suction – a withering and a scooping out of her will. She staggered, missing her aim, and slipped down the webbing. The creature scrambled after her, its flesh-skirts flapping and its beady eyes lit up with malice.

Isobel steadied herself, grabbed the long web-strand with one hand and thrust out again with her crackling blade. The tip punched straight into the creature's maw, severing its lolling tongue and silencing the barrage of psychic resonances. That made things easier – physically, the stringy horror was no match for her speed and strength. She laid into it, cutting and swiping, throwing scraps of its tormented muscle tissue wide and sending them tumbling back down towards the chamber's distant base. A final blow through its emaciated ribcage was enough to silence its residual wails and send its ravaged corpse bouncing down the long slide to the bottom.

Now she was breathing heavily, her heart pumping. She needed to keep moving, make use of her power armour's assistance to keep climbing. The Mechanicus warriors were toiling a long way down, burning their way through the increasingly demented psykers' attacks, but it was all too slow – only she had climbed up far enough to strike at the heart of the machine. Ortuyo sat above at the centre of the nexus like some vast and bloated spider, distended and distributed, still struggling to detach his unnatural bulk from the cables and milky strands that bound him in place. As she got closer, Isobel breathed in the full degradation of his transformation – the stench of decay masked with sweetness, the absolute cacophony of pain that blared from his locked-open jaws. It was overwhelming, overpowering, a tidal wave of despair that blotted out almost all else. It was like a fever, like fighting your way into the heart of some deranged dream where reality blended into increasingly esoteric layers of morbid fantasy.

She climbed as fast as she could, ignoring the siren calls of the monsters. Ortuyo had managed to get some of his many limbs free, and now slumped and twisted his way to meet her, slithering over the fronds in a welter of fermented slime. His gaping jaw was truly obscene up close, exposing a rippling well of pure ether-matter that popped and wobbled with his every movement. He was nothing but a conduit for it now, the unholy route through which the warp's malevolence had invaded the ship.

He lashed out at her, striking the lattice and making it swing. She nearly lost her footing again, and clung on hard, letting her body move with the impacts. The chance came, and she thrust upward again, blade extended, its disruptor field flaring as it came into proximity with the diseased flesh. Ortuyo dropped down at her, his enormous bulk flopping across the strands, and she had to scramble laterally to avoid being crushed by the flailing folds of tortured skin. She heard wild cries as she fought back – had Kuhl managed to clamber onto the webbing? Some of her crew? There was no time to glance back. She had to press on, fight her way through the lashing tendrils and filaments.

A tentacle whipped towards her – she sliced its tip off with a backhand swipe. A twelve-fingered hand reached out to throttle her and she stabbed it straight through the palm, making the digits snap closed in reflex and causing Ortuyo to yammer in pain. By then she was right up into the heart of his many appendages, clambering up into the living structure towards the swollen, pulsating heart. His gaping maw overshadowed her, spilling out every kind of psychic filth. Visions of excruciation flashed before her eyes like vid-picts – ribs snapping, skin unfurling from slick muscle, organs bursting and eyeballs lacerated.

'Damn you!' she cried, lashing out against the visions of horror. Fighting was the only thing now, the only means of defence against the psychic assault. If she stopped, even for a moment, the chorus would crowd into her mind completely, drenching it with every last diseased remnant of Ortuyo's failing, wretched consciousness. 'Damn you all!'

She cut and slashed, her flaming sword cooking the flaps of blubber and fat. Fingers came at her, dozens of them, aiming to freeze on her temples and cheeks, to drain the energy from her and replace it with terror. She swatted them away, her blade now moving faster than ever, her concentration total. Any error and she'd be enveloped by the squatting monster above her, sucked into his tormented embrace and turned into just one more voice in the choir. Ortuyo's shadow now fell across her, blocking out the rippling light of the warp above.

From below her she heard more shouts, more roars of aggression. They were human, not mechanical: so Kuhl had somehow managed to force an assault, to resist the wailing abominations and bring her crew into the fight. Good for her. Isobel pressed her own attack, clinging to the wildly oscillating fibrous strands while her sword whirled into the oncoming assault.

She wasn't immune to Ortuyo's siren call. It was brutally effective up close – a distilled shot of venom straight from the heart of the warp beyond the hull. The tug of madness was hard to resist. There was a temptation to simply relax her grip, fall back down towards the struggling masses on the deck below, to give up, to let others take the strain. What, after all, did she owe this ship? She was only a passenger, arriving on a whim, not one of those who had lived all their lives aboard it and wished to serve on it until death. The Ortuyo-creature was vile beyond reason, clogging her nostrils with his unholy stench and snagging at her sanity with his outrageous, tortured appearance. If the enemy could do this to one human, it could do the same to all of them, including her. She wasn't anything particularly special, not a master of combat like Maizad nor a commander of tempered skill like Kiastros. She was a healer, not a fighter.

'Ha!' she laughed, recognising the doubts for just what they were. A novice straight out of basic training might have listened to them for a moment, but she was too wily to be taken in now. She was human in all senses, a lover of life, as faithful a servant of the Immortal Throne as any who had ever taken up the banner. She would end this thing. She would silence its nightmare broadcasts. She would consign what remained of its addled soul to the deepest pits of forgetfulness.

She parried and she thrust, driving her crackling blade deeper into the living corpse of the beast. He screamed more wildly, he thrashed harder to dislodge her, and she just kept going, pushing back, slicing and severing. Her armour was coated with ichor and slime, smouldering as she carved into the centre of the beast's vast and splayed body. She could see his head now, rearing up with that horrific fixed-open mouth, far too big, fizzing with empyreal energies. What remained of the man's throat was exposed – a sweaty, glistening expanse of vibrating wattles, ripe for a single cut.

'I have you now!' she roared, reaching to pull herself closer. The mutant, in truth, wasn't any match for her – not physically. His entire structure, the whole point of his ludicrously ruined body, was to corrupt the psyche of the ship, not to fight at an individual level. As disgusting as he looked, as wretched and fear-inducing as his aura made it, she could kill him. She could plunge her blessed blade right through that scrawny neck and end the whole game. The ship would be made whole again. She could go back down the tunnels in triumph. She braced herself against the swinging lattice and pulled her arm back, the blade's tip levelled at the monster's exposed throat.

And suddenly, she was not alone. Unbelievably, Kuhl had clambered up beside her, braving the treacherous climb and the waves of psychic horror. She had taken her helm off at some point, exposing a face locked into a rictus of determination. She was sweating profusely, panting like a canid on the hunt, looking almost demented.

'Well met, my sister!' Isobel laughed, glorying in the absurdity of the sight. It was better this way – a member of crew to make the killing blow, a representative of those who had suffered most acutely from the madness. 'Together, then!'

Kuhl had taken up a turbo-drill with a lascutter muzzle – something usually carried by servitors due to its weight and complexity, but here she hauled it one-handed. She levelled it right at the gaping jawline of the Ortuyo-beast.

Then Kuhl swivelled it round to Isobel, and for the first time she noticed that the light in the woman's eyes was not just mortal determination.

'I will *not go back!*' Kuhl slurred, her face contorting into true madness. 'They came to take me away!'

Isobel hesitated, suddenly struck by a terrible fear. The creature had got to Kuhl – her sanity had gone.

'No, you–' she began.

Too late. Kuhl fired the drill, maximum power, point-blank range, and Isobel's world exploded into light and pain.

# Chapter Twenty-Eight

**INVINCIBLE**

**SUCH A LITTLE THING**

**TOO LATE**

The interrogator was hit by a whole flurry of strikes – projectiles, las-bolts, maybe half a dozen of them. He was wearing armour, and it weathered the impacts, but it knocked his aim off and sent him staggering back towards the open doorway. Kiastros' own shot missed too – he'd never considered himself a good marksman – but by then he was running, sprinting with the rest of his troops towards the entrance to the isolation halls.

As soon as the order had been given, as soon as the shots had started flying, everything seemed to blur. The world became a whirl of impressions, of warriors shouting and screaming, of guns opening up, of the crack and splinter of rockcrete being pulverised. His whole mob, all of them, had followed the order, surging forward and loosing everything at the enemy. That pleased him so much. They had been scared, dragged down here against all their instincts, but now that the moment had come they were responding as they'd been trained to. Some were officers – fine people, expert fighters – and others were the rabble of the lower decks, who had their own brutal methods of combat. It added up. The numbers made the difference.

Maybe the Inquisition should have locked themselves inside. Perhaps it had been arrogance that had brought them out into the open, or perhaps the – correct – assumption that he would have just blown up the doors. Maybe il-Moro thought he could intimidate them into withdrawing, or maybe his judgement was just as shot by spending too much time under a null-psi field. It didn't matter – the deed was done, the decision made, and now it all came down to strength of arms.

Kiastros raced to the doorway, surrounded by his retainers. Two of them were cut down, but not before forcing entry to the hall and pouring inside. The Inquisitorial retinue fell back before them, firing with discipline and dropping dozens, but once inside the first chamber the press of bodies made it harder. Two of them – death cult assassins, by their garb – switched to blades and started to create havoc. A figure wearing some kind of power armour laid into those closest to him with a claymore, cutting them apart. A woman with glittering eyes stretched out a closed fist and exploded the stomachs of two crew members coming at her. The interrogator's storm troopers were lethal too, sticking to their lasguns and reaping a heavy toll.

That should have broken the assault. That should have sent this rabble packing with their tails between their legs. The melee was so reckless, so open, so incautious, that by rights they should have all been sprinting into a slaughter.

But it didn't. Every death merely roused the others to greater heights. Kiastros felt his heart sing as the blood splattered across his face. He shot one of the storm troopers, and screamed with pleasure when a dozen other intersecting las-bolts cut the man down and threw his body backwards into a storage crate. He yelled aloud when one of the assassins was overwhelmed by a dozen bilge-rats working in concert. They rushed her, heedless of the glittering, artful blade, piling on top of her, crushing and throttling.

One of his junior officers targeted the null-psi field generator, and the chamber rocked with explosions. Others hurled krak charges into the stacked crates, blowing them up in clouds of spinning plascrete. The chambers immediately filled with smoke, cutting the visibility down for anyone not wearing a helm. The fight became a frenzied scrum, up close and claustrophobic, and more of them switched to blades. Kiastros strode through it all, laspistol in one hand, ceremonial power sword in the other, lashing out and taking shots when a target came too close.

He felt invincible. He felt majestic. This was what taking his realm back involved – assuming charge, getting his hands bloody again. He'd been sitting in the throne for too long, dealing out death from extreme range. This was better. This was what a Space Marine felt like. This was what service to the Throne demanded.

One of the storm troopers broke out of combat and barrelled towards him, firing snap-shots. They all missed, and Kiastros struck back with his sword, knocking the fighter backwards with one blow, slashing across his armour's neck seal with the next. As the trooper reeled, Kiastros spun his blade round, pushing it tip down into his body. It passed through the heavy armour with a flash of energy from the disruptor.

'By His will!' he roared, shaking the blood from his head and shoulders like a dog and casting the corpse aside.

He never stopped to consider how hard it should have been to kill a storm trooper. He never thought – not for a moment – how likely it was that every shot fired by an exceptionally trained killer should keep missing him. He never noticed how easily his ceremonial sword sliced through Inquisition-grade carapace plate. All he experienced was a surge of extreme and overwhelming confidence, a bow-wave of exuberance that fuelled his muscles and made his heart swell. There was a booming in his ears, a rush of sound like voices singing, urging him on, and he revelled in it.

'This is His ship!' he shouted. 'This is *my* ship! Kill them all!'

The mob was in a frenzy now. They charged at the retreating Inquisition forces, leaping over crates and bulkheads, shrugging off hits and piling in closer. They swarmed like rats, clambering over their fallen comrades just to get at the enemy. So many were killed, picked off by las-fire or torn apart by vicious blade-blows, but it didn't stop the rest. Kiastros could not have been prouder of them. Somehow the fear had gone, the enervating despair that made them all see visions and imagine monsters. He never thought why that change should have happened just then. He never thought – not for a moment – that the change had been so very sudden.

Because he was in his element. He charged on, pushing the surviving retinue back into the room beyond, singling out il-Moro even as his crew threw themselves at the rest.

'Regret your decision yet?' Kiastros taunted, feeling the trickle of sweat running down his forehead.

The interrogator stood his ground, and the two of them clashed, their blades crackling together. Il-Moro was taller, better-armoured, stronger, and yet he faltered first, pushed back against the far wall of the chamber.

'You don't see it, do you?' the interrogator snarled. 'You don't see it at all.'

Kiastros laughed, swinging his blade back heavily. 'I see everything. For the first time, I think. *Everything!*'

Il-Moro was powerful. He was dogged, and he was unyielding. Hatred had kindled in the man's dark eyes – unfeigned, real hatred. Kiastros saw that he was no longer pretending, no longer doubtful. He was fighting like a man who truly, truly wanted to kill him, to hurt him, to make him suffer. His bladework was sophisticated, the product of all that long Inquisition conditioning, and Kiastros found himself hammered back, knocked onto his heels and forced to work furiously to defend himself. Now that the man had no choices to make, pushed into defending the thing he had brought with him from the void, he was unrestrained, and it was hard to counter.

'You've been a fool!' il-Moro hissed at him. 'A blind, deaf fool! Keep to your orders. It's all you had to do.'

Kiastros pushed back, feeling his arms burn, his lungs labour. 'I don't know if it was malice or ignorance,' he panted. 'Doesn't matter now. The thing you guard is *hateful*.'

'Then why do you wish for it so badly?' il-Moro countered. 'Why must you *take* it? You could have destroyed this whole deck and nothing I could do would have stopped you.'

That halted Kiastros. He almost missed his parry, letting il-Moro's blade angle in to his chest, but corrected at the very last moment.

Why *did* he want to take it? Why hadn't he merely blasted the hangar level into scrap?

The roaring in his ears grew louder, more insistent. The fever in his blood ramped up again, flushing his skin dark, pulsing in his temples.

'*Everything* on this ship is mine,' he snarled, whirling back into the attack. He swiped and slashed, pushed and slammed, faster now, his motions propelled by righteous fury. 'By the Lex, by my divine right. You stand between me and my property, and the consequences shall be yours alone.'

'It can't be destroyed!' il-Moro shouted back. 'You understand that? You *cannot destroy it*. It must be kept safe, locked away. Cease this madness! *Listen!*'

That wasn't true. It couldn't be true. Everything could be destroyed, given enough time, enough power. He had a battle cruiser! He had galleries upon galleries of guns! What could possibly exist, small enough to fit in a standard cargo crate, that could withstand the volleys from those batteries?

Lies. Lies upon lies. That was all the Inquisition knew. It was all they had ever known.

He lashed out again. The strokes came in faster, too fast for the interrogator, who was suffering now. Kiastros smashed him backwards, bludgeoning him towards the open doorway into the chamber beyond. Il-Moro tried to resist, fighting hard and well, but Kiastros had never felt so good, so powerful, so completely in control of his body. He sent a truly vicious slash scything across the interrogator's guard, clattering his blade away and sending the crackling length of steel tumbling. Then he was in close, stabbing with venom, again and again, carving up the man's armour and throwing the shards and splinters spinning in all directions. Il-Moro still tried to fight back – he was brave, if nothing else – and pulled a dagger from his belt, but it was too late now. Kiastros whipped his sword back to take the interrogator's hand off at the wrist, then swivelled it round to drive the edge deep into his midriff. The armour plate had buckled there, so the killing edge sank right into the flesh, burning it up as it travelled.

Il-Moro collapsed, coughing up blood. Kiastros twisted the blade further in, relishing the vibrations as the energy field pulsed. The interrogator gave him one last look, an expression of pure loathing and contempt.

'Trai...tor,' he croaked, before finally crumpling to the deck.

Kiastros laughed out loud. What a ludicrous thing to say, right at the end.

He looked around. The last resistance had been snuffed out – the Inquisitorial retinue lay dead across the deck. They had exacted a terrible price – perhaps two-thirds of the mob Kiastros had brought with him were dead or incapacitated, but it had been enough. Something told him he ought to speak to those who remained, who were now looking rather aimless and dejected again. Many were badly wounded and needed immediate attention, and it wasn't clear how many officers remained to command them. He wondered where the Sister was. Hadn't she withdrawn from her assignment? Could she look after all this now?

Then his attention wandered. He turned back to look past il-Moro's still-twitching body to the open doorway. The chamber beyond was unoccupied, though full of the piles of equipment that Avati had told him about.

He started to walk towards the doorway. As he moved, he felt a pleasant warm glow spread over his body. It wasn't like the terrible overheating he'd experienced ever since the muster. It was inordinately comforting. He deserved to have a little respite, after all that had happened. He passed across the threshold, and the sensation only increased.

Standing before him, on the deck, was a large reinforced case. It didn't look like the rest of the storage units – it was entirely constructed of metal, possibly iron, and had an antique appearance. It was fairly large – over two yards long and one yard across, far too heavy for him to pick up. Its outer faces were covered in tiny inscriptions in an archaic form of Gothic. It hurt his eyes to look at those, and he made no attempt to read the scripts. Parchment scraps dotted every surface, held in place by wax seals, also covered in inscriptions. The entire thing seemed to be gently steaming, sending tiny trails of condensation spilling down its edges to the deck below. Its precise dimensions were curiously hard to pin down – one moment it seemed to be growing, the next to have snapped back to its original size.

That didn't matter much, because it was by far the most beautiful thing Kiastros had ever seen. He came up close, sheathing his sword and dropping to his knees. Just reaching out to touch it felt like a rare privilege – he expected electricity to snap between the iron mantle and his outstretched fingers.

He'd never have been able to open it had the locks still been in place. Just one look at those heavy shackles, wound about with protective runes, told him that. For some reason, though, the clasps were open. The lid was open. Had il-Moro done that? Had he been trying to do something with his precious cargo before being interrupted? Doubtful – Avati had been fairly sure they had no idea what it was. Strange, then, that it should be so easy for him to reach inside.

He hesitated. A tremor of fear rippled through him. He felt suddenly anxious, as if he'd forgotten something very important, something that everything depended on but that he'd mislaid somehow. He sensed the entire ship extending in all directions around him, vast and ancient, the custody of which had been his life's work and privilege. He remembered how small he was, how small all of them were, and how colossal was the place where they plied their trade.

This was his realm. His kingdom. The place he had sworn to guard against all ills. Now, suddenly, it seemed incredibly fragile, as if the structure itself were crying out, weeping, trying to speak to him, to say something important. He saw the expanse of it in his mind's eye – the great cannon galleries, the drive chambers, the engine halls, the high spires. So indomitable. So invincible. He couldn't imagine it would ever be ended. It *must* never be ended.

Then the vision left him, and the warmth returned. He blinked to clear his vision, reached out again. This time his fingers crossed the perimeter, entering the golden aura that gently emanated from the open casket. As if in a dream, he felt to grasp the contents within, and his grip closed on something hard and cool and abrasive.

He withdrew the object that lay within the chest, and stared at it for a long time. The world around him sank into nothing, and for a while all he could do was stare at it.

So this was what all the fuss was about, he thought.

'Such a little thing,' he said aloud, mesmerised by what he held. 'Such a little thing, for so much trouble.'

Avati knew she was doing something right when the ship tried to stop her going where she wanted to go. You couldn't pretend it wasn't happening now – corridors would end abruptly, doors would refuse to unlock, life-support failure warnings would suddenly kick in and prompt the bio-seal of whole sections. The crew around her – those still at their stations, those still sensate – were no use at all now.

She pressed on. It made a difference, how you reacted to it all. The moment you started to doubt, to start to think that you wouldn't make it, that was when you got stuck. You had to keep your eyes open and your scanners on, too – the changes didn't happen in front of you, not while you were actually watching, but out of sight, out of the corner of your eyes, a subtle rearrangement that seemed to depend a great deal on your own perception of events. Once you adapted to the essential strangeness of it all – the crippling fear that *the ship is being altered* – then it was possible to resist, to make compensations, to make progress. Whatever process had been unleashed, it wasn't complete yet. It was still fighting against the laws of physics, the heaviness of matter, so the game wasn't up. So she had to concentrate, to hold it together where everyone else was losing their mind. Never stop, just push on. The moment you sat back, took it all in, that was the moment it got you.

She wondered if Kiastros had reached his destination yet, and if he'd killed the interrogator. She sensed no change yet, so if he'd managed to reach the mysterious cargo already then it hadn't had any effect. In any case, she was increasingly sure that the spire was the source – the Imperial ship had aimed for it, after all. Nothing came back from Kuhl's comm now, not even the hiss of an empty channel. The whole place was sealed off from within, a vast tumour on the body of the ship that was sinking its tendrils deeper and deeper. What could be done about it? Could it be destroyed from the outside? That was the last chance, in all probability, unless the captain was right about il-Moro's treasure.

She went faster, jogging up the narrow ladders, sticking to the lit crawlways where she could. After a while she smelled it – the tang of incense that gave away the approaches to Santalina's demesne. There was no sign of the Navigator's attendants, and the corridors on the approach were strewn with refuse – smashed caskets, robes, even jewellery. Avati made her way carefully through it all, keeping her laspistol drawn. She could hear her own heavy breathing inside her helm's earpieces, feel her heart thumping. The atmosphere inside was even eerier than elsewhere – if you blinked, it looked like the walls were absolutely crawling.

The hum of the engines was very loud up here – Avati knew that resonance tubes ran all the way down to the main halls, giving the Navigator the constant ability to judge the health of the warp drives. They sounded chronic to Avati just then, like a sacrificial beast trapped in a vice and roaring to get out. All the antechambers were deserted too, with the same mess everywhere. The doors leading inside were open, though, which made accessing the core much easier – it would have been an inconvenience to have had to use charges.

Avati approached the great iron sphere, saw the locked hatch in its side. The access panel was open, its collection of runic tumblers exposed. Avati entered the code, and felt the locks clunk open. Santalina probably didn't know that both she and

Kiastros had means of access. Or perhaps she did, and didn't care about it. Navigators were powerful people with rules of their own, but a prudent captain preserved ways to get to them, if need be.

The heavy hatch swung open and a rich mist of smoky incense spilled across the threshold and over the deck. Avati ducked her head under the lintel and pushed herself through.

It was hazy inside, hard to breathe, hard to see much. The iron sphere was large, composed of a number of smaller interlocking spaces, so she picked her way carefully. Eventually she reached the very centre, the site of the Navigator's grand throne. The noise of the engines was louder in there, swelling like the sea in her ears. Santalina was sitting in her usual position, her limbs covered in input cables, her grand gown draped in ruffles of fine damask. Maybe she'd heard Avati approach, or maybe she'd paused her scrying, for her Seeing Eye was safely covered up. Her natural eyes were both closed, though she wasn't asleep. A faint smile played across her cracked lips.

'It's the spire,' Avati said, coming to stand before her. She kept her laspistol drawn.

Santalina's smile broadened. 'I know.'

'When did you know?'

'Not until a little while ago. When I heard Ortuyo screaming. Only it's not Ortuyo any more. It's something else. A conveyance into the warp itself.' The smile faded. 'What a fate for him. What an indignity for a man of his talents.'

'What happened?'

'I don't know exactly. Something broke in. Enough to overpower the choir. You saw the reports from Garrock? They tried a similar thing in the forward enginarium, I think, but the Space Marines prevented them. Those psykers were a gift to them, though. Powerful mutants, capable of causing so much mischief. Just like me.'

'The warp makes it worse.'

'The warp makes everything worse.'

'It's corrupting the whole ship.'

'It is, isn't it? Fascinating to watch.' Santalina turned her head towards Avati, opened her eyes. 'I can feel it, like water lapping slowly higher. We're being pulled in.'

'It has to stop.'

'You think it can be stopped?'

Avati had to go carefully now. Santalina had an edge of madness to her, just like everyone else. She was too old. Kiastros should have replaced her a decade ago, but then they'd always been so close, the two of them. The wrong word here, now, and everything could fall apart very quickly.

'Can you bring us out of the warp?' Avati asked.

'I could. But then we'd be vulnerable again. The captain ordered me to keep us out of the void.'

'Because there's a second ship.'

Santalina looked impressed. 'How do you know that?'

'You told me. Over the comm.'

'I did?'

'Were you right? Is there one?'

Santalina gave her a shrewd grin. 'But what difference would it make? Being destroyed in here, being destroyed out there? We have no guns left.'

Avati prepared herself. This was the essential sell.

'Because we have all been blinded. The intruder on the lower decks was an Imperial Astartes. The ships following us from the muster were Imperial ships. We destroyed one, but they were coming after us for a reason. They could see what we could not – that our hull had been compromised by something that had the power to take us over. They tried to prevent it, and we fought back. But one ship remains. One last hope. Now that we *know*, we can invite it close. They can board us, bring on troops to cut out the infection. Throne, they could even destroy it from the void, just as they tried to before. So we need to drop out. Lower our shields, come to full-stop. If it can track us like the other one did, it will know what it has to do.'

Santalina had been listening carefully. 'We shot its companion to pieces. Do you think they will wait to be attacked a second time?'

'Maybe not. They might open fire at once.' Avati shrugged. 'But better that, better a clean destruction, than to be eaten alive by this corruption. There are worse things than death in the void.'

Santalina thought about it. 'Does this come from the captain?'

There it was. Always back to Kiastros.

'He is busy.'

'Does he know you're here?'

'I cannot raise him. He gave me operational command.'

Santalina laughed. 'So that's it, eh? While the cat's away? You lost your chance for a new hull, I think, so you'll take this one. After all, who'd employ you after that catastrophe at the muster? It's over, so you're making the best of it.' She shook her head. 'Naughty, naughty. But then you've always been a scheming little bitch.'

Avati's blood rose, her trigger finger twitched. 'This has nothing to do with–'

'Oh, come on. You think he ran. At U-93. You think he's a fool, an old-fashioned martinet who deserves everything he gets. This is your *chance*, isn't it? You'll do anything to depose him, and if you need to do it this way, you won't hesitate.'

'You're insane.'

'We're all insane. That's what comes of drinking from the warp's cup. And we've all been doing it for far too long.'

Avati aimed her laspistol at Santalina's face. 'Then bring us out.'

'You'll *kill* me? And then how will you navigate?'

'There'll be a way. All I need is to get back to realspace. If I have to do it myself, I will.'

Santalina suddenly looked at her with something like respect. 'I believe you would, at that,' she murmured. Then the feyness returned. 'But it doesn't much matter now. Nothing much matters. You want proof? You want to see what's been after us all this time?'

Avati suddenly felt cold. The Navigator had a very odd expression on her withered face, one that properly alarmed her.

'Bring us out,' she ordered.

'No, let me *show* you,' said Santalina, reclining in the throne and flicking a switch.

Far above them both, where the curve of the sphere rose in a high dome, the locks on the warp-shutters slammed open.

'No!' screamed Avati, backing away.

'Too late!' giggled Santalina, as the lead panels slowly began to unfurl. 'Too late for us all!'

# Chapter Twenty-Nine

SO, SO CLOSE

PUT IT DOWN

NOT IN SPACE

Isobel fell. She fell for a very long time. On the way down, everything seemed to slow. She saw Maizad's face staring at her out of the whirling shadows, morose and reproachful.

'Why did you send me back out?' he asked her. 'Why didn't you fix me?'

Then that vision disappeared, to be replaced by Avati. The two of them were drinking a glass of wine together, laughing. Isobel had liked the first lieutenant. It had been a good evening.

Finally, she saw Kuhl. Dependable, competent Kuhl. She saw her as she had been before, in her enginarium fatigues, working away on the valves and the pistons.

'You *shot* me,' Isobel accused, outraged.

Then she hit the deck. Her armour took the brunt of the impact, but it was still horrific. Isobel felt her bones crack, the air expelled from her lungs, her blade sent flying off into the dark.

It was hard to breathe. Kuhl's shot had bored a hole into her chest. Blood was still pumping from it. She couldn't move her limbs – both her legs were agonising, her arms were heavy as lead. She tried to lift her head, and felt hot spikes of pain run down her neck.

She needed to get up. She needed to move again. It was so hard to see anything – the dark and haze and smoke swilled around her. For a while she only heard a high-pitched whine in her ears, but as that cleared she picked out the shouts and screams of combat. The psyker-creatures were still taking on the Mechanicus and enginarium crew. It sounded like the creatures were winning now. The atmosphere of dread had become crushing again, like a physical pall that seeped into every joint and pore.

She tried to rise again and managed to lift her head. She got an arm to move, shoved the crook of her elbow down, forcing her torso up a little. Everything was so painful, so slow. Her breastplate ran with blood which didn't seem to be clotting. She felt light-headed and empty, but had to keep moving. She peered upwards, trying to make out more of what was going on overhead. Everything was blurred – she thought she spotted the Ortuyo-mutant very high up, still bound tightly in those webs of cabling. Its jaws were still wide open, still spewing the silent screams that were turning the ship in on itself.

She would have killed it. She was so close.

'Damn you,' she grunted, bringing her other elbow in, trying to lift herself into a seated posture. Where would she get a weapon from? Could she get back up there? *'Damn you.'*

And then, out of the rolling shadow-banks, came Kuhl. She must have clambered down, and was panting roughly from the exertion. She limped up to Isobel, her improvised weapon still in her hand. Isobel tried to shuffle away from her, but it was no use – she was crippled, her body broken.

Kuhl crouched down, rested her drill on her knee.

'I'm so sorry,' Kuhl slurred. 'So, so sorry.'

'Why?' Isobel demanded. 'What... *madness* took you?'

Kuhl looked at the wound she'd caused. She was sorrowful, but only in the way a small child was sorrowful. 'I cannot allow you to kill it,' she said. 'That will end this, and they will take me back down. The Inquisition is here.'

It made no sense.

'Listen,' Isobel tried, feeling her strength ebb with every passing moment. She needed a weapon – would Kuhl's drill be enough? 'The scream is getting to you. You are not yourself. You have my protection, you know that? You have nothing to fear from anyone.'

Kuhl was listening. Her dull eyes wandered, her fingers twitched, but she listened.

Isobel pushed herself a little closer. 'That creature must be ended – you see that?' she urged. 'It's in your mind. That's what it does. It's what's making the ship transform. We have to kill it, you and me.'

Kuhl looked up. Howls of terror were still echoing throughout the chamber, punctuated by the electric crackle of the Mechanicus' weaponry. Ortuyo's mutated bulk could just be made out, a clot of blackness against the churn of smoke and steam. The naked warp roiled above it all, flooding the space with its foul multidimensional light, amplifying the madness, dragging their minds away from sanity.

Then she looked back at Isobel.

'There's nothing up there,' she said groggily, as if drugged. 'Just some damage to the dome. Everything can be fixed.'

Isobel clenched her fists. She'd have to move quickly, decisively – she was so weak still.

'Help me up. Help me to show you.'

Kuhl didn't move. 'I will be back in the enginarium,' she

mumbled, losing focus again. 'Safe in there. Part of the engines. The engines, part of me. I'll never leave them again.'

'Just help me up.' If she could get to Kuhl's drill, grab it from her, there was still a chance.

Kuhl looked away again.

'I still don't want to do it,' Kuhl said miserably.

'Want to do what, child?' asked Isobel softly, getting her hand in range to make the move.

'Kill you,' said Kuhl sadly, activating the drill's power pack again. 'Because you were nice to me.'

She fired a second time, driving a white-hot las-burst through the other side of Isobel's breastplate.

Isobel arched her back, impaled on the line of agony. She screamed out, thrashing her shattered arms, trying to reach Kuhl's neck. But it was no good – the drill-beam hammered through her, burning her up, torching away her life. Isobel felt tears of frustration prick at her open eyes – she had been *so close!* So close to ending the monster. She had been placed there, put in the location she needed to be in, given the chance to fulfil her potential, and she had failed.

'No!' she howled, feeling the darkness close in around her.

Kuhl was weeping, even as she poured on the power. Some small part of her might have known what was coming now, a tiny piece of her ravaged consciousness, aware that death was by far the best outcome compared to what was about to happen to the rest of the ship.

Isobel's consciousness began to fade, lost in a riot of pain and blood and horror. It wasn't enough. It wasn't a comfort. She had been so very, very close.

The back of her head hit the deck with a wet smack. Her last sight was of Ortuyo hanging above her, backlit by the fury of the warp. The astropath was laughing, laughing so hard that his jaws split even further apart, gaping wider and wider, a pit

into absolute oblivion, a fiery circlet around a blasphemous and
flickering tongue, and he laughed, and laughed, and laughed.

Garrock had run hard from the bridge to the garrison. Everywhere he went after leaving the bridge gave him fuel for nightmares. He'd once had to evacuate a deck that had been on fire, sprinting from station to station as the flames lapped around his ankles, and he had a similar sensation now. The anomalies were no longer just anomalies – the structure of the corridors and the crawlways and the transit shafts was rippling and flexing before his eyes. Lumen-pods were bursting, exposing wriggling nests of snakes in the sodium tubes. Ventilation panels were popping open, exposing inhuman screams filtered down from all decks and levels. The decking itself undulated like water, and the engine hum had become a stuttering growl, a slurring thunder that got into your head and made you want to smash it against the wall just to make it stop.

He recited the old litanies to himself as he ran. He'd never paid much attention to them before. Never liked a priest, never willingly gone to the grand services, but now, *now*, he was praying hard. It was so hard not to panic, to give in and let the madness swamp him, and that was the only way he could stay on his feet.

He'd managed to drag together a dozen armsmen, the few that he'd found who were still sane enough to follow an order and hale enough to get to their feet. He'd made sure they knew what was at stake.

'You see what's happening here,' he'd told them. 'The captain's decided that the cargo is the source. He's decided to seize it. He may be right. If he is, we go to aid him.'

Then he'd hesitated. It was still so hard to say.

'If he's not, if he's been driven mad by it, then we take it from him, deliver it to the first lieutenant. You get that? You understand what I'm saying?'

They did. Mutiny. Or at the very least, insurrection. If they were wrong, if this ever got out to fleet command, they'd all be liable for execution.

He'd almost laughed out loud, though, when that thought had occurred to him. What did it matter, when the warp was swilling freely through every vent? What could be *worse* than this?

So they ran, all of them, shotguns drawn and shields carried. They powered through the crowds of disorientated crew members, the faltering machinery, the empty picter lenses and the blaring vox-emitters. They chanted as they went – *Imperator Eterna, Imperator Eterna* – over and over again. They needed to. They needed to focus, to not look at the abominations blooming around them, to not listen to the strangled cries and imprecations from the dark. It still mattered, what you felt, what you *thought*. You could fight it, if you kept yourself together, your eyes on the target.

He had so very little idea what he was going to do when he got there. He still nurtured a hope – maybe a distant one – that the captain had landed on the solution, and that he'd already managed to take control. He kept imagining arriving at the isolation halls to find Kiastros in command of his senses, with a plan, with everything already turning for the better.

But he wasn't stupid. Whatever process had started, it was still rattling along. It had fooled them all, turned them into dupes, even Maizad.

Even Maizad. That had been the hardest blow. The hardest thing to witness.

'Keep running!' he shouted angrily. 'Keep running!'

They charged down the final long corridor, through the open blast doors, into the empty hangar where the system runner had been berthed. The isolation halls lay ahead past heaps of bodies. The corpses were mostly those of the crew – some senior ranks, most gun-deck rats. The halls' main entrance also lay open, and Garrock could already see more bodies slumped beyond the threshold.

He came to a halt, waved for those behind him to follow suit, then edged warily up to the entrance doorway. It smelled strongly of death already – some of the bodies appeared to be festering faster than normal. He heard the low buzz of insects.

He signalled for a rearguard to halt and stand watch over the gates, then beckoned the rest to come with him. They shuffled forward, guns aimed outward, going carefully.

The smell inside the hall was worse. More bodies lay everywhere, including all of the Inquisitorial retinue. They were a motley bunch, powerful no doubt, but they had died as easily as the others. No one left alive. It was eerily silent. Grimly, Garrock pressed on.

The chamber beyond was much the same, though the ever-present engine growl was replaced by a deeper sound in there – a deep, thrumming strobe that got under the fingernails. It wasn't mechanical. It was more like a heartbeat, or a great lung flexing. Every surface seemed to be running with static electricity.

Eventually he saw Kiastros standing, entirely alone, inside another room. The captain's back was turned. He was examining something in his hands. A large metal casket stood on the deck next to him, its lid open. The casket was emitting a steady light, a rich golden aura, though it wasn't wholesome – there was a greenish tinge to it, like a fine amulet tainted with patina.

'Lord captain,' said Garrock warily, holding his lasgun steady. 'Are you well?'

It took a while for Kiastros to turn around. When he did so, his face was so changed that Garrock barely recognised him. His skin had greyed and stiffened, the old lines had deepened, the eyes were ringed with red. A sheen of sweat covered it all, shining in the golden light. His gaze was unfocused for a moment, as if he had no idea where he was or whom he was addressing. Then some measure of recognition returned.

'Aris,' he said. 'Aris Garrock. My Captain of Armsmen.'

Garrock signalled those with him to stay back, stay ready. He could see no signs of life in the chamber, other than the captain, but the atmosphere of mortal danger was thick and pervasive.

'I ask you again, lord,' he said carefully. 'Are you well? Do you need assistance?'

The captain smiled, revealing teeth that had somehow aged and cracked. 'I am very well, Garrock. I am very well indeed. Everything is clear to me now. Everything. And I now see a great victory here. My victory. Our victory.'

It was hard to listen to. The words were like those of a priest's, with the same sense of declamation, the same unsettling certainty.

Now Garrock could see what he carried. It was a long blade, not metal but stone, napped and tarnished with age. It was covered in fresh blood, as were both Kiastros' forearms. It didn't look like any weapon Garrock had ever seen or used. It looked ancient, more than ancient, reeking of eternity, as if plucked from another age and unable to coexist with this one without causing massive structural damage. Kiastros' hands were blistered and weeping, but still he clutched at the blade. It fitted him, somehow, even though it seemed to be killing him. With a sudden flash of inspiration Garrock realised what he found so odd about the presentation – Kiastros wasn't wielding the blade; the blade was wielding him.

'I think you should put that down, lord,' he said carefully.

Kiastros laughed. 'Put it down? It's what I came for! And I took it. I killed its owner, just as he would have killed all of us. He lied, Aris. He lied about what he carried. And now he has paid for that. All is well. All is as it should be. I will return to the bridge.'

Garrock remained where he was. 'The first lieutenant told me you planned to destroy the cargo. She said it was the source of the sickness.'

'It is. In conjunction with some other outside interventions.

But it is also the cure. Because it will take us where we need to go.' Kiastros was looking ecstatic now, like a pict of an old saint. 'I had begun to doubt that we would make it. To our destination. But we can, now. We can get there.'

'I recommend you let go of it, lord,' said Garrock. 'It does not look... safe.'

'No. Not safe. Not safe at all. Neither am I, Aris. Neither is this ship. Nothing is safe. Nothing valuable ever is.' He looked down at the blade, to where his hands had been turned red raw from its touch. 'It is mine. It is my blade. Avati cannot have it. The Inquisition cannot have it. It is mine.'

What should he do? The captain was clearly mad now, just as Avati had feared. Garrock doubted he could be persuaded to give up the weapon. But to take it by force, to kill him, even...

'It must be destroyed,' Garrock told him. 'Expelled from the ship and destroyed by the guns. I can take it for you. If you give the order, I am ready now.'

Kiastros looked genuinely appalled. 'Destroyed? No, you are insane. Did Avati tell you to say that? No, you can stay where you are. I don't need you. I don't need anyone now. I am going back to the bridge. I am going to take command again. Things have been slack for far too long.'

So that was it. No chance of ending this through negotiation.

'No, lord captain,' Garrock said.

That made Kiastros stare. 'Did you say–'

'You will not go to the bridge with that thing. You will give it to me.'

Kiastros' mouth fell open. For a moment, an almost comical disbelief spread across his altered features. He'd never been countermanded. He'd never even had his orders questioned.

Then he ran his gaze across Garrock's forces, all of whom were standing with their weapons drawn on him. Then his eyes narrowed.

'So she's got to you too,' he murmured. 'Maybe she planned this all from the start.'

'No plans, lord captain,' said Garrock, keeping his tone low but firm. 'No tricks. I'll take the weapon, see that it's destroyed. That's all. Then we can put all this behind us.'

Kiastros chuckled darkly – it sounded like something had caught in his throat.

'I don't think you see the full picture. I don't think you see it at all. You had two journeys. One is nearly over. One is just beginning. How that second journey works out is up to you. Put your gun down. Come with me to the bridge. There are wonders ahead of us. Wonders beyond imagination.'

Garrock took aim at the captain's right kneecap. He knew that others would be following up – shooting to disable, not to kill. Even if some of them couldn't bring themselves to fire – very possible – there was no way out for him.

'Believe me, I don't want to do any of this,' Garrock told him. 'I really don't. But time's up. Hand it over.'

Kiastros' smile faded away. 'Very well. That is a shame.'

Kiastros leapt forward. Several guns fired, including Garrock's. None hit the target – because there was no target. Kiastros had momentarily disappeared, popping out of reality in a cloud of black spores, before reappearing a split second later, shifted by a yard or so. The captain whirled around, his every movement leaving trails of black inky motes, his limbs seeming to blur into nothing then shiver straight back into clarity. He swung the blade heavily, inexpertly, but that didn't matter – it was lethal. It flew at its targets like water sinking into soil, unstoppable, cleaving the very air around it.

'Bring him down!' Garrock roared, firing again, backing up, trying to get a clear shot.

His troops died horrifically quickly. The chamber filled with shouts of aggression and alarm, las-bursts spat and fizzed, but nothing landed, nothing stuck. Kiastros was like a flickering ghost, shifting and sliding in and out of view, using his blade in a way that he could never have been trained to do. Garrock fired again, aiming perfectly, only to see the las-beam punch straight through a bursting cloud of ink-blots and for Kiastros to spin back into instantiation just an arm's length away.

Kiastros wasn't fighting. He wasn't doing any of it – the *blade* was moving, carving through all resistance, slicing it up and spitting it out. Just looking at how it worked, how hard it drove him, told Garrock that Kiastros' body would be suffering. He couldn't maintain it for long without his sinews snapping and his muscles bursting, but then he didn't have to. It took the blade mere moments to cut its way through the mob – those few who had not accompanied Garrock into the innermost chamber ran now, their resolve broken at last.

Then it was just the two of them, facing one another. Garrock discarded his lasgun, and drew his combat knife. No point in trying to shoot him, but perhaps the thing that had been Kiastros might respect a more ancient form of weaponry.

'You didn't run, Aris,' Kiastros said, a trickle of blood running down his chin. 'Very good.'

The man was a wreck now. His uniform was torn, his breathing ragged. Did he even understand what was being done to him? Probably not. Avati had said his eyes were shining – they were still, glistening with mania.

'The blade is unholy,' Garrock said. 'You must see that. Put it down.'

'It came here for a reason.'

'It came here by chance.'

'There is no chance. It was all design. We were its vessel, ordained from the very start of time.'

'That is heresy.'

That stopped him in his tracks. For a split second, the old

Kiastros surfaced – the pious frown of disapproval, the hard-edged features embodying true certainty, the rigid captain at the helm of an Imperial voidship. He'd always cared about that so much. He'd always been the most faithful of them all.

Then it was gone again, and the shiny-eyed madness swept back in.

'Come with me now,' Kiastros said. 'I need a crew. I need you.'

'With respect,' said Garrock, tensing for the sudden shift, 'I don't think any of us will serve you now.'

'They will,' said Kiastros savagely. 'In life or in death, they *will*.'

Then he transposed again – a rapid switch, there one moment, then up against Garrock the next, his stone blade lashing in at his stomach.

Garrock had been waiting for the move, and dodged left, trailing his own blade and scoring the edge across Kiastros' chest. Black blood spilled over the captain's ripped uniform coat, smoking as it tumbled.

Garrock switched back, angling the knife to punch cleanly into the wound, but Kiastros had shifted again, darting out of range before sweeping in close. He felt the napped blade stab at him, the edge ripping through his armour like it was silk. The pain was indescribable – more than a wound, more like a disintegration. He could feel his flesh crisping up, atomising, turning into vapour, and tried to pull away.

Kiastros held him close, working the blade down into his entrails, embracing him the whole time.

'You were so good, Aris,' Kiastros whispered into his ears. 'So good. The best I ever served with.'

Unconsciousness was coming now. Garrock tried to break the hold, get his own knife into contact, but he no longer had control of his limbs.

'Perhaps you'll serve again,' said Kiastros, not unkindly. 'Perhaps I'll find a way.'

Garrock stared at him in horror. He'd meant that.

And then the blackness came for him, a crashing wave that rose up and swamped the last of his senses. He crumpled to the floor.

Kiastros watched him go. For a little while he looked somewhat forlorn. Then he looked around himself, at the bodies on the deck, at the open casket. Then he looked down at his blade, the one that he both loved and hated, that had turned the flesh of his palms into weeping scar tissue, that was burning up his soul faster than the great engines burned fuel.

'To the bridge, then,' he murmured, and started walking.

The shutters rose, and Avati tried to look away. She couldn't. Something compelled her to stare up, through the long mirrored shafts and out to where the Navigator's tower crested the ventral ridge of the ship. The warp flooded in, a sickening variegated swamp of colour. It was richer and more vivid than any colour she had ever seen before, an overabundance, saturated beyond possibility. As soon as you laid eyes on it, you were sucked in, unable to glance back, almost unable to blink. She started shivering, though it was fearsomely hot. She reached out to hold on to something, anything, but found nothing, and so swayed uncertainly before the kaleidoscope of horror, stricken into silence.

Behind her, Santalina unplugged herself and rose from her throne.

'Mesmeric, is it not?' she whispered, coming closer, her faded robes rustling on the stone. 'This is the realm you employed me to move through. This is where you made me look. Now it comes to you. All the shutters will open.'

'N-no,' Avati protested, weakly. 'The... *crew*...'

'They'll have to get used to it. Those who survive may even

come to relish it.' Santalina moved ahead, to where a series of levers controlled the aperture's orientation. 'You're not looking where I was looking, though,' she said, adjusting the settings. The mirrors and the lenses clunked and angled up above, filtering and directing the light. Avati couldn't avert her eyes, though she had to blink hard as the tears welled up.

'Shut it off,' she protested, but weakly now, because the more you looked, the more you were bathed in that ever-shifting light, the harder it was to contemplate not being able to see it.

'Remember what I said to you,' Santalina told her. 'The warp isn't a guide to the real. You see something in the empyrean, there's no exact correspondence. It might be there, it might not. Or it might have been there before, or will be in the future. Far and near, old and new, it means so much less.'

Avati couldn't look away. Something was swimming into her field of view. Something vast, a translucent blot on the seething mass. Its profile was familiar – deeply familiar.

'The second ship,' she breathed, watching it come closer.

'There was no second ship,' said Santalina. 'Just the one that we destroyed. But there was *this*. And what do you suppose that might be?'

It was enormous. A battleship. No, a battle cruiser. Despite all her long years in service, it was rare to see one so close. The guns had been run out, and she could see the barrels in their long sequence. The portholes were glimmering brightly. The high spires stood out in silhouette.

'Same displacement,' Avati said.

'Exactly the same. And look! It has suffered damage.'

It had. Heavy damage, although much of it seemed to have healed somehow, caked over like a flesh wound. For all that it looked so similar, it was also very different. It was palpably corrupted – the lights in its spires were spectral, the fires in its engines were ghosted with jarring resonances. It had no astro-paths' spire, just a jagged wound in the hull where the base of it should have been.

'It is us,' said Avati, finally understanding.

Santalina nodded. 'It has been shadowing us the whole time, creeping closer and closer, never falling back, never disap-pearing. And then I comprehended what it was. Not a ship in *space*, but a ship in *time*. Tracking us in order to overlap.' She grinned. 'That's the warp. That's the Seethe. You never know where you are with it, right up until it shows you.'

Avati felt the vice of fear clamp around her throat. She couldn't look away. Dimly, she thought of Isobel, of Garrock, of Kuhl, and wondered if they had succeeded in their missions.

They couldn't have. The ship was *there*, slipping over them. In a few moments it would be right on top of them, superimposed, ready to merge itself. Santalina was right. It had been getting closer to them all the time.

'Could we have prevented it?' she asked, more to herself than anything.

'I don't know. If Kuhl had worked faster, maybe. If the Space Marine had not been blinded. Does it matter now?'

Avati wanted to scream, but somehow couldn't. All she could do was watch it come.

'This will be hell for us,' she said. 'A living hell.'

Santalina nodded. 'It would be. If we lived through it.'

She looked at Avati. Avati looked back at her. Then she raised her laspistol again, aiming at Santalina's throat. The Navigator's hands crept up to her bandana.

'I never liked you much,' said Santalina wryly.

'Nor me, you,' replied Avati, giving her a salute in the Navy manner.

Above them, the ghostly image of their future state began to descend, merging with the physical counterpart as the ship churned through the living warp. Nothing could stop it now. The future had been set.

'For the Emperor,' said Santalina, taking off the thin layer of fabric that covered her Seeing Eye.

'For His people,' said Avati, squeezing the trigger.

# Epilogue

And then, the dream.

He never remembered much of it afterwards, just scattered impressions – screaming, weeping, his hand on the blade, moving in blurred procession from deck to deck. Justice was meted out, and now there was no one else left in command, so it was all up to him. So much had slipped, but this could not: discipline. Resolve. The essential elements of service.

There were still odd moments of clarity, of wakefulness – he'd suddenly see his reflection in a chamber's mirror, or catch the look on the face of someone he'd once known. Then he'd freeze, and pull his hand back, and a tidal wave of horror would surge up in his gorge, and he'd try to stop it all, the madness of it, the agony.

Those moments never lasted long. The voice would come back to him, the voice of forgetting, and the dream would resume, the long, long dream. He'd hear the engines grinding away, making him sleepy, reassuring him, folding him up in their warm embrace. He'd walk the long corridors, all dark now, and hear the noises of the vessel around him. He'd let his fingers graze on the walls, snagging on the patches of blood, tracing the desperate words carved into the plasteel.

He never ate. He never needed to eat. The warp sustained him, leaking in through every wound in the great ship's skin, sliding across the metal like spilled promethium. The longer the dream lasted, the more intense the warp's touch became. He could taste it in the air, hear it in the steady thrum of the failing systems, smell it under the oily puddles of human waste that sucked at his boots as he walked.

The functions of the ship carried on, erratically, weakly, but still there. The spars creaked, the immense iron skeleton flexed. As the vividness of the dream intensified, as the initial tasks of discipline were completed, he would see some of the crew still at their stations. They gazed into their terminal lenses, eyes unfocused, hands limp. Were they still doing anything much? Yes, they were. They were the faithful ones. He did not need to discipline them. They never looked up at him, never made the aquila. For some reason, he didn't mind that. He couldn't remember why not.

He never went to the spire, but he heard what came from it well enough now. He heard the song of the warp, picked up and amplified by the oh-so-clever mechanisms who dwelt there. He wondered at the resonance of it, the way the song radiated out through every shaft and chamber, coating every-thing in layers of sonic augmentation as thick as paint. Such a privilege, to have the services of such marvellous astropaths. If only he hadn't lost his Navigator. He missed her.

Not that it made much difference. The ship found its way well enough. It might have taken days, maybe months, pos-sibly even years, but it picked out the course in the end: to the objective, to the destination he had yearned to see for so long.

One night, he looked up, through the broken windows of the old bridge, out beyond the pale shimmer of the Geller fields, and saw the skies alive. He saw a world in perpetual torment, an unending struggle between the real and the unreal, a crash of psychic surf where unmaking surged against making. He saw stars burning darkly against a vermilion ground. He saw shoals of intelligences in the slurry of the void, surging, swirling, shrieking. He saw fires burning deep in the vaults, great wheels turning amid the nebulae of dreams.

He stood up. The blade was still in his hand, still burning his skin, still causing him such pain that he forever wanted to cry out from the agony and the joy of it, still caked in the blood of those he had corrected.

The ship carved its way through this New Void, the halls of nightmares, the melded place, and the chorus of the astropaths reached a new frenzy. For a long time there was nothing else – just that litany in his ears, the unfolding splendour of the realm around him, the emptiness, his dreaming.

And then, he saw it. Vast beyond imagination, swelling up out of the mottled dark, turrets and buttresses and grand galleries, all ranked and interspersed and terraced in an excess of impossible exuberance. Its flanks were as black as obsidian, sweeping up out of obscurity until its many prows filled all the forward viewers. Lightning crackled across its flanks, mere scampers of witchery against truly immense, sullenly reflective faces. The entire structure rotated with glacial slowness about its colossal central axis, churning up the matter of the warp like a flail.

He gazed up at it in a stupor. He had no word for what it might be. No class of voidship was that big. No object he had ever encountered over his long career had been even a fraction of its size. He just stared at it, the blade loose in his grasp, running his eyes across its gargantuan lines.

Slowly, very slowly, it swallowed him up. Great doors swung

open on colossal braces, each one trailing long lines of vapour and warp lightning as it moved. The ship passed within it, sliding under the shadow of the gaping aperture, absorbed into an even darker realm of iron and stone. For a while it remained in motion, and then there was a great echoing clang as docking clamps were deployed.

He remained stationary, staring out at newly blank viewers, glancing over at lenses filled with interference. The astropaths were silent, the song of the warp was muffled. He felt buried, entombed.

Then he started to walk. He went out of the bridge, down to the transit lanes, along the long passageways, and out into a new world. He never noticed the precise moment of threshold-crossing, but suddenly the surroundings changed – the walls were like black glass, forever moving with half-glimpsed reflections. The surface no longer smelled of blood, but had an aroma he could not place. It was quiet, but not silent – eerie cries echoed out from half-seen halls, distant crashes could be heard coming from the deep vaults. There were no crew, at least not for a long time. He walked, blade in hand, as if through an underworld of memory, tracing a route with certainty as if he'd rehearsed it since childhood.

This was not his home. It would never be his home. But he was meant to be here.

Eventually he arrived at a larger chamber, a grand viewing oculus set high on the roof of this esoteric world. He saw the vivid illumination of the warp spill through lead-framed windows, sinking into the black surfaces around him. Now there were other souls around him, chattering softly, limping and shuffling, their faces hidden with cowls, their spindly hands clutching at staves. Something was burning somewhere close – the air tasted of ashes. No one intervened – he just kept on walking. He passed along a straight channel cut into the obsidian floor that led up to a grand octagonal dais. More presences flitted and drifted around him, whispering with some agitation, glancing at him before swiftly averting their faces.

When he arrived at the dais, he halted. Two figures stood before him now. One was male, or had been male. He was painfully thin, emaciated almost, dressed in fine robes that slithered over corpse-like flesh. He had a hunted, empty expression on a sombre face. Semi-mechanical horrors clucked and hopped around him, pulling at his cloak, wafting incense from chain-hauled burners.

The other was female. She was younger, more human still, but the journey into change for her was well advanced nonetheless. Her skin was draining of colour, her eyes were darkening. She was adorned with jewels, hundreds of them, hanging from the incisions she had made into her flesh.

They both regarded him with intense interest. No hostility, no great welcome, but immense interest.

'What is your name?' the thin one asked. His voice was a horror all of its own, the voice of a destroyed mortal soul now sustained by power alone, the will to dominate and remodel, to destroy and remake.

'I am Iannis Kiastros, captain of His ship *Judgement of the Void*,' he said. 'Who are you?'

The woman was staring at him almost hungrily.

'He is Tenebrus,' she said. 'Hand of Abaddon. I am Yheng, his servant.'

'Do you know where you are?' asked Tenebrus.

'I brought the ship to where it needed to be,' he said.

'And where is that?'

'The Eye of Terror.'

Tenebrus nodded. 'Correct. A dark road, but now you have arrived. What guided you?'

He stiffened. 'Faith. Unbreakable faith. Others doubted, but

I never did. I had to kill some of them. I had to impose order when it was failing. I did it.'

'You did. And do you know why you had to come here?'

'To bring the fight to the enemy. As the primarch said. We are the spear-thrust into the darkest night. Fleet Secundus has the highest honour.'

Yheng looked at him with scorn, it felt like, but Tenebrus merely nodded again.

'So you say,' he said. 'Now give me the blade.'

He hung on to it for a little longer. He looked down at it. Then he looked up again, reluctant. He suddenly felt like a child faced with a demand to return a cherished toy. It was *his*. He had *earned* it.

'Do you know what it is?' Tenebrus asked patiently.

He shook his head.

'It is a shard of an older blade. A blade that has done more to alter the course of history than any other. Yours is the last to be found. Now you have become a part of an older drama, one that commenced long before the Imperium itself was born. Fortune, or misfortune – who can judge? It is done now.' Tenebrus looked down at it, and an avaricious light kindled in those soul-dead eyes. 'So hand it to me. You will feel better when you have done so.'

Still he resisted. He knew the danger. These monsters could kill him, surely. The blade could not protect him against such creatures. But it was *his*.

'And then, what next?' he asked numbly. 'What remains for me?'

'To serve,' said Yheng perfunctorily. 'On your ship. Is that not what you wished for, all your life? It will be eternal now.'

He shuddered to listen to that. Part of him was glad of it – intensely glad. But another part of him somehow knew, somehow divined more deeply, what it meant. He briefly saw the face of another woman in his mind, one whom he had once known, warning him, warning him of something terrible. Who had she been?

'But I did well, did I not?' he asked, glancing from one of them to the other. 'I was faithful, yes? When all others doubted?'

Tenebrus extended his clawed hand. 'The blade.'

So, in the end, he gave it up, trembling as the hot stone left his scarred hands. Tenebrus took it up. As he did so, the void beyond suddenly flared red, blooming out of the darkness and throwing bloody illumination across the obsidian chamber. The glow seared into Kiastros' chest, a branding iron fresh from a roaring flame, and stole his breath away.

He knew he had to leave now. He knew his part in this was played. He had so many questions, though. So much he wanted to know.

They wouldn't tell him anything. Even now they barely noticed he was still there. They were both staring at the blade, covetously, reverently.

'What is it for?' he ventured, holding little hope they would tell him.

Tenebrus' awful eyes rose to meet his again, just for a moment.

'When the time comes, you will know,' he said. 'When the time comes, the galaxy itself will know.'

And that was it. Nothing more. The end of his mission, the culmination of all his labour. He knew he should feel proud. He was still on his feet, the only one of his crew to endure. He had overcome. He had remained faithful. His cheeks were wet with tears suddenly, though he had no idea why. He should feel proud.

He turned on his heel, marched back the way he had come. His ship awaited. The *Judgement of the Void*, his life and his joy. He would command it again now, taking it to war again, though now with the song of the choir to guide him. Things would be better.

Behind, back at the dais, they were chanting now. Those words made him feel sick. He didn't want to know what they meant.

He walked faster. He would feel better on the ship.

He was weeping. Why was he weeping?

Better on the ship.

His hands were trembling, covered in blood and scars.

Best to get home now.

Best to get back to the dream.

# Appendix: Notes on the Crusade

## THE ROAD OF MARTYRS

Efforts to defend the approach to Terra from a Chaos attack led to the infamous, ongoing war named by those unfortunate enough to take part in it as 'The Road of Martyrs'.

## FLEET SECUNDUS

Following the opening of the Great Rift, there were those amongst the Lords of Terra who expected a coordinated attack from the galactic north towards the Throneworld. Although a manifestation of Neverborn was rumoured to have fallen upon the ancient capital, the expected mass assault by traitor forces did not come.

Why Abaddon the Despoiler did not immediately press home his advantage while the forces of the Imperium were in disarray has unsettled Imperial savants. Despite the lack of a concerted assault, that is not to say there was no threat. Thousands upon thousands of Chaos fleets poured out of the Eye of Terra through the collapsed Cadian Gate. Huge swathes of space, once considered to be the very heartlands of the Imperium, were laid waste, with trillions dead or enslaved by the servants of the Dark Gods.

Amidst all this though, coordination between the disparate followers of Chaos appeared lacking, with the daemon primarchs and greater warlords seemingly pursuing their own ambitions. As great priests and lords of the Imperium declared, the seeds of Chaos' destruction are sown by its very nature. Wiser heads disagreed.

Even without strategic organisation among the Chaos forces, it was clear Terra would come under serious threat sooner or later. When the primarch Roboute Guilliman returned and organised his grand endeavour to purge the stars, he gave the role of defending the north to Fleet Secundus. They would head towards the Eye, blunting further incursions, and retake worlds currently under the sway of the enemy.

Secundus was unusual in this regard. Most of the other fleets' battle groups were separated and sent all over the galaxy. Sending one entire fleet to perform a role was largely unheard of, though when one considers the vast area of space Secundus was to fight over it could perhaps be regarded differently.

Commanded by Fleetmaster Rasmatin Olythaddues Samil from his flagship *Thunder's Peal,* the fleet included the usual broad selection of representatives from numerous Imperial military organisations, notably the Mordian 84th, House Griegoris, and elements of the Black Templars and Minotaurs Space Marines chapters. Six battle groups were initially assembled, more joining the initial roll call later from other significant Imperial muster points, although some of the first six were almost immediately weakened upon assembly when several key assets were requisitioned by the understrength Fleet Septimus.

The fleet's primary role was to fight its way north to the Eye of Terra in order to stymie the flow of enemy assets into Imperium Sanctus. Taking the fight into the Eye itself was the ultimate aim put forward by some in the fleet's higher echelons, but remained a distant, unattainable ambition.

Fleet Secundus launched early, one of the first of the fleets to depart. A large part of its strength was assembled in Sol itself, and its massed battle groups broke out of the inner Segmentum Solar via the warp gate at Vorlese, which by that point was undergoing rapid fortification. From there, the fleet turned north, not heading solely towards the Eye, but pushing against multiple threats in a broad fan. Battle Group Betaris was given orders to head towards the key hive world of Armageddon, for example.

The fleet gathered reinforcements along the way, but very soon ran into formidable resistance. The majority of their engagements were against the forces of Chaos. Over time, their experiences of wars fought in areas of collapsing reality, facing the most hellish abominations and unspeakable atrocities, forged a hyper-religious zeal rarely matched in the other fleets.

Their faith was needed. The road north was gruelling, and thousands of Imperial systems needed retaking and securing. Although the Archenemy efforts were divided, the sheer number of armies and fleets coming out of the Eye of Terror meant relentless battle, and caused immense attrition of both personnel and machines. The work needed to establish supply networks required by the Officio Logisticarum was difficult and often ad hoc to begin with, as it was rare for systems to remain free from threats for long. A constant stream of reinforcements was required to keep the fleet fighting. Its number of battle groups grew. The efforts of a score of forge worlds and major industrial planets were dedicated solely to replenishing and expanding Fleet Secundus, while reconquered systems were tithed again and again for regiments of Astra Militarum. In addition to this, Chaos was not the fleet's only foe. Although intended as a thrust against the Archenemy, to the north-east the fleet often found itself opposed by orks. Furthermore, Fleet Secundus' role only became more important once the Nachmund Gauntlet was discovered.

### DEFENCE IN DEPTH

Despite all the obstacles and the horrendous cost in lives, progress was made. Fleet Secundus' battle groups edged closer and closer to the Eye, often working in conjunction with Fleet Primus, which was very active around Armageddon, Elysia and Fenris at this time. Five years into the Indomitus Crusade, it was deemed within the Officio Logisticarum that the standard pattern of hub fortresses, seeded in the wake of the fleets' reconquests, and existing fortress worlds that supported the fleets elsewhere, was insufficient to meet the challenges presented by the Eye of Terror and the Nachmund Gauntlet.

Two separate schemes were put into action. The first, the Sanctus Wall, was a series of heavily fortified systems at the Imperium Sanctus end of the Nachmund Gauntlet. The second, the Anaxian Line, was more extensive, comprising approximately two hundred systems across whole sectors, from Belis Corona to Agripinaa, and designed to provide a flexible, indepth defensive solution to the constant pressure from the Eye of Terror. The line was a combination of fortress worlds, specially sited Astropathic Relay stations, supply dumps and industrial worlds which allowed rapid response to Chaos incursions from the Eye, gave multiple fallback positions, and enabled reinforcements and supplies to be redeployed quickly. Although only a few were designated as primary sector strongholds or Hub Fortresses, all were garrisoned and ringed with defences.

Where the appropriate facilities did not exist, they were created, no matter the cost.

Poor diplomacy and the brutal methods forced upon the Imperium by the exigencies of galaxy-wide war provoked uprisings on some worlds designated to form the line. Establishing the network required further sacrifices on the part of Fleet Secundus, as the worlds needed holding while their capabilities and defences were upgraded, often in the face of significant enemy resistance. Whole populations were forced to labour upon the project, and many a planet suffered environmental devastation as they were transformed to suit their new purposes. Eventually, it was done.

The Anaxian Line was only ever a partial success. Dreams of pushing on to dead Cadia were put on indefinite hold. Such pressure was exerted by the endless tide of foes from the Eye that the leading edge of the line was prone to collapse, and the front moved back and forth many times. However, the line's creation did stabilise the situation in the Segmentum Solar somewhat, as it did shield systems behind it, and arguably contributed to Kor Phaeron's lack of success in destabilising the heart of the Imperium. Fleet Secundus too was afforded a degree of respite. At the end of the Road of Martyrs, they built a wall of suns and worlds, sanctified by the sacred dead of humanity. But though eased, the fleet's war would not cease, and attempts to win greater victories would often come to nought. For the time being, the Imperium had to be content with stalemate.

## ABOUT THE AUTHOR

**Chris Wraight** is the author of the Horus Heresy
novels *Warhawk, Scars* and *The Path of Heaven,* the
Primarchs novels *Leman Russ: The Great Wolf* and
*Jaghatai Khan: Warhawk of Chogoris,* the novellas
*Brotherhood of the Storm, Wolf King* and *Valdor:*
*Birth of the Imperium,* and the audio drama *The*
*Sigillite.* For Warhammer 40,000 he has written the
Space Wolves books *Blood of Asaheim, Stormcaller*
and *The Helwinter Gate,* as well as the Vaults of
Terra trilogy, *The Lords of Silence* and many more.
Additionally, he has many Warhammer novels
to his name, and the Warhammer Crime novel
*Bloodlines.* Chris lives and works in Bradford-on-
Avon, in south-west England.

# YOUR
# NEXT READ

### DARK IMPERIUM
**by Guy Haley**

The first phase of the Indomitus Crusade is over, and the conquering primarch, Roboute
Guilliman, sets his sights on home. The hordes of his traitorous brother, Mortarion,
march on Ultramar, and only Guilliman can hope to thwart their schemes with his
Primaris Space Marine armies.

---